THE

THE COLLECTED FANTASIES OF
CLARK ASHTON SMITH

VOLUME FIVE

THE Last Hieroglyph

THE COLLECTED FANTASIES OF
CLARK ASHTON SMITH

VOLUME FIVE

EDITED BY SCOTT CONNORS AND RON HILGER

WITH AN INTRODUCTION BY RICHARD A. LUPOFF

NIGHT SHADE BOOKS
NEW YORK

Night Shade books may be purchased in bulk at special discounts for sales promotion, corporate gifts, fund-raising, or educational purposes. Special editions can also be created to specifications. For details, contact the Special Sales Department, Night Shade Books, 307 West 36th Street, 11th Floor, New York, NY 10018 or info@skyhorsepublishing.com.

Night Shade Books® is a registered trademark of Skyhorse Publishing, Inc.®, a Delaware corporation.

Visit our website at www.nightshadebooks.com.

10 9 8 7 6 5 4 3 2 1

Library of Congress Cataloging-in-Publication Data

Names: Smith, Clark Ashton, 1893-1961, author. | Connors, Scott, editor. | Hilger, Ronald, editor.
Title: The last hieroglyph / Clark Ashton Smith ; edited by Scott Connors and Ron Hilger.
Description: New York : Night Shade Books, 2017. | Series: The collected fantasies of Clark Ashton Smith ; volume 5
Identifiers: LCCN 2016018020 | ISBN 9781597808835 (softcover)
Subjects: | BISAC: FICTION / Fantasy / Short Stories. | GSAFD: Science fiction. | Fantasy fiction. | Horror fiction.
Classification: LCC PS3537.M335 A6 2017 | DDC 813/.54--dc23
LC record available at https://lccn.loc.gov/2016018020

Cover artwork © 2010 by Jason Van Hollander
Cover design by Claudia Noble
Interior layout and design by Jeremy Lassen

ISBN: 978-1-59780-883-5

Printed in the United States of America

CONTENTS

INTRODUCTION

By Richard A. Lupoff

Of the many great names of those who wrote for *Weird Tales*, "The Unique Magazine," three stand above all. If you have access to a file of *Weird Tales*—or, lacking that, a cumulative bibliography of its near century of issues—you will find bylines ranging from such pioneers of modern science fiction and fantasy as Edmond Hamilton, Jack Williamson, and Catherine L. Moore to some far more surprising personalities: Tennessee Williams, Robert A. Heinlein, John D. MacDonald, and scores of others. And those, of course, represent only stories original to *Weird Tales*. Never mind the reprints.

Some of those writers are forgotten today, but they were acclaimed in their own time, and some of them—your guess is a good as mine, as to which—are due for a kind of literary resurrection, thanks especially to today's penchant for rediscovering long-neglected works and their creators. Will it be Henry S. Whitehead? Eli Colter? Donald E. Keyhoe, remembered now for his pioneering "nonfiction" work, *The Flying Saucers are Real,* but popular in an earlier decade for his pulpish gems?

Vincent Starrett, Seabury Quinn, E. Hoffmann Price?

Who can say?

Still, one returns inevitably to the three titans of *Weird Tales:* H. P. Lovecraft, "The Old Gentleman of Providence," Robert E. Howard, "Two Gun Bob," and Clark Ashton Smith, "The Emperor of Dreams."

Their lifetimes overlapped. Lovecraft: 1890–1937. Smith: 1893–1961. Howard: 1906–1936. They lived in widely separated sections of the United States: Lovecraft, in Providence, Rhode Island; Howard, in Cross Plains, Texas; Smith, in Auburn, California.

Excellent biographies have been written of Lovecraft and Howard. Donald Sidney-Fryer's splendid "bio-bibliography," *Emperor of Dreams,* is as close to a full-scale biography of Smith as has yet been achieved. In any case, I will not attempt to duplicate, in miniature form, the treatment that all three have been justly accorded. But I will point out that, despite their great differences, there were remarkable parallels among them.

As far as I have been able to determine, all three were sole offspring of their parents. All three had less than happy and conventional family lives. None of them followed the "standard model" of American life in their era. This model, as manifested in countless novels, radio dramas and motion pictures of the 1930s, called for an early and happy marriage, children, a steady job for the father, a contented career as homemaker and caregiver for the mother, and a cozy suburban home for the family.

How many families actually achieved this dreamlike existence is debatable. Certainly neither Howard Phillips Lovecraft nor Robert E. Howard nor Clark Ashton Smith came anywhere close.

Lovecraft's father went mad, was hospitalized, and died. Then Lovecraft's mother went mad, was hospitalized, and died. Raised by a pair of doting aunts, Lovecraft married a woman seven years his senior. After a couple of years he decided that marriage was not for him and returned to the quasi-maternal nest for the rest of his days.

Howard never married. He reportedly bragged of his sexual exploits but his claims were at best unsubstantiated. The details of Howard's suicide are well known. The reason or reasons may be more complicated than the following bald statement: His mother lay dying, her nurse told him that the end was near, he took a gun and put a bullet through his brain. Chronic depression, financial stress, a failed relationship, and what I am informed is now known as "Caregiver Stress Syndrome" may all have contributed to his act of self-destruction.

And Clark Ashton Smith spent most of his life struggling against poverty while caring for his own ill and elderly parents. Only after their death, and himself in late middle age and in failing health, did he marry.

Three brilliantly talented men, each of them a stranger in a world he never made nor lived in happily or comfortably. All three, perhaps surprisingly, expressed their pain and alienation in poetry. They were not unaware of this aspect in their natures. In a 1937 letter to R. H. Barlow, Smith said, "I could never live in any modern city, and am more of an 'outsider' than HPL. His 'outsideness' was principally in regard to time-period; mine is in space, too."

But even by the modest economic yardstick by which each lived, poetry could not provide sustenance. Each turned to creating fiction for the pulp magazines of the day—most notably, in all three cases, *Weird Tales*, a periodical that paid poorly even by the low standards of the pulps, but that welcomed offbeat and alienated world-views like those of these three tortured geniuses.

Lovecraft's visions were dark, moody, and pessimistic tales of old New England and cosmic doom that inevitably awaited all of humankind. Howard's tales were the most varied of the three, ranging from boxing yarns to sea stories to westerns, but most of all to tales of barbarian combat. Imbued with overwhelming violence and drenched in gore, they found a special niche and inspired a whole school of imitators.

But what of Clark Ashton Smith?

I suspect that, of the three writers under discussion, he was the most alienated from his surroundings. His fiction is the most remote from the mundane world. It is also, in a sense, the most remote from the fiction to which contemporary readers have become conditioned.

The modern novel, especially the modern genre novel, tends to be driven by a relentlessly urgent plot. The modern reader's attention is constantly sought by the demands of his work; his leisure life, by motion pictures filled with chases, gunfire, explosions, deadlines. Even as I sit at my computer working on this essay my telephone rings, a siren screams as an ambulance rockets past my house, there is little opportunity and regrettably little inclination to settle down for an uninterrupted hour with a book.

Clark Ashton Smith's prose—if prose it is!—is of a different sort. Every arcane word is chosen with care and purpose. Every glittering image demands our time and attention. We do not read these stories with an urgent need to find out what happens next, and what happens next, and always, always, what happens next.

Of course Clark Ashton Smith's works were not of uniform quality. I am by no means the first to point this out. But at his best each of his stories is like a glass of the finest—but also the strongest—of liquors. To gulp it down is to do injustice both to the liquor—the story!—and to the taster—the reader.

Instead, to appreciate the artistry of Clark Ashton Smith we must calm ourselves, settle into a comfortable chair, and shut out distractions and interruptions. It may be best to read Smith in silent surroundings. Or then again, one may put on music, but not the jarring, cacophonous sounds of contemporary popular composers and performers. The classical sounds of the eighteenth and nineteenth centuries are most appropriate. The specific works one chooses, I leave to each individual, although the appeal of the divine Mozart is eternal.

Let Smith's words carry you away to realms of glittering beauty—and evil and irony at times, yes. It does not matter whether you read a Smith tale set in a sumptuous Oriental court, a decadent world of the far future, or a remote, alien planet. These settings are arbitrary, and in my opinion they are really interchangeable.

I have my favorite stories in this collection. As the Romans said, *De gustibus, non est disputandum*. Still, I will indulge myself by mentioning just three.

"The Death of Malygris" is vintage Smith. Just see how he draws the reader into his world of whispers and of shadows:

> At the hour of interlunar midnight, when lamps burned rarely and far apart in Susran, and slow-moving autumn clouds had muffled the stars, King Gadeiron sent forth into the sleeping city twelve of his trustiest mutes. Like shadows gliding through oblivion, they vanished upon their various ways; each of them, returning presently to the darkened palace, led with him a shrouded figure no less silent and discreet than himself.
> In this manner, groping along tortuous alleys, through blind cypress-caverns in the royal gardens, and down subterranean halls and steps, twelve of the most powerful sorcerers of Susran were brought together in a vault of oozing, death-grey granite, far beneath the foundations of the palace.

What an opening scene! What irresistible imagery! It is impossible not to go on reading, not to want—no, to *need* to know about those twelve mutes and those twelve sorcerers and what plan is brewing in the mind of King Gadeiron.

Then there is "The Coming of the White Worm." Smith uses odd and intriguing words that weave an enchantment all their own, a kind of imagistic poetry whose very sound and texture is hypnotic, regardless even of their content:

> Evagh the warlock, dwelling beside the boreal sea, was aware of many strange and untimely portents in mid-summer. Frorely burned the sun above Mhu Thulan from a welkin clear and wannish as ice. At eve the aurora was hung from zenith to earth, like an arras in a high chamber of gods. Wan and rare were the poppies and small anemones in the cliff-sequestered vales lying behind the house of Evagh; and the fruits in his walled garden were pale of rind and green at the core. Also, he beheld by day the unseasonable flight of great multitudes of fowl, going southward from the hidden isles beyond Mhu Thulan; and by night he heard the distressful clamor of other passing multitudes. And always, in the loud wind and crying surf, he harkened to the weird whisper of voices from realms of perennial winter.

Nothing has happened. A character has been named but all that we know of him is his profession. No shots have rung out, no hoofs have pounded, no zombies have lurched, no bosoms have heaved. Instead, Smith has created a living, breathtakingly strange and fascinating place, and we are drawn to enter it and listen, our hearts pounding in our ears, while this male Scheherazade spins a thousand and second tale.

One more, "The Chain of Aforgomon." Curl up and let that insidious voice tell you this story:

> It is indeed strange that John Milwarp and his writings should have fallen so speedily into a sort of semi-oblivion. His books, treating of Oriental life in a somewhat flowery, romantic style, were popular a few months ago. But now, in spite of their range and penetration, their pervasive verbal sorcery, they are seldom mentioned; and they seem to have vanished unaccountably from the shelves of bookstores and libraries.
>
> Even the mystery of Milwarp's death, baffling to both law and science, has evoked but a passing interest, an excitement quickly lulled and forgotten.
>
> I was well acquainted with Milwarp over a term of years. But my recollection of the man is becoming strangely blurred, like an image in a misted mirror. His dark, half-alien personality, his preoccupation with the occult, his immense knowledge of Eastern life and lore, are things I remember with such effort and vagueness as attends the recovery of a dream. Sometimes I almost doubt that he ever existed. It is as if the man, and all that pertains to him, were being erased from human record by some mysterious acceleration of the common process of obliteration.

This is what academics refer to as recursive narration: a writer writing about a writer writing about a writer.... It is hard not to believe that this is Smith writing about Smith, if not the actual man struggling against a difficult fate on that hardscrabble mountainside above Auburn, California, then the Clark Ashton Smith of his own fantasies, the Emperor of Dreams.

"The Chain of Aforgomon" may not be the greatest of Smith's stories. It is certainly not the most famous. But it has a very special place in my personal list of favorites.

What, indeed, did Smith think of himself and his works? With what endorsement did he leave his remarkably extensive body of prose and poetry—and painting and sculpture!—to the world?

I recently came across the text of Charles Baudelaire's famous and scandalous volume, *Flowers of Evil*. Let me share with you just a few lines from Baudelaire's introduction:

> You know that I have always considered that literature and the arts pursue an aim independent of morality. Beauty of conception and style is enough for me. But this book, whose title (*Fleurs du mal*) says everything, is clad, as you will see, in a cold and sinister beauty. It was created with rage and patience. Besides, the proof of its positive

worth is in all the ill that they speak of it. The book enrages people ...(My detractors) deny me everything, the spirit of invention and even the knowledge of the French language. I don't care a rap about all these imbeciles, and I know that this book, with its virtues and its faults, will make its way in the memory of the lettered public, beside the best poems of V. Hugo, Th. Gautier and even Byron.

Just so, the collected works of Clark Ashton Smith will make their way into the memory of our own lettered public. They will stand on a plain with the best prose and poetry of Howard Phillips Lovecraft and Robert Ervin Howard. He was their equal; I am tempted to say more than that but will not. Each had his merits. Those of Clark Ashton Smith are lovingly displayed in this and its companion volumes of his collected fantasies.

In the same 1937 letter earlier cited, Smith referred to one of his stories, "The Death of Ilalotha," as "unusually poisonous and exotic." That story is included in this volume, and the reader is invited to consider it in the light of the author's assessment. How aptly the phrase applies to Smith—whose works, however glowingly lovely, were seldom optimistic and never Pollyan-naish—as well as to Baudelaire!

As you read this book or any collection of Smith's wondrous gems, do not hasten to the next story, the next scene, or even the next paragraph. Turn the clock to the wall. Put your wristwatch in a drawer. Disconnect the telephone and shut off your cell phone. Draw the blinds. Make yourself comfortable with the book in your lap, and perhaps with a glass of some fine, rare vintage at your elbow. Wade into the warm, scented sea of words. Give yourself over to the experience. Do not worry about emerging.

All too soon the world will summon you back to reality. The spell will be broken. When this happens, do not be ashamed to weep.

—Richard A. Lupoff
Berkeley, California
2010

A Note on the Texts

C lark Ashton Smith considered himself primarily a poet, but he began his publishing career with a series of Oriental *contes cruels* that were published in such magazines as the *Overland Monthly* and the *Black Cat*. He ceased the writing of short stories for many years, but, under the influence of his correspondent H. P. Lovecraft, he began experimenting with the weird tale when he wrote "The Abominations of Yondo" in 1925. His friend Genevieve K. Sully suggested that writing for the pulps would be a reasonably congenial way for him to earn enough money to support himself and his parents.

Between the years 1930 and 1935, Clark Ashton Smith was one of the most prolific contributors to *Weird Tales*. This prodigious output did not come at the price of sloppy composition, but was distinguished by its richness of imagination and expression. Smith put the same effort into one of his stories that he did into a bejeweled and gorgeous sonnet. Donald Sidney-Fryer has described Smith's method of composition in his 1978 bio-bibliography *Emperor of Dreams* (Donald M. Grant, West Kingston, R.I.) thus:

> First he would sketch the plot in longhand on some piece of note-paper, or in his notebook, *The Black Book*, which Smith used circa 1929–1961. He would then write the first draft, usually in longhand but occasionally directly on the typewriter. He would then rewrite the story 3 or 4 times (Smith's own estimate); this he usually did directly on the typewriter. Also, he would subject each draft to considerable alteration and correction in longhand, taking the ms. with him on a stroll and reading aloud to himself (19).

Unlike Lovecraft, who would refuse to allow publication of his stories without assurances that they would be printed without editorial alteration, Clark Ashton Smith would revise a tale if it would ensure acceptance. Smith was not any less devoted to his art than his friend, but unlike HPL he had to consider his responsibilities in caring for his elderly and infirm parents. He tolerated these changes to his carefully crafted short stories with varying degrees of resentment, and vowed that if he ever had the opportunity to collect them between hard covers he would restore the excised text. Unfortunately, he experienced severe eyestrain during the preparation of his first Arkham House collections, so he provided magazine tear sheets to August Derleth for his secretary to use in the preparation of a manuscript.

Lin Carter was the first of Smith's editors to attempt to provide the reader with pure Smith, but the efforts of Steve Behrends and Marc Michaud have revealed the extent to which Smith's prose was compromised. Through their series of pamphlets, the *Unexpurgated Clark Ashton Smith*, the reader and critic could see precisely the severity of these compromises; while, in the collections *Tales of Zothique* and *The Book of Hyperborea*, Behrends and Will Murray presented for the first time these stories just as Smith wrote them.

In establishing what the editors believe to be what Smith would have preferred, we were able to consult several repositories of Smith's manuscripts, most notably the Clark Ashton Smith Papers deposited at the John Hay Library of Brown University, but also including the Bancroft Library of the University of California at Berkeley, Special Collections of Brigham Young University, the California State Library, and several private collections. Priority was given to the latest known typescript prepared by Smith, except where he had indicated that the changes were made solely to satisfy editorial requirements. In these instances we compared the last version that satisfied Smith with the version sold. Changes made include the restoration of deleted material, except in those instances where the change of a word or phrase seems consistent with an attempt by Smith to improve the story, as opposed to the change of a word or phrase to a less Latinate, and less graceful, near-equivalent. This represents a hybrid or fusion of two competing versions, but it is the only way we see that Smith's intentions as author may be honored. In a few instances a word might be changed in the Arkham House collections that isn't indicated on the typescript.

We have also attempted to rationalize Smith's spellings and hyphenation practices. Smith used British spellings early in his career but gradually switched to American usage. He could also vary spelling of certain words from story to story, e.g., "eerie" and "eery." We have generally standardized on his later usage, except for certain distinct word choices such as "grey." In doing so we have deviated from the "style sheet" prepared by the late Jim Turner for his 1988 omnibus collection for Arkham House, *A Rendezvous in Averoigne*. Turner did not have access to such a wonderful scholarly tool as Boyd Pearson's website, www.eldritchdark.com. By combining its extremely useful search engine with consultation of Smith's actual manuscripts and typescripts, as well as seeing how he spelled a particular word in a poem or letter, the editors believe that they have reflected accurately Smith's idiosyncracies of expression.

However, as Emerson reminds us, "a foolish consistency is the hobgoblin of little minds." Smith may have deliberately varied his spelling and usages depending upon the particular mood or atmosphere that he was trying to achieve in a particular story. As he explained in a letter to H. P. Lovecraft sometime in November 1930:

> The problem of "style" in writing is certainly fascinating and profound. I find it highly important, when I begin a tale, to establish at once what might be called the appropriate "tone." If this is clearly determined at the start I seldom have much difficulty in maintaining it; but if it isn't, there is likely to be trouble. Obviously, the style of "Mohammed's Tomb" wouldn't do for "The Ghoul"; and one of my chief preoccupations in writing this last story was to *exclude* images, ideas and locutions which I would have used freely in a modern story. The same, of course, applies to "Sir John Maundeville," which is a deliberate study in the archaic. (*SL* 137)

Therefore we have allowed certain variations in spelling and usage that seem to us to be consistent with Smith's stated principles as indicated above.

Typescripts do not exist in some cases, notably "The Enchantress of Sylaire," while in other cases the existing typescript is incomplete, as is the case with "The Tomb-Spawn." An arsonist destroyed Smith's cabin in the 1950s, which resulted in some typescripts surviving only as burned fragments ("The Master of the Crabs," "Morthylla"). Still others survive only as earlier drafts that are noticeably less polished than the published texts ("Schizoid Creator," "Symposium of the Gorgon"). In the case of some stories that were only published long after Smith's death, several different versions exist, requiring the editors to use our best judgment in selecting a text that we hope would not displease Smith.

Three stories exist in versions that differ considerably from the published texts. We include the original version of "The Coming of the White Worm" without reference to the version published in *Stirring Science Stories*. We restore the cuts made to "Necromancy in Naat" while maintaining some very real improvements that Smith made when the tale was published in *Weird Tales*. On the other hand, the rejected version of "The Black Abbot of Puthuum" contained unsuccessful attempts at romantic comedy that detracted from the story's cumulative effect.

We regret that we cannot present a totally authoritative text for Smith's stories. Such typescripts do not exist. All that we can do is to apply our knowledge of Smith to the existing manuscripts and attempt to combine them to present what Smith would have preferred to publish were he not beset by editorial malfeasance in varying degrees. In doing so we hope to present Smith's own words in their purest form to date so that the reader might experience what Ray Bradbury described in his foreword to *A Rendezvous in Averoigne*: "Take one step across the threshold of his stories, and you plunge into color, sound, taste, smell, and texture—into language."

The editors wish to thank Douglas A. Anderson, Azédarac, Steve Behrends, Gregory Belt, Geoffrey Best, Joshua Bilmes, Christopher Crites, April Derleth, William A. Dorman, Alan Gullette, Don Herron, Margery Hill, Rah Hoffman, S. T. Joshi, Terence McVicker, Marc Michaud, Andrew Migliore, Will Murray, Boyd Pearson, John Pelan, Alan H. Pesetsky, Rob Preston, Robert M. Price, Dennis Rickard, Jim Rockhill, David E. Schultz, Donald Sidney-Fryer, James Thompson, Henry Vester, Jason Williams, and especially Martin Andersson for their help, support, and encouragement of this project, as well as Holly Snyder and the staff of the John Hay Library of Brown University, and D. S. Black of the Bancroft Library, University of California at Berkeley, for their assistance in the preparation of this collection. Needless to say, any errors are the sole responsibility of the editors.

THE DARK AGE

The laboratory was like a citadel. It stood on a steep eminence, overtopped only by the loftier mountains, and looked out across numberless fir-thick valleys and serried ridges. The morning sunlight came to it above peaks of perennial snow; and the sunsets burned beyond a rivered plain, where forest saplings had taken the battlefields of yesteryear, and skin-clad savages prowled amid the mounded ruins of sybaritic cities.

They who had built the laboratory, in the years when Earth's loftiest civilization was crumbling swiftly, had designed it for a fortress of science, in which something of man's lore and wisdom should be preserved throughout the long descent into barbaric night.

The walls were of squared boulders from a glacial moraine; and the woodwork was of mountain cedar, mightily beamed as that which was used in Solomon's temple. High above the main edifice there soared an observatory tower, from which the heavens and the surrounding lands could be watched with equal facility. The hill-top had been cleared of pine and fir. Behind the building there were sheer cliffs that forbade approach; and all around it a zone of repellent force, which could be made lethally destructive if desired, was maintained by machines that conserved the solar radiations and turned them into electricity.

The dwellers in the laboratory looked upon themselves as the priests of a sacred trust. They called themselves the Custodians. In the beginning they had numbered eight couples, men and women of the highest ability and attainment, specializing in all the main branches of science, who had withdrawn to this secluded place from a world ravaged by universal war, famine and disease, in which all other scientists and technicians were doomed to perish. The region about the laboratory was, at that time, unpeopled; and the building, reared with utmost secrecy, escaped destruction in the warfare

1

that wiped out whole cities and covered great empires with low-lying clouds of death.

Later, into the hills and valleys below the laboratory, there came a wretched remnant of city-dwellers from the plain. With these people, already brutalized by their sufferings and hardships, the handful of scientists held little commerce. Over a course of generations, the Custodians, intermarrying, decreased gradually in number through sterility; while the other fugitives multiplied, reverting more and more to a state of barbarism, and retaining only as a dim tribal legend the memory of the civilization from which they had fallen.

Living in mountain caves, or rude huts, hunting the forest animals with crudely made spears and bows, they lost all vestige of the high knowledge and mastery over nature possessed by their forefathers. They understood no longer the machines that rusted in the rotting cities. Through a sort of atavistic animism, they began to worship the elements that their fathers had subdued and controlled. At first they tried to assail the laboratory, impelled by a savage lust for loot and bloodshed; but, driven back with dire loss by the zone of deadly force, they soon abandoned their siege. In time they came to regard the Custodians as actual demigods, wielding mysterious, awful powers, and working incomprehensible miracles. Few of them now dared to approach the environs of the building, or to follow the wild boar and deer into the wooded valleys about it.

For many years, none of the Custodians was seen by the hill-people. Sometimes, by day, there were strange vapors that mounted to the clouds above the observatory; and at night the lofty windows burned like hill-descended stars. The Custodians, it was thought, were forging their thunderbolts in godlike secrecy.

Then, from the dreadful house on the height there came down one morning a single Custodian. He bore no weapon but carried an armful of heavy books. Approaching a small village of the tribesmen, he raised his right hand in the universal gesture of peace.

Many of the more timid fled before him, hiding themselves in their dark huts or amid the thick forest; and the other villagers received him with superstitious fear and suspicion. Speaking a language they could hardly understand, he told them that he had come to live among them. His name was Atullos. By degrees he won their confidence; and afterward he mated with a woman of the tribe. Like Prometheus, bringer of fire to ancient mankind, he sought to enlighten these savages; and undertook to reproduce for their benefit some of the inventions preserved in the laboratory. He told them nothing of his reasons for leaving the other Custodians, with whom he had held no communication since joining the hill-people.

Atullos had brought with him no other equipment than his few books. For lack of even the most rudimentary tools and materials, his scientific labors were fraught with immense difficulty. The savages, in their reversion, had lost even the knowledge of metals. Their weapons were those of the Stone Age; their ploughshares crooked sticks of fire-hardened wood. Atullos was compelled to spend whole years in mining and smelting the ores that he required for his tools and machines; and he even made long, hazardous journeys to obtain a supply of certain elements lacking in that region. From one of these journeys he failed to return; and it was believed that he had been slain by the warriors of a hostile and very brutal tribe upon whose territory he had intruded in his search.

He left behind him one child, the boy Torquane, whose mother had died shortly after the child's birth. Also, as a legacy to the tribe, he left a few tools of copper and iron, in whose forging he had instructed some of the more intelligent men. The machines on which he had labored with such pain and patience were only half-completed; and following his disappearance, no one was competent to finish them. They were designed for the development of electric power, and the use and control of certain cosmic radiations; but the tribesmen who had assisted Atullos knew nothing of their purpose and the principles involved.

Atullos had meant to instruct his son Torquane in all the lore of the Custodians; and thus the elder sciences, conserved so jealously by a few, might again have become in time the heritage of all mankind. Torquane had reached the age of four when Atullos vanished; and he had learned no more than the alphabet and a few simple rules of arithmetic. For lack of his father's guidance, this rudimentary knowledge was of little use to him; and, though naturally precocious and brilliant beyond his age, he could not continue for himself the education that Atullos had begun.

In the soul of Torquane, however, as he grew to manhood among primitive companions, there burned the spark of a restless aspiration, an inherited craving for knowledge, that set him apart from the others.

He remembered more of his father than most children recall when deprived of the parent at so early an age; and he learned from his fellows that Atullos had been one of the Custodians, who were looked upon by the tribe as beings with divine powers and attributes. It was commonly believed that the Custodians had banished Atullos from their midst because of his desire to help and enlighten the hill-people. Slowly, as his mind matured, there came to Torquane an understanding of the altruistic aims of his father, who had dreamt of restoring the old sciences in a darkened world.

Torquane lived the rude life of the tribesmen, hunting the hare, the boar and the deer, and climbing the precipitous crags and mountains. Excelling in all barbarous sports, he became very hardy and self-reliant. Outwardly he differed little from the other lads, except for his fairer skin and straighter features, and the dreaminess that filmed his bright eyes on occasion. As he neared his full growth, he became a leader among the youths, and was regarded with peculiar respect as the son of that Atullos who had become a sort of tutelary god for the hill-men after his death.

Often the boy visited the deep, dry cave which his father had used as a workshop. Here the tools, the half-built engines, the chemicals, books and manuscripts of Atullos were stored. Torquane examined them all with a great and growing wistfulness, trying vainly to guess the secret of the machines, and spelling painfully, letter by letter, the words in the mouldering volumes, whose meaning he could not divine. Like a man who dwells in a dark place, yearning blindly for the sun, he felt himself on the threshold of a luminous world; but light was denied him, and all his strivings ended only in deeper confusion.

Often, as he grew older, his thoughts turned to the mystery of the high and guarded citadel from which his father had come down to join the tribesmen. From certain vantage points on the higher hills he could see its observatory towers looming darkly above the cleared eminence. His comrades, like their forefathers, shunned the neighborhood as a place of supernatural peril, where the Custodians' thunderbolts would promptly strike down the intruder. For many years no one had beheld the Custodians; their voices which, it was said, had formerly spoken like the mountain thunder, threatening or warning the whole countryside, were no longer heard. But no man dreamt of penetrating their seclusion.

Torquane, however, knowing his kinship to the Custodians, wondered much concerning them. A strange curiosity drew him again and again to the hills below the laboratory. From such viewpoints, however, he could see nothing of the occupants or their activities. All was still and silent, and this very stillness, by degrees, emboldened the boy and drew him nearer to the dreaded eyrie.

Using all his stealth of woodcraft, and treading with utmost care lest a leaf or twig should crackle beneath him, he climbed one day the steep, heavily forested slope toward the building. Breathless with awe and apprehension, he peered at last from behind the bole of a gnarly pine that grew just beyond the verge of the laboratory grounds.

Grim, repellent, fortress-like, the rectilinear walls and square towers bulked above him against a heaven of light clouds. The windows glimmered blankly, withholding all their secrets. In the building's front an open doorway arched, beyond which, in silver flashes, Torquane discerned the leaping of fountains amid a sunlit court.

Sapling firs and pines had begun to invade the level, cleared area of the grounds. Some of them were already shoulder-high, while others rose only to a man's waist or knees, offering little obstruction to the view. Amid these miniature thickets Torquane heard a vengeful humming that might have been made by some invisible throng of bees. The sound maintained always the same position, the same pitch. Peering closely, he saw that there was a yard-wide line of bare, vacant soil running like a path amid the young co-nifers, and following the apparent course of the sound. This line, he knew suddenly, betokened the force-barrier beyond which no man could pass; and the humming was the noise made by the repellent, lethal power.

Much of the area between the saplings and the laboratory was filled with rows of vegetables, and there was also a small flower garden. The place bore evidence of careful tending and had been watered recently; but no one was in sight at the time. In the building itself, as Torquane stared and listened, there began a sonorous iron throbbing whose cause, in his complete ignorance of machinery, he could not imagine. Alarmed by the loudening noise, which seemed full of mysterious menace, Torquane fled on the wooded slope, and did not venture to return for many days.

Curiosity, and some emotion deeper than curiosity, whose nature and origin he could not have defined, impelled him to revisit the place in spite of his vague, half-superstitious fears and intuitions of danger.

Peering, as before, from the shelter of the ancient pines, he beheld for the first time one of the building's occupants. At a distance of no more than twenty yards from his hiding-place, a girl was stooping above the violets and pansies in the trimly plotted flower garden.

Torquane thought that he gazed upon a goddess: for, among all the village girls, there was none half so lovely and graceful as this incredible being. Clad in a gown of light April green, her hair falling in a luminous yellow cloud about her shoulders, she seemed to cast a brightness on the flowers as she moved among them.

Drawn by a strange fascination such as he had never before experienced, the boy leaned from behind the sheltering pine, forgetful of his fears, and unconscious that he was exposing himself to view. Only when the girl hap-pened to glance toward him, and gave a low, startled cry as her eyes met his, did he realize the indiscretion into which he had been betrayed.

Torquane was torn between the impulse of flight and a strong, unreasoned attraction that made him unwilling to go. This girl, he knew, was one of the Custodians; and the Custodians were demigods who wished no intercourse with men. Yet, through his father he was able to claim kinship with these lofty beings. And the girl was so beautiful, and her eyes, meeting his across the flower-plot, were so kind and gentle in spite of their startlement, that he ceased to apprehend the instant doom that his daring might perhaps have earned. Surely, even if he remained and spoke to her, she would not loose against him the dreadful lightning of the Custodians.

Raising his hand in a gesture of placation, he stepped forward among the seedling conifers, stopping only when he neared the vicious humming of the invisible force-barrier. The girl watched him with palpable amazement, her eyes widening, and her face paling and then reddening as she grew aware of Torquane's comeliness and the undisguised ardor of his gaze. For a moment it seemed that she would turn and leave the garden. Then, as if she had conquered her hesitancy, she came a little nearer to the barrier.

"You must go away," she said, in words that differed somewhat from those of the dialect familiar to Torquane. But he understood the words and to him their strangeness savored of divinity. Without heeding the admonition, he stood like one enchanted.

"Go quickly," warned the girl, a sharper note in her voice. "It is not allowable that any barbarian should come here."

"But I am not a barbarian," said Torquane proudly. "I am the son of Atullos, the Custodian. My name is Torquane. Can we not be friends?"

The girl was plainly surprised and perturbed. At the mention of Atullos' name, a shadow darkened her eyes; and behind the shadow an obscure terror seemed to lurk.

"No, no," she insisted. "It is impossible. You must not come here again. If my father knew—"

At that instant the humming of the barrier deepened, loud and angry as the buzzing of a million wasps, and Torquane felt in his flesh an electric tingling, such as he had felt during violent thunderstorms. All at once the air was lined with sparks and bright fiery threads, and was swept by a wave of ardent heat. Before Torquane the little pines and firs appeared to wither swiftly, and some of them leapt into sudden flame.

"Go! go!" he heard the crying of the girl, as he fell back before the moving barrier. She fled toward the laboratory, looking back over her shoulder as she went. Torquane, half-blinded by the weaving webs of fire, saw that a man had appeared in the portals, as if coming to meet her. The man was old and white-bearded, and his face was stern as that of some irate deity.

Torquane knew that this being had perceived his presence. His fate would be that of the seared saplings if he lingered. Again a superstitious terror rose within him, and he ran swiftly into the sheltering gloom of the ancient forest.

Heretofore Torquane had known only the aimless longings of adolescence. He had cared little for any of the savage though often not uncomely maidens of the hill-people. Doubtless he would have chosen one of them in time; but, having seen the fair daughter of the Custodian, he thought only of her, and his heart became filled with a turmoil of passion that was all the wilder because of its overweening audacity and apparent hopelessness.

Proud and reticent by nature, he concealed this love from his companions, who wondered somewhat at his gloomy moods and the fits of idleness that alternated with feverish toil and sport.

Sometimes he would sit for whole days in a deep study, contemplating the machines and volumes of Atullos; sometimes he would lead the younger men in the chase of some dangerous animal, risking his own life with a madder disregard than ever before. And often he would absent himself on lonely expeditions that he never explained to the others.

These expeditions were always to the region about the laboratory. For a youth of Torquane's ardor and courage, the peril of such visits became an excitant rather than a deterrent. He was careful, however, to keep himself hidden from view; and he maintained a respectful distance from the humming barrier.

Often he saw the girl as she moved about her garden labors, tending the blossoms and vegetables; and he fed his desperate longing on such glimpses, and dreamed wildly of carrying her away by force, or of making himself the master of the laboratory. He suspected, shrewdly, that the Custodians were few in number, since he had seen only the girl and the old man who was probably her father. But it did not occur to him that these two were the sole tenants of the massive citadel.

It seemed to Torquane, pondering with a lover's logic, that the girl had not disliked him. She had warned him to go away, had called him a barbarian. Nevertheless he felt that she had not been offended by his presumption in accosting her. He was sure that he could win her love if given the opportunity. Mating with a daughter of the Custodians, he would win admittance to that world of light and knowledge from which his father had come; that world which had tantalized his dreams. Tirelessly he schemed and plotted, trying to devise a way in which he could pass the force-barrier, or could communicate with the girl without bringing upon himself the Custodian's anger.

Once, by moonlight, he attempted to climb the cliffs behind the laboratory, working his way hazardously from coign to coign. He abandoned the attempt only when he came to an overhanging wall of rock that was smooth as beaten metal.

There came the day when Torquane, revisiting the woods that pressed close upon the laboratory garden, grew aware of an unwonted silence weighing oppressively upon all things. For a few instants he was puzzled, failing to comprehend the cause. Then he realized that the silence was due to a cessation of that humming noise which had signalized the presence of the barrier.

The grounds were deserted, and, for the first time, the building's heavy cedar portals had been closed. Nowhere was there any sound or visual sign of human occupation.

For awhile Torquane was suspicious, apprehending a trap with the instinct of a wild creature. Knowing nothing of machinery, it did not occur to him that the repellent power had failed through the wearing out of its hidden generators. Perplexed and wondering, he waited for hours, hoping to catch a glimpse of the girl. But the garden remained empty, and no one opened the frowning portals.

Alert and vigilant, the boy still watched. The forest's afternoon shadows began to lengthen, invading the laboratory grounds. Screaming harshly, a mountain blue-jay flashed from the pine above Torquane, and flew unharmed across the area that the lethal screen had formerly barred to all ingress of living things. An inquisitive squirrel raced among the saplings, over the bare path of the barrier, and chittered impudently in a plot of young corn and beans. Half incredulous, Torquane knew that the barrier was gone; but still his caution prevailed, and he went away at last.

"Varia, we cannot repair the generators," said the aged Phabar to his daughter. "The work is beyond my strength or yours. Also, metals are required which we cannot procure in their native state, and can no longer make with the weakening atomic transformers. Sooner or later the savages will learn that the force-barrier has ceased to exist. They will attack the laboratory—and will find only an old man and a girl to oppose them.

"The end draws near, for in any case I have not long to live. Alas! if there were only some younger man to assist me in my labors, and in defending the laboratory—some worthy and well-trained youth to whose care I could leave you, and could leave our heritage of science! But I am the last of the Custodians—and soon the darkness into which mankind has fallen will be complete, and none will remember the ancient knowledge."

"What of that boy who calls himself the son of Atullos?" ventured Varia timidly. "I am sure he is intelligent; and he would learn quickly if you were to receive him into the laboratory."

"Never!" cried Phabar, his quavering voice grown loud and deep with an old anger. "He is a mere savage, like the rest of mankind—and moreover I would rather receive a wild beast than the progeny of the false Atullos—that Atullos whom I drove from the laboratory because of his evil passion for your mother. One would think you were enamored of this young forest wolf. Speak not of him again."

He glared suspiciously at the girl, the rancor of unquenched enmity and jealousy toward Atullos glowing in his sunken eyes, and then turned with palsy-shaken fingers to the test-tubes and retorts among which he was still wont to busy himself in pottering experiments.

Torquane, returning the next day, verified his discovery of the barrier's failure. He could now approach the building if he wished, without peril of being blasted from existence at the first step. Boldly he went forward into the gardens and followed a little path that led to the shut portals. Coming in plain view of the windows, he laid his bow and arrows on the ground as a token of his peaceful intent.

When he neared the portals, a man appeared on one of the high towers and trained downward a long metal tube revolving on a pivot. It was the old man he had seen before. From the tube's mouth there leaped in swift succession a number of little shafts of silent flame that played around Torquane and blackened the soil and flower-beds wherever they struck. Phabar's aim was uncertain, due to his aging eyesight and trembling hands, for none of the fire-bolts found its mark. Torquane went away, concluding that his overtures were still undesired by the Custodians.

As he entered the woods, he was startled by a human shape that drew back stealthily into the shadows. It was the first time he had seen anyone lurking in that century-shunned locality. In that brief glimpse, Torquane knew the man for a stranger. He wore no garment except a wolf-skin, and carried for weapon only a crude spear tipped with flint. His features were brutal and degraded, and his forehead was striped with red and yellow earths, identifying him as a member of that extremely degenerate tribe which was believed to have slain Torquane's father.

Torquane hailed the man but received no answer other than the crackling of twigs and the sound of running footsteps. He dispatched an arrow after the intruder, and lost sight of him among the tree-trunks before he could notch a second arrow to the string. Feeling that the man's presence boded no good to the Custodians or his own people, he followed for some distance, trailing the stranger easily but failing to overtake him.

Disturbed and uneasy, he returned to the village. After that, for long hours daily, and sometimes by night, he watched the hills about the laboratory, glimpsing more than once the strange tribesman together with others plainly of the same clan. These savages were very furtive, and in spite of all his woodcraft they avoided any direct encounter with Torquane. It became manifest that the laboratory was the center of their interest, since he found them lurking always somewhere in its neighborhood. From day to day their numbers increased; and Torquane soon conceived the idea that they were planning an attack upon the building. Henceforth the torments of his baffled love became mingled with fears for the safety of its object.

He had kept this love and his trips and vigils secret from his comrades. Now, calling together the young men and boys who acknowledged him as their leader, he told them all that he had experienced and observed. Some, learning that the force-barrier was dead, urged an immediate assault upon the laboratory, and promised Torquane their assistance in capturing the girl. Torquane, however, shook his head, saying:

"A deed such as this would ill become the son of Atullos. I will take no woman against her will. Rather would I have you aid me in protecting the Custodians, who are now few and feeble, against the marauding of this alien tribe."

Torquane's followers were no less willing to fight the intruders than to assail the laboratory. Indeed, the alien clansmen were regarded as natural foes; and their slaying of Atullos had not been forgotten. When it became generally known that they were lurking about the laboratory, many of the tribe's older warriors pledged assistance to Torquane in repelling them; and the youth soon found himself the leader of a small army.

Scouts were sent out to watch closely the movements of the foreigners, who had grown bolder with daily re-enforcements. At midnight some of the scouts reported that they were gathering on the slope below the laboratory. Their exact number was hard to determine because of the thick forest. Some of them had been seen stripping a fallen pine of its boughs with stone axes; and it seemed plain that the attack was imminent, and that the pine would be used as a sort of battering-ram to break in the portals.

Torquane marshaled immediately his entire force, numbering close to a hundred men and boys. They were armed with copper knives or spears, well-seasoned oak or dogwood bows, and quivers filled with copper-tipped arrows. In addition to his own bow and knife, Torquane carried with much caution a small earthen jar filled with a grey powder, which he had taken from Atullos' workshop. Years before during his boyhood, prompted by a spirit of crude experimentation, he had dropped a pinch of the powder upon a bed of coals, and had been startled by the loud explosion that resulted. After that, realizing his complete ignorance of such matters, he had feared to experiment with any more of the chemicals prepared and stored by his father. Now, recalling the powder's properties, it occurred to him that he might make an effective use of it in the battle against the invaders.

Marching with all possible speed, the little army reached in an hour the starlit height on which stood the dark laboratory. The wooded slope was apparently clear of the alien savages who had swarmed upon it earlier that night; and Torquane began to fear that they had already assaulted and taken the building. However, when he and his men emerged from the forest on the edge of the gardens, they saw that the attack had just begun. The grounds swarmed with stealthy, silent shapes, dimly discernible, who moved with a concerted surging toward the still and unlit edifice. It was as if an army of shadows had beleaguered a phantom fortress. Then the eerie silence was shattered by a loud crashing together with an outburst of ferocious howling from the savages.

Torquane and his followers, rushing forward, saw the center of the dark horde surge backward a little. They knew that the battering-ram had failed to break in the cedar portals at its first impact and was being withdrawn for a second attempt.

Torquane, running well ahead of his men, ignited with a pitchy pine brand the fuse of tindery vegetable fiber which he had prepared for the earthen jar. The fuse burned perilously close to the jar's contents ere he came within hurling distance of that savage horde. He heard another and harsher crashing, followed by wild shouts of triumph, as if the door had given way. Then the jar, flung with all his strength, exploded with a great flash that lit the entire scene, together with a deafening detonation as of mountain thunder. Torquane, who had been prepared for some violent result, was hurled backward to the ground with stunning force; and his followers stood aghast, believing that they had witnessed the falling of a fiery bolt launched by some hidden Custodian.

A similar belief, it seemed, had been impressed even more powerfully upon the minds of the besiegers: for they fled on all sides in dire disorder. Some were speared in the darkness by Torquane's men, and the rest scattered amid the pines with frightful howls.

Thus, for the first time since the beginning of the dark era, gunpowder was used in battle.

Torquane, regaining his feet, found that the combat was already over. He advanced cautiously, and came upon the dismembered bodies of several of the invaders lying strewn about a garden plot that had been blasted and deeply pitted by the explosion. All the others, it seemed, had either escaped or been accounted for by his warriors. There was small likelihood that the savages would soon repeat their assault on the laboratory.

However, for the remainder of that night he and his followers kept watch about the building. Lest its inmates should mistake them for enemies, he went more than once to the portals, which had been shattered inward by the pine ram, and shouted aloud to declare his peaceful intentions. He had hoped for some sign from the girl: but in the courtyard beyond the broken door there was naught but the ghostly plashing of fountains. All the windows remained lightless; and a tomblike silence hung upon the building.

At earliest dawn, Torquane, accompanied by two of his warriors, ventured to enter the courtyard. In an angle of its opposite side, they came to an open doorway giving admission to a long empty hall illumined dimly by a single globe of mysterious blue light. They followed the hall, and Torquane shouted as they went but was answered only by hollow-sounding echoes. A little awed, and wondering if the silence might betoken some cunning trap, they reached the hall's end and paused on the threshold of an immense chamber.

The place was crowded with unknown, intricate machines. Tall dynamos towered to the skylighted roof; and everywhere, on wooden benches and shelves or stone-topped tables, there were huge and strangely shaped vessels, and vials and beakers filled with hueless or colored liquids. Gleaming, silent motors bulked in the corners. Apparatuses of a hundred forms, whose use the young barbarians could not imagine, littered the paved floor and were piled along the walls.

In the midst of all this paraphernalia, an old man sat before one of the vial-laden tables in a chair of cedarwood. The light of sunless morning, livid and ghastly, mingled with the glow of blue lamps on his sunken features. Beside him the girl stood, confronting the intruders with startled eyes.

"We come as friends," cried Torquane, dropping his bow on the floor.

The old Custodian, glowering with half-senile anger, made an effort to rise from his chair, but sank back as if the exertion were beyond his strength. He spoke faintly, and motioned with weak fingers to the girl, who, lifting from the table a glass filled with a water-clear liquid, held it firmly to his lips. He drank a portion of the liquid, and then, after a single convulsive shudder, he rested limply in the chair, his head lolling on his bosom and his body seeming to sag and shrivel beneath its garments.

For an instant, with dilated eyes and pallid features, the girl turned again toward Torquane. It seemed that she hesitated. Then, draining the remainder of the hueless liquid from the glass in her hand, she fell to the floor like a toppling statue.

Torquane and his companions, amazed and mystified, went forward into the room. A little doubtful of the strange contrivances that surrounded them, they ventured to inspect the fallen girl and the seated ancient. It was plain that both were dead; and it dawned upon them that the water-clear liquid must have been a poison more swift and violent than any with which they were familiar: a poison that was part of the lost science of the Custodians.

Torquane, peering down at the still, inscrutable face of Varia, was filled with a blind mingling of sorrow and bafflement. It was not thus that he had dreamt of entering the guarded citadel and winning the Custodian's daughter.

Never would he retrieve the mysterious lore of the Custodians or understand their machines, or read their ciphered books. It was not for him to finish the Promethean labors of Atullos, and re-illuminate the dark world with science. These things, with the girl Varia for mate and instructress, he might have done. But now, many centuries and cycles would pass, ere the lifting of the night of barbarism; and other hands than those of Torquane, or the sons of Torquane, would rekindle the lamp of ancient knowledge.

Still, though he knew it not in his sorrow and frustration, there remained other things: the clean, sweet lips of the simple hill-girl who would bear his children; the wild, free life of man, warring on equal terms with nature and maintaining her laws obediently; the sun and stars unclouded by the vapors of man's making; the air untainted by his seething cities.

THE DEATH OF MALYGRIS

At the hour of interlunar midnight, when lamps burned rarely and far apart in Susran, and slow-moving autumn clouds had muffled the stars, King Gadeiron sent forth into the sleeping city twelve of his trustiest mutes. Like shadows gliding through oblivion, they vanished upon their various ways; and each of them, returning presently to the darkened palace, led with him a shrouded figure no less silent and discreet than himself.

In this manner, groping along tortuous alleys, through blind cypress-caverns in the royal gardens, and down subterranean halls and steps, twelve of the most powerful sorcerers of Susran were brought together in a vault of oozing, death-grey granite, far beneath the foundations of the palace.

The entrance of the vault was guarded by earth-demons that obeyed the arch-sorcerer, Maranapion, who had long been the king's councillor. These demons would have torn limb from limb any who came unprepared to offer them a libation of fresh blood. The vault was lit dubiously by a single lamp, hollowed from a monstrous garnet, and fed with vipers' oil. Here Gadeiron, crownless, and wearing sackcloth dyed in sober purple, awaited the wizards on a seat of limestone wrought in the form of a sarcophagus. Maranapion stood at his right hand, immobile, and swathed to the mouth in the garments of the tomb. Before him was a tripod of orichalchum, rearing shoulder-high; and on the tripod, in a silver socket, there reposed the enormous blue eye of a slain Cyclops, wherein the archimage was said to behold weird visions. On this eye, gleaming balefully under the garnet lamp, the gaze of Maranapion was fixed with death-like rigidity.

From these circumstances, the twelve sorcerers knew that the king had convened them only because of a matter supremely grave and secret. The hour and fashion of their summoning, the place of meeting, the terrible elemental guards, the mufti worn by Gadeiron—all were proof of a need for

13

preternatural stealth and privity.

For awhile there was silence in the vault, and the twelve, bowing deferentially, waited the will of Gadeiron. Then, in a voice that was little more than a harsh whisper, the king spoke:

"What know ye of Malygris?"

Hearing that awful name, the sorcerers paled and trembled visibly; but, one by one, as if speaking by rote, several of the foremost made answer to Gadeiron's question.

"Malygris dwells in his black tower above Susran," said the first. "The night of his power is still heavy upon Poseidonis; and we others, moving in that night, are as shadows of a withered moon. He is overlord of all kings and sorcerers. Yea, even the triremes that fare to Tartessos, and the far-flown eagles of the sea, pass not beyond the black falling of his shadow."

"The demons of the five elements are his familiars," said the second. "The gross eyes of common men have beheld them often, flying like birds about his tower, or crawling lizard-wise on the walls and pavements."

"Malygris sits in his high hall," avowed the third. "Unto him, tribute is borne at the full moon from all the cities of Poseidonis. He takes a tithe of the lading of every galley. He claims a share of the silver and incense, of the gold and ivory sacred to the temples. His wealth is beyond the opulence of the sunken kings of Atlantis... even those kings who were thy forefathers, O Gadeiron."

"Malygris is old as the moon," mumbled a fourth. "He will live forever, armed against death with the dark magic of the moon. Death has become a slave in his citadel, toiling among other slaves, and striking only at the foes of Malygris."

"Much of this was true formerly," quoth the king, with a sinister hissing of his breath. "But now a certain doubt has arisen... for it may be that Malygris is dead."

A communicated shiver seemed to run about the assembly.

"Nay," said the sorcerer who had affirmed the immortality of Malygris. "For how can this thing have come to pass? The doors of his tower stood open today at sunset; and the priests of the ocean-god, bearing a gift of pearls and purple dyes, went in before Malygris, and found him sitting in his tall chair of the ivory of mastodons. He received them haughtily, without speaking, as is his wont; and his servants, who are half ape and half man, came in unbidden to carry away the tribute."

"This very night," said another, "I saw the stedfast lamps of the sable tower, burning above the city like the eyes of Taaran, god of Evil. The familiars have departed not from the tower as such beings depart at the dying of a wizard: for in that case, men would have heard their howling and lamentation in the dark."

"Aye," declared Gadeiron, "men have been befooled ere this. And Malygris was ever the master of illuding shows, of feints, and beguilements. But there is one among us who discerns the truth. Maranapion, through the eye of the Cyclops, has looked on remote things and hidden places. Even now, he peers upon his ancient enemy, Malygris."

Maranapion, shuddering a little beneath his shroud-like garments, seemed to return from his clairvoyant absorption. He raised from the tripod his eyes of luminous amber, whose pupils were black and impenetrable as jet.

"I have seen Malygris," he said, turning to the conclave. "Many times I have watched him thus, thinking to learn some secret of his close-hidden magic. I have spied upon him at noon, at evenfall, and through the drear, lampless vigils of midnight. And I have beheld him in the ashen dawn and the dawn of quickening fire. But always he sits in the great ivory chair, in the high hall of his tower, frowning as if with meditation. And his hands clutch always the basilisk-carven arms of the chair, and his eyes turn evermore, unshutting, unblinking, toward the orient window and the heavens beyond, where only high-risen stars and clouds go by.

"Thus have I beheld him for the space of a whole year and a month. And each day I have seen his monsters bring before him vessels filled with rare meat and drink; and later they have taken away the vessels untouched. And never have I discerned the least movement of his lips, nor any turning or tremor of his body.

"For these reasons, I deem that Malygris is dead; but by virtue of his supremacy in evil and in art magical, he sits defying the worm, still undecayed and incorrupt. And his monsters and his familiars attend him still, deceived by the lying appearance of life; and his power, though now an empty fraud, is still dark and awful upon Poseidonis."

Again, following the slow-measured words of Maranapion, there was silence in the vault. A dark, furtive triumph smouldered in the face of Gadeiron, on whom the yoke of Malygris had lain heavily, irking his pride. Among the twelve sorcerers, there was none who wished well to Malygris, nor any who did not fear him; and they received the annunciation of his demise with dreadful, half-incredulous joy. Some there were who doubted, holding that Maranapion was mistaken; and in the faces of all, as in somber mirrors, their awe of the master was still reflected.

Maranapion, who had hated Malygris above all others, as the one warlock whose art and power excelled his own, stood aloof and inscrutable like a poising vulture.

It was King Gadeiron who broke the gravid silence.

"Not idly have I called ye to this crypt, O sorcerers of Susran: for a work remains to be done. Verily, shall the corpse of a dead necromancer tyrannize over us all? There is mystery here, and a need to move cautiously, for the duration of his necromancy is yet unverified and untested. But I have called ye together in order that the hardiest among ye may take council with

Maranapion, and aid him in devising such wizardry as will now expose the fraud of Malygris, and evince his mortality to all men, as well as to the fiends that follow him still, and the ministering monsters."

A babble of disputation rose, and they who were most doubtful of this matter, and feared to work against Malygris in any fashion, begged Gadeiron's leave to withdraw. In the end, there remained seven of the twelve....

Swiftly, by dim and covert channels, on the day that followed, the death of Malygris was bruited throughout the isle Poseidonis. Many disbelieved the story, for the might of the wizard was a thing seared as with hot iron on the souls of them that had witnessed his thaumaturgies. However, it was recalled that during the past year few had beheld him face to face; and always he had seemed to ignore them, speaking not, and staring fixedly through the tower window, as if intent on far things that were veiled to others. During that time, he had called no man to his presence, and had sent forth no message, no oracle or decree; and they who had gone before him were mainly bearers of tribute and had followed a long-established custom.

When these matters became generally known, there were some who maintained that he sat thus in a long swoon of ecstasy or catalepsy, and would awaken therefrom in time. Others, however, held that he had died, and was able to preserve the deceitful aspect of life through a spell that endured after him. No man dared to enter the tall, sable tower; and still the shadow of the tower fell athwart Susran like the shadow of an evil gnomon moving on some disastrous dial; and still the umbrage of the power of Malygris lay stagnant as the tomb's night on the minds of men.

Now, among the five sorcerers who had begged Gadeiron's leave to depart, fearing to join their fellows in the making of wizardry against Malygris, there were two that plucked heart a little afterward, when they heard from other sources a confirmation of the vision beheld by Maranapion through the Cyclop's eye.

These two were brothers, named Nygon and Fustules. Feeling a certain shame for their timidity, and desiring to rehabilitate themselves in the regard of the others, they conceived an audacious plan.

When night had again fallen upon the city, bringing no moon, but only obscure stars and the scud of sea-born clouds, Nygon and Fustules went forth through the darkened ways and came to the steep hill at the heart of Susran, whereon, in half-immemorial years, Malygris had established his grim citadel.

The hill was wooded with close-grown cypresses, whose foliage, even to the full sun, was black and somber as if tarnished by wizard fumes. Crouching on either hand, they leaned like misshapen spirits of the night above the stairs of adamant that gave access to the tower. Nygon and Fustules, mounting the stairs, cowered and trembled when the boughs swung menacingly toward them in violent gusts of wind. They felt the dripping of heavy sea-dews, blown in their faces like a spittle of demons. The wood, it seemed, was full of execrably sighing voices, and weird whimpers and little moanings as of imp-children astray from Satanic dams.

The lights of the tower burned through the waving boughs, and seemed to recede unapproachably as they climbed. More than once, the two regretted their temerity. But at length, without suffering palpable harm or hindrance, they neared the portals, which stood eternally open, pouring the effulgence of still, unflaring lamps on the windy darkness.

Though the plan they had conceived was nefarious, they deemed it best to enter boldly. The purpose of their visit, if any should challenge or interrogate them, was the asking of an oracle from Malygris, who was famed throughout the isle as the most infallible of soothsayers.

Freshening momently from the sea beyond Susran, the wind clamored about the tower like an army of devils in flight from deep to deep, and the long mantles of the sorcerers were blown in their faces. But, entering the wide portals, they heard no longer the crying of the gale, and felt no more its pursuing rudeness. At a single step they passed into mausolean silence. Around them the lamplight fell unshaken on caryatides of black marble, on mosaics of precious gems, on fabulous metals and many-storied tapestries; and a tideless perfume weighed upon the air like a balsam of death.

They felt an involuntary awe, deeming the mortal stillness a thing that was hardly natural. But, seeing that the tower vestibule was unguarded by any of the creatures of Malygris, they were emboldened to go on and climb the marmorean stairs to the apartments above.

Everywhere, by the light of opulent lamps, they beheld inestimable and miraculous treasures. There were tables of ebony wrought with sorcerous runes of pearl and white coral; webs of silver and samite, cunningly pictured; caskets of electrum overflowing with talismanic jewels; tiny gods of jade and agate; and tall chryselephantine demons. Here was the loot of ages, lying heaped and mingled in utter negligence, without lock or ward, as if free for the taking of any casual thief.

Eyeing the riches about them with covetous wonder, the two sorcerers mounted slowly from room to room, unchallenged and unmolested, and came ultimately to that upper hall in which Malygris was wont to receive his visitors.

Here, as elsewhere, the portals stood open before them, and lamps burned as if in a trance of light. The lust of plunder was hot in their hearts. Made bolder still by the seeming desolation, and thinking now that the tower was unin-habited by any but the dead magician, they went in with little hesitancy.

Like the rooms below, the chamber was full of precious artifacts; and iron-bound volumes and brazen books of occult, tremendous necromancy, together with golden and earthen censers, and vials of unshatterable crystal, were strewn in weird confusion about the mosaic floor. At the very center, there sat the old archimage in his chair of primeval ivory, peering with stark, immovable eyes at the night-black window.

Nygon and Fustules felt their awe return upon them, remembering too clearly now the thrice-baleful mastery that this man had wielded, and the demon lore he had known, and the spells he had wrought that were irrefragable by other wizards. The specters of these things rose up before them as if by a final necromancy. With down-dropped eyes and humble mien, they went forward, bowing reverentially. Then, speaking aloud, in accordance with their predetermined plan, Fustules requested an oracle of their fortunes from Malygris.

There was no answer, and lifting their eyes, the brothers were greatly reassured by the aspect of the seated ancient. Death alone could have set the greyish pallor on the brow, could have locked the lips in a rigor as of fast-frozen clay. The eyes were like cavern-shadowed ice, holding no other light than a vague reflection of the lamps. Under the beard that was half silver, half sable, the cheeks had already fallen in as with beginning decay, showing the harsh outlines of the skull. The grey and hideously shrunken hands, whereon the eyes of enchanted beryls and rubies burned, were clenched inflexibly on the chair-arms, which had the form of arching basilisks.

"Verily," murmured Nygon, "there is naught here to frighten or dismay us. Behold, it is only the lich of an old man after all, and one that has cheated the worm of his due provender overlong."

"Aye," said Fustules. "But this man, in his time, was the greatest of all necromancers. Even the ring on his little finger is a sovereign talisman. The balas-ruby of the thumb-ring of his right hand will conjure demons from out the deep. In the volumes that lie about the chamber, there are secrets of perished gods and the mysteries of planets immemorial. In the vials, there are syrups that give strange visions, and philtres that can revive the dead. Among these things, it is ours to choose freely."

Nygon, eyeing the gems greedily, selected a ring that encircled the right forefinger with the sixfold coils of a serpent of orichalchum, bearing in its mouth a beryl shaped like a griffin's egg. Vainly, however, he tried to loosen the finger from its rigid clutch on the chair-arm, to permit the removal of the ring. Muttering impatiently, he drew a knife from his girdle and prepared to hew away the finger. In the meanwhile, Fustules had drawn his own knife as a preliminary before approaching the other hand.

"Is thy heart firm within thee, brother?" he inquired in a sort of sibilant whisper. "If so, there is even more to be gained than these talismanic rings. It is well known that a wizard who attains to such supremacy as Malygris, undergoes by virtue thereof a complete bodily transformation, turning his flesh into elements more subtle than those of common flesh. And whoso eats of his flesh even so much as a tiny morsel, will share thereafter in the powers owned by the wizard."

Nygon nodded as he bent above the chosen finger. "This, too, was in my thought," he answered.

Before he or Fustules could begin their ghoulish attack, they were startled by a venomous hissing that appeared to emanate from the bosom of Malygris. They drew back in amazement and consternation, while a small coral viper slid from behind the necromancer's beard, and glided swiftly over his knees to the floor like a sinuous rill of scarlet. There, coiling as if to strike, it regarded the thieves with eyes that were cold and malignant as two drops of frozen poison.

"By the black horns of Taaran!" cried Fustules. "It is one of Malygris' familiars. I have heard of this viper—"

Turning, the two would have fled from the room. But, even as they turned, the walls and portals seemed to recede before them, fleeing giddily and interminably, as if unknown gulfs had been admitted to the chamber. A vertigo seized them; reeling, they saw the little segments of mosaic under their feet assume the proportions of mighty flags. Around them the strewn books and censers and vials loomed enormous, rearing above their heads and barring their way as they ran.

Nygon, looking over his shoulder, saw that the viper had turned to a vast python, whose crimson coils were undulating swiftly along the floor. In a colossal chair, beneath lamps that were large as suns, there sat the colossal form of the dead archimage, in whose presence Nygon and Fustules were no more than pigmies. The lips of Malygris were still immobile beneath his beard; and his eyes still glared implacably upon the blackness of the far window. But at that instant a voice filled the awful spaces of the room, reverberating like thunder in the heavens, hollow and tremendous:

"Fools! ye have dared to ask me for an oracle. And the oracle is—death!"

Nygon and Fustules, knowing their doom, fled on in a madness of terror and desperation. Beyond the towering thuribles, the tomes that were piled like pyramids, they saw the threshold in intermittent glimpses, like a remote horizon. It withdrew before them, dim and unattainable. They panted as runners pant in a dream. Behind them, the vermilion python crawled; and overtaking them as they tried to round the brazen back of a wizard volume, it struck them down like fleeing dormice....

In the end, there was only a small coral viper, that crept back to its hiding-place in the bosom of Malygris....

Toiling by day and night, in the vaults under the palace of Gadeiron, with impious charms and unholy conjurations, and fouler chemistries, Maranapion and his seven coadjutors had nearly completed the making of their sorcery.

They designed an invultuation against Malygris, that would break the power of the dead necromancer by rendering evident to all the mere fact of his death. Employing an unlawful Atlantean science, Maranapion had created living plasm with all the attributes of human flesh, and had caused it to grow and flourish, fed with blood. Then he and his assistants, uniting their wills and convoking the forces that were blasphemy to summon, had compelled the shapeless, palpitating mass to put forth the limbs and members of a new-born child; and had formed it ultimately, after all the changes that man would undergo between birth and senescence, into an image of Malygris.

Now, carrying the process even further, they caused the simulacrum to die of extreme age, as Malygris had apparently died. It sat before them in a high chair, facing toward the east, and duplicating the very posture of the magician on his seat of ivory.

Nothing remained to be done. Forspent and weary, but hopeful, the sorcerers waited for the first signs of mortal decay in the image. If the spells they had woven were successful, a simultaneous decay would occur in the body of Malygris, incorruptible heretofore. Inch by inch, member by member, he would rot in the adamantine tower. His familiars would desert him, no longer deceived; and all who came to the tower would know his mortality; and the tyranny of Malygris would lift from Susran, and his necromancy be null and void as a broken pentacle in sea-girt Poseidonis.

For the first time since the beginning of their invultuation, the eight magicians were free to intermit their vigilance without peril of invalidating the charm. They slept soundly, feeling that their repose was well earned. On the morrow they returned, accompanied by King Gadeiron, to the vault in which they had left the plasmic image.

Opening the sealed door, they were met by a charnel odor, and were gratified to perceive in the figure the unmistakable signs of decomposition. A little later, by consulting the Cyclops' eye, Maranapion verified the paralleling of these marks in the features of Malygris.

A great jubilation, not unmingled with relief, was felt by the sorcerers and by King Gadeiron. Heretofore, not knowing the extent and duration of the powers wielded by the dead master, they had been doubtful of the efficacy of their own magic. But now, it seemed, there was no longer any reason for doubt.

On that very day it happened that certain sea-faring merchants went before Malygris to pay him, according to custom, a share of the profits of their latest voyage. Even as they bowed in the presence of the master, they became aware, by sundry disagreeable tokens, that they had borne tribute to a corpse. Not daring even then to refuse the long-exacted toll, they flung it down and fled from the place in terror.

Soon, in all Susran, there was none who doubted any longer the death of Malygris. And yet, such was the awe he had wrought through many lustrums, that few were venturous enough to invade the tower; and thieves were wary, and would not try to despoil its fabled treasures.

Day by day, in the blue, monstrous eye of the Cyclops, Maranapion saw the rotting of his dreaded rival. And upon him presently there came a strong desire to visit the tower and behold face to face that which he had witnessed only in vision. Thus alone would his triumph be complete.

So it was that he and the sorcerers who had aided him, together with King Gadeiron, went up to the sable tower by the steps of adamant, and climbed by the marble stairs, even as Nygon and Fustules before them, to the high room in which Malygris was seated…. But the doom of Nygon and Fustules, being without other witness than the dead, was wholly unknown to them.

Boldly and with no hesitation they entered the chamber. Slanting through the western window, the sun of late afternoon fell goldenly on the dust that had gathered everywhere. Spiders had woven their webs on the bright-jewelled censers, on the graven lamps, and the metal-covered volumes of sorcery. The air was stagnant with a stifling foulness of death.

The intruders went forward, feeling that impulse which leads the victors to exult over a vanquished enemy. Malygris sat unbowed and upright, his black and tattered fingers clutching the ivory chair-arms as of yore, and his empty orbits glowering still at the eastern window. His face was little more than a bearded skull; and his blackening brow was like worm-pierced ebony.

"O Malygris, I give thee greeting," said Maranapion in a loud voice of mockery. "Grant, I beseech thee, a sign, if thy wizardry still prevails, and hath not become the appanage of oblivion."

"Greeting, O Maranapion," replied a grave and terrible voice that issued from the maggot-eaten lips. "Indeed, I will grant thee a sign. Even as I, in death, have rotted upon my seat from that foul sorcery which was wrought in the vaults of King Gadeiron, so thou and thy fellows and Gadeiron, *living,* shall decay and putrefy wholly in an hour, by virtue of the curse that I put upon ye now."

Then the shrunken corpse of Malygris, fulminating the runes of an old Atlantean formula, cursed the eight sorcerers and King Gadeiron. The formula, at frequent intervals, was cadenced with fatal names of lethal gods; and in it were told the secret appellations of the black god of time, and the Nothingness that abides beyond time; and use was made of the titles of many tomb-lairing demons. Heavy and hollow-sounding were the runes, and in them one seemed to hear a noise of great blows on sepulchral doors, and a clangor of downfallen slabs. The air darkened as if with the hovering of seasonless night, and thereupon, like a breathing of the night, a chillness entered the chamber; and it seemed that the black wings of ages passed over the tower, beating prodigiously from void to void, ere the curse was done.

Hearing that maranatha, the sorcerers were dumb with the extremity of their dread; and even Maranapion could recall no counter-spell effectual in any degree against it.

All would have fled from the room ere the curse ended, but a mortal weakness was upon them, and they felt a sickness as of quick-coming death. Shadows were woven athwart their eyes; but through the shadows, each beheld dimly the instant blackening of the faces of his fellows, and saw the cheeks fall ruinously, and the lips curl back on the teeth like those of long-dead cadavers.

Trying to run, each was aware of his own limbs that rotted beneath him, pace by pace, and felt the quick sloughing of his flesh in corruption from the bone. Crying out with black tongues that shrivelled ere the cry was done, they fell down on the floor of the chamber. Life lingered in them, together with the dire knowledge of their doom, and they preserved something of hearing and sight. In the dark agony of their live corruption, they tossed feebly to and fro, and crawled inchmeal on the chill mosaic. And they still moved in this fashion, slowly and more imperceptibly, till their brains were turned to grey mould, and the sinews were parted from their bones, and the marrow was dried up.

Thus, in an hour, the curse was accomplished. The enemies of the necromancer lay before him, supine and shrunken, in the tomb's final posture, as if doing obeisance to a seated Death. Except for the garments, none could have told King Gadeiron from Maranapion, nor Maranapion from the lesser wizards.

The day went by, declining seaward; and, burning like a royal pyre beyond Susran, the sunset flung an aureate glare through the window, and then dropped away in red brands and funereal ashes. And in the twilight a coral viper glided from the bosom of Malygris, and weaving among the remnants of them that lay on the floor, and slipping silently down the stairs of marble, it passed forever from the tower.

THE TOMB-SPAWN

Evening had come from the desert into Faraad, bringing the last stragglers of caravans. In a wine-shop near the northern gate, many traveling merchants from outer lands, parched and weary, were refreshing themselves with the famed vintages of Yoros. To divert them from their fatigue, a story-teller spoke amid the clinking of the wine-cups:

"Great was Ossaru, being both king and wizard. He ruled over half the continent of Zothique. His armies were like the rolling sands, blown by the simoom. He commanded the genii of storm and of darkness, he called down the spirits of the sun. Men knew his wizardry as the green cedars know the blasting of levin.

"Half immortal, he lived from age to age, waxing in his wisdom and power till the end. Thasaidon, black god of evil, prospered his every spell and enterprise. And during his latter years he was companioned by the monster Nioth Korghai, who came down to Earth from an alien world, riding a fire-maned comet.

"Ossaru, by his skill in astrology, had foreseen the coming of Nioth Korghai. Alone, he went forth into the desert to await the monster. In many lands people saw the falling of the comet, like a sun that came down by night upon the waste; but only King Ossaru beheld the arrival of Nioth Korghai. He returned in the black, moonless hours before dawn, when all men slept, bringing the strange monster to his palace, and housing him in a vault beneath the throne-room, which he had prepared for Nioth Korghai's abode.

"Dwelling always thereafter in the vault, the monster remained unknown and unbeheld. It was said that he gave advice to Ossaru, and instructed him in the lore of the outer planets. At certain periods of the stars, women and young warriors were sent down as a sacrifice to Nioth Korghai; and these returned never to give account of that which they had seen. None could

23

surmise his aspect; but all who entered the palace heard ever in the vault beneath a muffled noise as of slow-beaten drums, and a regurgitation such as would be made by an underground fountain; and sometimes men heard an evil cackling as of a mad cockatrice.

"For many years King Ossaru was served by Nioth Korghai, and gave service to the monster in return. Then Nioth Korghai sickened with a strange malady, and men heard no more the cackling in the sunken vault; and the noises of drums and fountain-mouths grew fainter, and ceased. The spells of the wizard king were powerless to avert his death; but when the monster had died, Ossaru surrounded his body with a double zone of enchantment, circle by circle, and closed the vault. And later, when Ossaru died, the vault was opened from above, and the king's mummy was lowered therein by his slaves, to repose forever beside that which remained of Nioth Korghai.

"Cycles have gone by since then; and Ossaru is but a name on the lips of story-tellers. Lost now is the palace wherein he dwelt, and the city thereabout, some saying that it stood in Yoros, and some, in the empire of Cincor, where Yethlyreom was later built by the Nimboth dynasty. And this alone is certain, that somewhere still, in the sealed tomb, the alien monster abides in death, together with King Ossaru. And about them still is the inner circle of Ossaru's enchantment, rendering their bodies incorruptible throughout all the decay of cities and kingdoms; and around this is another circle, guarding against all intrusion: since he who enters there by the tomb's door will die instantly and will putrefy in the moment of death, falling to dusty corruption ere he strike the ground.

"Such is the legend of Ossaru and Nioth Korghai. No man has ever found their tomb; but the wizard Namirrha, prophesying darkly, foretold many ages ago that certain travellers, passing through the desert, would some day come upon it unaware. And he said that these travellers, descending into the tomb by another way than the door, would behold a strange prodigy. And he spoke not concerning the nature of the prodigy, but said only that Nioth Korghai, being a creature from some far world, was obedient to alien laws in death as in life. And of that which Namirrha meant, no man has yet guessed the secret."

The brothers Milab and Marabac, who were jewel-merchants from Ustaim, had listened raptly to the story-teller.

"Now truly this is a strange tale," said Milab. "However, as all men know, there were great wizards in the olden days, workers of deep enchantment and wonder; and also there were true prophets. And the sands of Zothique are full of lost tombs and cities."

"It is a good story," said Marabac, "but it lacks an ending. Prithee, O teller of tales, canst tell us no more than this? Was there no treasure of precious metals and jewels entombed with the monster and the king? I have seen sepulchers where the dead were walled with gold ingots, and sarcophagi that poured forth rubies like the gouted blood of vampires."

"I relate the legend as my fathers told it," affirmed the story-teller. "They who are destined to find the tomb must tell the rest—if haply they return from the finding."

Milab and Marabac had traded their store of uncut jewels, of carven talismans and small jasper and carnelian idols, making a good profit in Faraad. Now, laden with rosy and purple-black pearls from the southern gulfs, and the black sapphires and winy garnets of Yoros, they were returning northward toward Tasuun with a company of other merchants on the long, circuitous journey to Ustaim by the orient sea.

The way had led through a dying land. Now, as the caravan approached the borders of Yoros, the desert began to assume a profounder desolation. The hills were dark and lean, like recumbent mummies of giants. Dry waterways ran down to lake-bottoms leprous with salt. Billows of grey sand were driven high on the crumbling cliffs, where gentle waters had once rippled. Columns of dust arose and went by like fugitive phantoms. Over all, the sun was a monstrous ember in a charred heaven.

Into this waste, which was seemingly unpeopled and void of life, the caravan went warily. Urging their camels to a swift trot in the narrow, deep-walled ravines, the merchants made ready their spears and claymores and scanned the barren ridges with anxious eyes. For here, in hidden caves, there lurked a wild and half-bestial people, known as the Ghorii. Akin to the ghouls and jackals, they were eaters of carrion; and also they were anthropophagi, subsisting by preference on the bodies of travellers, and drinking their blood in lieu of water or wine. They were dreaded by all who had occasion to journey between Yoros and Tasuun.

The sun climbed to its meridian, searching with ruthless beams the nethermost umbrage of the strait, steep defiles. The fine ash-light sand was no longer stirred by any puff of wind. No lizards lifted or scurried on the rocks.

Now the road ran downward, following the course of some olden stream between acclivitous banks. Here, in lieu of former pools, there were pits of sand dammed up by riffles or boulders, in which the camels floundered knee-deep. And here, without the least warning, in a turn of the sinuous bed, the gully swarmed and seethed with the hideous earth-brown bodies of the Ghorii, who appeared instantaneously on all sides, leaping wolfishly from the rocky slopes or flinging themselves like panthers from the high ledges.

These ghoulish apparitions were unspeakably ferocious and agile. Uttering no sound, other than a sort of hoarse coughing and spitting, and armed only with their double rows of pointed teeth and their sickle-like talons, they poured over the caravan in a climbing wave. It seemed that there were scores of them to each man and camel. Several of the dromedaries were thrown to earth at once, with the Ghorii gnawing their legs and haunches and chines, or hanging dog-wise at their throats. They and their drivers were buried from sight by the ravenous monsters, who began to devour them immediately. Boxes of jewels and bales of rich fabrics were torn open in the melée, jasper and onyx idols were strewn ignominiously in the dust, pearls and rubies, unheeded, lay weltering in puddled blood; for these things were of no value to the Ghorii.

Milab and Marabac, as it happened, were riding at the rear. They had lagged behind, somewhat against their will, since the camel ridden by Milab had gone lame from a stone-bruise; and thus, by good fortune, they evaded the ghoulish onset. Pausing aghast, they beheld the fate of their companions, whose resistance was overcome with horrible quickness. The Ghorii, however, did not perceive Milab and Marabac, being wholly intent on devouring the camels and merchants they had dragged down, as well as those members of their own band that were wounded by the swords and lances of the travellers.

The two brothers, levelling their spears, would have ridden forward to perish bravely and uselessly with their fellows. But, terrified by the hideous tumult, by the odor of blood and the hyena-like scent of the Ghorii, their dromedaries balked and bolted, carrying them back along the route into Yoros.

During this unpremeditated flight they soon saw another band of the Ghorii, who had appeared far off on the southern slopes and were running to intercept them. To avoid this new peril Milab and Marabac turned their camels into a side ravine. Traveling slowly because of the lameness of Milab's dromedary, and thinking to find the swift Ghorii on their heels at any moment, they went eastward for many miles with the sun lowering behind them, and came at mid-afternoon to the low and rainless water-shed of that immemorial region.

Here they looked out over a sunken plain, wrinkled and eroded, where the white walls and domes of some innominate city gleamed. It appeared to Milab and Marabac that the city was only a few leagues away. Deeming they had sighted some hidden town of the outer sands, and hopeful now of escaping their pursuers, they began the descent of the long slope toward the plain.

For two days, on a powdery terrain that was like the bituminous dust of mummies, they traveled toward the ever-receding domes that had seemed so near. Their plight became desperate; for between them they possessed only a handful of dried apricots and a water-bag that was three-fourths empty. Their provisions, together with their stock of jewels and carvings, had been lost with the pack-dromedaries of the caravan. Apparently there was no pursuit from the Ghorii; but about them there gathered the red demons of thirst, the black demons of hunger. On the second morning Milab's camel refused to rise and would not respond either to the cursing of its master or the prodding of his spear. Thereafter, the two shared the remaining camel, riding together or by turns.

Often they lost sight of the gleaming city, which appeared and disappeared like a mirage. But an hour before sunset, on the second day, they followed the far-thrown shadows of broken obelisks and crumbling watch-towers into the olden streets.

The place had once been a metropolis; but now many of its lordly mansions were scattered shards or heaps of downfallen blocks. Great dunes of sand had poured in through proud triumphal arches, had filled the pavements and courtyards. Lurching with exhaustion, and sick at heart with the failure of their hope, Milab and Marabac went on, searching everywhere for some well or cistern that the long desert years had haply spared.

In the city's heart, where the walls of temples and lofty buildings of state still served as a barrier to the engulfing sand, they found the ruins of an old aqueduct, leading to cisterns dry as furnaces. There were dust-choked fountains in the market places; but nowhere was there anything to betoken the presence of water.

Wandering hopelessly on, they came to the ruins of a huge edifice which, it appeared, had been the palace of some forgotten monarch. The mighty walls, defying the erosion of ages, were still extant. The portals, guarded on either hand by green brazen images of mythic heroes, still frowned with unbroken arches. Mounting the marble steps, the jewelers entered a vast, roofless hall where cyclopean columns towered as if to bear up the desert sky.

The broad pavement flags were mounded with debris of arches and architraves and pilasters. At the hall's far extreme there was a dais of black-veined marble on which, presumably, a royal throne had once reared. Nearing the dais, Milab and Marabac both heard a low and indistinct gurgling as of some hidden stream or fountain, that appeared to rise from underground depths below the palace pavement.

Eagerly trying to locate the source of the sound, they climbed the dais. Here a huge block had fallen from the wall above, perhaps recently, and the marble had cracked beneath its weight, and a portion of the dais had broken through into some underlying vault, leaving a dark and jagged aperture. It was from this opening that the water-like regurgitation rose, incessant and regular as the beating of a pulse.

The jewelers leaned above the pit, and peered down into webby darkness shot with a doubtful glimmering that came from an indiscernible source. They could see nothing. A dank and musty odor touched their nostrils, like the breath of some long-sealed reservoir. It seemed to them that the steady fountain-like noise was only a few feet below in the shadows, a little to one side of the opening.

Neither of them could determine the depth of the vault. After a brief consultation they returned to their camel, which was waiting stolidly at the palace entrance; and removing the camel's harness they knotted the long reins and leather body-bands into a single thong that would serve them in lieu of rope. Going back to the dais, they secured one end of this thong to the fallen block, and lowered the other into the dark pit.

Milab descended hand over hand into the depths for ten or twelve feet before his toes encountered a solid surface. Still gripping the thong cautiously, he found himself on a level floor of stone. The day was fast waning beyond the palace walls; but a wan glimmer was afforded by the hole in the pavement above; and the outlines of a half-open door, sagging at a ruinous angle, were revealed at one side by the feeble twilight that entered the vault from unknown crypts or stairs beyond.

While Marabac came nimbly down to join him, Milab peered about for the source of the water-like noise. Before him in the undetermined shadows he discerned the dim and puzzling contours of an object that he could liken only to some enormous clepsydra or fountain surrounded with grotesque carvings.

The light seemed to fail momently. Unable to decide the nature of the object, and having neither torch nor candle, he tore a strip from the hem of his hempen burnoose, and lit the slow-burning cloth and held it aloft at arm's length before him. By the dull, smouldering luminance thus obtained, the jewelers beheld more clearly the thing that bulked prodigious and monstrous, rearing above them from the fragment-littered floor to the shadowy roof.

The thing was like some blasphemous dream of a mad devil. Its main portion or body was urn-like in form and was pedestaled on a queerly tilted block of stone at the vault's center. It was palish and pitted with innumerable small apertures. From its bosom and flattened base many arm-like and leg-like projections trailed in swollen nightmare segments to the ground; and two other members, sloping tautly, reached down like roots into an open and seemingly empty sarcophagus of gilded metal, graven with weird archaic ciphers, that stood beside the block.

The urn-shaped torso was endowed with two heads. One of these heads was beaked like a cuttle-fish and was lined with long oblique slits where the eyes should have been. The other head, in close juxtaposition on the narrow shoulders, was that of an aged man, dark and regal and terrible, whose burning eyes were like balas-rubies and whose grizzled beard had grown to the length of jungle moss on the loathsomely porous trunk. This trunk, on the side below the human head, displayed a faint outline as of ribs; and some of the members ended in human hands and feet, or possessed anthropomorphic jointings.

Through heads, limbs and body there ran recurrently the mysterious noise of regurgitation that had drawn Milab and Marabac to enter the vault. At each repetition of the sound a slimy dew exuded from the monstrous pores and rilled sluggishly down in endless drops.

The jewelers were held speechless and immobile by a clammy terror. Unable to avert their gaze, they met the baleful eyes of the human head, glaring upon them from its unearthly eminence. Then, as the hempen strip in Milab's fingers burned slowly away and failed to a red smoulder, and darkness gathered again in the vault, they saw the blind slits in the other head open gradually, pouring forth a hot, yellow, intolerably flaming light as they expanded to immense round orbits. At the same time they heard a singular drum-like throbbing, as if the heart of the huge monster had become audible.

They knew only that a strange horror not of earth, or but partially of earth, was before them. The sight deprived them of thought and memory. Least of all did they remember the story-teller in Faraad, and the tale he had told concerning the hidden tomb of Ossaru and Nioth Korghai, and the prophecy of the tomb's finding by those who should come to it unaware.

Swiftly, with a dreadful stretching and straightening, the monster lifted its foremost members, ending in the brown, shrivelled hands of an old man, and reached out toward the jewelers. From the cuttle-fish beak there issued a shrill demonian cackling; from the mouth of the kingly greybeard head a sonorous voice began to utter words of solemn cadence, like some enchanter's rune, in a tongue unknown to Milab and Marabac.

They recoiled before the abhorrently groping hands. In a frenzy of fear and panic, by the streaming light of its incandescent orbs, they saw the anomaly rise and lumber forward from its stone seat, walking clumsily and uncertainly on its ill-assorted members. There was a trampling of elephantine pads—and a stumbling of human feet inadequate to bear up their share of the blasphemous hulk. The two stiffly sloping tentacles were withdrawn from the gold sarcophagus, their ends muffled by empty, jewel-sewn cloths of a precious purple, such as would be used for the winding of some royal mummy. With a ceaseless and insane cackling, a malign thundering as of curses that broke to senile quavers, the double-headed horror leaned toward Milab and Marabac.

Turning, they ran wildly across the roomy vault. Before them, illumined now by the pouring rays from the monster's orbits, they saw the half-open door of somber metal whose bolts and hinges had rusted away, permitting it to sag inward. The door was of cyclopean height and breadth, as if designed for beings huger than man. Beyond it were the dim reaches of a twilight corridor.

Five paces from the doorway there was a faint red line that followed the chamber's conformation on the dusty floor. Marabac, a little ahead of his brother, crossed the line. As if checked in mid-air by some invisible wall, he faltered and stopped. His limbs and body seemed to melt away beneath the burnoose—the burnoose itself became tattered as with incalculable age. Dust floated on the air in a tenuous cloud, and there was a momentary gleaming of white bones where his outflung hands had been. Then the bones too were gone—and an empty heap of rags lay rotting on the floor.

A faint odor as of corruption rose to the nostrils of Milab. Uncomprehending, he had checked his own flight for an instant. Then, on his shoulders, he felt the grasp of slimy, withered hands. The cackling and muttering of the heads was like a demon chorus behind him. The drum-like beating, the noise of rising fountains, were loud in his ears. With one swiftly dying scream he followed Marabac over the red line.

The enormity that was both man and star-born monster, the nameless amalgam of an unearthly resurrection, still lumbered on and did not pause. With the hands of that Ossaru who had forgotten his own enchantment, it reached for the two piles of empty rags. Reaching, it entered the zone of death and dissolution which Ossaru himself had established to guard the vault forever. For an instant, on the air, there was a melting as of misshapen cloud, a falling as of light ashes. After that the darkness returned, and with the darkness, silence.

Night settled above that nameless land, that forgotten city; and with its coming the Ghorii, who had followed Milab and Marabac over the desert plain. Swiftly they slew and ate the camel that waited patiently at the palace entrance. Later, in the old hall of columns, they found that opening in the dais through which the jewelers had descended. Hungrily they gathered about the hole, sniffing at the tomb beneath. Then, baffled, they went away, their keen nostrils telling them that the scent was lost, that the tomb was empty either of life or death.

THE WITCHCRAFT OF ULUA

Sabmon the anchorite was famed no less for his piety than for his prophetic wisdom and knowledge of the dark art of sorcery. He had dwelt alone for two generations in a curious house on the rim of the northern desert of Tasuun: a house whose floor and walls were built from the large bones of dromedaries, and whose roof was a wattling composed of the smaller bones of wild dogs and men and hyenas. These ossuary relics, chosen for their whiteness and symmetry, were bound securely together with well-tanned thongs, and were joined and fitted with marvellous closeness, leaving no space for the blown sand to penetrate. This house was the pride of Sabmon, who swept it daily with a besom of mummy's hair, till it shone immaculate as polished ivory both within and without.

Despite his remoteness and reclusion, and the hardships that attended a journey to his abode, Sabmon was much consulted by the people of Tasuun, and was even sought by pilgrims from the further shores of Zothique. However, though not ungracious or inhospitable, he often ignored the queries of his visitors, who, as a rule, wished merely to divine the future or to ask advice concerning the most advantageous government of their temporal affairs. He became more and more taciturn with age, and spoke little with men in his last years. It was said, perhaps not untruly, that he preferred to talk with the ever-murmuring palms about his well, or the desert-wandering stars that went over his hermitage.

In the summer of Sabmon's ninety-third year, there came to him the youth Amalzain, his great-nephew, and the son of a niece that Sabmon had loved dearly in days before his retirement to a gymnosophic seclusion. Amalzain, who had spent all of his one-and-twenty years in the upland home of his parents, was on his way to Miraab, the capital of Tasuun, where he would serve as a cupbearer to Famorgh the king. This post, obtained for him by

31

influential friends of his father, was much coveted among the youth of the land, and would lead to high advancement if he were fortunate enough to win the king's favor. In accord with his mother's wish, he had come to visit Sabmon and to ask the counsel of the sage regarding various problems of worldly conduct.

Sabmon, whose eyes were undimmed by age and astronomy and much poring over volumes of archaic ciphers, was pleased with Amalzain and found in the boy something of his mother's beauty. And for this reason he gave freely of his hoarded wisdom; and, after uttering many profound and pertinent maxims, he said to Amalzain:

"It is indeed well that you have come to me: for, innocent of the world's turpitude, you fare to a city of strange sins and strange witcheries and sorceries. There are numerous evils in Miraab. Its women are witches and harlots, and their beauty is a foulness wherein the young, the strong, the valiant, are limed and taken."

Then, ere Amalzain departed, Sabmon gave to him a small amulet of silver, graven curiously with the migniard skeleton of a girl. And Sabmon said:

"I counsel you to wear this amulet at all times henceforward. It contains a pinch of ashes from the pyre of Yos Ebni, sage and archimage, who won supremacy over men and demons in elder years by defying all mortal temptation and putting down the insubordination of the flesh. There is a virtue in these ashes, and they will protect you from such evils as were overcome by Yos Ebni. And yet, peradventure, there are ills and enchantments in Miraab from which the amulet cannot defend you. In such case you must return to me. I shall watch over you carefully, and shall know all that occurs to you in Miraab: for I have long since become the owner of certain rare faculties of sight and hearing whose exercise is not debarred or limited by mere distance."

Amalzain, being ignorant of the matters at which Sabmon hinted, was somewhat bewildered by this peroration. But he received the amulet gratefully. Then, bidding Sabmon a reverential farewell, he resumed his journey to Miraab, wondering much as to the fortune that would befall him in that sinful and many-legended city.

II

Famorgh, who had grown old and senile amid his debaucheries, was the ruler of an aging, semi-desert land; and his court was a place of far-sought luxury, of obliquitous refinement and corruption. The youth Amalzain, accustomed only to the simple manners, the rude virtues and vices of country-dwelling folk, was dazzled at first by the sybaritic life around him. But a certain innate strength of character, fortified by the moral teachings of his parents and the precepts of his great-uncle, Sabmon, preserved him from any grave errors or lapses.

Thus it was that he served as a cupbearer at bacchanalian revels, but remained abstemious throughout, pouring night after night in the ruby-crusted cup of Famorgh the maddening wines that were drugged with cannabis and the stupefying arrack with its infusion of poppy. With untainted heart and flesh he beheld the infamous mummeries whereby the courtiers, vying with each other in shamelessness, attempted to lighten the king's ennui. Feeling only wonder or disgust, he watched the nimble and lascivious contortions of black dancers from Dooza Thom in the north, or saffron-bodied girls from the southern isles. His parents, who believed implicitly in the superhuman goodness of monarchs, had not prepared him for this spectacle of royal vice; but the reverence they had instilled so thoroughly into Amalzain led him to regard it all as being the peculiar but mysterious prerogative of the kings of Tasuun.

During his first month in Miraab, Amalzain heard much of the Princess Ulua, sole daughter of Famorgh and Queen Lunalia; but since the women of the royal family seldom attended the banquets or appeared in public, he did not see her. The huge and shadowy palace, however, was filled with whispers concerning her amours. Ulua, he was told, had inherited the sorceries of her mother Lunalia, whose dark, luxurious beauty, so often sung by bewitched poets, was now fallen to a haggish decrepitude. The lovers of Ulua were innumerable, and she often procured their passion or insured their fidelity by other charms than those of her person. Though little taller than a child, she was exquisitely formed and endowed with the loveliness of some female demon that might haunt the slumbers of youth. She was feared by many and her ill will was deemed a dangerous thing. Famorgh, no less blind to her sins and witcheries than he had been to those of Lunalia, indulged her in all ways and denied her nothing.

Amalzain's duties left him much idle time, for Famorgh usually slept the double sleep of age and intoxication after the evening revels. Much of this time he gave to the study of algebra and the reading of olden poems and romances. One morning, while he was engaged with certain algebraic calculations, there came to Amalzain a huge negress who had been pointed out to him as one of Ulua's waiting-women. She told him peremptorily that he was to follow her to the apartments of Ulua. Bewildered and amazed by this singular interruption of his studies, he was unable to reply for a moment. Thereupon, seeing his hesitation, the great black woman lifted him in her naked arms and carried him easily from the room and through the palace halls. Angry, and full of discomfiture, he found himself deposited in a chamber hung with shameless designs, where, amid the fuming of aphrodisiac vapors, the princess regarded him with luxurious gravity from a couch of fire-bright scarlet. She was small as a woman of the elf-folk, and voluptuous as a coiled lamia. The incense floated about her like sinuous veils.

"There are other things than the pouring of wine for a sottish monarch, or the study of worm-eaten volumes," said Ulua in a voice that was like the flowing of hot honey. "Sir cupbearer, your youth should have a better employment than these."

"I ask no employment, other than my duties and studies," replied Amalzain ungraciously. "But tell me, O princess, what is your will? Why has your serving-woman brought me here in a fashion so unseemly?"

"For a youth so erudite and clever, the question should be needless," answered Ulua, smiling obliquely. "See you not that I am beautiful and desirable? Behold! my arms are the portals of strange felicities. The pleasures I give are keener than the pangs of a fiery death. The dead kings of Tasuun will whisper enviously of our love to their dead queens in the immemorial granite vaults below Chaon Gacca. Thasaidon, the black, shadowy lord of hell, grown jealous of our raptures, will wish to become incarnate in a mortal body."

The vapors, mounting thickly from golden thuribles before the couch, were parted with a motion as of drawn draperies; and Amalzain saw that Ulua was clad only in breast-cups of coral and mother-of-pearl, and bracelets and anklets of jet....

"The matters whereof you speak are nothing to me," said the youth, untempted.

Ulua laughed lightly, and the vapors undulated as if in unison with her laughter, and were shaped dimly into obscene forms.

"Soon you will answer otherwise," she told the youth. "Few men have denied me long—and these few have regretted their refusal in the end. You may go now: but you will return to me presently—of your own accord."

For many days thereafter, Amalzain, going about his duties as usual, was aware of a strange haunting. It seemed now that Ulua was everywhere. Appearing at the revels, as if by some new caprice, she flaunted her evil beauty in the eyes of the young cupbearer; and often, by day, he met her in the palace gardens and corridors. All men spoke of her, as if conspiring tacitly to keep her in his thoughts; and it seemed that even the heavy arrases whispered her name as they rustled in the lost winds that wandered through the gloomy and interminable halls.

This, however, was not all: for her undesired image began to trouble his nightly dreams; and awakening, he heard the warm, dulcet languor of her voice, and felt the caress of light and subtle fingers in the darkness. Peering at the pale moon that waxed beyond the windows, above the black cypresses, he saw her dead, corroded face assume the living features of Ulua. The lithe and migniard form of the young witch appeared to move among the fabulous queens and goddesses that thronged the opulent hangings with their amours. Beheld as if through enchantment, her face leaned beside his in the mirrors; and she came and vanished, phantom-like, with seductive murmurs and wanton gestures, as he bent over his books. But though he was perturbed by these appearances, in which he could scarce distinguish the real from the illusory, Amalzain was still indifferent toward Ulua, being surely protected from her charms by the amulet containing the ashes of Yos Ebni, saint and sage and archimage. From certain curious flavors detected more than once in his food and drink, he suspected that the love-potions for which she had become infamous were being administered to him; but beyond a light and passing qualmishness, he experienced no ill effect whatever; and he was wholly ignorant of the spells woven against him in secret, and the thrice-lethal invultuations that were designed to wound his heart and senses.

Now (though he knew it not) his indifference was a matter of much gossip at the court. Men marvelled greatly at such exemption: for all whom the princess had chosen heretofore, whether captains, cupbearers or high dignitaries, or common soldiers and grooms, had yielded easily to her bewitchments. So it came to pass that Ulua was angered, since all men knew that her beauty was scorned by Amalzain, and her sorcery was impotent to ensnare him. Thereupon she ceased to appear at the revels of Famorgh; and Amalzain beheld her no longer in the halls and gardens; and neither his dreams nor his waking hours were haunted any more by the spell-wrought semblance of Ulua. So, in his innocence, he rejoiced as one who has encountered a grave peril and has come forth unharmed.

Then, later, on a certain night, as he lay sleeping tranquilly in the moonless hours before dawn, there came to him in his dream a figure muffled from crown to heel with the vestments of the tomb. Tall as a caryatid, awful and menacing, it leaned above him in silence more malignant than any curse; and the cerements fell open at the breast, and charnel-worms and death-scarabs and scorpions, together with shreds of rotting flesh, rained down upon Amalzain. Then, as he awoke from his nightmare, sick and stifled, he breathed a carrion fetor, and felt against him the pressure of a still, heavy body. Affrighted, he rose and lit the lamp; but the bed was empty. Yet the odor of putrefaction still lingered; and Amalzain could have sworn that the corpse of a woman, two weeks dead and teeming with maggots, had lain closely at his side in the darkness.

Thereafter, for many nights, his slumbers were broken by such foulnesses as this. Hardly could he sleep at all for the horror of that which came and went, invisible but palpable, in his chamber. Always he awoke from ill dreams, to find about him the stiffened arms of long-dead succubi, or to feel at his side the amorous trembling of fleshless skeletons. He was choked by the natron and bitumen of mummied breasts; he was crushed by the unremoving weight of gigantic liches; he was kissed nauseously by lips that were oozing tatters of corruption.

Nor was this all; for other abominations came to him by day, visible, and perceived through all his senses, and more loathsome even than the dead. Things that seemed as the leavings of leprosy crawled before him at high noon in the halls of Famorgh; and they rose up from the shadows and sidled toward him, leering whitely with faces that were no longer faces, and trying to caress him with their half-eaten fingers. About his ankles, as he went to and fro, there clung lascivious empusæ with breasts that were furred like the bat; and serpent-bodied lamiæ minced and pirouetted before his eyes, like the dancers before the king.

No longer could he read his books or solve his problems of algebra in peace: for the letters changed from moment to moment beneath his scrutiny and were twisted into runes of evil meaning; and the signs and ciphers he had written were turned into devils no bigger than large emmets, that writhed foully across the paper as if on a field, performing those rites which are acceptable only to Alila, queen of perdition and goddess of all iniquities.

Thus plagued and bedevilled, the youth Amalzain was near to madness; yet he dared not complain or speak to others of aught that he beheld; for he knew that these horrors, whether immaterial or substantial, were perceived only by himself. Nightly, for the full period of a moon, he lay with dead things in his chamber; and daily, in all his comings and goings, he was besought by abhorrent specters. And he doubted not that all these were the sendings of Ulua, angered by his refusal of her love; and he remembered that Sabmon had hinted darkly of certain enchantments from which the ashes of Yos Ebni, preserved in the silver amulet, might be powerless to defend him. And, knowing that such enchantments were upon him now, he recalled the final injunction of the old archimage.

So, feeling that there was no help for him save in the wizardry of Sabmon, he went before King Famorgh and begged a short leave of absence from the court. And Famorgh, who was well pleased with the cupbearer, and moreover had begun to note his thinness and pallor, granted the request readily.

Mounted on a palfrey chosen for speed and endurance, Amalzain rode northward from Miraab on a sultry morning in autumn. A strange heaviness had stilled all the air; and great coppery clouds were piled like towering, many-domed palaces of genii on the desert hills. The sun appeared to swim in molten brass. No vultures flew on the silent heavens; and the very jackals had retired to their lairs, as if in fear of some unknown doom. But Amalzain, riding swiftly toward Sabmon's hermitage, was haunted still by leprous larvæ that rose before him, posturing foully on the dun sands; and he heard the desirous moaning of succubi under the hooves of his horse.

The night waylaid him, airless and starless, as he came to a well amid dying palms. Here he lay sleepless, with the curse of Ulua still upon him: for it seemed that the dry, dusty liches of desert tombs reclined rigidly at his side; and bony fingers wooed him toward the unfathomable sand-pits from which they had risen.

Weary and devil-ridden, he reached the wattled house of Sabmon at noon of the next day. The sage greeted him affectionately, showing no surprise, and listened to his story with the air of one who harkens a twice-told tale.

"These things, and more, were known to me from the beginning," he said to Amalzain. "I could have saved you from the sendings of Ulua ere now; but it was my wish that you should come to me at this time, forsaking the court of the dotard Famorgh and the evil city of Miraab, whose iniquities are now at the full. The imminent doom of Miraab, though unread by her astrologers, has been declared in the heavens; and I would not that you should share the doom.

"It is needful," he went on, "that the spells of Ulua should be broken on this very day, and the sendings returned to her that sent them; since otherwise they would haunt you forever, remaining as a visible and tangible plague when the witch herself has gone to her black lord, Thasaidon, in the seventh hell."

Then, to the wonderment of Amalzain, the old magician brought forth from a cabinet of ivory an elliptic mirror of dark and burnished metal and placed it before him. The mirror was held aloft by the muffled hands of a veiled image; and peering within it, Amalzain saw neither his own face nor the face of Sabmon, nor aught of the room itself reflected. And Sabmon enjoined him to watch the mirror closely, and then repaired to a small oratory that was curtained off from the chamber with long and queerly painted rolls of camel-parchment.

Watching the mirror, Amalzain was aware that certain of the sendings of Ulua still came and went beside him, striving ever to gain his attention with unclean gestures such as harlots use. But resolutely he fixed his eyes on the void and unreflecting metal; and anon he heard the voice of Sabmon chanting without pause the powerful words of an antique formula of exorcism; and now from between the oratory curtains there issued the intolerable pungency of burning spices, such as are employed to drive away demons.

Then Amalzain perceived, without lifting his eyes from the mirror, that the sendings of Ulua had all vanished like vapors blown away by the desert wind. But in the mirror a scene limned itself darkly, and he seemed to look on the marble towers of the city of Miraab beneath overlooming bastions of ominous cloud. Then the scene shifted, and he saw the palace-hall where Famorgh nodded in wine-stained purple, senile and drunken, amid his ministers and sycophants. Again the mirror changed, and he beheld a room with tapestries of shameless design, where, on a couch of fire-bright crimson, the Princess Ulua sat with her latest lovers amid the fuming of golden thuribles.

Marvelling as he peered within the mirror, Amalzain witnessed a strange thing: for the vapors of the thuribles, mounting thickly and voluminously, took from instant to instant the form of those very apparitions by which he had been bedevilled so long. Ever they rose and multiplied, till the chamber teemed with the spawn of hell and the vomitings of the riven charnel. Betwixt Ulua and the lover at her right hand, who was a captain of the king's guard, there coiled a monstrous lamia, enfolding them both in its serpentine volumes and crushing them with its human bosom; and close at her left hand appeared a half-eaten corpse, leering with lipless teeth, from whose cerements worms were sifted upon Ulua and her second lover, who was a royal equerry. And, swelling like the fumes of some witches' vat, those other abominations pressed about the couch of Ulua with obscene mouthings and fingerings.

At this, like the mark of a hellish branding, horror was printed on the features of the captain and the equerry; and a terror rose in the eyes of Ulua like a pale flame ignited in sunless pits; and her breasts shuddered beneath the breast-cups. And now, in a trice, the mirrored room began to rock violently, and the censers were overturned on the tilting flags, and the shameless hangings shook and bellied like the blown sails of a vessel in storm. Great cracks appeared in the floor; and beside the couch of Ulua a chasm deepened swiftly, and then widened from wall to wall. The whole chamber was riven asunder, and the Princess and her two lovers, with all her loathly sendings about them, were hurled tumultuously into the chasm.

After that, the mirror darkened, and Amalzain beheld for a moment the pale towers of Miraab, tossing and falling on heavens black as adamant. The mirror itself trembled, and the veiled image of metal supporting it began to totter and seemed about to fall; and the wattled house of Sabmon shook in the passing earthquake, but, being stoutly built, stood firm while the mansions and palaces of Miraab went down in ruin.

When the earth had ceased its long trembling, Sabmon issued from the oratory.

"It is needless to moralize on what has happened," he said. "You have learned the true nature of carnal desire, and have likewise beheld the history of mundane corruption. Now, being wise, you will turn early to those things which are incorruptible and beyond the world."

Thereafter, till the death of Sabmon, Amalzain dwelt with him, and became his only pupil in the science of the stars and the hidden arts of enchantment and sorcery.

THE COMING OF THE WHITE WORM
(Chapter IX of the Book of Eibon)*

E vagh the warlock, dwelling beside the boreal sea, was aware of many strange and untimely portents in mid-summer. Frorely burned the sun above Mhu Thulan from a welkin clear and wannish as ice. At eve the aurora was hung from zenith to earth, like an arras in a high chamber of gods. Wan and rare were the poppies and small the anemones in the cliff-sequestered vales lying behind the house of Evagh; and the fruits in his walled garden were pale of rind and green at the core. Also, he beheld by day the unseasonable flight of great multitudes of fowl, going southward from the hidden isles beyond Mhu Thulan; and by night he heard the distressful clamor of other passing multitudes. And always, in the loud wind and crying surf, he harkened to the weird whisper of voices from realms of perennial winter.

Now Evagh was troubled by these portents, even as the rude fisher-folk on the shore of the haven below his house were troubled. Being a past-master of all sortilege, and a seer of remote and future things, he made use of his arts in an effort to divine their meaning. But a cloud was upon his eyes through the daytime; and a darkness thwarted him when he sought illumination in dreams. His most cunning horoscopes were put to naught; his familiars were silent or answered him equivocally; and confusion was amid all his geomancies and hydromancies and haruspications. And it seemed to Evagh that an unknown power worked against him, mocking and making impotent in such fashion the sorcery that none had defeated heretofore. And Evagh knew, by certain tokens perceptible to wizards, that the power was an evil power, and its boding was of bale to man.

Day by day, through the middle summer, the fisher-folk went forth in their coracles of elk-hide and willow, casting their seines. But in the seines they drew dead fishes, blasted as if by fire or extreme cold; and they drew living

* Rendered from the Old French manuscript of Gaspard du Nord.

monsters, such as their eldest captains had never beheld: things triple-headed and tailed and finned with horror; black, shapeless things that turned to a liquid foulness and ran from the net; or headless things like bloated moons with green, frozen rays about them; or things leprous-eyed and bearded with stiffly-oozing slime.

Then, out of the sea-horizoned north, where ships from Cerngoth were wont to ply among the Arctic islands, a galley came drifting with idle oars and aimlessly veering helm. The tide beached it among the boats of the fishermen, which fared no longer to sea but were drawn up on the sands below the cliff-built house of Evagh. And, thronging about the galley in awe and wonder, the fishers beheld its oarsmen still at the oars and its captain at the helm. But the faces and hands of all were stark as bone, and were white as the flesh of leprosy; and the pupils of their open eyes had faded strangely, being indistinguishable now from the whites; and a blankness of horror was within them, like ice in deep pools that are fast frozen to the bottom. And Evagh himself, descending later, also beheld the galley's crew, and pondered much concerning the import of this prodigy.

Loath were the fishers to touch the dead men; and they murmured, saying that a doom was upon the sea, and a curse upon all sea-faring things and people. But Evagh, deeming that the bodies would rot in the sun and would breed pestilence, commanded them to build a pile of driftwood about the galley; and when the pile had risen above the bulwarks, hiding from view the dead rowers, he fired it with his own hands.

High flamed the pile, and smoke ascended black as a storm-cloud, and was borne in windy volumes past the tall towers of Evagh on the cliff. But later, when the fire sank, the bodies of the oarsmen were seen sitting amid the mounded embers; and their arms were still outstretched in the attitude of rowing, and their fingers were clenched: though the oars had now dropped away from them in brands and ashes. And the captain of the galley stood upright still in his place: though the burnt helm had fallen beside him. Naught but the raiment of the corpses had been consumed; and they shone white as moon-washed marble above the charrings of wood; and nowhere upon them was there any blackness from the fire.

Deeming this thing an ill miracle, the fishers were all aghast, and they fled swiftly to the uppermost rocks. There remained with Evagh only his two servants, the boy Ratha and the ancient crone Ahilidis, who had both witnessed many of his conjurations and were thus well inured to sights of magic. And, with these two beside him, the sorcerer awaited the cooling of the brands.

Quickly the brands darkened; but smoke arose from them still throughout the noon and afternoon; and still they were over-hot for human treading when the hour drew toward sunset. So Evagh bade his servants to fetch water in urns from the sea and cast it upon the ashes and charrings. And after the smoke and the hissing had died, he went forward and approached the pale corpses. Nearing them, he was aware of a great coldness, such as would emanate from trans-Arctic ice; and the coldness began to ache in his hands and ears, and smote sharply through his mantle of fur. Going still closer, he touched one of the bodies with his forefinger-tip; and the finger, though lightly pressed and quickly withdrawn, was seared as if by flame.

Evagh was much amazed: for the condition of the corpses was a thing unknown to him heretofore; and in all his science of wizardry there was naught to enlighten him. He bethought him that a spell had been laid upon the dead: an ensorcelling such as the wan polar demons might weave, or the chill witches of the moon might devise in their caverns of snow. And he deemed it well to retire for the time, lest the spell should now take effect upon others than the dead.

Returning to his house ere night, he burned at each door and window the gums that are most offensive to the northern demons; and at each angle where a spirit might enter, he posted one of his own familiars to guard against all intrusion. Afterwards, while Ratha and Ahilidis slept, he perused with sedulous care the writings of Pnom, in which are collated many powerful exorcisms. But ever and anon, as he read again, for his comfort, the old rubrics, he remembered ominously the saying of the prophet Lith, which no man had understood: "There is One that inhabits the place of utter cold, and One that respireth where none other may draw breath. In the days to come He shall issue forth among the isles and cities of men, and shall bring with Him as a white doom the wind that slumbereth in His dwelling."

Though a fire burned in the chamber, piled with fat pine and terebinth, it seemed that a deadly chill began to invade the air toward midnight. Then, as Evagh turned uneasily from the parchments of Pnom, and saw that the fires blazed high as if in no need of replenishment, he heard the sudden turmoil of a great wind full of sea-birds eerily shrieking, and the cries of land-fowl driven on helpless wings, and over all a high laughter of diabolic voices. Madly from the north the wind beat upon his square-based towers; and birds were cast like blown leaves of autumn against the stout-paned windows; and devils seemed to tear and strain at the granite walls. Though the room's door was shut and the windows were tight-closed, an icy gust went round and round, circling the table where Evagh sat, snatching the broad parchments of Pnom from beneath his fingers, and plucking at the lamp-flame.

Vainly, with numbing thoughts, he strove to recall that counter-charm which is most effective against the spirits of the boreal quarter. Then, strangely, it seemed that the wind fell, leaving a mighty stillness about the house. The chill gust was gone from the room, the lamp and the fire burned steadily, and something of warmth returned slowly into the half-frozen marrow of Evagh.

Soon he was made aware of a light shining beyond his chamber windows, as if a belated moon had now risen above the rocks. But Evagh knew that the moon was at that time a thin crescent, declining with eventide. It seemed that the light shone from the north, pale and frigid as fire of ice; and going to the window he beheld a great beam that traversed all the sea, coming as if from the hidden pole. In that light the rocks were paler than marble, and the sands were whiter than sea-salt, and the huts of the fishermen were as white tombs. The walled garden of Evagh was full of the beam, and all the green had departed from its foliage and its blossoms were like flowers of snow. And the beam fell bleakly on the lower walls of his house, but left still in shadow the wall of that upper chamber from which he looked.

He thought that the beam poured from a pale cloud that had mounted above the sea-line, or else from a white peak that had lifted skyward in the night; but of this he was uncertain. Watching, he saw that it rose higher in the heavens but climbed not upon his walls. Pondering in vain the significance of the mystery, he seemed to hear in the air about him a sweet and wizard voice. And, speaking in a tongue that he knew not, the voice uttered a rune of slumber. And Evagh could not resist the rune, and upon him fell such numbness of sleep as overcomes the outworn watcher in a place of snow.

Waking stiffly at dawn, he rose up from the floor where he had lain, and witnessed a strange marvel. For, lo, in the harbor there towered an ice-berg such as no vessel had yet sighted in all its sea-faring to the north, and no legend had told of among the dim Hyperborean isles. It filled the broad haven from shore to shore, and sheered up to a height immeasurable with piled escarpments and tiered precipices; and its pinnacles hung like towers in the zenith above the house of Evagh. It was higher than the dread mountain Achoravomas, which belches rivers of flame and liquid stone that pour unquenched through Tscho Vulpanomi to the austral main. It was steeper than the mountain Yarak, which marks the site of the boreal pole; and from it there fell a wan glittering on sea and land. Deathly and terrible was the glittering, and Evagh knew that this was the light he had beheld in the darkness.

Scarce could he draw breath in the cold that was on the air; and the light of the huge ice-berg seared his eyeballs with an exceeding froreness. Yet he perceived an odd thing, that the rays of the glittering fell indirectly and to either side of his house; and the lower chambers, where Ratha and Ahilidis slept, were no longer touched by the beam as in the night; and upon all his house there was naught but the early sun and the morning shadows.

On the shore below he saw the charrings of the beached galley, and amid them the white corpses incombustible by fire. And along the sands and rocks, the fisher-folk were lying or standing upright in still, rigid postures, as if they had come forth from their hiding-places to behold the pale beam and had been smitten by a magic sleep. And the whole harbor-shore, and the garden of Evagh, even to the front threshold of his house, was like a place where frost has fallen thickly over all.

Again he remembered the saying of Lith; and with much foreboding he descended to the ground story. There, at the northern windows, the boy Ratha and the hag Ahilidis were leaning with faces turned to the light. Stiffly they stood, with wide-open eyes, and a pale terror was in their regard, and upon them was the white death of the galley's crew. And, nearing them, the sorcerer was stayed by the terrible chillness that smote upon him from their bodies.

He would have fled from the house, knowing his magic wholly ineffectual against this thing. But it came to him that death was in the direct falling of the rays from the ice-berg, and, leaving the house, he must perforce enter that fatal light. And it came to him also that he alone, of all who dwelt on that shore, had been exempted from the death. He could not surmise the reason of his exemption; but in the end he deemed it best to remain patiently and without fear, waiting whatever should befall.

Returning to his chamber he busied himself with various conjurations. But his familiars had gone away in the night, forsaking the angles at which he had posted them; and no spirit either human or demoniacal made reply to his questions. And not in any way known to wizards could he learn aught of the ice-berg or divine the least inkling of its secret.

Presently, as he labored with his useless cantraips, he felt on his face the breathing of a wind that was not air but a subtler and rarer element cold as the moon's ether. His own breath forsook him with agonies unspeakable, and he fell down on the floor in a sort of waking swoon that was near to death. In the swoon he was doubtfully aware of voices uttering unfamiliar spells. Invisible fingers touched him with icy pangs; and about him came and went a bleak radiance, like a tide that flows and ebbs and flows again. Intolerable was the radiance to all his senses; but it brightened slowly, with briefer ebbings; and in time his eyes and his flesh were tempered to endure it. Full upon him now was the light of the ice-berg through his northern windows; and it seemed that a great Eye regarded him in the light. He would have risen to confront the Eye; but his swoon held him like a palsy.

After that, he slept again for a period. Waking, he found in all his limbs their wonted strength and quickness. The strange light was still upon him, filling all his chamber; and peering out he witnessed a new marvel. For, lo, his garden and the rocks and sea-sands below it were visible no longer. In their stead were level spaces of ice about his house, and tall ice-pinnacles that rose like towers from the broad battlements of a fortress. Beyond the verges of the ice he beheld a sea that lay remotely and far beneath; and beyond the sea the low looming of a dim shore.

Terror came to Evagh now, for he recognized in all this the workings of a sorcery plenipotent and beyond the power of all mortal wizards. For plain it was that his high house of granite stood no longer on the coast of Mhu

Thulan, but was based now on some upper crag of the ice-berg. Trembling, he knelt then and prayed to the Old Ones, who dwell secretly in subterrene caverns, or abide under the sea or in the supermundane spaces. And even as he prayed, he heard a loud knocking at the door of his house.

In much fear and wonder he descended and flung wide the portals. Before him were two men, or creatures who had the likeness of men. Both were strange of visage and bright-skinned, and they wore for mantles such rune-woven stuffs as wizards wear. The runes were uncouth and alien; but when the men bespoke him he understood something of their speech, which was in a dialect of the Hyperborean isles.

"We serve the One whose coming was foretold by the prophet Lith," they said. "From spaces beyond the limits of the north he hath come in his floating citadel, the ice-mountain Yikilth, to voyage the mundane oceans and to blast with a chill splendor the puny peoples of humankind. He hath spared us alone amid the inhabitants of the broad isle Thulask, and hath taken us to go with him in his sea-faring upon Yikilth. He hath tempered our flesh to the rigor of his abode, and hath made respirable for us the air in which no mortal man may draw breath. Thee also he hath spared and hath acclimated by his spells to the coldness and the thin ether that go everywhere with Yikilth. Hail, O Evagh, whom we know for a great wizard by this token: since only the mightiest of warlocks are thus chosen and exempted."

Sorely astonished was Evagh; but seeing that he had now to deal with men who were as himself, he questioned closely the two magicians of Thulask. They were named Dooni and Ux Loddhan, and were wise in the lore of the elder gods. The name of the One that they served was Rlim Shaikorth, and he dwelt in the highest summit of the ice-mountain. They told Evagh nothing of the nature or properties of Rlim Shaikorth; and concerning their own service to this being they avowed only that it consisted of such worship as is given to a god, together with the repudiation of all bonds that had linked them heretofore to mankind. And they told Evagh that he was to go with them before Rlim Shaikorth, and perform the due rite of obeisance, and accept the bond of final alienage.

So Evagh went with Dooni and Ux Loddhan and was led by them to a great pinnacle of ice that rose unmeltable into the wan sun, beetling above all its fellows on the flat top of the berg. The pinnacle was hollow, and climbing therein by stairs of ice, they came at last to the chamber of Rlim Shaikorth, which was a circular dome with a round block at the center, forming a dais. And on the dais was that being whose advent the prophet Lith had foretold obscurely.

At sight of this entity, the pulses of Evagh were stilled for an instant by terror; and, following quickly upon the terror, his gorge rose within him through excess of loathing. In all the world there was naught that could be likened for its foulness to Rlim Shaikorth. Something he had of the semblance of a fat white worm; but his bulk was beyond that of the sea-elephant. His half-coiled tail was thick as the middle folds of his body; and his front reared upward from the dais in the form of a white round disk, and upon it were imprinted vaguely the lineaments of a visage belonging neither to beast of the earth nor ocean-creature. And amid the visage a mouth curved uncleanly from side to side of the disk, opening and shutting incessantly on a pale and tongueless and toothless maw. The eye-sockets of Rlim Shaikorth were close together between his shallow nostrils; and the sockets were eyeless, but in them appeared from moment to moment globules of a blood-colored matter having the form of eyeballs; and ever the globules broke and dripped down before the dais. And from the ice-floor of the dome there ascended two masses like stalagmites, purple and dark as frozen gore, which had been made by the ceaseless dripping of the globules.

Dooni and Ux Loddhan prostrated themselves before the being, and Evagh deemed it well to follow their example. Lying prone on the ice, he heard the red drops falling with a splash as of heavy tears; and then, in the dome above him, it seemed that a voice spoke; and the voice was like the sound of some hidden cataract in a glacier hollow with caverns.

"Behold, O Evagh," said the voice. "I have preserved thee from the doom of thy fellow-men, and have made thee as they that inhabit the bourn of cold-ness, and they that inhale the airless void. Wisdom ineffable shall be thine, and mastery beyond the conquest of mortals, if thou wilt but worship me and become my thrall. With me thou shalt voyage amid the kingdoms of the north, and shalt pass among the green southern islands, and see the white falling of death upon them in the light from Yikilth. Our coming shall bring eternal frost on their gardens, and shall set upon their people's flesh the seal of that gulf whose rigor paleth one by one the most ardent stars, and putteth rime at the core of suns. All this thou shalt witness, being as one of the lords of death, supernal and immortal; and in the end thou shalt return with me to that world beyond the uttermost pole, in which is mine abiding empire. For I am he whose coming even the gods may not oppose."

Now, seeing that he was without choice in the matter, Evagh professed himself willing to yield worship and service to the pale worm. Beneath the instruction of Dooni and Ux Loddhan, he performed the sevenfold rite that is scarce suitable for narration here, and swore the threefold vow of unspeakable alienation.

Thereafter, for many days and nights, he sailed with Rlim Shaikorth a-down the coast of Mhu Thulan. Strange was the manner of that voyaging, for it seemed that the great ice-berg was guided by the sorcery of the worm, prevailing ever against wind and tide. And always, by night or day, like the beams of a deathly beacon, the chill splendor smote afar from Yikilth. Proud galleys were overtaken as they fled southward, and their crews were blasted at the oars; and often ships were caught and embedded in the new bastions of ice that formed daily around the base of that ever-growing mountain.

The fair Hyperborean ports, busy with maritime traffic, were stilled by the passing of Rlim Shaikorth. Idle were their streets and wharves, idle was the shipping in their harbors, when the pale light had come and gone. Far inland fell the rays, bringing to the fields and gardens a blight of trans-Arctic winter; and forests were frozen, and the beasts that roamed them were turned as if into marble, so that men who came long afterwards to that region found the elk and bear and mammoth still standing in all the postures of life. But, dwelling upon Yikilth, the sorcerer Evagh was immune to the icy death; and, sitting in his house or walking abroad on the berg, he was aware of no sharper cold than that which abides in summer shadows.

Now, beside Dooni and Ux Loddhan, the sorcerers of Thulask, there were five other wizards that went with Evagh on that voyage, having been chosen by Rlim Shaikorth. They too had been tempered to the coldness by Yikilth, and their houses had been transported to the berg by unknown enchantment. They were outlandish and uncouth men, called Polarians, from islands nearer the pole than broad Thulask; and Evagh could understand little of their ways; and their sorcery was foreign to him; and their speech was unintelligible; nor was it known to the Thulaskians.

Daily the eight wizards found on their tables all the provender necessary for human sustenance; though they knew not the agency by which it was supplied. All were united in the worship of the white worm; and all, it seemed, were content in a measure with their lot, and were fain of that unearthly lore and dominion which the worm had promised them. But Evagh was uneasy at heart, and rebelled in secret against his thralldom to Rlim Shaikorth; and he beheld with revulsion the doom that went forth eternally from Yikilth upon lovely cities and fruitful ocean-shores. Ruthfully he saw the blasting of flower-girdled Cerngoth, and the boreal stillness that descended on the thronged streets of Leqquan, and the frost that seared with sudden whiteness the garths and orchards of the sea-fronting valley of Aguil. And sorrow was in his heart for the fishing-coracles and the biremes of trade and warfare that floated manless after they had met Yikilth.

Ever southward sailed the great ice-berg, bearing its lethal winter to lands where the summer sun rode high. And Evagh kept his own counsel, and followed in all ways the custom of Dooni and Ux Loddhan and the others. At intervals that were regulated by the motions of the circumpolar stars, the eight warlocks climbed to that lofty chamber in which Rlim Shaikorth abode perpetually, half-coiled on his dais of ice. There, in a ritual whose cadences corresponded to the falling of those eyelike tears that were wept by the worm, and with genuflections timed to the yawning and shutting of his mouth, they yielded to Rlim Shaikorth the required adoration. Sometimes the worm was silent, and sometimes he bespoke them, renewing vaguely the promises he had made. And Evagh learned from the others that the worm slept for a period at each darkening of the moon; and only at that time did the sanguine tears suspend their falling, and the mouth forbear its alternate closing and gaping.

At the third repetition of the rites of worship, it came to pass that only seven wizards climbed to the tower. Evagh, counting their number, perceived that the missing man was one of the five outlanders. Afterwards, he questioned Dooni and Ux Loddhan regarding this matter, and made signs of inquiry to the four northrons; but it seemed that the fate of the absent warlock was a thing mysterious to all. Nothing was seen or heard of him from that time; and Evagh, pondering long and deeply, was somewhat disquieted. For, during the ceremony in the tower chamber, it had seemed to him that the worm was grosser of bulk and girth than on any prior occasion.

Covertly he asked what manner of nutriment was required by Rlim Shaikorth. Concerning this, there was much dubiety and dispute: for Ux Loddhan maintained that the worm fed on nothing less unique than the hearts of white Arctic bears; while Dooni swore that his rightful nourishment was the liver of whales. But, to their knowledge, the worm had not eaten during their sojourn upon Yikilth; and both averred that the intervals between his times of feeding were longer than those of any terrestrial creature, being computable not in hours or days but in whole years.

Still the ice-berg followed its course, ever vaster and more prodigious beneath the heightening sun; and again, at the star-appointed time, which was the forenoon of every third day, the sorcerers convened in the presence of Rlim Shaikorth. To the perturbation of all, their number was now but six; and the lost warlock was another of the outlanders. And the worm had greatened still more in size; and the increase was visible as a thickening of his whole body from head to tail.

Deeming these circumstances an ill augury, the six made fearful supplication to the worm in their various tongues, and implored him to tell them the fate of their absent fellows. And the worm answered; and his speech was intelligible to Evagh and Ux Loddhan and Dooni and the three northrons, each thinking that he had been addressed in his native language.

"This matter is a mystery concerning which ye shall all receive enlightenment in turn. Know this: the two that have vanished are still present; and they and ye also shall share even as I have promised in the ultramundane lore and empery of Rlim Shaikorth."

Afterwards, when they had descended from the tower, Evagh and the two Thulaskians debated the interpretation of this answer. Evagh maintained that the import was sinister, for truly their missing companions were present only in the worm's belly; but the others argued that these men had undergone a more mystical translation and were now elevated beyond human sight and hearing. Forthwith they began to make ready with prayer and austerity, in expectation of some sublime apotheosis which would come to them in due turn. But Evagh was still fearful; and he could not trust the equivocal pledges of the worm; and doubt remained with him.

Seeking to assuage his doubt and peradventure find some trace of the lost Polarians, he made search of the mighty berg, on whose battlements his own house and the houses of the other warlocks were perched like the tiny huts of fishers on ocean-cliffs. In this quest the others would not accompany him, fearing to incur the worm's displeasure. From verge to verge of Yikilth he roamed unhindered, as if on some broad plateau with peaks and horns; and he climbed perilously on the upper scarps, and went down into deep crevasses and caverns where the sun failed and there was no other light than the strange luster of that unearthly ice. Embedded here in the walls, as if in the stone of nether strata, he saw dwellings such as men had never built, and vessels that might belong to other ages or worlds; but nowhere could he detect the presence of any living creature; and no spirit or shadow gave response to the necromantic evocations which he uttered oftentimes as he went along the chasms and chambers.

So Evagh was still apprehensive of the worm's treachery; and he resolved to remain awake on the night preceding the next celebration of the rites of worship; and at eve of that night he assured himself that the other wizards were all housed in their separate mansions, to the number of five. And, having ascertained this, he set himself to watch without remission the entrance of Rlim Shaikorth's tower, which was plainly visible from his own windows.

Weird and chill was the shining of the berg in the darkness; for a light as of frozen stars was effulgent at all times from the ice. A moon that was little past the full arose early on the orient seas. But Evagh, holding vigil at his window till midnight, saw that no visible form emerged from the tall tower, and none entered it. At midnight there came upon him a sudden drowsiness, such as would be felt by one who had drunk some opiate wine; and he could not sustain his vigil any longer but slept deeply and unbrokenly throughout the remainder of the night.

On the following day there were but four sorcerers who gathered in the ice-dome and gave homage to Rlim Shaikorth. And Evagh saw that two more of the outlanders, men of bulk and stature dwarfish beyond their fellows, were now missing.

One by one thereafter, on nights preceding the ceremony of worship, the companions of Evagh vanished. The last Polarian was next to go; and it came to pass that only Evagh and Ux Loddhan and Dooni went to the tower; and then Evagh and Ux Loddhan went alone. And terror mounted daily in Evagh, for he felt that his own time drew near; and he would have hurled himself into the sea from the high ramparts of Yikilth, if Ux Loddhan, who perceived his intention, had not warned him that no man could depart therefrom and live again in solar warmth and terrene air, having been habituated to the coldness and thin ether. And Ux Loddhan, it seemed, was wholly oblivious to his doom, and was fain to impute an esoteric significance to the ever-growing bulk of the white worm and the vanishing of the wizards.

So, at that time when the moon had waned and darkened wholly, it occurred that Evagh climbed before Rlim Shaikorth with infinite trepidation and loath, laggard steps. And, entering the dome with downcast eyes, he found himself the sole worshipper.

A palsy of fear was upon him as he made obeisance; and scarcely he dared to lift his eyes and regard the worm. But soon, as he began to perform the customary genuflections, he became aware that the red tears of Rlim Shaikorth no longer fell on the purple stalagmites; nor was there any sound such as the worm was wont to make by the perpetual opening and shutting of his mouth. And venturing at last to look upward, Evagh beheld the abhorrently swollen mass of the monster, whose thickness was such as to overhang the dais' rim; and he saw that the mouth and eye-holes of Rlim Shaikorth were closed as if in slumber; and thereupon he recalled how the wizards of Thulask had told him that the worm slept for an interval at the darkening of each moon; which was a thing he had forgotten temporarily in his extreme dread and apprehension.

Now was Evagh sorely bewildered; for the rites he had learned from his fellows could be fittingly performed only while the tears of Rlim Shaikorth fell down and his mouth gaped and closed and gaped again in a measured alternation. And none had instructed him as to what rites were proper and suitable during the slumber of the worm. And, being in much doubt, he said softly:

"Wakest thou, O Rlim Shaikorth?"

In reply, he seemed to hear a multitude of voices that issued obscurely from out the pale, tumid mass before him. The sound of the voices was weirdly muffled, but among them he distinguished the accents of Dooni and Ux Loddhan; and there was a thick muttering of outlandish words which Evagh knew for the speech of the five Polarians; and beneath this he caught, or seemed to catch, innumerable undertones that were not the voices of men or beasts, nor such sounds as would be emitted by earthly demons. And the voices rose and clamored, like those of a throng of prisoners in some profound oubliette.

Anon, as he listened in horror ineffable, the voice of Dooni became articulate above the others; and the manifold clamor and muttering ceased, as if a multitude were hushed to hear its own spokesman. And Evagh heard the tones of Dooni, saying:

"The worm sleepeth, but we whom the worm hath devoured are awake. Direly has he deceived us, for he came to our houses in the night, devouring us bodily one by one as we slept under the enchantment he had wrought. He has eaten our souls even as our bodies, and verily we are part of Rlim Shaikorth, but exist only as in a dark and noisome dungeon; and while the worm wakes we have no separate or conscious being, but are merged wholly in the ultraterrestrial being of Rlim Shaikorth.

"Hear then, O Evagh, the truth which we have learned from our oneness with the worm. He has saved us from the white doom and has taken us upon Yikilth for this reason, because we alone of all mankind, who are sorcerers of high attainment and mastery, may endure the lethal ice-change and become breathers of the airless void, and thus, in the end, be made suitable for the provender of such as Rlim Shaikorth.

"Great and terrible is the worm, and the place wherefrom he cometh and whereto he returneth is not to be dreamt of by living men. And the worm is omniscient, save that he knows not the waking of them he has devoured, and their awareness during his slumber. But the worm, though ancient beyond the antiquity of worlds, is not immortal and is vulnerable in one particular. Whosoever learneth the time and means of his vulnerability and hath heart for the undertaking, may slay him easily. And the time for the deed is during his term of sleep. Therefore we adjure thee now by the faith of the Old Ones to draw the sword thou wearest beneath thy mantle and plunge it in the side of Rlim Shaikorth: for such is the means of his slaying.

"Thus alone, O Evagh, shall the going forth of the pale death be ended; and only thus shall we, thy fellow-sorcerers, obtain release from our blind thralldom and incarceration; and with us many that the worm hath betrayed and eaten in former ages and upon distant worlds. And only by the doing of this thing shalt thou escape the wan and loathly mouth of the worm, nor abide henceforward as a doubtful ghost among other ghosts in the evil blackness of his belly. But know, however, that he who slayeth Rlim Shaikorth must necessarily perish in the slaying."

Evagh, being wholly astounded, made question of Dooni and was answered readily concerning all that he asked. And oftentimes the voice of Ux Loddhan replied to him; and sometimes there were unintelligible murmurs or outcries from certain others of those foully enmewed phantoms. Much did Evagh learn of the worm's origin and essence; and he was told the secret of Yikilth, and the manner wherein Yikilth had floated down from trans-Arctic gulfs to voyage the seas of Earth. Ever, as he listened, his abhorrence greatened: though deeds of dark sorcery and conjured devils had long indurated his flesh and soul, making him callous to more than common horrors. But of that which he learned it were ill to speak now.

At length there was silence in the dome; for the worm slept soundly, and Evagh had no longer any will to question the ghost of Dooni; and they that were imprisoned with Dooni seemed to wait and watch in a stillness of death.

Then, being a man of much hardihood and resolution, Evagh delayed no more but drew from its ivory sheath the short but well-tempered sword of bronze which he carried always at his baldric. Approaching the dais closely, he plunged the blade in the over-swelling mass of Rlim Shaikorth. The blade entered easily with a slicing and tearing motion, as if he had stabbed a monstrous bladder, and was not stayed even by the broad pommel; and the whole right hand of Evagh was drawn after it into the wound.

He perceived no quiver or stirring of the worm; but out of the wound there gushed a sudden torrent of black liquescent matter, swiftening and deepening irresistibly till the sword was caught from Evagh's grasp as if in a mill-race. Hotter far than blood, and smoking with strange steam-like vapors, the liquid poured over his arms and splashed his raiment as it fell. Quickly the ice was a-wash about his feet; but still the fluid welled as if from some inexhaustible spring of foulness; and it spread everywhere in pools and runlets that came together.

Evagh would have fled then; but the sable liquid, mounting and flowing, was above his ankles when he neared the stair-head; and it rushed adown the stairway before him like a cataract in some steeply pitching cavern. Hotter and hotter it grew, boiling, bubbling; while the current strengthened, and clutched at him and drew him like malignant hands. He feared to essay the downward stairs; nor was there any place now in all the dome where he could climb for refuge. He turned, striving against the tide for bare foothold, and saw dimly through the reeking vapors the throned mass of Rlim Shaikorth. The gash had widened prodigiously, and a stream surged from it like the waters of a broken weir, billowing outward around the dais; and yet, as if in further proof of the worm's unearthly nature, *his bulk was in no wise diminished thereby*. And still the black liquid came in an evil flood; and it rose swirling about the knees of Evagh; and the vapors seemed to take the forms of a myriad press of phantoms, wreathing obscurely together and dividing once more as they went past him. Then, as he tottered and grew giddy on the stair-head, he was swept away and was hurled to his death on the ice-steps far below.

That day, on the sea to eastward of middle Hyperborea, the crews of certain merchant galleys beheld an unheard-of thing. For, lo, as they sped north, returning from far ocean-isles with a wind that aided their oars, they sighted in the late forenoon a monstrous ice-berg whose pinnacles and crags loomed high as mountains. The berg shone in part with a weird light; and from its loftiest pinnacle poured an ink-black torrent; and all the ice-cliffs and buttresses beneath were a-stream with rapids and cascades and sheeted falls of the same blackness, that fumed like boiling water as they plunged oceanward; and the sea around the berg was clouded and streaked for a wide interval as if with the dark fluid of the cuttle-fish.

The mariners feared to sail closer; but, full of awe and marvelling, they stayed their oars and lay watching the berg; and the wind dropped, so that their galleys drifted within view of it all that day. They saw that the berg dwindled swiftly, melting as though some unknown fire consumed it; and the air took on a strange warmth, and the water about their ships grew tepid. Crag by crag the ice was runneled and eaten away; and huge portions fell off with a mighty splashing; and the highest pinnacle collapsed; but still the blackness poured out as from an unfathomable fountain. The watchers thought, at whiles, that they beheld houses ruining seaward amid the loosened fragments; but of this they were uncertain because of those ever-mounting vapors. By sunset-time the berg had diminished to a mass no larger than a common floe; yet still the welling blackness overstreamed it; and it sank low in the wave; and the weird light was quenched altogether. Thereafter, the night being moonless, it was lost to vision; and a gale rose, blowing strongly from the south; and at dawn the sea was void of any remnant.

Concerning the matters related above, many and various legends have gone forth throughout Mhu Thulan and all the extreme hyperborean kingdoms and archipelagoes, even to the southmost isle of Oszhtror. The truth is not in such tales: for no man has known the truth heretofore. But I, the sorcerer Eibon, calling up through my necromancy the wave-wandering specter of Evagh, have learned from him the veritable history of the worm's advent. And I have written it down in my volume with such omissions as are needful for the sparing of mortal weakness and sanity. And men will read this record, together with much more of the elder lore, in days long after the coming and melting of the great glacier.

THE SEVEN GEASES

The Lord Ralibar Vooz, high magistrate of Commoriom and third cousin to King Homquat, had gone forth with six-and-twenty of his most valorous retainers in quest of such game as was afforded by the black Eiglophian Mountains. Leaving to lesser sportsmen the great sloths and vampire-bats of the intermediate jungle, as well as the small but noxious dinosauria, Ralibar Vooz and his followers had pushed rapidly ahead and had covered the distance between the Hyperborean capital and their objective in a day's march. The glassy scaurs and grim ramparts of Mount Voormithadreth, highest and most formidable of the Eiglophians, had beetled above them, wedging the sun with dark scoriac peaks at mid-afternoon, and walling the blazonries of sunset wholly from view. They had spent the night beneath its lowermost crags, keeping a ceaseless watch, piling dead cryptomeria branches on their fires, and hearing on the grisly heights above them the wild and dog-like ululations of those subhuman savages, the Voormis for which the mountain was named. Also, they heard the bellowing of an alpine catoblepas pursued by the Voormis, and the mad snarling of a saber-tooth tiger assailed and dragged down; and Ralibar Vooz had deemed that these noises boded well for the morrow's hunting.

He and his men rose betimes; and having breakfasted on their provisions of dried bear-meat and a dark sour wine that was noted for its invigorative qualities, they began immediately the ascent of the mountain, whose upper precipices were hollow with caves occupied by the Voormis. Ralibar Vooz had hunted these creatures before; and a certain room of his house in Commoriom was arrased with their thick and shaggy pelts. They were usually deemed the most dangerous of the Hyperborean fauna; and the mere climbing of Voormithadreth, even without the facing of its inhabitants, would have been a feat attended by more than sufficient peril: but Ralibar Vooz, having tasted of such sport, could now satisfy himself with nothing tamer.

He and his followers were well armed and accoutered. Some of the men bore coils of rope and grappling-hooks to be employed in the escalade of the steeper crags. Some carried heavy crossbows; and many were equipped with long-handled and saber-bladed bills which, from experience, had proved the most effective weapons in close-range fighting with the Voormis. The whole party was variously studded with auxiliary knives, throwing-darts, two-handed scimitars, maces, bodkins and saw-toothed axes. The men were all clad in jerkins and hose of dinosaur-leather, and were shod with brazen-spiked buskins. Ralibar Vooz himself wore a light suiting of copper chain-mail, which, flexible as cloth, in no wise impeded his movements. In addition he carried a buckler of mammoth-hide with a long bronze spike in its center that could be used as a thrusting-sword; and, being a man of huge stature and strength, his shoulders and baldric were hung with a whole arsenal of weaponries.

The mountain was of volcanic origin, though its four craters were suppos-edly all extinct. For hours the climbers toiled upward on the fearsome scarps of black lava and obsidian, seeing the sheerer heights above them recede interminably into a cloudless zenith, as if not to be approached by man. Far faster than they the sun climbed, blazing torridly upon them and heating the rocks till their hands and feet were scorched as if by the walls of a furnace. But Ralibar Vooz, eager to flesh his weapons, would permit no halting in the shady chasms nor under the scant umbrage of rare junipers.

That day, however, it seemed that the Voormis were not abroad upon Mount Voormithadreth. No doubt they had feasted too well during the night, when their hunting-cries had been heard by the Commorians. Perhaps it would be necessary to invade the warren of caves in the loftier crags: a procedure none too palatable even for a sportsman of such hardihood as Ralibar Vooz. Few of these caverns could be reached by men without the use of ropes; and the Voormis, who were possessed of quasi-human cunning, would hurl blocks and rubble upon the heads of the assailants. Most of the caves were narrow and darksome, thus putting at a grave disadvantage the hunters who entered them; and the Voormis would fight redoubtably in defense of their young and their females, who dwelt in the inner recesses; and the females were fiercer and more pernicious, if possible, than the males.

Such matters as these were debated by Ralibar Vooz and his henchmen as the escalade became more arduous and hazardous, and they saw far above them the pitted mouths of the lower dens. Tales were told of brave hunters who had gone into those dens and had not returned; and much was said of the vile feeding-habits of the Voormis and the uses to which their captives were put before death and after it. Also, much was said regarding the genesis of the Voormis, who were popularly believed to be the offspring of women and certain atrocious creatures that had come forth in primal days from a tenebrous cavern-world in the bowels of Voormithadreth. Somewhere beneath that four-coned mountain, the sluggish and baleful god Tsathoggua, who had come down from Saturn in years immediately following the Earth's creation, was fabled to reside; and during the rite of worship at his black altars, the devotees were always careful to orient themselves toward Voormithadreth. Other and more doubtful beings than Tsathoggua slept below the extinct volcanoes, or ranged and ravened throughout that hidden underworld; but of these beings few men, other than the more adept or abandoned wizards, professed to know anything at all.

Ralibar Vooz, who had a thoroughly modern disdain of the supernatural, avowed his skepticism in no equivocal terms when he heard his henchmen regaling each other with these antique legendries. He swore with many ribald blasphemies that there were no gods anywhere, above or under Voormithadreth. As for the Voormis themselves, they were indeed a misbegotten species; but it was hardly necessary, in explaining their generation, to go beyond the familiar laws of nature. They were merely the remnant of a low and degraded tribe of aborigines, who, sinking further into brutehood, had sought refuge in those volcanic fastnesses after the coming of the true Hyperboreans.

Certain grizzled veterans of the party shook their heads and muttered at these heresies; but because of their respect for the high rank and prowess of Ralibar Vooz, they did not venture to gainsay him openly.

After several hours of heroic climbing, the hunters came within measurable distance of those nether caves. Below them now, in a vast and dizzying prospect, were the wooded hills and fair, fertile plains of Hyperborea. They were alone in a world of black, riven rock, with innumerable precipices and chasms above, beneath and on all sides. Directly overhead, in the face of an almost perpendicular cliff, were three of the cavern-mouths, which had the aspect of volcanic fumaroles. Much of the cliff was glazed with obsidian, and there were few ledges or handgrips. It seemed that even the Voormis, agile as apes, could scarcely climb that wall; and Ralibar Vooz, after studying it with a strategic eye, decided that the only feasible approach to the dens was from above. A diagonal crack, running from a shelf just below them to the summit, no doubt afforded ingress and egress to their occupants.

First, however, it was necessary to gain the precipice above: a difficult and precarious feat in itself. At one side of the long talus on which the hunters were standing, there was a chimney that wound upward in the wall, ceasing thirty feet from the top and leaving a sheer, smooth surface. Working along the chimney to its upper end, a good alpinist could hurl his rope and grappling-hook to the summit-edge.

The advisability of bettering their present vantage was now emphasized by a shower of stones and offal from the caverns. They noted certain human relics, well-gnawed and decayed, amid the offal. Ralibar Vooz, animated by wrath against these miscreants, as well as by the fervor of the huntsman, led his six-and-twenty followers in the escalade. He soon reached the chimney's termination, where a slanting ledge offered bare foothold at one side. After the third cast, his rope held; and he went up hand over hand to the precipice.

He found himself on a broad and comparatively level-topped buttress of the lowest cone of Voormithadreth, which still rose for two thousand feet above him like a steep pyramid. Before him on the buttress, the black lava-stone was gnarled into numberless low ridges and strange masses like the pedestals of gigantic columns. Dry, scanty grasses and withered alpine flowers grew here and there in shallow basins of darkish soil; and a few cedars, levin-struck or stunted, had taken root in the fissured rock. Amid the black ridges, and seemingly close at hand, a thread of pale smoke ascended, serpentining oddly in the still air of noon and reaching an unbelievable height ere it vanished. Ralibar Vooz inferred that the buttress was inhabited by some person nearer to civilized humanity than the Voormis, who were quite ignorant of the use of fire. Surprised by this discovery, he did not wait for his men to join him, but started off at once to investigate the source of the curling smoke-thread.

He had deemed it merely a few steps away, behind the first of those grotesque furrows of lava. But evidently he had been deceived in this: for he climbed ridge after ridge and rounded many broad and curious dolmens and great dolomites which rose inexplicably before him where, an instant previous, he had thought there were only ordinary boulders; and still the pale, sinuous wisp went skyward at the same seeming interval.

Ralibar Vooz, high magistrate and redoubtable hunter, was both puzzled and irritated by this behavior of the smoke. Likewise, the aspect of the rocks around him was disconcertingly and unpleasantly deceitful. He was wasting too much time in an exploration idle and quite foreign to the real business of the day; but it was not his nature to abandon any enterprise, no matter how trivial, without reaching the set goal. Halloing loudly to his men, who must have climbed the cliff by now and were doubtless wondering what had happened to their master, he went on toward the elusive smoke.

It seemed to him, once or twice, that he heard the answering shouts of his followers, very faint and indistinct, as if across some mile-wide chasm. Again he called lustily, but this time there was no audible reply. Going a little further, he began to detect among the rocks beside him a peculiar conversational droning and muttering in which four or five different voices appeared to take part. Seemingly they were much nearer at hand than the smoke, which had now receded like a mirage. One of the voices was clearly that of a Hyperborean; but the others possessed a timbre and accent which Ralibar Vooz, in spite of his varied ethnic knowledge, could not associate with any branch or sub-division of mankind. They affected his ears in a most unpleasant fashion, suggesting by turns the hum of great insects, the murmurs of fire and water, and the rasping of metal.

Ralibar Vooz emitted a hearty and somewhat ireful bellow to announce his coming to whatever persons were convened amid the rocks. His weapons and accouterments clattering loudly, he scrambled over a sharp lava-ridge toward the voices.

Topping the ridge, he looked down on a scene that was both mysterious and unexpected. Below him in a circular hollow there stood a rude hut of boulders and stone fragments roofed with cedar boughs. In front of this hovel, on a large flat block of obsidian, a fire burned with flames alternately blue, green and white; and from it rose the pale thin spiral of smoke whose situation had illuded him so strangely.

An old man, withered and disreputable-looking, in a robe that appeared no less antique and unsavory than himself, was standing near to the fire. He was not engaged in any visible culinary operations; and, in view of the torrid sun, it hardly seemed that he required the warmth given by the queer-colored blaze. Aside from this individual, Ralibar Vooz looked in vain for the participants of the muttered conversation he had just overheard. He thought there was an evanescent fluttering of dim, grotesque shadows around the obsidian block; but the shadows faded and vanished in an instant; and, since there were no objects nor beings that could have cast them, Ralibar Vooz deemed that he had been victimized by another of those highly disagreeable optic illusions in which that part of the mountain Voormithadreth seemed to abound.

The old man eyed the hunter with a fiery gaze and began to curse him in fluent but somewhat archaic diction as he descended into the hollow. At the same time, a lizard-tailed and sooty-feathered bird, which seemed to belong to some night-flying species of archaeopterix, began to snap its toothed beak and flap its digited wings on the objectionably shapen stela that served it for a perch. This stela, standing on the lee side of the fire and very close to it, had not been perceived by Ralibar Vooz at first glance.

"May the ordure of demons bemire you from heel to crown!" cried the venomous ancient. "O lumbering, bawling idiot! you have ruined a most promising and important evocation. How you came here I cannot imagine. I have surrounded this place with twelve circles of illusion, whose effect is multiplied by their myriad intersections; and the chance that any intruder would ever find his way to my abode was mathematically small and insignificant. Ill was that chance which brought you here: for They that you have frightened away will not return till the high stars repeat a certain rare and quickly passing conjunction; and much wisdom is lost to me in the interim."

"How now, varlet!" said Ralibar Vooz, astonished and angered by this greeting, of which he understood little save that his presence was unwelcome to the old man. "Who are you that speak so churlishly to a magistrate of Commoriom and a cousin to King Homquat? I advise you to curb such insolence:

for, if so I wish, it lies in my power to serve you even as I serve the Voormis. Though methinks," he added, "your pelt is far too filthy and verminous to merit room amid my trophies of the chase."

"Know that I am the sorcerer Ezdagor," proclaimed the ancient, his voice echoing among the rocks with dreadful sonority. "By choice I have lived remote from cities and men; nor have the Voormis of the mountain troubled me in my magical seclusion. I care not if you are the magistrate of all swinedom or a cousin to the king of dogs. In retribution for the charm you have shattered, the business you have undone by this oafish trespass, I shall put upon you a most dire and calamitous and bitter geas."

"You speak in terms of outmoded superstition," said Ralibar Vooz, who was impressed against his will by the weighty oratorical style in which Ezdagor had delivered these periods.

The old man seemed not to hear him.

"Harken then to your geas, O Ralibar Vooz," he fulminated. "For this is the geas, that you must cast aside all your weapons and go unarmed into the dens of the Voormis; and fighting bare-handed against the Voormis and against their females and their young, you must win to that secret cave in the bowels of Voormithadreth, beyond the dens, wherein abides from eldermost aeons the god Tsathoggua. You shall know Tsathoggua by his great girth and his batlike furriness and the look of a sleepy black paddock which he has eternally. He will rise not from his place even in the ravening of hunger, but will wait in divine slothfulness for the sacrifice. And, going close to Lord Tsathoggua, you must say to him: 'I am the blood-offering sent by the sorcerer Ezdagor.' Then, if it be his pleasure, Tsathoggua will avail himself of the offering.

"In order that you may not go astray, the bird Raphtontis, who is my familiar, will guide you in your wanderings on the mountain-side and through the caverns." He indicated with a peculiar gesture the night-flying archaeopterix on the foully symbolic stela, and added as if in afterthought: "Raphtontis will remain with you till the accomplishment of the geas and the end of your journey below Voormithadreth. He knows the secrets of the underworld and the lairing-places of the Old Ones. If our Lord Tsathoggua should disdain the blood-offering, or, in his generosity, should send you on to his brethren, Raphtontis will be fully competent to lead the way whithersoever is ordained by the god."

Ralibar Vooz found himself unable to answer this more than outrageous peroration in the style which it manifestly deserved. In fact, he could say nothing at all: for it seemed that a sort of lockjaw had afflicted him. Moreover, to his exceeding terror and bewilderment, this vocal paralysis was accompanied by certain involuntary movements of a most alarming type. With a sense of nightmare compulsion, together with the horror of one who feels that he is going mad, he began to divest himself of the various weapons which he carried. His bladed buckler, his mace, broadsword, hunting-knife, ax and needle-tipped anelace jingled on the ground before the obsidian block.

"I shall permit you to retain your body-armor and helmet," said Ezdagor at this juncture. "Otherwise, I fear that you will not reach Tsathoggua in the state of corporeal intactness proper for a sacrifice. The teeth and nails of the Voormis are sharp even as their appetites."

Muttering certain half-inaudible and doubtful-sounding words, the wizard turned from Ralibar Vooz and began to quench the tri-colored fire with a mixture of dust and blood from a shallow brass basin. Deigning to vouchsafe no farewell or sign of dismissal he kept his back toward the hunter, but waved his left hand obliquely to the bird Raphtontis. This creature, stretching his murky wings and clacking his saw-like beak, abandoned his perch and hung poised in air with one ember-colored eye malignly fixed on Ralibar Vooz. Then, floating slowly, his long snakish neck reverted and his eye maintaining its vigilance, the bird flew among the lava-ridges toward the pyramidal cone of Voormithadreth; and Ralibar Vooz followed, driven by a compulsion that he could neither understand nor resist.

Evidently the demon fowl knew all the turnings of that maze of delusion with which Ezdagor had environed his abode; for the hunter was led with comparatively little indirection across the enchanted buttress. He heard the far-off shouting of his men as he went; but his own voice was faint and thin as that of a flittermouse when he sought to reply. Soon he found himself at the bottom of a great scarp of the upper mountain, pitted with cavern-mouths. It was a part of Voormithadreth that he had never visited before.

Raphtontis rose toward the lowest cave, and hovered at its entrance while Ralibar Vooz climbed precariously behind him amid a heavy barrage of bones and glass-edged flints and other oddments of less mentionable nature hurled by the Voormis. These low, brutal savages, fringing the dark mouths of the dens with their repulsive faces and members, greeted the hunter's progress with ferocious howlings and an inexhaustible supply of garbage. However, they did not molest Raphtontis, and it seemed that they were anxious to avoid hitting him with their missiles; though the presence of this hovering, wide-winged fowl interfered noticeably with their aim as Ralibar Vooz began to near the nethermost den.

Owing to this partial protection, the hunter was able to reach the cavern without serious injury. The entrance was rather strait; and Raphtontis flew upon the Voormis with open beak and flapping wings, compelling them to withdraw into the interior while Ralibar Vooz made firm his position on the threshold-ledge. Some, however, threw themselves on their faces to allow the passage of Raphtontis; and, rising when the bird had gone by, they assailed the Commorian as he followed his guide into the fetid gloom. They stood only half erect, and their shaggy heads were about his thighs and hips, snarling and snapping like dogs; and they clawed him with hook-shaped nails that caught and held in the links of his chain-armor.

Weaponless he fought them in obedience to his geas, striking down their hideous faces with his mailed fists in a veritable madness that was not akin to the ardor of a huntsman. He felt their nails and teeth break on the close-woven links as he hurled them loose; but others took their place when he won onward a little into the murky cavern; and their females struck at his legs like darting serpents; and their young beslavered his ankles with mouths wherein the fangs were as yet ungrown.

Before him, for his guidance, he heard the clanking of the wings of Raphtontis, and the harsh cries, half hiss, half caw, that were emitted by this bird at intervals. The darkness stifled him with a thousand stenches; and his feet slipped in blood and filth at every step. But anon he knew that the Voormis had ceased to assail him. The cave sloped downward; and he breathed an air that was edged with sharp, acrid mineral odors.

Groping for awhile through sightless night and descending a steep incline, he came at length to a sort of underground hall in which neither day nor darkness prevailed. Here the archings of rock were visible by an obscure glow such as hidden moons might yield. Thence, through declivitous grottoes and along perilously skirted gulfs, he was conducted ever downward by Raphtontis into the world beneath the mountain Voormithadreth. Everywhere was that dim, unnatural light whose source he could not ascertain. Wings that were too broad for those of the bat flew vaguely overhead; and at whiles, in the shadowy caverns, he beheld great, fearsome bulks having a likeness to those behemoths and giant reptiles which burdened the Earth in earlier times, but because of the dimness he could not tell if these were living shapes or forms that the stone had taken.

Strong was the compulsion of his geas on Ralibar Vooz; and a numbness had seized his mind; and he felt only a dulled fear and a dazed wonder. It seemed that his will and his thoughts were no longer his own, but were become those of some alien person. He was going down to some obscure but predestined end, by a route that was darksome but foreknown.

At last the bird Raphtontis paused and hovered significantly in a cave distinguished from the others by a most evil potpourri of smells. Ralibar Vooz deemed at first that the cave was empty. Going forward to join Raphtontis, he stumbled over certain attenuated remnants on the floor, which appeared to be the skin-clad skeletons of men and various animals. Then, following the coal-bright gaze of the demon bird, he discerned in a dark recess the formless bulking of a couchant mass. And the mass stirred a little at his approach, and put forth with infinite slothfulness a huge and toad-shaped head. And the head opened its eyes very slightly, as if half-awakened from slumber, so that they were visible as two slits of oozing phosphor in the black, browless face.

Ralibar Vooz perceived an odor of fresh blood amid the many fetors that rose to besiege his nostrils. A horror came upon him therewith; for, looking down, he beheld lying before the shadowy monster the lean husk of a thing that was neither man, beast, nor Voormi. He stood hesitant, fearing to go closer yet powerless to retreat. But, admonished by an angry hissing from the archaeopterix, together with a slashing stroke of its beak between his shoulder-blades, he went forward till he could see the fine dark fur on the dormant body and sleepily porrected head.

With new horror, and a sense of hideous doom, he heard his own voice speaking without volition: "O Lord Tsathoggua, I am the blood-offering sent by the sorcerer Ezdagor."

There was a sluggish inclination of the toad-like head; and the eyes opened a little wider, and light flowed from them in viscous tricklings on the creased under-lids. Then Ralibar Vooz seemed to hear a deep, rumbling sound; but he knew not whether it reverberated in the dusky air or in his own mind. And the sound shaped itself, albeit uncouthly, into syllables and words:

"Thanks are due to Ezdagor for this offering. But, since I have fed lately on a well-blooded sacrifice, my hunger is appeased for the present, and I require not the offering. However, it may be that others of the Old Ones are athirst or famished. And, since you came here with a geas upon you, it is not fitting that you should go hence without another. So I place you under this geas, to betake yourself downward through the caverns till you reach, after long descent, that bottomless gulf over which the spider-god Atlach-Nacha weaves his eternal webs. And there, calling to Atlach-Nacha, you must say: 'I am the gift sent by Tsathoggua.'"

So, with Raphtontis leading him, Ralibar Vooz departed from the presence of Tsathoggua by another route than that which had brought him there. The way steepened more and more; and it ran through chambers that were too vast for the searching of sight; and along precipices that fell sheer for an unknown distance to the black, sluggish foam and somnolent murmur of underworld seas.

At last, on the verge of a chasm whose farther shore was lost in darkness, the night-flying bird hung motionless with level wings and down-dropping tail. Ralibar Vooz went close to the verge and saw that great webs were attached to it at intervals, seeming to span the gulf with their multiple crossing and reticulations of grey, rope-thick strands. Apart from these, the chasm was bridgeless. Far out on one of the webs he discerned a darksome form, big as a crouching man but with long spider-like members. Then, like a dreamer who hears some nightmare sound, he heard his own voice crying loudly: "O Atlach-Nacha, I am the gift sent by Tsathoggua."

The dark form ran toward him with incredible swiftness. When it came near he saw that there was a kind of face on the squat ebon body, low down amid the several-jointed legs. The face peered up with a weird expression of doubt and inquiry; and terror crawled through the veins of the bold hunts-man as he met the small, crafty eyes that were circled about with hair.

Thin, shrill, piercing as a sting, there spoke to him the voice of the spider-god Atlach-Nacha: "I am duly grateful for the gift. But, since there is no one else to bridge this chasm, and since eternity is required for the task, I cannot spend my time in extracting you from those curious shards of metal. However, it may be that the antehuman sorcerer Haon-Dor, who abides beyond the gulf in his palace of primal enchantments, can somehow find a use for you. The bridge I have just now completed runs to the threshold of his abode; and your weight will serve to test the strength of my weaving. Go then, with this geas upon you, to cross the bridge and present yourself before Haon-Dor, saying: 'Atlach-Nacha has sent me.'"

With these words, the spider-god withdrew his bulk from the web and ran quickly from sight along the chasm-edge, doubtless to begin the construction of a new bridge at some remoter point.

Though the third geas was heavy and compulsive upon him, Ralibar Vooz followed Raphtontis none too willingly over the night-bound depths. The weaving of Atlach-Nacha was strong beneath his feet, giving and swaying only a little; but between the strands, in unfathomable space below, he seemed to descry the dim flitting of dragons with claw-tipped wings; and, like a seething of the darkness, fearful hulks without name appeared to heave and sink from moment to moment.

However, he and his guide came presently to the gulf's opposite shore, where the web of Atlach-Nacha was joined to the lowest step of a mighty stairway. The stairs were guarded by a coiled snake whose mottlings were broad as bucklers and whose middle volumes exceeded in girth the body of a stout warrior. The horny tail of this serpent rattled like a sistrum, and he thrust forth an evil head with fangs that were long as bill-hooks. But, seeing Raphtontis, he drew his coils aside and permitted Ralibar Vooz to ascend the steps.

Thus, in fulfillment of the third geas, the hunter entered the thousand-columned palace of Haon-Dor. Strange and silent were those halls hewn from the grey, fundamental rock of Earth. In them were faceless forms of smoke and mist that went uneasily to and fro, and statues representing monsters with myriad heads. In the vaults above, as if hung aloof in night, lamps burned with inverse flames that were like the combustion of ice and stone. A chill spirit of evil, ancient beyond all conception of man, was abroad in those halls; and horror and fear crept throughout them like invisible serpents, unknotted from sleep.

Threading the mazy chambers with the surety of one accustomed to all their windings, Raphtontis conducted Ralibar Vooz to a high room whose walls described a circle broken only by the one portal, through which he entered. The room was empty of furnishment, save for a five-pillared seat rising so far aloft without stairs or other means of approach, that it seemed only a winged being could ever attain thereto. But on the seat was a figure shrouded with thick, sable darkness, and having over its head and features a caul of grisly shadow.

The bird Raphtontis hovered ominously before the columned chair. And Ralibar Vooz, in astonishment, heard a voice saying: "O Haon-Dor, Atlach-Nacha has sent me." And not till the voice had ceased speaking did he know it for his own.

For a long time the silence seemed infrangible. There was no stirring of the high-seated figure. But Ralibar Vooz, peering trepidantly at the walls about him, beheld their former smoothness embossed with a thousand faces, twisted and a-wry like those of mad devils. The faces were thrust forward on necks that lengthened; and behind the necks malshapen shoulders and bodies emerged inch by inch from the stone, craning toward the huntsman. And beneath his feet the very floor was now cobbled with other faces, turning and tossing restlessly, and opening ever wider their demoniacal mouths and eyes.

At last the shrouded figure spoke; and though the words were of no mortal tongue, it seemed to the listener that he comprehended them darkly:

"My thanks are due to Atlach-Nacha for this sending. If I appear to hesitate, it is only because I am doubtful regarding what disposition I can make of you. My familiars, who crowd the walls and floors of this chamber, would devour you all too readily; but you would serve only as a morsel amid so many. On the whole, I believe that the best thing I can do is to send you on to my allies, the serpent-people. They are scientists of no ordinary attainment; and perhaps you might provide some special ingredient required in their chemistries. Consider, then, that a geas has been put upon you, and take yourself off to the caverns in which the serpent-people reside."

Obeying this injunction, Ralibar Vooz went down through the darkest strata of that primeval underworld, beneath the palace of Haon-Dor. The guidance of Raphtontis never failed him; and he came anon to the spacious caverns in which the serpent-men were busying themselves with a multitude of tasks. They walked lithely and sinuously erect on pre-mammalian members, their pied and hairless bodies bending with great suppleness. There was a loud and constant hissing of formulae as they went to and fro. Some were smelting the black nether ores; some were blowing molten obsidian into forms of flask and urn; some were measuring chemicals; others were decanting strange liquids and curious colloids. In their intense preoccupation, none of them seemed to notice the arrival of Ralibar Vooz and his guide.

After the hunter had repeated many times the message given him by Haon-Dor, one of the walking reptiles at last perceived his presence. This being eyed him with cold but highly disconcerting curiosity, and then emitted a sonorous hiss that was audible above all the noises of labor and converse. The other serpent-men ceased their toil immediately and began to crowd around Ralibar Vooz. From the tone of their sibilations, it seemed that there was much argument among them. Certain of their number sidled close to the Commorian, touching his face and hands with their chill, scaly digits, and prying beneath his armor. He felt that they were anatomizing him with methodical minuteness. At the same time, he perceived that they paid no attention to Raphtontis, who had perched himself on a large alembic.

After a while, some of the chemists went away and returned quickly, bearing among them two great jars of glass filled with a clear liquid. In one of the jars there floated upright a well-developed and mature male Voormi; in the other, a large and equally perfect specimen of Hyperborean manhood, not without a sort of general likeness to Ralibar Vooz himself. The bearers of these specimens deposited their burdens beside the hunter and then each of them delivered what was doubtless a learned dissertation on comparative biology.

This series of lectures, unlike many such, was quite brief. At the end the reptilian chemists returned to their various labors, and the jars were removed. One of the scientists then addressed himself to Ralibar Vooz with a fair though somewhat sibilant approximation of human speech:

"It was thoughtful of Haon-Dor to send you here. However, as you have seen, we are already supplied with an exemplar of your species; and, in the past, we have thoroughly dissected others and have learned all that there is to learn regarding this very uncouth and aberrant life-form.

"Also, since our chemistry is devoted almost wholly to the production of powerful toxic agents, we can find no use in our tests and manufactures for the extremely ordinary matters of which your body is composed. They are without pharmaceutic value. Moreover, we have long abandoned the eating of impure natural foods, and now confine ourselves to synthetic types of aliment. There is, you must realize, no place for you in our economy.

"However, it may be that the Archetypes can somehow dispose of you. At least you will be a novelty to them, since no example of contemporary human evolution has so far descended to their stratum. Therefore we shall put you under that highly urgent and imperative kind of hypnosis which, in the parlance of warlockry, is known as a geas. And, obeying the hypnosis, you will go down to the Cavern of the Archetypes."

The region to which the magistrate of Commoriom was now conducted lay at some distance below the ophidian laboratories. The air of the gulfs and grottoes along his way began to increase markedly in warmth, and was moist and steamy as that of some equatorial fen. A primordial luminosity, such as might have dawned before the creation of any sun, seemed to surround and pervade everything.

All about him, in this thick and semi-aqueous light, the hunter discerned the rocks and fauna and vegetable forms of a crassly primitive world. These shapes were dim, uncertain, wavering, and were all composed of loosely organized elements. Even in this bizarre and more than doubtful terrain of the under-

Earth, Raphtontis seemed wholly at home, and he flew on amid the sketchy plants and cloudy-looking boulders as if at no loss whatever in orienting himself. But Ralibar Vooz, in spite of the spell that stimulated and compelled him onward, had begun to feel a fatigue by no means unnatural in view of his prolonged and heroic itinerary. Also, he was much troubled by the elasticity of the ground, which sank beneath him at every step like an oversodded marsh, and seemed insubstantial to a quite alarming degree.

To his further disconcertion, the hunter soon found that he had attracted the attention of a huge foggy monster with the rough outlines of a tyrannosaurus. This creature pursued him amid the archetypal ferns and club-mosses; and overtaking him after five or six bounds, it proceeded to ingest him with the celerity of any latter-day saurian of the same species. Luckily, the ingestment was not permanent: for the tyrannosaurus' body-plasm, though fairly opaque, was more astral than material; and Ralibar Vooz, protesting stoutly against his confinement in its maw, felt the dark walls give way before him and tumbled out on the deeply resilient ground.

After its third attempt to devour him, the monster must have decided that he was inedible. It turned and went away with immense leapings in search of comestibles on its own plane of matter. Ralibar Vooz continued his progress through the Cavern of the Archetypes: a progress often delayed by the alimentary designs of crude, misty-stomached allosaurs, pterodactyls, pteranodons, stegosaurs, and other carnivora of the prime.

At last, following his experience with a most persistent megalosaur, he beheld before him two entities of vaguely human outline. These creatures were gigantic, with bodies almost globular in form, and they seemed to float rather than walk. Their features, though shadowy to the point of inchoateness, appeared to express aversion and hostility. They drew near to the Commorian, and he became aware that one of them was addressing him. The language used was wholly a matter of primitive vowel-sounds; but a meaning was forcibly, though indistinctly, conveyed:

"We, the originals of mankind, are dismayed by the sight of a copy so coarse and egregiously perverted from the true model. We disown you with sorrow and indignation. Your presence here is an unwarrantable intrusion; and it is obvious that you are not to be assimilated even by our most esurient dinosaurs. Therefore we put you under a geas: depart without delay from the Cavern of the Archetypes, and seek out the slimy gulf in which Abhoth, father and mother of all cosmic uncleanness, eternally carries on Its repugnant fission. We consider that you are fit only for Abhoth, which will perhaps mistake you for one of Its own progeny and devour you in accordance with the custom which It follows."

The weary hunter was led by the untirable Raphtontis to a deep cavern on the same level as that of the Archetypes. Possibly it was a kind of annex to the latter. At any rate, the ground was much firmer there, even though the air was murkier; and Ralibar Vooz might have recovered a little of his customary aplomb, if it had not been for the ungodly and disgusting creatures which he soon began to meet. There were things which he could liken only to monstrous one-legged toads, and immense myriad-tailed worms, and miscreated lizards. They came flopping or crawling through the gloom in a ceaseless procession; and there was no end to the loathsome morphologic variations which they displayed. Unlike the Archetypes, they were formed of all too solid matter, and Ralibar Vooz was both fatigued and nauseated by the constant necessity of kicking them away from his shins. He was somewhat relieved to find, however, that these wretched abortions became steadily smaller as he continued his advance.

The dusk about him thickened with hot, evil steam that left an oozy deposit on his armor and bare face and hands. With every breath he inhaled an odor noisome beyond imagining. He stumbled and slipped on the crawling foulnesses underfoot. Then, in that reeky twilight, he saw the pausing of Raphtontis; and below the demoniac bird he descried a sort of pool with a margin of mud that was marled with obscene offal; and in the pool a greyish, horrid mass that nearly choked it from rim to rim.

Here, it seemed, was the ultimate source of all miscreation and abomination. For the grey mass quobbed and quivered, and swelled perpetually; and from it, in manifold fission, were spawned the anatomies that crept away on every side through the grotto. Things there were like bodiless legs or arms that flailed in the slime, or heads that rolled, or floundering bellies with fishes' fins; and all manner of things malformed and monstrous, that grew in size as they departed from the neighborhood of Abhoth. And those that swam not swiftly ashore when they fell into the pool from Abhoth, were devoured by mouths that gaped in the parent bulk.

Ralibar Vooz was beyond thought, beyond horror, in his weariness: else he would have known intolerable shame, seeing that he had come to the bourn ordained for him by the Archetypes as most fit and proper. A deadness near to death was upon all his faculties; and he heard as if remote and high above him a voice that proclaimed to Abhoth the reason of his coming; and he did not know that the voice was his own.

There was no sound in answer; but out of the lumpy mass there grew a member that stretched and lengthened toward Ralibar Vooz where he stood waiting on the pool's margin. The member divided to a flat, webby hand, soft and slimy, which touched the hunter and went over his person slowly from foot to head. Having done this, it seemed that the thing had served its use: for it dropped quickly away from Abhoth and wriggled into the gloom like a serpent together with the other progeny.

Still waiting, Ralibar Vooz felt in his brain a sensation as of speech heard without words or sound. And the import, rendered in human language, was somewhat as follows:

"I, who am Abhoth, the coeval of the oldest gods, consider that the Archetypes have shown a questionable taste in thus recommending you to me. After careful inspection, I fail to recognize you as one of my relatives or progeny; though I must admit that I was nearly deceived at first by certain biologic similarities. You are quite alien to my experience; and I do not care to endanger my digestion with untried articles of diet.

"Who you are, or whence you have come, I cannot surmise; nor can I thank the Archetypes for troubling the profound and placid fertility of my existence with a problem so vexatious as the one that you offer. Get hence, I adjure you. There is a bleak and drear and dreadful limbo, known as the Outer World, of which I have heard dimly; and I think that it might prove a suitable objective for your journeying. I settle an urgent geas upon you: go seek this Outer World with all possible expedition."

Apparently Raphtontis realized that it was beyond the physical powers of his charge to fulfill the seventh geas without an interim of repose. He led the hunter to one of the numerous exits of the grotto inhabited by Abhoth: an exit giving on regions altogether unknown, opposite to the Cavern of the Archetypes. There, with significant gestures of his wings and beak, the bird indicated a sort of narrow alcove in the rock. The recess was dry and by no means uncomfortable as a sleeping-place. Ralibar Vooz was glad to lay himself down; and a black tide of slumber rolled upon him with the closing of his eyelids. Raphtontis remained on guard before the alcove, discouraging with strokes of his bill the wandering progeny of Abhoth that tried to assail the sleeper.

Since there was neither night nor day in that subterrene world, the term of oblivion enjoyed by Ralibar Vooz was hardly to be measured by the usual method of time-telling. He was aroused by the noise of vigorously flapping wings, and saw beside him the fowl Raphtontis, holding in his beak an unsavory object whose anatomy was that of a fish rather than anything else. Where or how he had caught this creature during his constant vigil, was a more than dubious matter; but Ralibar Vooz had fasted too long to be squeamish. He accepted and devoured the proffered breakfast without ceremony.

After that, in conformity with the geas laid upon him by Abhoth, he resumed his journey back to the outer Earth. The route chosen by Raphtontis was presumably a short-cut. Anyhow, it was remote from the cloudy cave of the Archetypes, and the laboratories in which the serpent-men pursued their arduous toils and toxicological researches. Also, the enchanted palace of Haon-Dor was omitted from the itinerary. But, after long, tedious climbing through a region of desolate crags and over a sort of underground plateau, the traveller came once more to the verge of that far-stretching, bottomless chasm which was bridged only by the webs of the spider-god Atlach-Nacha.

For some time past he had hurried his pace because of certain of the progeny of Abhoth, who had followed him from the start and had grown steadily bigger after the fashion of their kind, till they were now large as young tigers or bears. However, when he approached the nearest bridge, he saw that a ponderous and sloth-like entity, preceding him, had already begun to cross it. The posteriors of this being were studded with unamiable eyes, and Ralibar Vooz was unsure for a little regarding its exact orientation. Not wishing to tread too closely upon the reverted talons of its heels, he waited till the monster had disappeared in the darkness; and by that time the spawn of Abhoth were hard upon him.

Raphtontis, with sharp admonitory cawings, floated before him above the giant web; and he was impelled to a rash haste by the imminently slavering snouts of the dark abnormalities behind. Owing to such precipitancy, he failed to notice that the web had been weakened and some of its strands torn or stretched by the weight of the sloth-like monster. Coming in view of the chasm's opposite verge, he thought only of reaching it, and redoubled his pace. But at this point the web gave way beneath him. He caught wildly at the broken, dangling strands, but could not arrest his fall. With several pieces of Atlach-Nacha's weaving clutched in his fingers, he was precipitated into that gulf which no one had ever voluntarily tried to plumb.

This, unfortunately, was a contingency that had not been provided against by the terms of the seventh geas.

THE CHAIN OF AFORGOMON

It is indeed strange that John Milwarp and his writings should have fallen so speedily into a sort of semi-oblivion. His books, treating of Oriental life in a somewhat flowery, romantic style, were popular a few months ago. But now, in spite of their range and penetration, their pervasive verbal sorcery, they are seldom mentioned; and they seem to have vanished unaccountably from the shelves of bookstores and libraries.

Even the mystery of Milwarp's death, baffling to both law and science, has evoked but a passing interest, an excitement quickly lulled and forgotten.

I was well acquainted with Milwarp over a term of years. But my recollection of the man is becoming strangely blurred, like an image in a misted mirror. His dark, half-alien personality, his preoccupation with the occult, his immense knowledge of Eastern life and lore, are things I remember with such effort and vagueness as attends the recovery of a dream. Sometimes I almost doubt that he ever existed. It is as if the man, and all that pertains to him, were being erased from human record by some mysterious acceleration of the common process of obliteration.

In his will, he appointed me his executor. I have vainly tried to interest publishers in the novel he left among his papers: a novel surely not inferior to anything he ever wrote. They say that his vogue has passed. Now I am publishing as a magazine story the contents of the diary kept by Milwarp for a period preceding his demise.

Perhaps, for the open-minded, this diary will serve to explain the enigma of his death. It would seem that the circumstances of that death are virtually forgotten, and I repeat them here as part of my endeavor to revive and perpetuate Milwarp's memory.

Milwarp had returned to his house in San Francisco after a long sojourn in Indo-China. We who knew him gathered that he had gone into places seldom visited by Occidentals. At the time of his demise he had just finished correcting the typescript of a novel which dealt with the more romantic and mysterious aspects of Burma.

On the morning of April 2nd, 1933, his housekeeper, a middle-aged woman, was startled by a glare of brilliant light which issued from the half-open door of Milwarp's study. It was as if the whole room were in flames. Horrified, the woman hastened to investigate. Entering the study, she saw her master sitting in an armchair at the table, wearing the rich, somber robes of Chinese brocade which he affected as a dressing-gown. He sat stiffly erect, a pen clutched unmoving in his fingers on the open pages of a manuscript volume. About him, in a sort of nimbus, glowed and flickered the strange light; and her only thought was that his garments were on fire.

She ran toward him, crying out a warning. At that moment the weird nimbus brightened intolerably, and the wan early dayshine, the electric bulbs that still burned to attest the night's labor, were alike blotted out. It seemed to the housekeeper that something had gone wrong with the room itself; for the walls and table vanished, and a great, luminous gulf opened before her; and on the verge of the gulf, in a seat that was not his cushioned armchair but a huge and rough-hewn seat of stone, she beheld her master stark and rigid. His heavy brocaded robes were gone, and about him, from head to foot, were blinding coils of pure white fire, in the form of linked chains. She could not endure the brilliance of the chains, and cowering back, she shielded her eyes with her hands. When she dared to look again, the weird glowing had faded, the room was as usual; and Milwarp's motionless figure was seated at the table in the posture of writing.

Shaken and terrified as she was, the woman found courage to approach her master. A hideous smell of burnt flesh arose from beneath his garments, which were wholly intact and without visible trace of fire. He was dead, his fingers clenched on the pen and his features frozen in a stare of tetanic agony. His neck and wrists were completely encircled by frightful burns that had charred them deeply. The coroner, in his examination, found that these burns, preserving an outline as of heavy links, were extended in long unbroken spirals around the arms and legs and torso. The burning was apparently the cause of Milwarp's death: it was as if iron chains, heated to incandescence, had been wrapped about him.

Small credit was given to the housekeeper's story of what she had seen. No one, however, could suggest an acceptable explanation of the bizarre mystery. There was, at the time, much aimless discussion; but, as I have hinted, people soon turned to other matters. The efforts made to solve the riddle were somewhat perfunctory. Chemists tried to determine the nature of a queer drug, in the form of a grey powder with pearly granules, to whose use Milwarp had become addicted. But their tests merely revealed the presence of an alkaloid whose source and attributes were obscure to Western science.

Day by day, the whole incredible business lapsed from public attention; and those who had known Milwarp began to display the forgetfulness that was no less unaccountable than his weird doom. The housekeeper, who had held steadfastly in the beginning to her story, came at length to share the common dubiety. Her account, with repetition, became vague and contradictory; detail by detail, she seemed to forget the abnormal circumstances that she had witnessed with overwhelming horror.

The manuscript volume, in which Milwarp had apparently been writing at the time of death, was given into my charge with his other papers. It proved to be a diary, its last entry breaking off abruptly. Since reading the diary, I have hastened to transcribe it in my own hand, because, for some mysterious reason, the ink of the original is already fading and has become almost illegible in places.

The reader will note certain lacunæ, due to passages written in an alphabet which neither I nor any scholar of my acquaintance can transliterate. These passages seem to form an integral part of the narrative, and they occur mainly toward the end, as if the writer had turned more and more to a language remembered from his ancient avatar. To the same mental reversion one must attribute the singular dating, in which Milwarp, still employing English script, appears to pass from our contemporary notation to that of some premundane world.

I give hereunder the entire diary, which begins with an undated footnote:

This book, unless I have been misinformed concerning the qualities of the drug *souvara*, will be the record of my former life in a lost cycle. I have had the drug in my possession for seven months, but fear has prevented me from using it. Now, by certain tokens, I perceive that the longing for knowledge will soon overcome the fear.

Ever since my earliest childhood I have been troubled by intimations, dim, unplaceable, that seemed to argue a forgotten existence. These intimations partook of the nature of feelings rather than ideas or images: they were like the wraiths of dead memories. In the background of my mind there has lurked a sentiment of formless, melancholy desire for some nameless beauty long perished out of time. And, coincidentally, I have been haunted by an equally formless dread, an apprehension as of some bygone but still imminent doom.

Such feelings have persisted, undiminished, throughout my youth and maturity, but nowhere have I found any clue to their causation. My travels in the mystic Orient, my delvings into occultism have merely convinced me that these shadowy intuitions pertain to some incarnation buried under the wreck of remotest cycles.

Many times, in my wanderings through Buddhistic lands, I had heard of the drug *souvara*, which is believed to restore, even for the uninitiate, the memory of other lives. And at last, after many vain efforts, I managed to procure a supply of the drug. The manner in which I obtained it is a tale sufficiently remarkable in itself, but of no special relevance here. So far—perhaps because of that apprehension which I have hinted—I have not dared to use the drug.

March 9th, 1933. This morning I took *souvara* for the first time, dissolving the proper amount in pure distilled water as I had been instructed to do. Afterwards I leaned back easily in my chair, breathing with a slow, regular rhythm. I had no preconceived idea of the sensations that would mark the drug's initial effect, since these were said to vary prodigiously with the temperament of the users; but I composed myself to await them with tranquillity, after formulating clearly in my mind the purpose of the experiment.

For awhile there was no change in my awareness. I noticed a slight quickening of the pulse, and modulated my breathing in conformity with this. Then, by slow degrees, I experienced a sharpening of visual perception. The Chinese rugs on the floor, the backs of the serried volumes in my bookcases, the very wood of chairs, table and shelves, began to exhibit new and unimagined colors. At the same time there were curious alterations of outline, every object seeming to extend itself in a hitherto unsuspected fashion. Following this, my surroundings became semi-transparent, like moulded shapes of mist. I found that I could see through the marbled cover the illustrations in a volume of John Martin's edition of *Paradise Lost*, which lay before me on the table.

All this, I knew, was a mere extension of ordinary physical vision. It was only a prelude to those apperceptions of occult realms which I sought through *souvara*. Fixing my mind once more on the goal of the experiment, I became aware that the misty walls had vanished like a drawn arras. About me, like reflections in rippled water, dim sceneries wavered and shifted, erasing one another from instant to instant. I seemed to hear a vague but ever-present sound, more musical than the murmurs of air, water or fire, which was a property of the unknown element that environed me.

With a sense of troublous familiarity, I beheld the blurred unstable pictures which flowed past me upon this never-resting medium. Orient temples, flashing with sun-struck bronze and gold; the sharp, crowded gables and spires of medieval cities; tropic and northern forests; the costumes and physiognomies of the Levant, of Persia, of old Rome and Carthage, went by like blown, flying mirages. Each succeeding tableau belonged to a more ancient period than the one before it—and I knew that each was a scene from some former existence of my own.

Still tethered, as it were, to my present self, I reviewed these visible memories, which took on tri-dimensional depth and clarity. I saw myself as warrior and troubadour, as noble and merchant and mendicant. I trembled with dead fears, I thrilled with lost hopes and raptures, and was drawn by ties that death and Lethe had broken. Yet never did I fully identify myself with those other avatars: for I knew well that the memory I sought pertained to some incarnation of older epochs.

Still the phantasmagoria streamed on, and I turned giddy with vertigo ineffable before the vastness and diuturnity of the cycles of being. It seemed that I, the watcher, was lost in a grey land where the homeless ghosts of all dead ages went fleeing from oblivion to oblivion.

The walls of Nineveh, the columns and towers of unnamed cities, rose before me and were swept away. I saw the luxuriant plains that are now the Gobi desert. The sea-lost capitals of Atlantis were drawn to the light in unquenched glory. I gazed on lush and cloudy scenes from the first continents of Earth. Briefly I relived the beginnings of terrestrial man—and knew that the secret I would learn was ancienter even than these.

My visions faded into black voidness—and yet, in that void, through fathomless eons, it seemed that I existed still like a blind atom in the space between the worlds. About me was the darkness and repose of that night which antedated the earth's creation. Time flowed backward with the silence of dreamless sleep....

The illumination, when it came, was instant and complete. I stood in the full, fervid blaze of day amid royally towering blossoms in a deep garden, beyond whose lofty, vine-clad walls I heard the confused murmuring of the great city called Kalood. Above me, at their vernal zenith, were the four small suns that illumed the planet Hestan. Jewel-colored insects fluttered about me, lighting without fear on the rich habiliments of gold and black, enwrought with astronomic symbols, in which I was attired. Beside me was a dial-shaped altar of zoned agate, carved with the same symbols, which were those of the dreadful omnipotent time-god, Aforgomon, whom I served as a priest.

I had not even the slightest memory of myself as John Milwarp, and the long pageant of my terrestrial lives was as something that had never been—or was yet to be. Sorrow and desolation choked my heart as ashes fill some urn consecrated to the dead; and all the hues and perfumes of the garden about me were redolent only of the bitterness of death. Gazing darkly upon the altar, I muttered blasphemy against Aforgomon, who, in his inexorable course, had taken away my beloved and had sent no solace for my grief. Separately I cursed the signs upon the altar: the stars, the worlds, the suns, the moons, that meted and fulfilled the processes of time. Belthoris, my betrothed, had died at the end of the previous autumn: and so, with double maledictions, I cursed the stars and planets presiding over that season.

I became aware that a shadow had fallen beside my own on the altar, and knew that the dark sage and sorcerer Atmox had obeyed my summons. Fearfully but not without hope I turned toward him, noting first of all that he bore under his arm a heavy, sinister-looking volume with covers of black steel and hasps of adamant. Only when I had made sure of this did I lift my eyes to his face, which was little less somber and forbidding than the tome he carried.

"Greeting, O Calaspa," he said harshly. "I have come against my own will and judgment. The lore that you request is in this volume; and since you saved me in former years from the inquisitorial wrath of the time-god's priests, I cannot refuse to share it with you. But understand well that even I, who have called upon names that are dreadful to utter, and have evoked forbidden presences, shall never dare to assist you in this conjuration. Gladly would I help you to hold converse with the shadow of Belthoris, or to animate her still unwithered body and draw it forth from the tomb. But that which you purpose is another matter. You alone must perform the ordained rites, must speak the necessary words: for the consequences of this thing will be direr than you deem."

"I care not for the consequences," I replied eagerly, "if it be possible to bring back the lost hours which I shared with Belthoris. Think you that I could content myself with her shadow, wandering thinly back from the Borderland? Or that I could take pleasure in the fair clay that the breath of necromancy has troubled and has made to arise and walk without mind or soul? Nay, the Belthoris I would summon is she on whom the shadow of death has never yet fallen!"

It seemed that Atmox, the master of doubtful arts, the vassal of umbrageous powers, recoiled and blenched before my vehement declaration.

"Bethink you," he said with minatory sternness, "that this thing will constitute a breach of the sacred logic of time and a blasphemy against Aforgomon, god of the minutes and the cycles. Moreover, there is little to be gained: for not in its entirety may you bring back the season of your love, but only one single hour, torn with infinite violence from its rightful period in time…. Refrain, I adjure you, and content yourself with a lesser sorcery."

"Give me the book," I demanded. "My service to Aforgomon is forfeit. With due reverence and devotion I have worshipped the time-god, and have done in his honor the rites ordained from eternity; and for all this the god has betrayed me."

Then, in that high-climbing, luxuriant garden beneath the four suns, Atmox opened the adamantine clasps of the steel-bound volume; and, turning to a certain page, he laid the book reluctantly in my hands. The page, like its fellows, was of some unholy parchment streaked with musty discolorations and blackening at the margin with sheer antiquity; but upon it shone unquenchably the dread characters a primal archimage had written with an ink bright as the new-shed ichor of demons. Above this page I bent in my madness, conning it over and over till I was dazzled by the fiery runes; and, shutting my eyes, I saw them burn on a red darkness, still legible, and writhing like hellish worms.

Hollowly, like the sound of a far bell, I heard the voice of Atmox: "You have learned, O Calaspa, the unutterable name of that One whose assistance can alone restore the fled hours. And you have learned the incantation that will rouse that hidden power, and the sacrifice needed for its propitiation. Knowing these things, is your heart still strong and your purpose firm?"

The name I had read in the wizard volume was that of the chief cosmic power antagonistic to Aforgomon; the incantation and the required offering were those of a foul demonolatry. Nevertheless, I did not hesitate, but gave resolute affirmative answer to the somber query of Atmox.

Perceiving that I was inflexible, he bowed his head, trying no more to dissuade me. Then, as the flame-runed volume had bade me do, I defiled the altar of Aforgomon, blotting certain of its prime symbols with dust and spittle. While Atmox looked on in silence, I wounded my right arm to its deepest vein on the sharp-tipped gnomon of the dial; and, letting the blood drip from zone to zone, from orb to orb on the graven agate, I made unlawful sacrifice, and intoned aloud, in the name of the Lurking Chaos, Xexanoth, an abominable ritual composed by a backward repetition and jumbling of litanies sacred to the time-god.

Even as I chanted the incantation, it seemed that webs of shadow were woven foully athwart the suns; and the ground shook a little, as if colossal demons trod the world's rim, striding stupendously from abysses beyond. The garden walls and trees wavered like a wind-blown reflection in a pool; and I grew faint with the loss of that life-blood I had poured out in demonolatrous offering. Then, in my flesh and in my brain, I felt the intolerable racking of a vibration like the long-drawn shock of cities riven by earthquake, and coasts crumbling before some chaotic sea; and my flesh was torn and harrowed infinitely, and my brain shuddered with the toneless discords sweeping through me from deep to deep.

I faltered, and confusion gnawed at my inmost being. Dimly I heard the prompting of Atmox, and dimmer still was the sound of my own voice that made answer to Xexanoth, naming the impious necromancy which was to be effected only through its power. Madly I implored from Xexanoth, in despite of time and its ordered seasons, one hour of that bygone autumn which I had shared with Belthoris; and imploring this, I named no special hour: for all, in memory, had seemed of an equal joy and gladness.

As the words ceased upon my lips, I thought that darkness fluttered in the air like a great wing; and the four suns went out, and my heart was stilled as if in death. Then the light returned, falling obliquely from suns mellow with full-tided autumn; and nowhere beside me was there any shadow of Atmox; and the altar of zoned agate was bloodless and undefiled. I, the lover of Belthoris, witting not of the doom and sorrow to come, stood happily with my beloved before the altar, and saw her young hands crown its ancient dial with the flowers we had plucked from the garden.

Dreadful beyond all fathoming are the mysteries of time. Even I, the priest and initiate, though wise in the secret doctrines of Aforgomon, know little enough of that elusive, ineluctable process whereby the present becomes the past and the future resolves itself into the present. All men have pondered the riddles of duration and transience; have wondered, vainly, to what bourn the lost days and the sped cycles are consigned. Some have dreamt that the past abides unchanged, becoming eternity as it slips from our mortal ken; and others have deemed that time is a stairway whose steps crumble one by one behind the climber, falling into a gulf of nothing.

Howsoever this may be, I know that she who stood beside me was the Belthoris on whom no shadow of mortality had yet descended. The hour was one newborn in a golden season; and the minutes to come were pregnant with all wonder and surprise belonging to the untried future.

Taller was my beloved than the frail, unbowed lilies of the garden. In her eyes was the sapphire of moonless evenings sown with small golden stars. Her lips were strangely curved, but only blitheness and joy had gone to their shaping.

She and I had been betrothed from our childhood, and the time of the marriage-rites was now approaching. Our intercourse was wholly free, according to the custom of that world. Often she came to walk with me in my garden and to decorate the altar of that god whose revolving moons and suns would soon bring the season of our felicity.

The moths that flew about us, winged with aerial cloth-of-gold, were no lighter than our hearts. Making blithe holiday, we fanned our frolic mood to a high flame of rapture. We were akin to the full-hued, climbing flowers, the swift-darting insects, and our spirits blended and soared with the perfumes that were drawn skyward in the warm air. Unheard by us was the loud murmuring of the mighty city of Kalood lying beyond my garden walls; for us the many-peopled planet known as Hestan no longer existed; and we dwelt alone in a universe of light, in a blossomed heaven. Exalted by love in the high harmony of those moments, we seemed to touch eternity; and even I, the priest of Aforgomon, forgot the blossom-fretting days, the system-devouring cycles.

In the sublime folly of passion, I swore then that death or discord could never mar the perfect communion of our hearts. After we had wreathed the altar, I sought the rarest, the most delectable flowers: frail-curving cups of wine-washed pearl, of moony azure and white with scrolled purple lips; and these I twined, between kisses and laughter, in the black maze of Belthoris' hair; saying that another shrine than that of time should receive its due offering.

Tenderly, with a lover's delay, I lingered over the wreathing; and, ere I had finished, there fluttered to the ground beside us a great, crimson-spotted moth whose wing had somehow been broken in its airy voyaging through the garden. And Belthoris, ever tender of heart and pitiful, turned from me and took up the moth in her hands; and some of the bright blossoms dropped from her hair unheeded. Tears welled from her deep blue eyes; and seeing that the moth was sorely hurt and would never fly again, she refused to be comforted; and no longer would she respond to my passionate wooing. I, who grieved less for the moth than she, was somewhat vexed; and between her sadness and my vexation, there grew between us some tiny, temporary rift....

Then, ere love had mended the misunderstanding; then, while we stood before the dread altar of time with sundered hands, with eyes averted from each other, it seemed that a shroud of darkness descended upon the garden. I heard the crash and crumbling of shattered worlds, and a black flowing of ruinous things that went past me through the darkness. The dead leaves of winter were blown about me, and there was a falling of tears or rain.... Then the vernal suns came back, high-stationed in cruel splendor; and with them came the knowledge of all that had been, of Belthoris' death and my sorrow, and the madness that had led to forbidden sorcery. Vain now, like all other hours, was the resummoned hour; and doubly irredeemable was my loss. My blood dripped heavily on the dishallowed altar, my faintness grew deathly, and I saw through murky mist the face of Atmox beside me; and the face was like that of some comminatory demon....

March 13th. I, John Milwarp, write this date and my name with an odd dubiety. My visionary experience under the drug *souvara* ended with that rilling of my blood on the symboled dial, that glimpse of the terror-distorted face of Atmox. All this was in another world, in a life removed from the present by births and deaths without number; and yet, it seems, not wholly have I returned from the twice-ancient past. Memories, broken but strangely vivid and living, press upon me from the existence of which my vision was a fragment; and portions of the lore of Hestan, and scraps of its history, and words from its lost language, arise unbidden in my mind.

Above all, my heart is still shadowed by the sorrow of Calaspa. His desperate necromancy, which would seem to others no more than a dream within a dream, is stamped as with fire on the black page of recollection. I know the awfulness of the god he had blasphemed, and the foulness of the demonolatry he had done, and the sense of guilt and despair under which he swooned. It is *this* that I have striven all my life to remember, this which I have been doomed to re-experience. And I fear with a great fear the farther knowledge which a second experiment with the drug will reveal to me.

EDITOR'S NOTE. The next entry of Milwarp's diary begins with a strange dating in English script: "The second day of the moon Occalat, in the thousand-and-ninth year of the Red Aeon." This dating, perhaps, is repeated in the language of Hestan: for, directly beneath it, a line of unknown ciphers is set apart. Several lines of the subsequent text are in the alien tongue; and then, as if by an unconscious reversion, Milwarp continues the diary in English. There is no reference to another experiment with *souvara*: but apparently such had been made, with a continued revival of his lost memories.

...What genius of the nadir gulf had tempted me to this thing and had caused me to overlook the consequences? Verily, when I called up for myself and Belthoris an hour of former autumn, with all that was attendant upon the hour, *that bygone interim was likewise evoked and repeated for the whole world Hestan, and the four suns of Hestan.* From the full midst of spring, all men had stepped backward into autumn, keeping only the memory of things prior to the hour thus resurrected, and knowing not the events future to the hour. But, returning to the present, they recalled with amazement the unnatural necromancy; and fear and bewilderment were upon them; and none could interpret the meaning.

For a brief period, the dead had lived again; the fallen leaves had returned to the bough; the heavenly bodies had stood at a long-abandoned station; the flower had gone back into the seed, the plant into the root. Then, with eternal disorder set among all its cycles, time had resumed its delayed course.

No movement of any cosmic body, no year or instant of the future, would be precisely as it should have been. The error and discrepancy I had wrought would bear fruit in ways innumerable. The suns would find themselves at fault; the worlds and atoms would go always a little astray from their appointed bourns.

It was of these matters that Atmox spoke, warning me, after he had staunched my bleeding wound. For he too, in that relumined hour, had gone back and had lived again through a past happening. For him the hour was one in which he had descended into the nether vaults of his house. There, standing in a many-pentacled circle, with burning of unholy incense and uttering of accurst formulæ, he had called up a malign spirit from the bowels of Hestan and had questioned it concerning the future. But the spirit, black and voluminous as the fumes of pitch, refused to answer him directly and pressed furiously with its clawed members against the confines of the circle. It said only: "Thou hast summoned me at thy peril. Potent are the spells thou hast used, and strong is the circle to withstand me, and I am restrained by time and space from the wreaking of my anger upon thee. *But haply thou shalt summon me again, albeit in the same hour of the same autumn;* and in that summoning the laws of time shall be broken, and a rift shall be made in space; and through the rift, though with some delay and divagation, I shall yet win to thee."

Saying no more, it prowled restlessly about the circle; and its eyes burned down upon Atmox like embers in a high-lifted sooty brazier; and ever and anon its fanged mouth was flattened on the spell-defended air. And in the end he could dismiss it only after a double repetition of the form of exorcism.

As he told me this tale in the garden, Atmox trembled; and his eyes searched the narrow shadows wrought by the high suns; and he seemed to listen for the noise of some evil thing that burrowed toward him beneath the earth.

Fourth day of the moon Occalat …. Stricken with terrors beyond those of Atmox, I kept apart in my mansion amid the city of Kalood. I was still weak with the loss of the blood I had yielded to Xexanoth; my senses were full of strange shadows; my servitors, coming and going about me, were as phantoms, and scarcely I heeded the pale fear in their eyes or heard the dreadful things they whispered…. Madness and chaos, they told me, were abroad in Kalood; the divinity of Aforgomon was angered. All men thought that some baleful doom impended because of that unnatural confusion which had been wrought among the hours of time.

This afternoon they brought me the story of Atmox's death. In bated tones they told me how his neophytes had heard a roaring as of a loosed tempest in the chamber where he sat alone with his wizard volumes and paraphernalia. Above the roaring, for a little, human screams had sounded, together with a clashing as of hurled censers and braziers, a crashing as of overthrown tables and tomes. Blood rilled from under the shut door of the chamber, and, rilling, it took from instant to instant the form of dire ciphers that spelt an unspeakable name. After the noises had ceased the neophytes waited a long while ere they dared to open the door. Entering at last, they saw the floor and the walls heavily bespattered with blood, and rags of the sorcerer's raiment mingled everywhere with the sheets of his torn volumes of magic, and the shreds and manglings of his flesh strewn amid broken furniture, and his brains daubed in a horrible paste on the high ceiling.

Hearing this tale, I knew that the earthly demon feared by Atmox had found him somehow and had wreaked its wrath upon him. In ways unguessable, it had reached him through the chasm made in ordered time and space by one hour repeated through necromancy. And because of that lawless chasm, the magician's power and lore had utterly failed to defend him from the demon….

Fifth day of the moon Occalat. Atmox, I am sure, had not betrayed me: for in so doing, he must have betrayed his own implicit share in my crime…. Howbeit, this evening the priests came to my house ere the setting of the westernmost sun: silent, grim, with eyes averted as if from a foulness innominable. Me, their fellow, they enjoined with loath gestures to accompany them…. Thus they took me from my house and along the thoroughfares of Kalood toward the lowering suns. The streets were empty of all other passers, and it seemed that no man desired to meet or behold the blasphemer…. Down the avenue of gnomon-shaped pillars, I was led to the portals of Aforgomon's fane: those awfully gaping portals arched in the likeness of some devouring chimera's mouth….

Sixth day of the moon Occalat. They had thrust me into an oubliette beneath the temple, dark, noisome and soundless except for the maddening, measured drip of water beside me. There I lay and knew not when the night passed and the morning came. Light was admitted only when my captors opened the iron door, coming to lead me before the tribunal....

...Thus the priests condemned me, speaking with one voice in whose dreadful volume the tones of all were indistinguishably blended. Then the aged high-priest Helpenor called aloud upon Aforgomon, offering himself as a mouth-piece to the god, and asking the god to pronounce through him the doom that was adequate for such enormities as those of which I had been judged guilty by my fellows.

Instantly, it seemed, the god descended into Helpenor; and the figure of the high-priest appeared to dilate prodigiously beneath his mufflings; and the accents that issued from his mouth were like thunders of the upper heaven:

"O Calaspa, thou hast set disorder amid all future hours and aeons through this evil necromancy. Thereby, moreover, thou hast wrought thine own doom: fettered art thou forever to the hour thus unlawfully repeated, apart from its due place in time. According to hieratic rule, thou shalt meet the death of the fiery chains: but deem not that this death is more than the symbol of thy true punishment. Thou shalt pass hereafter through other lives in Hestan, and shalt climb midway in the cycles of the world subsequent to Hestan in time and space. But through all thine incarnations the chaos thou hast invoked will attend thee, widening ever like a rift. And always, in all thy lives, the rift will bar thee from reunion with the soul of Belthoris; and always, though merely by an hour, thou shalt miss the love that should otherwise have been oftentimes regained.

"At last, when the chasm has widened overmuch, thy soul shall fare no farther in the onward cycles of incarnation. At that time it shall be given thee to remember clearly thine ancient sin; and remembering, thou shalt perish out of time. Upon the body of that latter life shall be found the charred imprint of the chains, as the final token of thy bondage. But they that knew thee will soon forget, and thou shalt belong wholly to the cycles limited for thee by thy sin."

March 29th. I write this date with infinite desperation, trying to convince myself that there is a John Milwarp who exists on Earth, in the twentieth century. For two days running, I have not taken the drug *souvara*: and yet I have returned twice to that oubliette of Aforgomon's temple, in which the priest Calaspa awaits his doom. Twice I been immersed in its stagnant darkness, hearing the slow drip of water beside me, like a clepsydra that tells the black ages of the damned.

Even as I write this at my library table, it seems that an ancient midnight plucks at the lamp. The bookcases turn to walls of oozing, nighted stone.

There is no longer a table… nor one who writes… and I breathe the noisome dankness of a dungeon lying unfathomed by any sun, in a lost world.

Eighteenth day of the moon Occalat. Today, for the last time, they took me from my prison. Helpenor, together with three others, came and led me to the adytum of the god. Far beneath the outer temple we went, through spacious crypts unknown to the common worshippers. There was no word spoken, no glance exchanged between the others and me; and it seemed that they already regarded me as one cast out from time and claimed by oblivion.

We came ultimately to that sheer-falling gulf in which the spirit of Aforgomon is said to dwell. Lights, feeble and far-scattered, shone around it like stars on the rim of cosmic vastness, shedding no ray into the depths. There, in a seat of hewn stone overhanging the frightful verge, I was placed by the executioners; and a ponderous chain of black unrusted metal, stapled in the solid rock, was wound about and about me, circling my naked body and separate limbs, from head to foot.

To this doom, others had been condemned for heresy or impiety… though never for a sin such as mine. After the chaining of the victim, he was left alone for a stated interim, to ponder his crime—and haply to confront the dark divinity of Aforgomon. At length, from the abyss into which his position forced him to peer, a light would dawn, and a bolt of strange flame would leap upward, striking the many-coiled chain about him and heating it instantly to the whiteness of candescent iron. The source and nature of the flame were mysterious, and many ascribed it to the god himself rather than to mortal agency….

Even thus they have left me, and have gone away. Long since the burden of the massy links, cutting deeper and deeper into my flesh, has become an agony. I am dizzy from gazing downward into the abyss—and yet I cannot fall. Beneath, immeasurably beneath, at recurrent intervals, I hear a hollow and solemn sound. Perhaps it is the sigh of sunken waters… of cavern-straying winds… or the respiration of One that abides in the darkness, meting with his breath the slow minutes, the hours, the days, the ages…. My terror has become heavier than the chain, my vertigo is born of a twofold gulf….

Aeons have passed by and all the worlds have ebbed into nothingness, like wreckage borne on a chasm-falling stream, taking with them the lost face of Belthoris. I am poised above the gaping maw of the Shadow…. Somehow, in another world, an exile phantom has written these words… a phantom who must fade utterly from time and place, even as I, the doomed priest Calaspa. I cannot remember the name of the phantom.

Beneath me, in the black depths, there is an awful brightening….

The Primal City

In these after-days, when all things are touched with insoluble doubt and dereliction, I am not sure of the purpose that had taken us into that little-visited land. I recall, however, that we had found explicit mention, in a volume of which we possessed the one existing copy, of certain vast prehuman ruins lying amid the bare plateaus and stark pinnacles of the region. How we had acquired the volume I do not remember: but Sebastian Polder and I had given our youth and much of our manhood to the quest of hidden knowledge; and this book was a compendium of all things that men have forgotten or ignored in their desire to repudiate the inexplicable.

We, being enamored of mystery, and seeking ever for the clues that material science has disregarded, pondered much upon those pages written in an antique alphabet. The location of the ruins was clearly stated, though in terms of an obsolete geography; and I remember our excitement when we had marked the position on a terrestrial globe. We were consumed by a wild eagerness to behold the alien city, and certain of our ability to find it. Perhaps we wished to verify a strange and fearful theory which we had formed regarding the nature of the earth's primal inhabitants; perhaps we sought to recover the buried records of a lost science... or perhaps there was some other and darker objective....

I recall nothing of the first stages of our journey, which must have been long and arduous. But I recall distinctly that we traveled for many days amid the bleak, treeless uplands that rose rapidly like a many-tiered embankment toward the range of high pyramidal summits guarding our destination. Our guide was a native of the country, sodden and taciturn, with intelligence little above that of the llamas who carried our supplies. He had never visited the ruins, but we had been assured that he knew the way, which was a secret remembered by few of his fellow countrymen. Rare and scant was the local legendry concerning the place and its builders; and, after many queries, we could add nothing to the knowledge gained from the immemorial volume. The city, it seemed, was nameless; and the region about it was untrodden by man.

Desire and curiosity raged within us like a calenture; and we gave no heed to the hazards and travails of exploration. Over us stood the eternal azure of vacant heavens, matching in their desolation the empty landscape. The route steepened; and above us now was a wilderness of cragged and chasmed rock, where nothing dwelt but the sinister wide-winged condors.

Often we lost sight of certain eminent peaks that had served us for landmarks. But it seemed that our guide knew the way, as if led by an instinct more subtle than memory or intelligence; and at no time did he hesitate. At intervals we came to the broken fragments of a paved road that had formerly traversed the whole of this rugged region: broad, cyclopean flags of gneiss, channeled as if by the storms of cycles older than human history. And in some of the deeper chasms we saw the eroded piers of great bridges that had spanned them in other time. These ruins reassured us; for in the primordial volume there was mention of a highway and of mighty bridges, leading to the fabulous city.

Polder and I were exultant; and yet I think that we both shivered with a curious terror when we tried to read certain inscriptions that were still deeply engraved on the worn stones. No living man, though erudite in all the tongues of Earth, could have deciphered those characters; and perhaps it was their very alienage that frightened us. We had sought diligently during many laborious years for all that transcends the dead level of mortality through age or remoteness or strangeness; we had longed ardently for the esoteric and bizarre: but such longing was not incompatible with fear and repulsion. Better than those who had walked always in the common paths, we knew the perils that might attend our exorbitant and solitary researches.

Often we had debated, with variously fantastic conjectures, the enigma of the mountain-builded city. But, toward our journey's end, when the vestiges of that pristine people multiplied around us, we fell into long periods of silence, sharing the taciturnity of our stolid guide. Thoughts came to us that were overly strange for utterance; the chill of elder aeons entered our hearts from the ruins—and did not depart.

We toiled on between the desolate rocks and the sterile heavens, breathing an air that became thin and painful to the lungs, as if with some admixture of cosmic ether. At high noon we reached an open pass, and saw before and above us, at the end of a long and vertiginous perspective, the city that had been described as an unnamed ruin in a volume antedating all other known books.

The place was built on an inner peak of the range, surrounded by snowless summits little sterner and loftier than itself. On one side the peak fell in a thousand-foot precipice from the overhanging ramparts; on another, it was terraced with wild cliffs; but the third side, facing toward us, was a steep acclivity with broken-down scarps and chimneys that would offer small difficulty to expert mountaineers. The rock of the whole mountain was strangely ruinous and black; but the city walls, though gapped and worn to a like dilapidation, were conspicuous above it at a distance of leagues.

Polder and I beheld the bourn of our world-wide search with thoughts and emotions which we did not voice. The Indian made no comment, pointing impassively toward the far summit with its crown of ruins. We hurried on, wishing to complete our journey by daylight; and, after plunging into an abysmal valley, we began at mid-afternoon the ascent of the slope toward the city.

We were impressed anew by the abnormal blackness and manifold cleavages of the rock. It was like climbing amid the overthrown and fire-blasted blocks of a Titan citadel. Everywhere the slope was rent into huge, obliquely angled masses, often partly vitrified, which made the ascent a more arduous problem than we had expected. Plainly, at some former time, it had been subjected to the action of intense heat; and yet there were no volcanic craters amid the nearby mountains. Puzzling greatly, I recalled a passage in that old volume, hinting ambiguously at the dark fate that long ago destroyed the city's inhabitants: "For the people of that city had reared its walls and towers too high amid the region of the clouds; and the clouds came down in their anger and smote the city with dreadful fires; and thereafter the place was peopled no more by those primal giants who had built it, but had only the clouds for inhabitants and custodians." But from this passage I could still draw no definite conclusion: for the ideation was too fantastic to be understood as anything more than a dubious figure of speech.

We had left our three llamas at the slope's bottom, merely taking with us provisions for a night. Thus unhampered, we made fair progress in spite of the ever-varying obstacles offered by the shattered scarps. After a while we came to the hewn steps of a stairway mounting toward the summit; but the steps had been wrought for the feet of colossi, and, in many places, they were part of the heaved and tilted ruin; so they did not greatly facilitate our climbing.

The sun was still high above the western pass behind us; and for this reason, as we went on, I was much surprised by a sudden deepening of the char-like blackness on the rocks. Turning, I saw that several greyish vapory masses, which might have been either clouds or smoke, were drifting idly about the summits that overlooked the pass; and one of these masses, rearing like a limbless figure, upright and colossal, had interposed itself between us and the sun.

Sebastian and the guide had also noted this phenomenon. Clouds were almost unheard-of amid those arid mountains in summer; and the presence of smoke would have been equally hard to explain. Moreover, the grey masses were wholly detached from each other and showed a peculiar opacity and sharpness of outline. At second glance they did not really resemble any cloud-forms we had ever seen; for about them there was a baffling suggestion of weight and solidity. Moving sluggishly into the heavens above the pass, they preserved their original contours and their separateness. They seemed to swell and tower, coming toward us on the blue air from which, as yet, no lightest stirring of wind had reached us. Floating thus, they maintained the rectitude of massive columns or of giants marching on a broad plain.

I think we all felt an alarm that was none the less urgent for its vagueness. Somehow, from that instant, it seemed that we were penned up by unknown powers and were cut off from all possibility of retreat. All at once, the dim legends of the ancient volume had assumed a menacing reality. We had ventured into a place of hidden peril—and the peril was upon us. In the movement of the clouds there was something alert, deliberate and implacable. Polder spoke with a sort of horror in his voice, uttering the thought which had already occurred to me:

"They are the sentinels who guard this region—and they have espied us!"

We heard a harsh cry from the Indian. Following his gaze, we saw that several of the unnatural cloud-shapes had appeared on the summit toward which we were climbing, above the megalithic ruins. Some arose half hidden by the walls, as if from behind a breastwork; others stood, as it were, on the topmost towers and battlements, bulking in portentous menace, like the cumuli of a thunder-storm.

Then, with terrifying swiftness, many more of the cloud-presences towered simultaneously from the four quarters, emerging from behind the gaunt peaks or assuming sudden visibility in mid-air. With equal and effortless speed, as if convoked by an unheard command, they gathered in converging lines upon the eyrie-like ruins. We the climbers, and the whole slope about us and the valley below, were plunged in a twilight weird and awesome as that of central eclipse.

The air was still windless, but it weighed upon us as if burdened with the wings of a thousand cacodemons. I remembered that I was conscious of our exposed position, for we had paused on a wide landing of the mountain-hewn steps. We could have concealed ourselves amid the huge fragments on the surrounding slope; but, for the nonce, we were incapable of the simplest movement. The rarity of the air had left us weak and gasping. And the chill of altitude crept into us.

In a close-ranged army, the clouds mustered above and around us. They rose into the very zenith, swelling to insuperable vastness, and darkening like Tartarean gods. The sun had disappeared, leaving no faintest beam to prove that it still hung unfallen and undestroyed in the heavens.

I felt that I was crushed into the very stone by the eyeless regard of that awful assemblage, judging and condemning. We had trespassed upon a region conquered long ago by strange elemental entities; we had approached their very citadel—and now we must meet the doom our rashness had invited. Such thoughts, like a black lightning, flared in my brain.

Now, for the first time, I became aware of sound—if the word can be applied to a sensation so anomalous. It was as if the oppression that weighed upon me had become audible; as if palpable thunders poured over and past me. I felt, I *heard* them in every nerve, and they roared through my brain like torrents from the opened floodgates of some tremendous weir in a world of genii.

Downward upon us, with limbless Atlantean stridings, there swept the cloudy cohorts. Their swiftness was that of mountain-sweeping winds. The air was riven as if by the tumult of a thousand tempests, was rife with an unmeasured elemental malignity. I recall but partially the events that ensued; but the impression of insufferable darkness, of demonic clamor and trampling, and the pressure of thunderous burdenous onset, remains forever indelible. Also, there were voices that called out with the stridor of clarions in a war of gods, uttering ominous syllables that the ears of man could never seize.

Before those vengeful Shapes, we could not stand for an instant. We hurled ourselves madly down the darkly shadowed steps of the giant stairs. Polder and the guide were a little ahead of me, to the left hand, and I saw them in that baleful twilight through sheets of sudden rain, on the verge of a deep chasm, which, in our ascent, had compelled us to much circumambulation. I saw them leap together—and yet I swear that they did not fall into the chasm: for one of the Shapes was upon them, whirling and stooping over them, even as they sprang. There was a blasphemous, unthinkable fusion as of forms beheld in delirium: for an instant the two men were like vapors that swelled and swirled, towering high as the thing that had covered them; and the thing itself was a misty Janus, with two heads and bodies melting, no longer human, into its unearthly column....

After that, I remember nothing more, except the sense of vertiginous falling. By some miracle I must have reached the edge of the chasm and flung myself into its depths without being overtaken as the others had been. How I escaped the pursuit of those cloudy Guardians is forevermore an enigma. Perhaps, for some inscrutable reason of their own, they permitted me to go.

When I returned to awareness, stars were peering down upon me like chill incurious eyes between black and jagged lips of rock. The air had turned sharp with the coldness of nightfall in a mountain land. My body ached with a hundred bruises and my right forearm was limp and useless when I tried to raise myself. A dark mist of horror stifled my thoughts. Struggling to my feet with pain-racked effort, I called aloud, though I knew that none would answer me. Then, striking match after match, I searched the chasm and found myself, as I had expected, alone. Nowhere was there any trace of my companions: they had vanished utterly—as clouds vanish....

Somehow, by night, with a broken arm, I must have climbed from the steep fissure, I must have made my way down the frightful mountain-side and out of that namelessly haunted and guarded land. I remember that the sky was clear, that the stars were undimmed by any semblance of cloud; and that somewhere in the valley I found one of our llamas, still laden with its stock of provisions....

Plainly I was not pursued by the Guardians. Perhaps They were concerned only with the warding of that mysterious primal city from human intrusion. Never shall I learn the secret of those ruinous walls and crumbling keeps, nor the fate of my companions. But still, through my nightly dreams and diurnal visions, the dark Shapes move with the tumult and thunder of a thousand storms; and my soul is crushed into the earth with the burden of Their imminence; and They pass over me with the speed and vastness of vengeful gods; and I hear Their voices calling like clarions in the sky, with ominous, world-shaking syllables that the ear can never seize.

XEETHRA

Subtle and manifold are the nets of the Demon, who followeth his chosen from birth to death and from death to birth, throughout many lives.

—*The Testaments of Carnamagos*

Long had the wasting summer pastured its suns, like fiery red stallions, on the dun hills that crouched before the Mykrasian Mountains in wild easternmost Cincor. The peak-fed torrents were become tenuous threads or far-sundered, fallen pools; the granite boulders were shaled by the heat; the bare earth was cracked and creviced; and the low, meager grasses were seared even to the roots.

So it occurred that the boy Xeethra, tending the black and piebald goats of his uncle Pornos, was obliged to follow his charges farther each day on the combes and hill-tops. In an afternoon of late summer he came to a deep, craggy valley which he had never before visited. Here a cool and shadowy tarn was watered by hidden well-springs; and the ledgy slopes about the tarn were mantled with herbage and bushes that had not wholly lost their vernal greenness.

Surprised and enchanted, the young goatherd followed his capering flock into this sheltered paradise. There was small likelihood that the goats of Pornos would stray afield from such goodly pasturage; so Xeethra did not trouble himself to watch them any longer. Entranced by his surroundings, he began to explore the valley, after quenching his thirst at the clear waters that sparkled like golden wine.

To him, the place seemed a veritable garden-pleasance. Everywhere there were new charms to beguile him onward: flowers that the fell suns had spared, tiny and pale as the stars of evening; spicy ferns like fretted jade, growing in the moist shadows of boulders; and even a few edible orange berries, lingering past their season in this favorable reclusion.

Forgetting the distance he had already come, and the wrath of Pornos if the flock should return late for the milking, he wandered deeper among the winding crags that protected the valley. On every hand the rocks grew sterner and wilder; the valley straitened; and he stood presently at its end, where a rugged wall forbade further progress. Here, however, he found something that allured him even more than the flowers, the ferns, and the berries.

Before him, in the base of the sheer wall, he perceived the mysterious yawning of a cavern. It seemed that the rock must have opened only a little while before his coming: for the lines of cleavage were clearly marked, and the cracks made in the surrounding surface were unclaimed by the moss that grew plentifully elsewhere. From the cavern's creviced lip there sprang a stunted tree, with its newly broken roots hanging in air; and the stubborn taproot was in the rock at Xeethra's feet, where, it was plain, the tree had formerly stood.

Wondering and curious, the boy peered into the inviting gloom of the cavern, from which, unaccountably, a soft balmy air now began to blow, touching his face like a perfumed sigh. There were strange odors in the air such as he had never known except in nocturnal dreams, suggesting the pungency of temple incense, the languor and luxury of opiate blossoms. They disturbed the senses of Xeethra; and, at the same time, they seduced him with their promise of unbeholden marvellous things. It seemed that the cavern was the portal of some undiscovered world—and the portal had opened expressly to permit his entrance. Being of a nature both venturesome and visionary, he was undeterred by the fears that others might have felt in his place. Overpowered by a great curiosity, he soon entered the cave, carrying for a torch a dry, resinous bough that had fallen from the tree in the cliff.

Beyond the mouth he was swallowed by a rough-arched passage that pitched downward like the gorge of some monstrous dragon. The torch's flame blew back, flaring and smoking in the warm aromatic wind that strengthened from unknown depths. The cave steepened perilously; but Xeethra continued his exploration, climbing down by the stair-like coigns and projections of the stone.

Like a dreamer in a dream, he was wholly absorbed by the mystery on which he had stumbled; and at no time did he recall his abandoned duty. He lost all reckoning of the time consumed in his descent. Then suddenly, his torch was extinguished by a hot gust that blew upon him like the expelled breath of some prankish demon.

The enthralling spell was shattered for an instant, as he tottered in darkness and sought to secure his footing on the dangerous incline. He felt the assailment of a black panic; but, ere he could relume the blown-out torch, he saw that the night around him was not complete, but was tempered by a wan, golden glimmering from the depths below. Forgetting his alarm in a new wonder, he descended toward the mysterious light.

At the bottom of the long incline, Xeethra passed through a low cavern-mouth and emerged into sun-bright radiance. Dazzled and bewildered, he thought for a little while that his subterranean wanderings had brought him back to the outer air in some unsuspected land lying among the Mykrasian hills. Yet surely the region before him was no part of summer-stricken Cincor: for he saw neither hills nor mountains nor the black sapphire heavens from which the aging but despotic sun glared down with implacable drouth on the many kingdoms of Zothique.

Instead, he seemed to stand on the threshold of a fertile plain that lapsed illimitably into golden distance under the measureless arch of a golden vault. Far-off, through the misty radiance, he beheld the dim towering of unidentifiable masses that might have been spires and domes and ramparts. A level meadow lay at his feet, covered with close-grown curling sward that had the greenness of verdigris; and the sward, at intervals, was studded with strange blossoms appearing to turn and move like living eyes beneath the regard of the young goatherd. Near at hand, beyond the meadow, was an orchard-like grove of tall, amply spreading trees, amid whose lush leafage he descried the burning of numberless dark-red fruits. The plain, to all seeming, was empty of human life; and no birds flew in the fiery air or perched on the laden boughs. There was no sound other than the sibilant sighing of leaves in the perfume-burdened wind: a sound that had an elusive, troublous undertone such as might be made by the hissing of many small hidden serpents.

To the boy from the parched hill-country, this cavern-portalled realm was an Eden of untasted delights, alluring him with the promise of its fruited boughs and verdurous ground. But, for a little while, he was stayed by the strangeness of it all, and by the sense of weird and preternatural vitality which informed the whole landscape. Flakes of fire appeared to descend and melt in the rippling air; the grasses coiled with verminous writhings; the flowery eyes returned his regard intently; the trees palpitated as if a sanguine ichor flowed within them in lieu of sap; and the undernote of adder-like hissings amid the foliage grew louder and sharper.

In spite of all that was mysterious in his surroundings, Xeethra was deterred only by the thought that a region so fair and fertile must belong to some jealous owner who would resent his intrusion. He scanned the unpeopled plain with much circumspection. Then, deeming himself secure from observation, he yielded to the craving that had been roused within him by the red, luxuriant fruit.

The turf was elastic beneath him, like a living substance, as he ran forward to the nearest trees. Bowed with their shining globes, the branches drooped around him. He plucked several of the largest fruits and stored them thriftily in the bosom of his threadbare tunic. Then, unable to resist his appetence any longer, he lifted one of the fruits to his mouth. The rind broke easily under his teeth, and it seemed that a royal wine, sweet and puissant, was poured into his mouth from an overbrimming cup. He felt in his throat and bosom a swift warmth that almost suffocated him; and a strange fever sang in his ears and wildered his senses. It passed quickly, and he was startled from his bemusement by the sound of voices falling as if from an airy height above the trees.

He knew instantly that the voices were not those of men. They filled his ears with a rolling as of baleful drums, heavy with ominous echoes; yet it seemed that they spoke in articulate words, albeit of a strange language. Looking up between the thick boughs, he beheld a sight that inspired him with terror. Two beings of colossean stature, tall as the watch-towers of the mountain people, stood waist-high above the near tree-tops. It was as if they had appeared by sorcery from the green ground or the gold heavens: for surely the clumps of vegetation, dwarfed into bushes by their bulk, could never have concealed them from Xeethra's discernment.

The figures were completely clad in black armor, lusterless and gloomy, such as demons might wear in the service of Thasaidon, lord of the bottomless underworlds. Xeethra felt sure that they had seen him; and perhaps their unintelligible converse concerned his presence. He trembled, thinking now that he had trespassed on the gardens of genii. More and more he was terrified by the aspect of the giant shapes; for he could discern no features beneath the frontlets of the dark helms that were bowed toward him: but eyelike spots of yellowish-red fire, restless as marsh-lights, shifted to and fro in void shadow where the faces should have been.

It seemed to Xeethra that the rich foliage could afford no shelter from the scrutiny of these beings, the guardians of the land on which he had so rashly intruded. He was overwhelmed by a consciousness of guilt: the sibilant leaves, the drum-like voices of the giants, the eye-shaped flowers—all appeared to accuse him of trespass and thievery. At the same time he was perplexed by a queer and unwonted vagueness in regard to his own identity: somehow it was not Xeethra the goatherd... but another... who had found the bright garden-realm and had eaten the blood-dark fruit. This alien self was without name or formulable memory; but there was a flickering of confused lights, a murmur of indistinguishable voices, amid the stirred shadows of his mind. Again he felt the weird warmth, the swift-mounting fever, that had followed the devouring of the fruit.

From all this, he was aroused by a livid flash of light that clove downward toward him across the branches. Whether a bolt of levin had issued from the clear vault, or whether one of the armored beings had brandished a great sword, he was never quite sure afterwards. The light seared his vision, he recoiled in uncontrollable fright, and found himself running, half blind, across the open turf. Through whirling bolts of color he saw before him, in a sheer, topless cliff, the cavern-mouth through which he had come. Behind him he heard a long rumbling as of summer thunder... or the laughter of colossi.

Without pausing to retrieve the still-burning brand he had left at the entrance, Xeethra plunged incontinently into the dark cave. Through Stygian murk he managed to grope his way upward on the perilous incline. Reeling, stumbling, bruising himself at every turn, he came at last to the outer exit, in the hidden valley behind the hills of Cincor.

To his consternation, twilight had fallen during his absence in the world beyond the cave. Stars crowded above the grim crags that walled the valley; and the skies of burnt-out purple were gored by the sharp horn of an ivory moon. Still fearing the pursuit of the giant guardians, and apprehending also the wrath of his uncle Pornos, Xeethra hastened back to the little tarn, collected his flock, and drove it homeward through the long, gloomy miles.

During that journey, it seemed that a fever burned and died within him at intervals, bringing strange fancies. He forgot his fear of Pornos, forgot, indeed, that he was Xeethra, the humble and disregarded goatherd. He was returning to another abode than the squalid hut of Pornos, built of clay and brushwood. In a high-domed city, gates of burnished metal would open for him, and fiery-colored banners would stream on the perfumed air; and silver trumpets and the voices of blonde odalisques and black chamberlains would greet him as king in a thousand-columned hall. The ancient pomp of royalty, familiar as air and light, would surround him, and he, the King Amero, who had newly come to the throne, would rule as his fathers had ruled over all the kingdom of Calyz by the orient sea. Into his capital, on shaggy camels, the fierce southern tribesmen would bring a levy of date-wine and desert sapphires; and galleys from isles beyond the morning would burden his wharves with their semi-annual tribute of spices and strange-dyed fabrics....

Such were the wild fantasies that thronged the mind of Xeethra, surging and fading like pictures of delirium. Clearer than the memories of his daily life, the madness came and went; and once again he was the nephew of Pornos, returning belated with the flock, and full of confused apprehension and wonder.

Like a downward-thrusting blade, the red moon had fixed itself in the somber hills when Xeethra reached the rough wooden pen in which Pornos kept his goats. Even as Xeethra had expected, the old man was waiting at the gate, bearing in one hand a clay lantern and in the other a staff of briar-wood. He began to curse the boy with half-senile vehemence, waving the staff, and threatening to beat him for his tardiness.

Xeethra did not flinch before the staff. Again, in his fancy, he was Amero, the young king of Calyz. Bewildered and astonished, he saw before him by the light of the shaken lantern a foul and rancid-smelling ancient whom he could not remember. Hardly could he understand the speech of Pornos; the man's anger puzzled but did not frighten him; and his nostrils, as if accustomed only to delicate perfumes, were offended by the goatish stench. As if for the first time, he heard the bleating of the tired flock, and gazed in wild surprise at the wattled pen and the hut beyond.

"Is it for this," cried Pornos, "that I have reared my sister's orphan at great expense? Accursed moon-calf! thankless whelp! If you have lost a milch-goat or a single kid, I shall flay you from thigh to shoulder."

Deeming that the silence of the youth was due to mere obstinacy, Pornos began to beat him with the staff. At the first blow, the bright cloud lifted from Xeethra's mind. Dodging the briar-wood with agility, he tried to tell Pornos of the new pasture he had found hidden among the barren hills. At this the old man suspended his blows, and Xeethra went on to tell of the strange cave that had conducted him to an unguessed garden-land. To support his story, he reached within his tunic for the blood-red apples he had stolen; but, to his confoundment, the fruits were gone, and he knew not whether he had lost them in the dark, or whether, perhaps, they had vanished by virtue of some indwelling necromancy.

Pornos, interrupting the boy with frequent scoldings, heard him at first with open unbelief. But he grew silent as the youth went on; and when the story was done, he cried out in a trembling voice:

"Ill was this day, for you have wandered among enchantments. Verily, there is no tarn such as you have described amid the hills; nor, at this season, has any herder found such pasturage. These things were illusions, designed to lead you astray; and the cave, I wot, was no honest cave but an entrance into hell. I have heard my fathers tell that the gardens of Thasaidon, king of the seven underworlds, lie near to the earth's surface in this region; and caves have opened ere this, like a portal, and the sons of men, trespassing unaware on the gardens, have been tempted by the fruit and have eaten it. But madness comes thereof and much sorrow and long damnation: for the Demon, they say, forgetting not one stolen apple, will exact his price in the end. Woe! woe! the goat-milk will be soured for a whole moon by the grass of such wizard pasture; and, after all the food and care you have cost me, I must find another stripling to ward the flocks."

Once more, as he listened, the burning cloud of delirium returned upon Xeethra.

"Old man, I know you not," he said perplexedly. Then, using soft words of a courtly speech but half-intelligible to Pornos: "It would seem that I have gone astray. Prithee, where lies the kingdom of Calyz? I am king thereof, being newly crowned in the high city of Shathair, over which my fathers have ruled for a thousand years."

"Ai! Ai!" wailed Pornos. "The boy is daft. These notions have come through the eating of the Demon's apple. Cease your maundering, and help me to milk the goats. You are none other than the child of my sister Askli, who was delivered these nineteen years agone after her husband, Outhoth, had died of a dysentery. Askli lived not long, and I, Pornos, have reared you as a son, and the goats have mothered you."

"I must find my kingdom," persisted Xeethra. "I am lost in darkness, amid uncouth things, and how I have wandered here I cannot remember. Old man,

I would have you give me food and lodging for the night. In the dawn I shall journey toward Shathair, by the orient main."

Pornos, shaking and muttering, lifted his clay lantern to the boy's face. It seemed that a stranger stood before him, in whose wide and wondering eyes the flame of golden lamps was somehow reflected. There was no wildness in Xeethra's demeanor, but merely a sort of gentle pride and remoteness; and he wore his threadbare tunic with a strange grace. Surely, however, he was demented; for his manner and speech were past understanding. Pornos, mumbling under his breath, but no longer urging the boy to assist him, turned to the milking....

Xeethra woke betimes in the white dawn, and peered with amazement at the mud-plastered walls of the hovel in which he had dwelt since birth. All was alien and baffling to him; and especially was he troubled by his rough garments and by the sun-swart tawniness of his skin: for such were hardly proper to the young King Amero, whom he believed himself to be. His circumstances were wholly inexplicable; and he felt an urgency to depart at once on his homeward journey.

He rose quietly from the litter of dry grasses that had served him for a bed. Pornos, lying in a far corner, still slept the sleep of age and senescence; and Xeethra was careful not to awaken him. He was both puzzled and repelled by this unsavory ancient, who had fed him on the previous evening with coarse millet-bread and the strong milk and cheese of goats, and had given him the hospitality of a fetid hut. He had paid little heed to the mumblings and objurgations of Pornos; but it was plain that the old man doubted his claims to royal rank, and, moreover, was possessed of peculiar delusions regarding his identity.

Leaving the hovel, Xeethra followed an eastward-winding footpath amid the stony hills. He knew not whither the path would lead: but reasoned that Calyz, being the easternmost realm of the continent Zothique, was situated somewhere below the rising sun. Before him, in vision, the verdant vales of his kingdom hovered like a fair mirage, and the swelling domes of Shathair were as morning cumuli piled in the orient. These things, he deemed, were memories of yesterday. He could not recall the circumstances of his departure and his absence; but surely the land over which he ruled was not remote.

The path turned among lessening ridges, and Xeethra came to the small village of Cith, to whose inhabitants he was known. The place was alien to him now, seeming no more than a cirque of low, filthy hovels that reeked and festered under the sun. The people gathered about him, calling him by name, and staring and laughing oafishly when he inquired the road to Calyz. No one, it appeared, had ever heard of this kingdom or of the city of Shathair. Noting a strangeness in Xeethra's demeanor, and deeming that his queries were those of a madman, the people began to mock him. Children pelted

him with dry clods and pebbles; and thus he was driven from Cith, following an eastern road that ran from Cincor into the neighboring lowlands of
the country of Zhel.

Sustained only by the vision of his lost kingdom, the youth wandered for
many moons throughout Zothique. People derided him when he spoke of his
kingship and made inquiry concerning Calyz; but many, thinking madness
a sacred thing, offered him shelter and sustenance. Amid the far-stretching
fruitful vineyards of Zhel, and into Istanam of the myriad cities; over the
high-winding passes of Ymorth, where snow tarried at the autumn's beginning; and across the salt-pale desert of Dhir, and through the python-haunted
jungles of Ongath, Xeethra followed that bright imperial dream which had
now become his only memory. Always eastward he went, traveling sometimes
with caravans whose members hoped that a madman's company would bring
them good fortune; but oftener he went as a solitary wayfarer.

At whiles, for a brief space, his dream deserted him, and he was only the
simple goatherd, lost in foreign realms, and homesick for the barren hills
of Cincor. Then, once more, he remembered his kingship, and the opulent
gardens of Shathair and the proud palaces, and the names and faces of them
that had served him following the death of his father, King Eldamaque, and
his own succession to the throne. More often than other memories, there
came to him the thought of a vernal evening, when he had walked alone on
an eastward terrace of the palace, breathing the perfumes of languid flowers
mingled with sharp sea-balsams, and watching the mighty star Canopus,
which had climbed midway between the low skyline and the zenith. There
he had stood, feeling a mystic joy and an obscure pain, while the night assumed a profounder purple, and the lesser stars came out thronging around
Canopus.

At midwinter, in the far city of Sha-Karag, Xeethra met certain sellers of
amulets from Ustaim, who smiled oddly when he asked if they could direct
him to Calyz. Winking among themselves when he spoke of his royal rank,
the merchants told him that Calyz was situated several hundred leagues
beyond Sha-Karag, below the orient sun.

"Hail, O King," they said with mock ceremony. "Long and merrily may you
reign in Shathair, over all the peoples of Calyz."

Very joyful was Xeethra, hearing word of his lost kingdom for the first
time. And he did not heed the laughter and whispering that passed among
the merchants of Ustaim as he left them.

Tarrying no longer in Sha-Karag, he journeyed on with all possible haste.
In his thin rags he dared the heavy rains of winter; and he passed perilously
over the salt marshes of an island sea, and across the stony wilderness lying
beyond, wherein no people dwelt but a clashing and tumult as of unseen
armies was heard by the traveller. Through this he came with safety to the

land of certain half-barbarous tribesmen, who treated him with kindness but could not understand his speech. Afterwards he arrived in the four cities of Athoad, whose inhabitants informed him, with a curious derision in their manner, that Calyz was still a full month's journey to the east.

Now, as he went on, Xeethra began to marvel because he met no travellers from his own country. He recalled that merchants were wont to traffic between Calyz and the vicinal regions; and dimly he remembered hearing of the cities of Athoad as far outland places. Everywhere men eyed him strangely when he asked for news of his kingdom; and some laughed openly, and others, in tones of irony, wished him well of his journeying.

When the first moon of spring was a frail crescent at eve, he knew that he neared his destination. For Canopus burned high in the eastern heavens, mounting gloriously amid the smaller stars even as he had once seen it from his palace-terrace in Shathair.

His heart leapt with the gladness of homecoming; but much he marvelled at the wildness and sterility of the region through which he passed. It seemed that there were no travellers coming and going from Calyz; and he met only a few nomads, who fled at his approach like the creatures of the waste. The highway was overgrown with grasses and cacti, and was rutted only by the winter rains. Beside it, anon, he came to a stone terminus carved in the form of a rampant lion, that had marked the western boundary of Calyz. The lion's features had crumbled away, and his paws and body were lichened, and it seemed that long ages of desolation had gone over him. A chill dismay was born in Xeethra's heart: for only yesteryear, if his memory served him rightly, he had ridden past the lion with his father Eldamaque, hunting hyenas, and had remarked then the newness of the carving.

Now, from the high ridge of the border, he gazed down upon Calyz, which had lain like a long verdant scroll beside the sea. To his wonderment and consternation, the wide fields were sere as if with autumn; the rivers were thin threads that wasted themselves in sand; the hills were gaunt as the ribs of unceremented mummies; and there was no greenery other than the scant herbage which a desert bears in spring. Far off, by the purple main, he thought that he beheld the shining of the marble domes of Shathair; and, fearing that some blight of hostile sorcery had fallen upon his kingdom, he hastened toward the city.

Everywhere, as he wandered heartsick through the vernal day, he found that the desert had established its empire. Void were the fields, unpeopled the villages. The cots had tumbled into midden-like heaps of ruin; and it seemed that a thousand seasons of drouth had withered the fruitful orchards, leaving only a few black and decaying stumps.

In the late afternoon he entered Shathair, which had been the white mistress of the orient sea. The streets and the harbor were alike empty, and silence sat on the broken housetops and the ruining walls. The great bronze obelisks

were greened with antiquity; the massy marmorean temples of the gods of
Calyz leaned and slanted to their fall.

Tardily, as one who fears to confirm an expected thing, Xeethra came to the
palace of the monarchs. Not as he recalled it, a glory of soaring marble half
veiled by flowering almonds and trees of spice and high-pulsing fountains;
but, in stark dilapidation amid blasted gardens, the palace awaited him, while
the brief, illusory rose of sunset faded upon its dome, leaving them wan as
mausoleums.

How long the place had lain desolate, he could not know. Confusion filled
him, and he was whelmed by utter loss and despair. It seemed that none remained to greet him amid the ruins; but, nearing the portals of the west wing,
he saw, as it were, a fluttering of shadows that appeared to detach themselves
from the gloom beneath the portico; and certain dubious beings, clothed in
rotten tatters, came sidling and crawling before him on the cracked pavement. Pieces of their raiment dropped from them as they moved; and about
them was an unnamed horror of filth, of squalor and disease. When they
neared him, Xeethra saw that most of them were lacking in some member
or feature, and that all were marked by the gnawing of leprosy.

His gorge rose within him, and he could not speak. But the lepers hailed him
with hoarse cries and hollow croakings, as if deeming him another outcast
who had come to join them in their abode amid the ruins.

"Who are ye that dwell in my palace of Shathair?" he inquired at length.
"Behold! I am King Amero, the son of Eldamaque, and I have returned from
a far land to resume the throne of Calyz."

At this, a loathsome cackling and tittering arose among the lepers. "We
alone are the kings of Calyz," one of them told the youth. "The land has been
a desert for centuries, and the city of Shathair had long lain unpeopled save
by such as we, who were driven out from other places. Young man, you are
welcome to share the realm with us: for another king, more or less, is a small
matter here."

Then, with obscene cachinnations, the lepers jeered at Xeethra and derided
him; and he, standing amid the dark fragments of his dream, could find no
words to answer them. However, one of the oldest lepers, well-nigh limbless
and faceless, shared not in the mirth of his fellows, but seemed to ponder
and reflect; and he said at last to Xeethra, in a voice issuing thickly from the
black pit of his gaping mouth:

"I have heard something of the history of Calyz, and the names of Amero
and Eldamaque are familiar to me. In bygone ages certain of the rulers were
named thus; but I know not which of them was the son and which the father.
Haply both are now entombed, with the rest of their dynasty, in the deep-
lying vaults beneath the palace."

Now, in the greying twilight, other lepers emerged from the shadowy ruin
and gathered about Xeethra. Hearing that he laid claim to the kingship of

the desert realm, certain of their number went away and returned presently, bearing vessels filled with rank water and mouldy victuals, which they proffered to Xeethra, bowing low with a mummery as of chamberlains serving a monarch.

Xeethra turned from them in loathing, though he was famished and athirst. He fled through the ashen gardens, among the dry fountain-mouths and dusty plots. Behind him he heard the hideous mirth of the lepers; but the sound grew fainter, and it seemed that they did not follow him. Rounding the vast palace in his flight, he met no more of these creatures. The portals of the south wing and the east wing were dark and empty, but he did not care to enter them, knowing that desolation and things worse than desolation were the sole tenants.

Wholly distraught and despairing, he came to the eastern wing and paused in the gloom. Dully, and with a sense of dreamlike estrangement, he became aware that he stood on that very terrace above the sea, which he had remembered so often during his journey. Bare were the ancient flower-beds; the trees had rotted away in their sunken basins; and the great flags of the pavement were runneled and broken. But the veils of twilight were tender upon the ruin; and the sea sighed as of yore under a purple shrouding; and the mighty star Canopus climbed in the east, with the lesser stars still faint around him.

Bitter was the heart of Xeethra, thinking himself a dreamer beguiled by some idle dream. He shrank from the high splendor of Canopus, as if from a flame too bright to bear; but, ere he could turn away, it seemed that a column of shadow, darker than the night and thicker than any cloud, rose upward before him from the terrace and blotted out the effulgent star. Out of the solid stone the shadow grew, towering tall and colossal; and it took on the outlines of a mailed warrior; and it seemed that the warrior looked down upon Xeethra from a great height with eyes that shone and shifted like fireballs in the darkness of his face under the lowering helmet.

Confusedly, as one who recalls an old dream, Xeethra remembered a boy who had herded goats upon summer-stricken hills; and who, one day, had found a cavern that opened portal-like on a garden-land of strangeness and marvel. Wandering there, the boy had eaten a blood-dark fruit and had fled in terror before the black-armored giants who warded the garden. Again he was that boy; and still he was the King Amero, who had sought for his lost realm through many regions; and, finding it in the end, had found only the abomination of desolation.

Now, as the trepidation of the goatherd, guilty of theft and trespass, warred in his soul with the pride of the king, he heard a voice that rolled through the heavens like thunder from a high cloud in the spring night:

"I am the Emissary of Thasaidon, who sends me in due course to all who have passed the nether portals and have tasted the fruit of His garden. No man, having eaten the fruit, shall remain thereafter as he was before; but to some the fruit brings oblivion, and to others, memory. Know, then, that in another birth, ages agone, you were indeed the young King Amero. The memory, being strong upon you, has effaced the remembrance of your present life, and has driven you forth to seek your ancient kingdom."

"If this be true, then doubly am I bereft," said Xeethra, bowing sorrowfully before the shadow. "For, being Amero, I am throneless and realmless; and, being Xeethra, I cannot forget my former royalty and regain the content which I knew as a simple goatherd."

"Hearken, for there is another way," said the shadow, its voice muted like the murmur of a far ocean. "Thasaidon is the master of all sorceries, and a giver of magic gifts to those who serve Him and acknowledge Him as their lord. Pledge your allegiance, promise your soul to Him; and in fee thereof, the Demon will surely reward you. If it be your wish, He can wake again the buried past with His necromancy. Again, as King Amero, you shall reign over Calyz; and all things shall be as they were in the perished years; and the dead faces and the fields now desert shall bloom again; and not one petal shall be wanting from your gardens, nor one block or segment of mosaic from the high-builded glory of Shathair."

"I accept the bond," said Xeethra. "I plight my fealty to Thasaidon, and I promise my soul to Him if He, in return, will give me back my kingdom."

"There is more to be said," resumed the shadow. "Not wholly have you remembered your other life, but merely those years that correspond to your present youth. Living again as Amero, perhaps you will regret your royalty in time; and if such regret should overcome you, leading you to forget a monarch's duty, then the whole necromancy shall end and vanish like vapor."

"So be it," said Xeethra. "This too I accept as part of the bargain."

When the words ended, he beheld no longer the shadow towering against Canopus. The star flamed with a pristine splendor, as if no cloud had ever dimmed it; and, without sense of change or transition, he who watched the star was none other than King Amero; and the goatherd Xeethra, and the Emissary, and the pledge given to Thasaidon, were as things that had never been. The ruin that had come upon Shathair was no more than the dream of some mad prophet; for in the nostrils of Amero the perfume of languorous flowers mingled with salt sea-balsams; and in his ears the grave murmur of ocean was pierced by the amorous plaint of lyres and a shrill laughter of slave-girls from the palace behind him. He heard the myriad noises of the nocturnal city, where his people feasted and made jubilee; and, turning from the star with a mystic pain and an obscure joy in his heart, Amero beheld the effulgent portals and windows of his fathers' house, and the far-mounting light from a thousand flambeaux that paled the stars in mid-heaven as they passed over Shathair.

It is written in the old chronicles that King Amero reigned for many prosperous years. Peace and abundance were upon all the realm of Calyz; the drouth came not from the desert, nor violent gales from the main; and tribute was sent at the ordained seasons to Amero from the subject isles and outlying lands. And Amero was well content, dwelling superbly in rich-arrased halls, feasting and drinking royally, and hearing the praise of his lute-players and his chamberlains and his lemans.

When his life was a little past the meridian years, there came at whiles to Amero something of that satiety which lies in wait for the minions of fortune. At such times he turned from the cloying pleasures of the court and found delight in blossoms and leaves and the verses of olden poets. Thus was satiety held at bay; and, since the duties of the realm rested lightly upon him, Amero still found his kingship a goodly thing.

Then, in a latter autumn, it seemed that the stars looked disastrously upon Calyz. Murrain and blight and pestilence rode abroad as if on the wings of unseen dragons. The coast of the kingdom was beset and sorely harried by pirate galleys. Upon the west, the caravans coming and going through Calyz were assailed by redoubtable bands of robbers; and certain fierce desert peoples made war on the villages lying near to the southern border. The land was filled with turmoil and death, with lamentation and many miseries.

Deep was Amero's concern, hearing the distressful complaints that were brought before him daily. Being but little skilled in kingcraft, and wholly untried by the ordeals of dominion, he sought counsel of his courtlings but was ill advised by them. The troubles of the realm multiplied upon him; uncurbed by authority, the wild peoples of the waste grew bolder, and the pirates gathered like vultures of the sea. Famine and drouth divided his realm with the plague; and it seemed to Amero, in his sore perplexity, that such matters were beyond all medication; and his crown was become a too onerous burden.

Striving to forget his own impotence and the woeful plight of his kingdom, he gave himself to long nights of debauch. But the wine refused its oblivion, and the kisses of his lemans no longer stirred him to rapture. He sought other divertissements, calling before him strange maskers and mummers and buffoons, and assembling outlandish singers, and the players of uncouth instruments. Daily he made proclamation of a high reward to any that could bemuse him from his cares.

Wild songs and sorcerous ballads of yore were sung to him by immortal minstrels; the black girls of the north, with amber-dappled limbs, danced before him their weird lascivious measures; the blowers of the horns of chimeras played a mad and secret tune; and savage drummers pounded a troublous music on drums made from the skin of cannibals; while men clothed with the scales and pelts of half-mythic monsters ramped or crawled grotesquely through the halls of the palace. But all these were vain to beguile the king from his grievous musings.

One afternoon, as he sat heavily in his hall of audience, there came to him a player of pipes who was clad in tattered homespun. The eyes of the man were bright as newly stirred embers, and his face was burned to a cindery blackness, as if by the ardor of outland suns. Hailing Amero with small servility, he announced himself as a goatherd who had come to Shathair from a region of valleys and mountains lying sequestered beyond the bourn of sunset.

"O King, I know the melodies of oblivion," he said, "and I would play for you, though I desire not the reward you have offered. If haply I succeed in diverting you, I shall take my own guerdon in due time."

"Play, then," said Amero, feeling a faint interest rise within him at the bold speech of the piper.

Forthwith, on his pipes of reed, the black goatherd began a music that was like the falling and rippling of water in quiet vales, and the passing of wind over lonely hill-tops. Subtly the pipes told of freedom and peace and forgetfulness lying beyond the sevenfold purple of outland horizons. Dulcetly they sang of a place where the years came not with an iron trampling, but were soft of tread as a zephyr shod with flower petals. There the world's turmoil and troubling were lost upon measureless leagues of silence, and the burdens of empire were blown away like thistledown. There the goatherd, tending his flock on solitary fells, was possessed of tranquillity sweeter than the power of monarchs.

As he listened to the piper, a sorcery crept upon the mind of Amero. The weariness of kingship, the cares and perplexities, were as dream-bubbles lapsing in some Lethean tide. He beheld before him, in sun-bright verdure and stillness, the enchanted vales evoked by the music; and he himself was the goatherd, following grassy paths, or lying oblivious of the vulture hours by the margin of lulled waters.

Hardly he knew that the low piping had ceased. But the vision darkened, and he who had dreamt of a goatherd's peace was again a troubled king.

"Play on!" he cried to the black piper. "Name your own guerdon—and play."

The eyes of the goatherd burned like embers in a dark place at evening. "Not till the passing of ages and the falling of kingdoms shall I require of you my reward," he said enigmatically. "Howbeit, I shall play for you once more."

So, through the afternoon, King Amero was beguiled by that sorcerous piping which told ever of a far land of ease and forgetfulness. With each playing it seemed that the spell grew stronger upon him; and more and more was his royalty a hateful thing; and the very grandeur of his palace oppressed and stifled him. No longer could he endure the heavily jewelled yoke of duty; and madly he envied the carefree lot of the goatherd.

At twilight he dismissed the ministrants who attended him, and held speech alone with the piper.

"Lead me to this land of yours," he said, "where I too may dwell as a simple herder."

Clad in mufti, so that his people might not recognize him, the king stole from the palace through an unguarded postern, accompanied by the piper. Night, like a formless monster with the crescent moon for its lowered horn, was crouching beyond the town; but in the streets the invading shadows were thrust back by a flaming of myriad cressets. Amero and his guide were unchallenged by any man as they went toward the outer darkness. And the king repented not his forsaken throne: though he saw in the city a continual passing of biers laden with the victims of the plague; and faces gaunt with famine rose up from the shadows as if to accuse him of recreancy. These he heeded not: for his eyes were filled with the dream of a green, silent valley, in a land lost beyond the turbid flowing of time with its wreckage and tumult.

Now, as Amero followed the black piper, there descended upon him a sudden dimness; and he faltered in weird doubt and bewilderment. The street-lights flickered before him, and swiftly they expired in the gloom. The loud murmuring of the city fell away in a vast silence; and, like the shifting of some disordered dream, it seemed that the tall houses crumbled stilly and were gone even as shadows, and the stars shone over broken walls. Confusion filled the thoughts and the senses of Amero; and in his heart was a black chill of unutterable desolation; and he seemed to himself as one who had known the lapse of long empty years, and the loss of high splendor; and who stood now amid the extremity of age and decay. In his nostrils was a dry mustiness such as the night draws from olden ruin; and it came to him, as a thing foreknown and now remembered obscurely, that the desert was lord in his proud capital of Shathair.

"Where have you led me?" cried Amero to the piper.

For all reply, he heard a laughter that was like the peal of derisive thunder. The muffled shape of the goatherd towered colossally in the gloom, changing, growing, till its outlines were transformed to those of a giant warrior in sable armor. Strange memories thronged the mind of Amero, and he seemed to recall darkly something of another life…. Somehow, somewhere, for a time, he had been the goatherd of his dreams, content and forgetful… somehow, somewhere, he had entered a strange bright garden and had eaten a blood-dark fruit….

Then, in a flaring as of infernal levin, he remembered all, and knew the mighty shadow that towered above him like a Terminus reared in hell. Beneath his feet was the cracked pavement of the seaward terrace; and the stars above the Emissary were those that precede Canopus; but Canopus himself was blotted out by the Demon's shoulder. Somewhere in the dusty darkness, a leper laughed and coughed thickly, prowling about the ruined palace in which had once dwelt the kings of Calyz. All things were even as they had been before the making of that bargain through which a perished kingdom had been raised up by the powers of hell.

Anguish choked the heart of Xeethra as if with the ashes of burnt-out pyres and the shards of heaped ruin. Subtly and manifoldly had the Demon tempted him to his loss. Whether these things had been dream or necromancy or verity he knew not with sureness; nor whether they had happened once or had happened often. In the end there was only dust and dearth; and he, the doubly accurst, must remember and repent forevermore all that he had forfeited.

He cried out to the Emissary: "I have lost the bargain that I made with Thasaidon. Take now my soul and bear it before Him where He sits aloft on His throne of ever-burning brass; for I would fulfill my bond to the uttermost."

"There is no need to take your soul," said the Emissary, with an ominous rumble as of departing storm in the desolate night. "Remain here with the lepers, or return to Pornos and his goats, as you will: it matters little. At all times and in all places your soul shall be part of the dark empire of Thasaidon."

THE LAST HIEROGLYPH

The world itself, in the end, shall be turned to a round cipher.
—Old prophecy of Zothique

Nushain the astrologer had studied the circling orbs of night from many far-separated regions, and had cast, with such skill as he was able to command, the horoscopes of a myriad men, women and children. From city to city, from realm to realm he had gone, abiding briefly in any place: for often the local magistrates had banished him as a common charlatan; or elsewise, in due time, his consultants had discovered the error of his predictions and had fallen away from him. Sometimes he went hungry and shabby; and small honor was paid to him anywhere. The sole companions of his precarious fortunes were a wretched mongrel dog that had somehow attached itself to him in the desert town of Zul-Bha-Sair, and a mute, one-eyed negro whom he had bought very cheaply in Yoros. He had named the dog Ansarath, after the canine star, and had called the negro Mouzda, which was a word signifying darkness.

In the course of his prolonged itinerations, the astrologer came to Xylac and made his abode in its capital, Ummaos, which had been built above the shards of an elder city of the same name, long since destroyed by a sorcerer's wrath. Here Nushain lodged with Ansarath and Mouzda in a half-ruinous attic of a rotting tenement; and from the tenement's roof, Nushain was wont to observe the positions and movements of the sidereal bodies on evenings not obscured by the fumes of the city. At intervals some housewife or jade, some porter or huckster or petty merchant, would climb the decaying stairs to his chamber, and would pay him a small sum for the nativity which he plotted with immense care by the aid of his tattered books of astrological science.

When, as often occurred, he found himself still at a loss regarding the significance of some heavenly conjunction or opposition after poring over his books, he would consult Ansarath, and would draw profound auguries

from the variable motions of the dog's mangy tail or his actions in searching for fleas. Certain of these divinations were fulfilled, to the considerable
benefit of Nushain's renown in Ummaos. People came to him more freely
and frequently, hearing that he was a soothsayer of some note; and, moreover,
he was immune from prosecution, owing to the liberal laws of Xylac, which
permitted all the sorcerous and mantic arts.

It seemed, for the first time, that the dark planets of his fate were yielding
to auspicious stars. For this fortune, and the coins which accrued thereby to
his purse, he gave thanks to Vergama who, throughout the whole continent
of Zothique, was deemed the most powerful and mysterious of the genii, and
was thought to rule over the heavens as well as the earth.

On a summer night, when the stars were strewn thickly like a fiery sand on
the black azure vault, Nushain went up to the roof of his lodging-place. As
was often his custom, he took with him the negro Mouzda, whose one eye
possessed a miraculous sharpness and had served well, on many occasions,
to supplement the astrologer's own rather near-sighted vision. Through a
well codified system of signs and gestures, the mute was able to communicate
the result of his observations to Nushain.

On this night the constellation of the Great Dog, which had presided over
Nushain's birth, was ascendant in the east. Regarding it closely, the dim eyes
of the astrologer were troubled by a sense of something unfamiliar in its
configuration. He could not determine the precise character of the change
till Mouzda, who evinced much excitement, called his attention to three new
stars of the second magnitude which had appeared in close proximity to the
Dog's hindquarters. These remarkable novæ, which Nushain could discern
only as three reddish blurs, formed a small equilateral triangle. Nushain and
Mouzda were both certain that they had not been visible on any previous
evening.

"By Vergama, this is a strange thing," swore the astrologer, filled with
amazement and dumbfoundment. He began to compute the problematic
influence of the novæ on his future reading of the heavens, and perceived
at once that they would exert, according to the law of astral emanations, a
modifying effect on his own destiny, which had been so largely controlled
by the Dog.

He could not, however, without consulting his books and tables, decide
the particular trend and import of this supervening influence; though he felt
sure that it was most momentous, whether for his bale or welfare. Leaving
Mouzda to watch the heavens for other prodigies, he descended at once to
his attic. There, after collating the opinions of several old-time astrologers
on the power exerted by novæ, he began to re-cast his own horoscope. Painfully and with much agitation he labored throughout the night, and did not
finish his figurings till the dawn came to mix a deathly greyness with the
yellow light of the candles.

There was, it seemed, but one possible interpretation of the altered heavens. The appearance of the triangle of novæ in conjunction with the Dog signified clearly that Nushain was to start ere long on an unpremeditated journey which would involve the transit of no less than three elements. Mouzda and Ansarath were to accompany him; and three guides, appearing successively, at the proper times, would lead him toward a destined goal. So much his calculations had revealed, but no more: there was nothing to foretell whether the journey would prove auspicious or disastrous, nothing to indicate its bourn, purpose or direction.

The astrologer was much disturbed by this somewhat singular and equivocal augury. He was ill pleased by the prospect of an imminent journey, for he did not wish to leave Ummaos, among whose credulous people he had begun to establish himself not without success. Moreover, a strong apprehension was roused within him by the oddly manifold nature and veiled outcome of the journey. All this, he felt, was suggestive of the workings of some occult and perhaps sinister providence; and surely it was no common traveling which would take him through three elements and would require a triple guidance.

During the nights that followed, he and Mouzda watched the mysterious novæ as they went over toward the west behind the bright-flaming Dog. And he puzzled interminably over his charts and volumes, hoping to discover some error in the reading he had made. But always, in the end, he was compelled to the same interpretation.

More and more, as time went on, he was troubled by the thought of that unwelcome and mysterious journey which he must make. He continued to prosper in Ummaos, and it seemed that there was no conceivable reason for his departure from that city. He was as one who awaited a dark and secret summons, not knowing whence it would come, nor at what hour. Throughout the days, he scanned with fearful anxiety the faces of his visitors, deeming that the first of the three star-predicted guides might arrive unheralded and unrecognized among them.

Mouzda and the dog Ansarath, with the intuition of dumb things, were sensible of the weird uneasiness felt by their master. They shared it palpably, the negro showing his apprehension by wild and demoniac grimaces, and the dog crouching under the astrologer's table or prowling restlessly to and fro with his half-hairless tail between his legs. Such behavior, in its turn, served to reconfirm the inquietude of Nushain, who deemed it a bad omen.

On a certain evening, Nushain pored for the fiftieth time over his horoscope, which he had drawn with sundry-colored inks on a sheet of papyrus. He was much startled when, on the blank lower margin of the sheet, he saw a curious character which was no part of his own scribbling. The character was a hieroglyph written in dark bituminous brown, and seeming to represent a mummy whose shroudings were loosened about the legs and whose feet were set in the posture of a long stride. It was facing toward that quarter of the chart where stood the sign indicating the Great Dog, which, in Zothique, was a House of the zodiac.

Nushain's surprise turned to a sort of trepidation as he studied the hieroglyph. He knew that the margin of the chart had been wholly clear on the previous night; and during the past day he had not left the attic at any time. Mouzda, he felt sure, would never have dared to touch the chart; and, moreover, the negro was little skilled in writing. Among the various inks employed by Nushain, there was none that resembled the sullen brown of the character, which seemed to stand out in a sad relief on the white papyrus.

Nushain felt the alarm of one who confronts a sinister and unexplainable apparition. No human hand, surely, had inscribed the mummy-shapen character, like the sign of a strange outer planet about to invade the Houses of his horoscope. Here, as in the advent of the three novæ, an occult agency was suggested. Vainly, for many hours, he sought to unriddle the mystery: but in all his books there was naught to enlighten him; for this thing, it seemed, was wholly without precedent in astrology.

During the next day he was busied from morn till eve with the plotting of those destinies ordained by the heavens for certain people of Ummaos. After completing the calculations with his usual toilsome care, he unrolled his own chart once more, albeit with trembling fingers. An eeriness that was nigh to panic seized him when he saw that the brown hieroglyph no longer stood on the margin, but was now placed like a striding figure in one of the lower Houses, where it still fronted toward the Dog, as if advancing on that ascendant sign.

Henceforth the astrologer was fevered with the awe and curiosity of one who watches a fatal but inscrutable portent. Never, during the hours that he pondered above it, was there any change in the intruding character; and yet, on each successive evening when he took out the chart, he saw that the mummy had strode upward into a higher House, drawing always nearer to the House of the Dog....

There came a time when the figure stood on the Dog's threshold. Portentous with mystery and menace that were still beyond the astrologer's divining, it seemed to wait while the night wore on and was shot through with the grey wefting of dawn. Then, overworn with his prolonged studies and vigils, Nushain slept in his chair. Without the troubling of any dream he slept; and Mouzda was careful not to disturb him; and no visitors came to the attic on that day. So the morn and the noon and the afternoon went over, and their going was unheeded by Nushain.

He was awakened at eve by the loud and dolorous howling of Ansarath, which appeared to issue from the room's farthest corner. Confusedly, ere he opened his eyes, he became aware of an odor of bitter spices and piercing natron. Then, with the dim webs of sleep not wholly swept from his vision, he beheld, by the yellowy tapers that Mouzda had lighted, a tall, mummy-like form that waited in silence beside him. The head, arms and body of the shape were wound closely with bitumen-colored cerements; but the folds were loosened from the hips downward, and the figure stood like a walker, with one brown, withered foot in advance of its fellow.

Terror quickened in Nushain's heart, and it came to him that the shrouded shape, whether lich or phantom, resembled the weird, invasive hieroglyph that had passed from House to House through the chart of his destiny. Then, from the thick swathings of the apparition, a voice issued indistinctly, saying: "Prepare yourself, O Nushain, for I am the first guide of that journey which was foretold to you by the stars."

Ansarath, cowering beneath the astrologer's bed, was still howling his fear of the visitant; and Nushain saw that Mouzda had tried to conceal himself in company with the dog. Though a chill as of imminent death was upon him, and he deemed the apparition to be death itself, Nushain arose from his chair with that dignity proper to an astrologer, which he had maintained through all the vicissitudes of his lifetime. He called Mouzda and Ansarath from their hiding-place, and the two obeyed him, though with many cringings before the dark, muffled mummy.

With the comrades of his fortune behind him, Nushain turned to the visitant. "I am ready," he said, in a voice whose quavering was almost imperceptible. "But I would take with me certain of my belongings."

The mummy shook his mobled head. "It were well to take with you nothing but your horoscope: for this alone shall you retain in the end."

Nushain stooped above the table on which he had left his nativity. Before he began to roll the open papyrus, he noticed that the hieroglyph of the mummy had vanished. It was as if the written symbol, after moving athwart his horoscope, had materialized itself in the figure that now attended him. But on the chart's nether margin, in remote opposition to the Dog, was the sea-blue hieroglyph of a quaint merman with carp-like tail and head half human, half apish; and behind the merman was the black hieroglyph of a small barge.

Nushain's fear, for a moment, was subdued by wonder. But he rolled the chart carefully, and stood holding it in his right hand.

"Come," said the guide. "Your time is brief, and you must pass through the three elements that guard the dwelling-place of Vergama from unseasonable intrusion."

These words, in a measure, confirmed the astrologer's divinations. But the mystery of his future fate was in no wise lightened by the intimation that he must enter, presumably at the journey's end, the dim House of that being called Vergama, whom some considered the most secret of all the gods, and others, the most cryptical of demons. In all the lands of Zothique, there were rumors and fables regarding Vergama; but these were wholly diverse and contradictory, except in their common attribution of almost omnipotent powers to this entity. No man knew the situation of his abode; but it was believed that vast multitudes of people had entered it during the centuries and millenniums, and that none had returned therefrom.

Ofttimes had Nushain called upon the name of Vergama, swearing or protesting thereby as men are wont to do by the cognomens of their shrouded lords. But now, hearing the name from the lips of his macabre visitor, he was filled with the darkest and most eerie apprehensions. He sought to subdue these feelings, and to resign himself to the manifest will of the stars. With Mouzda and Ansarath at his heels, he followed the striding mummy, which seemed little hampered, if at all, by its trailing cerements.

With one regretful backward glance at his littered books and papers, he passed from the attic room and down the tenement stairs. A wannish light seemed to cling about the swathings of the mummy; but, apart from this, there was no illumination; and Nushain thought that the house was strangely dark and silent, as if all its occupants had died or had gone away. He heard no sound from the evening city; nor could he see aught but close-encroaching darkness beyond the windows that should have gazed on a litten street. Also, it seemed that the stairs had changed and lengthened, giving no more on the courtyard of the tenement, but plunging deviously into an unsuspected region of stifling vaults and foul, dismal, nitrous corridors.

Here the air was pregnant with death, and the heart of Nushain failed him. Everywhere, in the shadow-curtained crypts and deep-shelved recesses, he felt the innumerable presence of the dead. He thought that there was a sad sighing of stirred cerements, a breath exhaled by long-stiffened cadavers, a dry clicking of lipless teeth beside him as he went. But darkness walled his vision, and he saw nothing save the luminous form of his guide, who stalked onward as if through a natal realm.

It seemed to Nushain that he passed through boundless catacombs in which were housed the mortality and corruption of all the ages. Behind him still he heard the shuffling of Mouzda, and at whiles the low, frightened whine of Ansarath; so he knew that the twain were faithful to him. But upon him, with a chill of lethal damps, there grew the horror of his surroundings; and he shrank with all the repulsion of living flesh from the shrouded thing that he followed, and those other things that mouldered round about in the fathomless gloom.

Half thinking to hearten himself by the sound of his own voice, he began to question the guide; though his tongue clove to his mouth as if palsied. "Is it indeed Vergama, and none other, who has summoned me forth upon this journey? For what purpose has he called me? And in what land is his dwelling?"

"Your fate has summoned you," said the mummy. "In the end, at the time appointed and no sooner, you shall learn the purpose. As to your third question, you would be no wiser if I should name the region in which the house of Vergama is hidden from mortal trespass: for the land is not listed on any terrene chart, nor map of the starry heavens."

These answers seemed equivocal and disquieting to Nushain, who was possessed by frightful forebodings as he went deeper into the subterranean charnels. Dark, indeed, he thought, must be the goal of a journey whose first stage had led him so far amid the empire of death and corruption; and dubious, surely, was the being who had called him forth and had sent to him as the first guide a sere and shrunken mummy clad in the tomb's habiliments.

Now, as he pondered these matters almost to frenzy, the shelfy walls of the catacomb before him were outlined by a dismal light, and he came after the mummy into a chamber where tall candles of black pitch in sockets of tarnished silver burned about an immense and solitary sarcophagus. Upon the blank lid and sides of the sarcophagus, as Nushain neared it, he could see neither runes nor sculptures nor hieroglyphs engraven; but it seemed, from the proportions, that a giant must lie within.

The mummy passed athwart the chamber without pausing. But Nushain, seeing that the vaults beyond were full of darkness, drew back with a reluctance that he could not conquer; and though the stars had decreed his journey, it seemed to him that human flesh could go no farther. Prompted by a sudden impulse, he seized one of the heavy yard-long tapers that burned stilly about the sarcophagus; and, holding it in his left hand, with his horoscope still firmly clutched in the right, he fled with Mouzda and Ansarath on the way he had come, hoping to retrace his footsteps through the gloomy caverns and return to Ummaos by the taper's light.

He heard no sound of pursuit from the mummy. But ever, as he fled, the pitch candle, flaring wildly, revealed to him the horrors that darkness had curtained from his eyes. He saw the bones of men that were piled in repugnant confusion with those of fell monsters, and the riven sarcophagi from which protruded the half-decayed members of innominate beings; members which were neither heads nor hands nor feet. And soon the catacomb divided and redivided before him, so that he must choose his way at random, not knowing whether it would lead him back to Ummaos or into the untrod depths.

Presently he came to the huge, browless skull of an uncouth creature, which reposed on the ground with upward-gazing orbits; and beyond the skull was the monster's mouldy skeleton, wholly blocking the passage. Its ribs were cramped by the narrowing walls, as if it had crept there and had died in the darkness, unable to withdraw or go forward. White spiders, demon-headed and large as monkeys, had woven their webs in the hollow arches of the bones; and they swarmed out interminably as Nushain approached; and the skeleton seemed to stir and quiver as they seethed over it abhorrently and dropped to the ground before the astrologer. Behind them others poured in a countless army, crowding and mantling every ossicle. Nushain fled with his companions; and running back to the forking of the caverns, he followed another passage.

Here he was not pursued by the demon spiders. But, hurrying on lest they or the mummy overtake him, he was soon halted by the rim of a great pit which filled the catacomb from wall to wall and was overwide for the leaping of man. The dog Ansarath, sniffing certain odors that arose from the pit, recoiled with a mad howling; and Nushain, holding the taper outstretched above it, discerned far down a glimmer of ripples spreading circle-wise on some unctuous black fluid; and two blood-red spots appeared to swim with a weaving motion at the center. Then he heard a hissing as of some great cauldron heated by wizard fires; and it seemed that the blackness boiled upward, mounting swiftly and evilly to overflow the pit; and the red spots, as they neared him, were like luminous eyes that gazed malignantly into his own....

So Nushain turned away in haste; and, returning upon his steps, he found the mummy awaiting him at the junction of the catacombs.

"It would seem, O Nushain, that you have doubted your own horoscope," said the guide, with a certain irony. "However, even a bad astrologer, on occasion, may read the heavens aright. Obey, then, the stars that decreed your journey."

Henceforward, Nushain followed the mummy without recalcitrance. Returning to the chamber in which stood the immense sarcophagus, he was enjoined by his guide to replace in its socket the black taper he had stolen. Without other light than the phosphorescence of the mummy's cerements, he threaded the foul gloom of those profounder ossuaries which lay beyond. At last, through caverns where a dull dawning intruded upon the shadows, he came out beneath shrouded heavens, on the shore of a wild sea that clamored in mist and cloud and spindrift. As if recoiling from the harsh air and light, the mummy drew back into the subterrane, and it said:

"Here my dominion ends, and I must leave you to await the second guide."

Standing with the poignant sea-salt in his nostrils, with his hair and garments outblown on the gale, Nushain heard a metallic clangor, and saw that a door of rusty bronze had closed in the cavern-entrance. The beach was walled by unscalable cliffs that ran sheerly to the wave on each hand. So perforce the astrologer waited; and from the torn surf he beheld erelong the emergence of a sea-blue merman whose head was half human, half apish; and behind the merman there hove a small black barge that was not steered or rowed by any visible being. At this, Nushain recalled the hieroglyphs of the sea-creature and the boat which had appeared on the margin of his nativity; and unrolling the papyrus, he saw with wonderment that the figures were both gone; and he doubted not that they had passed, like the mummy's hieroglyph, through all the zodiacal Houses, even to that House which presided over his destiny; and thence, mayhap, they had emerged into material being. But in their stead now was the burning hieroglyph of a fire-colored salamander, set opposite to the Great Dog.

The merman beckoned to him with antic gestures, grinning deeply, and showing the white serrations of his shark-like teeth. Nushain went forward and entered the barge in obedience to the signs made by the sea-creature; and Mouzda and Ansarath, in faithfulness to their master, accompanied him. Thereupon the merman swam away through the boiling surf; and the barge, as if oared and ruddered by mere enchantment, swung about forthwith, and warring smoothly against wind and wave, was drawn straightly over that dim, unnamable ocean.

Half-seen amid rushing foam and mist, the merman swam steadily on before. Time and space were surely outpassed during that voyage; and as if he had gone beyond mortal existence, Nushain experienced neither thirst nor hunger. But it seemed that his soul drifted upon seas of strange doubt and direst alienation; and he feared the misty chaos about him even as he had feared the nighted catacombs. Often he tried to question the mer-creature concerning their destination, but received no answer. And the wind blowing from shores unguessed, and the tide flowing to unknown gulfs, were alike filled with whispers of awe and terror.

Nushain pondered the mysteries of his journey almost to madness; and the thought came to him that, after passing through the region of death, he was now traversing the grey limbo of uncreated things; and, thinking this, he was loath to surmise the third stage of his journey; and he dared not reflect upon the nature of its goal.

Anon, suddenly, the mists were riven, and a cataract of golden rays poured down from a high-seated sun. Near at hand, to the lee of the driving barge, a tall island hove with verdurous trees and light, shell-shaped domes, and blossomy gardens hanging far up in the dazzlement of noon. There, with a sleepy purling, the surf was lulled on a low, grassy shore that had not known the anger of storm; and fruited vines and full-blown flowers were pendent above the water. It seemed that a spell of oblivion and slumber was shed from the island, and that any who landed thereon would dwell inviolable forever in sun-bright dreams. Nushain was seized with a longing for its green, bowery refuge; and he wished to voyage no further into the dreadful nothingness of the mist-bound ocean. And between his longing and his terror, he quite forgot the terms of that destiny which had been ordained for him by the stars.

There was no halting nor swerving of the barge; but it drew still nearer to the isle in its coasting; and Nushain saw that the intervening water was clear and shallow, so that a tall man might easily wade to the beach. He sprang into the sea, holding his horoscope aloft, and began to walk toward the island; and Mouzda and Ansarath followed him, swimming side by side.

Though hampered somewhat by his long wet robes, the astrologer thought to reach that alluring shore; nor was there any movement on the part of the merman to intercept him. The water was midway between his waist and his armpits; and now it lapped at his girdle; and now at the knee-folds of his garment; and the island vines and blossoms drooped fragrantly above him.

Then, being but a step from that enchanted beach, he heard a great hissing, and saw that the vines, the boughs, the flowers, the very grasses, were intertwined and mingled with a million serpents, writhing endlessly to and fro in hideous agitation. From all parts of that lofty island the hissing came, and the serpents, with foully mottled volumes, coiled, crept and slithered upon it everywhere; and no single yard of its surface was free from their defilement, or clear for human treading.

Turning seaward in his revulsion, Nushain found the merman and the barge waiting close at hand. Hopelessly he re-entered the barge with his followers, and the magically driven boat resumed its course. And now, for the first time, the merman spoke, saying over his shoulder in a harsh, half-articulate voice, not without irony: "It would seem, O Nushain, that you lack faith in your own divinations. However, even the poorest of astrologers may sometimes cast a horoscope correctly. Cease, then, to rebel against that which the stars have written."

The barge drove on, and the mists closed heavily about it, and the noon-bright island was lost to view. After a vague interim the muffled sun went down behind inchoate waters and clouds; and a darkness as of primal night lay everywhere. Presently, through the torn rack, Nushain beheld a strange heaven whose signs and planets he could not recognize; and at this there came upon him the black horror of utmost dereliction. Then the mists and clouds returned, veiling that unknown sky from his scrutiny. And he could discern nothing but the merman, who was visible by a wan phosphor that clung always about him in his swimming.

Still the barge drove on; and in time it seemed that a red morning rose stifled and conflagrant behind the mists. The boat entered the broadening light, and Nushain, who had thought to behold the sun once more, was dazzled by a strange shore where flames towered in a high unbroken wall, feeding perpetually, to all appearances, on bare sand and rock. With a mighty leaping and a roar as of blown surf the flames went up, and a heat like that of many furnaces smote far on the sea. Swiftly the barge neared the shore; and the merman, with uncouth gestures of farewell, dived and disappeared under the waters.

Nushain could scarcely regard the flames or endure their heat. But the barge touched the strait tongue of land lying between them and the sea; and before Nushain, from the wall of fire, a blazing salamander emerged, having the form and hue of that hieroglyph which had last appeared on his horoscope. And he knew, with ineffable consternation, that this was the third guide of his threefold journey.

"Come with me," said the salamander, in a voice like the crackling of fagots. Nushain stepped from the barge to that strand which was hot as an oven beneath his feet; and behind him, though with palpable reluctance, Mouzda and Ansarath still followed. But, approaching the flames behind the salamander, and half swooning from their ardor, he was overcome by the weakness of mortal flesh; and seeking again to evade his destiny, he fled along the narrow scroll of beach between the fire and the water. But he had gone only a few paces when the salamander, with a great fiery roaring and racing, intercepted him; and it drove him straight toward the fire with terrible flailings of its dragon-like tail, from which showers of sparks were emitted. He could not face the salamander, and he thought the flames would consume him like paper as he entered them: but in the wall there appeared a sort of opening, and the fires arched themselves into an arcade, and he passed through with his followers, herded by the salamander, into an ashen land where all things were veiled with low-hanging smoke and steam. Here the salamander observed with a kind of irony: "Not wrongly, O Nushain, have you interpreted the stars of your horoscope. And now your journey draws to an end, and you will need no longer the services of a guide." So saying, it left him, going out like a quenched fire on the smoky air.

Nushain, standing irresolute, beheld before him a white stairway that mounted amid the veering vapors. Behind him the flames rose unbroken, like a topless rampart; and on either hand, from instant to instant, the smoke shaped itself into demon forms and faces that menaced him. He began to climb the stairs, and the shapes gathered below and about, frightful as a wizard's familiars, and keeping pace with him as he went upward, so that he dared not pause or retreat. Far up he climbed in the fumy dimness, and came unaware to the open portals of a house of grey stone rearing to unguessed height and amplitude.

Unwillingly, but driven by the thronging of the smoky shapes, he passed through the portals with his companions. The house was a place of long, empty halls, tortuous as the folds of a sea-conch. There were no windows, no lamps; but it seemed that bright suns of silver had been dissolved and diffused in the air. Fleeing from the hellish wraiths that pursued him, the astrologer followed the winding halls and emerged ultimately in an inner chamber where space itself was immured. At the room's center a cowled and muffled figure of colossal proportions sat upright on a marble chair, silent, unstirring. Before the figure, on a sort of table, a vast volume lay open.

Nushain felt the awe of one who approaches the presence of some high demon or deity. Seeing that the phantoms had vanished, he paused on the room's threshold: for its immensity made him giddy, like the void interval that lies between the worlds. He wished to withdraw; but a voice issued from the cowled being, speaking softly as the voice of his own inmost mind:

"I am Vergama, whose other name is Destiny; Vergama, on whom you have called so ignorantly and idly, as men are wont to call on their hidden lords; Vergama, who has summoned you on the journey which all men must make at one time or another, in one way or another way. Come forward, O Nushain, and read a little in my book."

The astrologer was drawn as by an unseen hand to the table. Leaning above it, he saw that the huge volume stood open at its middle pages, which were covered with a myriad signs written in inks of various colors, and representing men, gods, fishes, birds, monsters, animals, constellations and many other things. At the end of the last column of the right-hand page, where little space was left for other inscriptions, Nushain beheld the hieroglyphs of an equal-sided triangle of stars, such as had lately appeared in proximity to the Dog; and, following these, the hieroglyphs of a mummy, a merman, a barge and a salamander, resembling the figures that had come and gone on his horoscope, and those that had guided him to the house of Vergama.

"In my book," said the cowled figure, "the characters of all things are written and preserved. All visible forms, in the beginning, were but symbols written by me; and at the last they shall exist only as the writing of my book. For a season they issue forth, taking to themselves that which is known as substance.... It was I, O Nushain, who set in the heavens the stars that foretold your journey; I, who sent the three guides. And these things, having served their purpose, are now but infoliate ciphers, as before."

Vergama paused, and an infinite silence returned to the room, and a measureless wonder was upon the mind of Nushain. Then the cowled being continued:

"Among men, for a while, there was that person called Nushain the astrologer, together with the dog Ansarath and the negro Mouzda, who followed his fortunes.... But now, very shortly, I must turn the page, and before turning it, must finish the writing that belongs thereon."

Nushain thought that a wind arose in the chamber, moving lightly with a weird sigh, though he felt not the actual breath of its passing. But he saw that the fur of Ansarath, cowering close beside him, was ruffled by the wind. Then, beneath his marvelling eyes, the dog began to dwindle and wither, as if seared by a lethal magic; and he lessened to the size of a rat, and thence to the smallness of a mouse and the lightness of an insect, though preserving still his original form. After that, the tiny thing was caught up by the sighing air, and it flew past Nushain as a gnat might fly; and, following it, he saw that the hieroglyph of a dog was inscribed suddenly beside that of the salamander, at the bottom of the right-hand page. But, apart from this, there remained no trace of Ansarath.

Again a wind breathed in the room, touching not the astrologer, but fluttering the ragged raiment of Mouzda, who crouched near to his master, as if appealing for protection. And the mute became shrunken and shrivelled, turning at the last to a thing light and thin as the black, tattered wing-shard of a beetle, which the air bore aloft. And Nushain saw that the hieroglyph of a one-eyed negro was inscribed following that of the dog; but, aside from this, there was no sign of Mouzda.

Now, perceiving clearly the doom that was designed for him, Nushain would have fled from the presence of Vergama. He turned from the outspread volume and ran toward the chamber door, his worn, tawdry robes of an astrologer flapping about his thin shanks. But softly in his ear, as he went, there sounded the voice of Vergama:

"Vainly do men seek to resist or evade that destiny which turns them to ciphers in the end. In my book, O Nushain, there is room even for a bad astrologer."

Once more the weird sighing arose, and a cold air played upon Nushain as he ran; and he paused midway in the vast room as if a wall had arrested him. Gently the air breathed on his lean, gaunt figure, and it lifted his greying locks and beard, and it plucked softly at the roll of papyrus which he still held in his hand. To his dim eyes, the room seemed to reel and swell, expanding infinitely. Borne upward, around and around, in a swift vertiginous swirling, he beheld the seated shape as it loomed ever higher above him in cosmic vastness. Then the god was lost in light; and Nushain was a weightless and exile thing, the withered skeleton of a lost leaf, rising and falling on the bright whirlwind.

In the book of Vergama, at the end of the last column of the right-hand page, there stood the hieroglyph of a gaunt astrologer, carrying a furled nativity.

Vergama leaned forward from his chair, and turned the page.

NECROMANCY IN NAAT

Dead longing, sundered evermore from pain:
How dim and sweet the shadow-hearted love,
The happiness that perished lovers prove
In Naat, far beyond the sable main.

—Song of the Galley-Slaves.

Yadar, prince of a nomad people in the half-desert region known as Zyra, had followed throughout many kingdoms a clue that was often more elusive than broken gossamer. For thirteen moons he had sought Dalili, his betrothed, whom the slave traders of Sha-Karag, swift and cunning as desert falcons, had reft from the tribal encampment with nine other maidens while Yadar and his men were hunting the black gazelles of Zyra. Fierce was the grief of Yadar, and fiercer still his wrath, when he came back at eve to the ravaged tents. He had sworn then a great oath to find Dalili, whether in slave-mart or brothel or harem, whether dead or living, whether tomorrow or after the lapse of grey years.

The tracks of the slavers' camels ran plainly toward the iron gates of Sha-Karag, lying many leagues away in the west. Because of similar raidings, the nomads had long been at war with the people of that infamous market-place where women were the chief merchandise. Knowing that the high-walled city was impregnable to assault by his little band of followers, Yadar disguised himself as a rug-merchant; and accompanied by four of his men in like attire, with certain hoarded heirlooms of the tribe for a stock-in-trade, he appeared before the shut gates and was admitted without challenge by the guards. Listening discreetly to the gossip of the bazaars, he learned that the raiders had not remained in Sha-Karag; but, after selling most of their captives to local dealers, they had gone on without delay toward the great empires of the sunset, taking with them Dalili and her fairest companions. It was said that they hoped to sell Dalili to some opulent king or emperor who would pay a city's ransom for the wild, rare beauty of the outland princess.

Weary and perilous was the quest to which Yadar and his followers now dedicated themselves. Still disguised as rug-merchants, they joined a caravan that was departing on the route taken by the slavers. From realm to realm they followed a doubtful trail, sometimes led astray by vain rumors.

In Tinarath, hearing that a nomad girl of strange loveliness had lately been purchased by the king, they entered the palace harem on a night of storm, slaying the griffon-like monsters who warded its balconies, and braving the hideous pitfalls that had been set for intruders in the inner halls. They found the girl, who was not Dalili but another of the maidens reaved from Yadar's people; and swiftly, amid the bewildered hubbub of the awakening palace, they carried her away into the darkness and storm. She knew little of the fate of Dalili, saying that the princess had been parted from her in Tinarath and had gone with the slave-traders toward Zul-Bha-Sair: for the king of Tinarath had refused to pay the vast sum demanded for Dalili.

Now, when they were safely beyond the borders of Tinarath, Yadar sent the girl back toward Zyra with one of his tribesmen; and he and the others resumed their search and were brought near to death amid the springless dunes of the waste lying between Tinarath and Zul-Bha-Sair. And in Zul-Bha-Sair, Yadar learned that Dalili had been offered to the king who, caring not for a sun-dark beauty, had declined to buy her; and, after that, the princess and her captors had gone northward to an undeclared destination. But, before the nomads could follow, Yadar's companions were seized by a strange fever and died swiftly; and their bodies, according to custom, were claimed by the priesthood of a great temple-dwelling ghoul who was worshipped in that city. So Yadar went on alone, and after much random wandering, he came to Oroth, a western sea-port of the land of Xylac.

There, for the first time in several moons, he heard a rumor that might concern Dalili: for the people of Oroth were still gossiping about the departure of a rich galley bearing a lovely outland girl who had been bought by the emperor of Xylac and sent to the ruler of the far southern kingdom of Yoros as a gift concluding a treaty between these realms.

Yadar, who had almost yielded to despair, was now hopeful of finding his beloved: since, by the description the people had given, he thought that the girl was indeed none other than Dalili. Nothing remained of the precious weavings of the tribe which he had brought with him to sell as merchandise; but, through the sale of his camels, he procured money with which to engage his passage on a ship that was about to sail for Yoros.

The ship was a small merchant galley, laden with grain and wine, that was wont to coast up and down, hugging closely the winding western shores of the continent Zothique and venturing never beyond eyeshot of land. On a clear blue summer day it departed from Oroth with all auguries for a safe and tranquil voyage. But on the third morn after leaving port, a tremendous wind blew suddenly from the low-lying sandy shore they were then skirting; and with it, blotting the heavens and sea, there came a blackness as of night thickened with clouds. The sails and oars could win no headway against the gale, and the vessel was swept far out to sea, going with the blind tempest.

After two days, the wind fell from its ravening fury and was soon no more than a vague whisper; and the skies cleared, leaving a bright azure vault from horizon to horizon. But nowhere was there any land visible, only a waste of waters that still roared and tossed turbulently without wind, pouring ever westward in a cataracting tide that was too swift and strong for the galley to stem. And the galley was borne on irresistibly by that strange current, even as by the hurricane.

Yadar, who was the sole passenger, marvelled much at this thing; and he was struck by the pale terror on the faces of the captain and crew. And, looking again at the sea, he remarked a singular darkening of its waters, which assumed from moment to moment a hue as of old blood commingled with more and more of blackness: though above it the sun shone untarnished. So he made inquiry of the captain, a greybeard from Yoros, named Agor, who had sailed the ocean for forty summers; and the captain answered, with many seafaring oaths:

"This I had apprehended when the storm bore us westwardly: for know now that we have fallen into the grip of that terrible ocean-stream which is called by mariners the Black River. Evermore the stream surges and swiftens toward the fabled place of the sun's outermost setting, till it pours at last from the world's rim. Between us now and that final verge, there is no land, saving the evil land of Naat, which is called also the Isle of Necromancers. And I know not which were the worse fate, to be wrecked on that infamous isle or hurled into space with the waters falling eternally from earth's edge. From either place there is no return for living men such as we. And from the Isle of Naat none go forth except the ill sorcerers who people it, and the dead who are raised up and controlled by their sorcery. In magical ships that breast the full current of the Black River, the sorcerers sail at will to other strands; and beneath their necromancy, to fulfill their wicked errands, the dead men swim without pause for many days and nights whithersoever the masters may send them."

Yadar, who knew little of sorcerers and necromancy, was somewhat incredulous concerning the matters whereof the captain spoke. But he saw that the blackening waters streamed always more wildly and torrentially toward the skyline, as if pouring adown some submarine slope of earth that steepened to the final rim; and verily there was small hope that the galley could regain its southward course. And he was troubled chiefly by the thought that he should never reach the kingdom of Yoros, where he had dreamt to find Dalili.

All that day the vessel was borne on without respite by the dark seas racing weirdly beneath an airless and immaculate heaven. It followed the silent orange sunset into a night filled with large, unquivering stars; and at length it was overtaken by the stilly flying amber morn. But still there was no abating of the waters; and neither land nor cloud was discernible in the vastness about the galley.

Yadar held little converse with Agor and the crew, after questioning them vainly as to the reason of the ocean's blackness, which was a thing that no man understood. Despair was upon him; but, standing at the bulwark, he watched the sky and wave with an alertness born of his nomad life. Toward middle afternoon he descried far-off a strange vessel, rigged with funereal purple sails, that drove steadily on an eastering course against the mighty current. At this, he cried out in wonder, calling the captain's attention to the vessel; and the captain, with a muttering of outlandish oaths, told him that it was a ship belonging to the necromancers of Naat, whose malign magic was more cogent than the tide of the Black River.

Soon the purple sails were lost to vision; but a little later, Yadar perceived certain objects, queerly resembling human heads, that passed in the high-billowing water to the galley's leeward, as if swimming easily toward Zothique on the route of that necromantic ship. Deeming that no mortal living men could swim thus, and remembering that which the captain had told him concerning the dead swimmers who went forth from Naat, Yadar shivered a little with such trepidation as a brave man may feel in the presence of preternatural things; and he did not speak of the matter. And seemingly the head-like objects were not noticed by any of his companions.

Still the galley drove on, its oarsmen sitting idle at the oars, and the captain standing listless beside the untended helm.

Now, as the sun declined above that tumultuous ebon ocean, it seemed that a great bank of thunder-cloud arose from the west, long and low-lying at first, but surging rapidly skyward with mountainous domes and craggy battlements. Ever higher it loomed, revealing the menace as of piled cliffs and somber awful sea-capes; but its form changed not in the manner of clouds; and Yadar, watching it closely, knew it at last for an island bulking far aloft in the long-rayed sunset. From it, a chill effluence of evil came like a sighing breath; and a shadow was thrown for leagues, darkening still more the sable waters, as if with the fall of untimely night; and in the shadow, the foam-crests flashing upon hidden reefs were white as the bared teeth of Death. And Yadar needed not the shrill, frightened cries of his companions to tell him that this was the terrible Isle of Naat.

Direly the current swiftened, raging, as it raced onward for battle with the rock-fanged shore; and the voices of the mariners, praying loudly to their gods, were drowned by its clamor. Yadar, standing in the prow, gave only a silent prayer to the dim, fatal deity of his tribe; and his eyes searched the towering isle like those of a sea-flown hawk, seeing the bare horrific crags, and the spaces of sullen forest creeping seaward between the crags, and the white mounting of breakers on a shadowy strand. And he discerned, on the lofty downs behind the shore, the furtive scattered roofs of houses pale amid cypress-trees that clotted the gloom with funereal umbrage.

Shrouded, and ominous of bale was the island's aspect, and the heart of

Yadar sank like a plummet in unsunned seas. As the galley drew nearer to land, he thought that he beheld people moving darkly, visible in the lapsing of surges on a low beach, and then hidden once more by foam and spindrift. Ere he saw them a second time, the galley was hurled with thunderous crashing and grinding on a reef covered by the torrent waters. The whole forepart of its prow and bottom were broken in, and being lifted from the reef by a great comber, it filled instantly and sank. And of those who had sailed from Oroth in the vessel, Yadar alone leapt free ere its foundering; but, since he was little skilled as a swimmer, he was drawn under quickly and was like to have drowned in the maelstroms of that evil sea.

His senses left him, and in his brain, like a lost sun returned from yesteryear, he beheld the face of Dalili; and with Dalili, in a bright phantasmagoria, there came the happy days that had been ere his bereavement. The visions passed, and he awoke struggling, with the bitterness of the sea in his mouth, and its loudness in his ears, and its rushing darkness all about him. And, as his senses quickened, he became aware of a form that swam close behind him, and arms that supported him amid the waters.

He lifted his head in the twilight, and saw dimly the pale neck and half-averted face of his rescuer, and the long black hair that floated from wave to wave. Touching the body at his side, he knew it for that of a woman. Mazed and wildered though he was by the sea's buffeting, a sense of something familiar stirred within him; and he thought that he had known, somewhere, at some former time, a girl with like hair and similar curving of cheek; but he could not remember clearly. And, trying to remember, he touched the woman again, and felt in his fingers a strange coldness from her naked body. At this, he wondered a little, but forgot his wonder in the wildness of that sea through which he was borne by the swimmer.

Miraculous was the woman's strength and skill, for she rode easily the dreadful mounting and falling of the surges. Yadar, floating as in a cradle upon her arm, beheld the nearing shore from the billows' summits; and hardly it seemed that any swimmer, however able, could win alive through the ponderous cataracting of that surf on the stony strand. Dizzily, at the last, they were hurled upward, as if the surf would fling them against the highmost crag; but, as if checked by some enchantment, the wave fell with a slow, lazy undulation; and Yadar and his rescuer, released by its ebbing, lay unhurt on a shelfy beach.

Uttering no word, nor turning to look at Yadar, the woman rose swiftly to her feet; and, beckoning the nomad prince to follow, she moved away in the deathly blue dusk that had fallen upon Naat. Yadar, arising and following the woman, heard a strange and eerie chanting of voices above the sea's tumult, and saw a fire that burned weirdly, with the colors of driftwood, at some distance before him in the dusk. Straightly, toward the fire and the voices, the woman walked in the fashion of a somnambulist, and Yadar, with eyes grown used to that doubtful twilight, saw that the fire blazed in the mouth of a low-sunken cleft between crags that overloomed the beach; and behind the fire, like tall, evilly posturing shadows, there stood the dark-clad figures of those who chanted.

Now memory returned to him of that which the galley's captain had said regarding the people of Naat and their necromantic practices; and with the memory came misgiving. For the very sound of that chanting, albeit in an unknown language, seemed to suspend the heartward flowing of his veins, and to set the tomb's chillness in his marrow. And though he was little learned in such matters, the thought came to him that the words uttered were of sorcerous import and power.

Going forward, the woman bowed low before the chanters, in such fashion as a slave, and stood waiting submissively. The men, who were three in number, continued their incantation without pausing, and they seemed not to perceive the presence of Yadar as he entered the firelight. Gaunt as starved herons they were, and great of stature, with a common likeness, as of brothers; and sharply ridged were their faces, where shadows inhabited their hollow cheeks, and their sunk eyes were visible only by red sparks reflected within them from the blaze. And their eyes, as they chanted, seemed to glare afar on the darkling sea and on things hidden by dusk and distance. And Yadar, coming before them, was aware of swift horror and repugnance that made his gorge rise as if he had encountered, in a place given wholly to death, the powerful evil ripeness of corruption.

High leaped the fire as he neared it, with a writhing of tongues that were like blue and green serpents coiling amid serpents of yellow. And the light flickered brightly on the face and breasts of that woman who had saved him from the Black River; and Yadar, beholding her clearly, knew why she had stirred within him a dim remembrance: for she was none other than his lost love, Dalili!

Forgetting the presence of the dark chanters, and the ill renown of that isle to which the seas had brought him, he sprang forward to clasp his beloved, crying out her name in an agony of rapture. But she answered not his cry, and responded to his embrace only with a faint trembling. And Yadar, sorely perplexed and dismayed, was aware of the deathly coldness that crept into his fingers and smote through his very raiment from her flesh. Mortally pale and languid were the lips that he kissed, and it seemed that no breath emerged between them, nor was there any rising and falling of the wan bosom against his. In the wide, beautiful eyes that she turned to him, he found only a drowsy voidness, and such recognition as a sleeper gives when but half awakened, relapsing quickly into slumber thereafter.

"Art thou indeed Dalili?" he said. And she answered somnolently, in a toneless, indistinct voice, "I am Dalili."

To Yadar, baffled by mystery, chilled, forlorn and aching, it was as if she had spoken from a land farther away than all the weary leagues of his search throughout Zothique. Fearing to understand the change that had come upon her, he said tenderly:

"Surely thou knowest me, for I am thy lover, the Prince Yadar, who has sought thee through half the kingdoms of Earth, and has sailed afar for thy sake on the unshored sea." And she replied like one bemused by some heavy drug, in a soulless voice, as if echoing his words without true comprehension: "Surely I know thee." And to Yadar there was no comfort in her reply; and his concernment was not allayed by the parrotings with which she answered all his other loving speeches and queries.

He knew not that the three chanters had all ceased their incantation; and verily, he had forgotten their presence in his finding of Dalili. But as he stood holding the girl closely, the men came toward him, and one of them clutched his arm. And the man hailed him by name and addressed him, albeit uncouthly, in a language commonly spoken throughout many parts of Zothique, saying: "We bid thee welcome to the Isle of Naat, from which no living traveller may return."

Yadar, feeling a dread suspicion, interrogated the man fiercely: "What manner of beings are ye? And why is Dalili in this place? And what have ye done to her?"

"I am Vacharn, a necromancer," the man replied readily, "and these others with me are my sons, Vokal and Uldulla, who are also necromancers. We dwell in a house behind the crags, and are attended by the drowned people that our sorcery has called up from the sea to a semblance of life and animation. Among our servants is this girl, Dalili, together with the whole crew of that ship in which she sailed from Oroth. For, like the vessel in which thou camest later, the ship was blown far asea and was taken by the ineluctable Black River, and was wrecked finally on the reefs of Naat. And my sons and I, chanting that powerful formula which requires no use of circle or pentacle, summoned ashore the drowned company: even as we have now summoned the crew of that other vessel, from which thou alone wert saved alive by the necromantic swimmer at our command, for a certain purpose."

Vacharn ended, and stood peering into the dusk intently; and Yadar at that moment heard behind him a noise of slow footsteps coming upward across the shingle from the surf. Turning, he saw emerge from the livid twilight the old captain of that merchant galley in which he had voyaged so unwillingly to Naat; and behind the captain were the sailors and oarsmen. With the paces of sleep-walkers they approached the firelight, the sea-water dripping heavily from their raiment and hair, and drooling from their mouths. Some were sorely bruised, and others came stumbling or dragging with limbs broken by the rocks on which that torrential sea had flung them; and on all their faces was the ghastly look of men who have suffered the doom of drowning.

Stiffly, like automatons, they made obeisance in a body before Vacharn and his sons, acknowledging thus their thralldom to those who had raised them from deep death. In their glassily staring eyes there was no recognition of Yadar, no awareness of outward things; and they spoke only in dull, rote-like recognition of certain obscure words addressed to them by the necromancers.

To Yadar, it was as if he too stood and moved like the living dead in a dark, hollow, half-conscious dream. Even thus, walking side by side with Dalili, and followed by those others, he was led by the enchanters through a dusky ravine that wound secretly toward the uplands of Naat. Obediently he went: but in his heart there was small joy at the finding of Dalili; and his love was companioned by a sick despair.

Vacharn lit the way with a brand of driftwood plucked from the fire; and Yadar beheld vaguely, by its flickering, the black and cruel precipices of a steepening gorge, and the dwarfish crooked pines that leaned malignantly from high ledges, as if to cast with wizard hands a malediction upon the wayfarers. Anon a bloated moon rose red as with sanies-mingled blood behind them, over the wild, racing sea; and, ere its orb had cleared to a death-like paleness, they emerged from the gorge on a stony fell where stood the house of the three necromancers.

Long and low-lying was the house, built of dark granite, with crouching wings half hidden amid the foliage of close-grown cypresses. Behind it a cliff beetled, overhanging it starkly; and above the cliff were somber slopes and ridges piled in the moonlight, rising afar toward the mountainous center of Naat.

To Yadar, it seemed that the mansion was a place pre-empted by death: for no lights burned in its portals and windows; and a silence came from it to meet the stillness of the wan heavens. But, when the necromancers neared the threshold, a word was spoken by Vacharn, echoing distantly in the inner halls and chambers; and as if in answer, lamps were illumined suddenly everywhere, filling the house as with monstrous yellow eyes; and people appeared instantly within the portals like bowing shadows. But the faces of these beings were blanched by the tomb's pallor, and some were mottled with green decay, or marked by the tortuous gnawing of maggots....

Later, in a great hall of the house, Yadar was bidden to seat himself at a table where Vacharn and Vokal and Uldulla were wont to sit alone during their meals. The table stood on a sort of dais formed of gigantic flagstones; and below, in the main hall, the dead were gathered about other tables, numbering nearly twoscore; and among them sat the girl Dalili, looking never toward Yadar. He, though sorely sick at heart, would have joined her, unwilling to be parted from her side: but a deep languor was upon him, as if an unspoken spell had enthralled his limbs, and he could no longer move at his own volition but must obey in all things the will of Vacharn.

Dully he sat, observing with small wonder the grimness and taciturnity of his hosts, who, dwelling always with the silent dead, had apparently assumed no little part of their manner and similitude. And he saw more clearly than before the common likeness of the three: for all, it seemed, were as brothers of one birth rather than parent and sons; and all were like ageless things, being neither old nor young in the fashion of ordinary men. Yadar could distinguish Vacharn from his sons only by the darker hue of his garments, and the greater breadth of brow and shoulders; and he knew Vokal from Uldulla merely by a sharper pitch of voice and a deeper hollowing of the gaunt cheeks. And more and more was he aware of that weird evil which emanated from the three, powerful and abhorrent as an exhalation of hidden death.

In the thralldom that weighed upon him, he scarcely marvelled at the serving of the strange supper that followed: though meats were brought in by no palpable agency, and wines poured out as if by the air itself; and the passing of the bearers to and fro was betrayed only by a rustle of doubtfully dying footsteps, and a light chillness that came and went.

Mutely, with stiff gestures and movements, the dead began to eat at their laden tables. But the necromancers refrained from the victuals before them, in an attitude of waiting; and Vacharn, in explanation, said to the nomad: "There are still others who will sup with us tonight." And Yadar, for the first time, perceived that a vacant chair had been set beside the chair of Vacharn.

Then, from an inner doorway, there entered the hall with hasty strides a man of great thews and stature, naked, and brown almost to blackness. Savage of aspect was the man, and his eyes were dilated as if with rage or terror, and little flecks of foam were on his thick purple lips. And close behind him, lifting in menace their heavy, rusted scimitars, there came two liches, like guards who attend a prisoner.

"This man is a cannibal," said Vacharn. "Our servants have captured him for us in the forest beyond the mountains, which is peopled mainly by such savages." Then, with a dark irony couching behind the words, he added: "Only the strong and courageous are summoned living to this mansion, and are suffered to eat with my sons and me at our table…. Not idly, O Prince Yadar, wert thou chosen for this honor among all who sailed in the merchant galley from Oroth. Observe closely all that follows."

The giant savage had paused within the threshold, as if fearing the hall's occupants more than the wicked weapons of his guards. At a signal from Vacharn, one of the liches slashed his left shoulder with the rusty blade, and blood rilled copiously from a deep wound as the cannibal came forward beneath that prompting. Convulsively he trembled, in such wise as a frightened animal, looking wildly to either side for an avenue of escape; and only after a second prompting did he mount the dais and approach the necromancers' table. But, after certain hollow-sounding words had been uttered by Vacharn, the man seated himself, still trembling, in the chair beside the master, opposite to Yadar. And behind him, with high-raised weapons, there stationed themselves the ghastly guards, whose features were those of men a fortnight dead.

"There is still another guest," said Vacharn, "a guest who prefers to sup when others have supped. He will come at his own time."

Without further ceremony, he began to eat, and Yadar, though with little appetence, followed suit. Hardly did the prince perceive the savor of those viands with which his plate was piled; nor could he have sworn whether the vintages he drank were sour or dulcet. For his thoughts were divided between Dalili and the strangeness and horror about him. The utterances of Vacharn, and the presence of the cannibal, and the reason of his own presence at that table, were obscure to him; and he felt in all this the incumbence of an ill mystery. And, seeing that there was no longer a vacant place at the table, he was perplexed by the necromancer's reference to the coming of still another guest. As he ate and drank, it seemed that his senses were sharpened weirdly, so that he grew aware of eldritch shadows moving between the lamps, and heard the chill sibilance of whispers that checked his very blood. And there came to him, from the peopled hall, every odor that is exhaled by mortality between the recentness of death and the end of corruption.

Vacharn and his sons addressed themselves to the meal with the unconcern of those long habituated to such surroundings. But the cannibal, whose fear was still palpable in his features and members, ate only a few scant mouthfuls, and these at the direct prompting of Vacharn, who appeared very solicitous of his guest's appetite. Blood, in two heavy rills, ran unceasingly down his bosom from his wounded shoulders, and fell at last on the stone flags with an audible dripping. But of this, in his sore terror, he seemed unaware.

Finally, at the urging of Vacharn, who spoke to him in the cannibal's own language, he was persuaded to drink from a cup of wine that had long stood before him untasted. This wine, Yadar perceived, was not the same that had been served to the rest of the company, being of a violet color, dark as the nightshade's blossom, while the other wine was a poppy red. Hardly had the man tasted it, when he sank back in his chair with the appearance of one smitten helpless by palsy. The wine-cup, rilling the remnant of its contents, was still clutched in his rigid fingers; there was no movement, no trembling of his limbs; and his eyes were wide open and staring, as if consciousness still remained within him.

A dire suspicion sprang up in Yadar, and no longer could he eat the food and drink the wine of the necromancers. And much was he puzzled by the actions of Vacharn and Vokal and Uldulla, who, abstaining likewise, turned in their chairs and peered steadfastly at a certain portion of the floor behind Vacharn, between the table and the hall's inner end. Rising a little in his seat, Yadar looked down across the table and saw that all three were staring at a small hole in one of the flagstones, which he had not hitherto perceived. The hole was such as might be inhabited by some tiny animal: but Yadar could not surmise the nature of a beast that burrowed in solid granite.

Now, in a loud clear voice, Vacharn spoke the single word, "Esrit," as if calling the name of one that he wished to summon. Not long thereafter, two little sparks of fire appeared in the darkness of the hole, and from it sprang a creature having somewhat the size and likeness of a weasel, but even longer and thinner of body. The fur of the creature was a rusted black, and its paws were like tiny hairless hands; and its beaded eyes of flaming fulvous yellow seemed to hold the malign wisdom and malevolence of a demon. Swiftly, with writhing movements that gave it the air of a furred serpent, it ran forward beneath the chair occupied by the cannibal, and began to drink greedily the pool of blood that had dripped down on the floor from his wounds.

Then, while horror fastened upon the heart of Yadar, it leapt to the knees of the huge savage, and thence to his left shoulder, where the deepest wound had been inflicted. And there the thing applied itself to the still bleeding cut, from which it sucked in the fashion of a weasel; and the blood ceased to flow down on the man's body. And the man stirred not in his chair; but his eyes still widened, slowly, with a horrible glaring, till the balls were isled in livid white; and his lips fell slackly apart, showing teeth that were strong and pointed as those of a shark.

The necromancers had resumed their eating, with eyes attentive on the small bloodthirsty monster; and it came to Yadar that this was the other guest expected by Vacharn. Whether the thing was an actual weasel, or a sorcerer's familiar, he knew not: but anger followed upon his horror before the plight of the cannibal; and, drawing a sword he had carried through all his travels and voyagings, he sprang to his feet and would have tried to kill the monster. But Vacharn described in the air a peculiar sign with his forefinger; and it seemed that the prince's arm was suspended in mid-stroke, and his fingers became weak as those of a newborn babe, and the sword fell from his hand, ringing loudly on the dais. Thereafter, as if by the unspoken will of Vacharn, he was constrained to seat himself again at the table.

Insatiable, to all appearance, was the thirst of the weasel-like creature: for, after many minutes had gone by in that hall of abominations, it continued to suck the blood of the savage. And from moment to moment the man's mighty thews became strangely shrunken, and the bones and taut sinews showed starkly beneath wrinkling folds of skin. His face was like the chapless face of death, his limbs were lean as those of an old mummy: but the thing that battened upon him had increased in girth only so much as a stoat increases by sucking the blood of some farmyard fowl.

By this token, Yadar knew that the thing was indeed a demon, and was no doubt the familiar of Vacharn. Entranced with terror, he sat regarding it, till the creature dropped from the dry skin and bones of the cannibal, and ran with an evil writhing and slithering to its hole in the flagstone.

Weird was the life that now began for Yadar in the house of the necromancers. Upon him there rested by day and night the malign thralldom that had overpowered him during that first supper, and he moved as one who could not wholly awake from some benumbing dream. It seemed that his volition was in some way controlled by those masters of the living dead. But, more than this, he was held by the old enchantment of his love for Dalili: though the love had now turned to a spell of despair.

He ate at the table of the necromancers, and slept in a chamber adjoining that of Vacharn: a chamber unlocked, and without tangible bars to hinder his going. Dully he foresaw the fate designed for him: since Vacharn spoke seldom except with grim ironies, referring to the doom of the cannibal, and of the thirst of the weasel-like familiar, whose name was Esrit. And he learned that Esrit had undertaken to serve Vacharn for a certain term, receiving in guerdon thereof, at the full of each moon, the blood of a living man chosen for redoubtable strength and valor. And it was clear to Yadar that, in default of some miracle, or sorcery beyond that of the necromancers, his days of life were limited by the moon's period. For, other than himself and the masters, there was no person in all that mansion who had not already passed through the bitter gates of death, thereby becoming unacceptable to Esrit.

Lonely was the house, standing far apart from all neighbors. Other necromancers dwelt on the shores of Naat, served mainly by the people they had evoked from drowning after shipwreck; but betwixt these and the hosts of Yadar there was little intercourse. And beyond the wild mountains that divided the isle, there dwelt only certain tribes of anthropophagi, who warred perpetually with each other in the black woods of pine and cypress, but feared the necromancers and their thralls.

The dead were housed in deep catacomb-like caves of the cliff behind the mansion, lying all night in rows of stone coffins, and coming forth in daily resurrection to do the tasks ordained by the masters. Some were compelled to till the rocky gardens on a slope sequestered from sea-wind; others tended the sable goats and cattle of the isle; and still others were sent out as divers for pearls in the sea that raged and ravened prodigiously, not to be dared by living swimmers, on the bleak atolls and headlands horned with granite. Of such pearls, Vacharn had amassed a mighty store through years exceeding the common span of life. And sometimes, in a ship that sailed contrary to the Black River, he or one of his sons would voyage to Zothique with certain of the dead for crew, and would trade the pearls for such things as their magic was unable to raise up in Naat.

Strange it was to Yadar, to see the companions of his voyage passing to and fro with the other liches, recognizing him not, or greeting him only in mindless echo of his own salutations. And bitter it was, yet never without a dim, sorrowful sweetness, to behold Dalili and speak with her, trying vainly to revive the lost ardent love in a heart that had gone fathom-deep into oblivion and had not returned therefrom. And always, with a desolate yearning, he seemed to grope toward her across a gulf more terrible than the stemless tide that poured forever about the Isle of the Necromancers.

Dalili, who had swum from childhood in the sunken lakes of Zyra, was among those enforced to dive for pearls in that ebon water. Often Yadar would accompany her to the shore and await her return from the mad surges; and at whiles he was tempted to fling himself after her, and find, if such were possible, the peace of very death. This he would surely have done: but, amid the eerie wilderments of his plight, and the grey webs of sorcery woven about him, it seemed that his old strength and resolution were wholly lacking.

Now, night by night, the moon was sharpened above the craggy isle, and it became a heavy scythe and then a thin scimitar. And, after the interlunar dusk, it broadened from a frail saber to a sickle, and, digit by digit, swelled toward the gibbous orb and the plenilune. Yadar, supping with the sorcerers as it changed, was not unregardful of that burrow in the granite flag, from which the weasel-demon, Esrit, had slithered forth to suck the blood of the cannibal. But, beneath his extreme languor and lethargy, he hardly feared that verminous death which would dart upon him at the time of the moon's fullness.

One day, toward sunset-time, as the month drew to its end, Vokal and Uldulla approached the prince where he stood waiting on a rock-walled beach while Dalili dived after pearls far out in the torrent waters. Speaking no word, they beckoned to him with furtive signs; and Yadar, vaguely curious as to their intent, suffered them to lead him from the beach and by perilous paths that wound from crag to crag above the curving sea-shore. Ere the fall of darkness, they came suddenly to a small landlocked harbor whose existence had been heretofore unsuspected by the nomad. In that placid bay, beneath the deep umbrage of the isle, there rode a galley with somber purple sails, resembling the ship that Yadar had discerned moving steadily toward Zothique against the full tide of the Black River.

Yadar was much bewondered, nor could he divine why they had brought him to the hidden harbor, nor the import of their gestures as they pointed out the strange vessel. Then, in a hushed and covert whisper, as if fearing to be overheard in that remote place, Vokal said to him:

"If thou wilt aid my brother and me in the execution of a certain plan which we have conceived, thou shalt have the use of yonder galley in quitting Naat. And with thee, if such be thy desire, thou shalt take the girl Dalili whom thou lovest, together with certain of the dead mariners for oarsmen. Favored by the powerful gales which our enchantments will evoke for thee, thou shalt sail against the Black River and return to Zothique…. But if thou helpest us not, then shall the weasel Esrit suck thy blood, till the last, least member of thy body has been emptied thereof; and Dalili shall remain forever as the bondslave of Vacharn, toiling for his avarice by day in the dark waters… and perchance serving his lust by night."

At the promise of Vokal, Yadar felt something of hope and manhood revive within him, and it seemed that the baleful sorcery of Vacharn was lifted from his mind; and an indignation against Vacharn was awakened in him by Vokal's hintings. And he said quickly: "I will aid thee in thy plan, whatever it may be, if such aid is within my power to give."

Then, with many fearful glances about and behind him, Uldulla took up the furtive whispering.

"It is our thought that Vacharn has lived beyond the allotted term, and has imposed his authority upon us for an excessive length of years. We, his sons, grow old: and we deem it no more than rightful that we should inherit the stored treasures and the magical supremacy of our father ere age has wholly debarred us from their enjoyment. Therefore we seek thy help in the slaying of the necromancer."

Though Yadar was somewhat surprised, it came to him after brief reflection that the killing of the necromancer should be held in all ways a righteous deed, and one to which he could lend himself without demeaning his valor or his manhood. So he said without demur: "I will aid thee."

Then, seeming greatly emboldened by Yadar's consent, Vokal spoke again in his turn, saying: "This thing must be accomplished ere tomorrow's eve, which will bring a full-rounded moon from the Black River upon Naat, and will call the weasel-demon Esrit from his burrow. And tomorrow's forenoon is the only time when we can take Vacharn unaware in his chamber. During those hours, as is his wont, he will peer entranced on a magic mirror that yields visions of the outer sea, and the ships sailing over the sea, and the lands lying beyond. And we must slay him before the mirror, striking swiftly and surely ere he awakens from his trance."

At the hour set for the deed, Vokal and Uldulla came to Yadar where he stood awaiting them in the mansion's outer hall. Each of the brothers bore in his right hand a long and coldly glittering scimitar; and Vokal also carried in his left a like weapon, which he offered to the prince, explaining that these scimitars had been tempered to a muttering of lethal runes, and inscribed afterward with unspeakable deathspells. Yadar, preferring his own sword, declined the wizard weapon; and, delaying no more, the three went hastily and with all possible stealth toward Vacharn's chamber.

The house was empty at that hour, for the dead had all gone forth to their labors; nor was there any whisper or shadow of those invisible beings, whether sprites of the air or mere phantoms, that waited upon Vacharn and served him in sundry ways. In silence and, as they thought, wholly unperceived, the three came to the portals of the chamber, where entrance was barred only by a black arras wrought with the Signs of night in silver, and bordered all about with a repetition of the fives names of the archfiend Thasaidon in scarlet thread. The brothers paused before the arras, as if fearing to lift it; but Yadar, unhesitating, held it aside and passed into the chamber; and the twain followed him quickly as if for shame of their poltroonery.

Large and high vaulted was the room, and lit by a dim window looking forth between unpruned cypresses toward the black sea. No flames arose from the myriad lamps to assist that baffled daylight; and shadows brimmed the place like a spectral fluid, through which the vessels of wizardry used by Vacharn, the great censers and alembics and braziers, seemed to quiver and move like animate things. A little past the room's center, his back to the doorway, Vacharn sat on an ebon trivet before the mirror of clairvoyance, which was wrought from electrum in the form of a huge delta, and was held obliquely aloft by a serpentining copper arm. The mirror flamed brightly in the shadow, as if lit by some splendor of unknown source; and the intruders were dazzled by glimpsings of its radiance as they went forward.

It seemed that Vacharn had indeed been overcome by the wonted trance, for he peered rigidly into the mirror, immobile as a seated mummy. The brothers held back, while Yadar, thinking them close behind him, stole toward the necromancer with lifted blade. As he drew nearer, he perceived that Vacharn held a great scimitar across his knees; and deeming that the sorcerer was perhaps forewarned, Yadar ran quickly up behind him and aimed a powerful stroke at his neck, meaning to hew off the head with that single blow. But, even while he aimed, his eyes were wholly blinded by the strange brightness of the mirror, as though a sun had blazed into them from its depth across the shoulder of Vacharn; and the blade swerved and bit slantingly into the collar-bone, so that the necromancer, though sorely wounded, was saved from decapitation.

Now it seemed likely that Vacharn had foreknown the attempt to slay him, and had thought to do battle with his assailers when they came, and kill the three without injury to himself, by virtue of his superiority in swordsmanship and in magic. But, sitting at the mirror in pretended trance, he had no doubt been overpowered against his will by the weird brilliancy; and was aroused from that mantic slumber only by the lethal biting of Yadar's sword through flesh and bone.

Fierce and swift as a wounded tiger, he leapt from the trivet, swinging his scimitar aloft as he turned upon Yadar. The prince, still blinded, could neither strike again nor avoid the stroke of Vacharn; and the scimitar clove deeply into his right shoulder, and he fell mortally wounded and lay with his head upheld a little against the base of the snakish copper arm that supported the mirror.

Lying there, with his life ebbing slowly, he beheld how Vokal, who stood somewhat in advance of Uldulla, sprang forward as with the desperation of one who sees imminent death, and hewed mightily into the neck of Vacharn ere the sorcerer could turn. The head, almost sundered from the body, toppled and hung by a strip of flesh and skin: yet Vacharn, reeling, did not fall or die at once, as any mortal man should have done: but, still animated by the wizard power within him, he ran about the chamber, striking great blows at the parricides. Blood gushed from his neck like a fountain as he ran; and his head swung to and fro like a monstrous pendulum on his breast. And all his blows went wild because he could no longer see to direct them, and his sons avoided him agilely, hewing into him oftentimes as he went past. And sometimes he stumbled over the fallen Yadar, or struck the mirror of electrum with his sword, making it ring like a deep bell. And sometimes the battle passed beyond sight of the dying prince, toward the dim window that looked seaward; and he heard the strange crashings, as if some of the magic furniture were shattered by the strokes of the warlock; and there were loud breathings from the sons of Vacharn, and the dull sound of blows that went home as they still pursued their father. And anon the fight returned before Yadar, and he watched it with dimming eyes.

Dire beyond telling was that combat, and Vokal and Uldulla panted like spent runners ere the end. But, after a while, the power seemed to fail in Vacharn with the draining of his life-blood. He staggered from side to side as he ran, and his paces halted, and his blows became enfeebled. His raiment hung upon him in blood-soaked rags from the slashings of his sons, and certain of his members were half sundered, and his whole body was hacked and overscored like an executioner's block. At last, with a dexterous blow, Vokal severed the thin strip by which the head still depended; and the head dropped and rolled with many reboundings about the floor.

Then, with a wild tottering, as if still fain to stand erect, the body of Vacharn toppled down and lay thrashing like a great, headless fowl, heaving itself up and dropping back again, incessantly. Never, with all its rearings, did the body quite regain its feet: but the scimitar was still held firmly in the right hand, and the corpse laid blindly about it, striking from the floor with sidelong slashes, or slicing down as it rose half-way to a standing posture. And the head still rolled, unresting, about the chamber, and maledictions came from its mouth in a pipy voice no louder than that of a child.

At this, Yadar saw that Vokal and Uldulla drew back, as if somewhat aghast; and they turned toward the door, manifestly intending to quit the room. But before Vokal, going first, had lifted the portal-arras, there slithered beneath its folds the long, black, snakish body of the weasel-familiar, Esrit. And the familiar launched itself in air, reaching at one bound the throat of Vokal; and it clung there with teeth fastened in his flesh, sucking his blood steadily, while he staggered about the room and strove in vain to tear it away with maddened fingers.

Uldulla, it seemed, would have made some attempt to kill the creature; for he cried out, adjuring Vokal to stand firm, and raised his sword as if waiting for a chance to strike at the weasel-thing. But Vokal seemed to hear him not, or was too frenzied to obey his adjuration. And at that instant the head of Vacharn, in its rolling, bounded against Uldulla's feet; and the head, snarling ferociously, caught the hem of his robe with its teeth and hung there as he sprang back in panic fright. And though he sliced wildly at the head with his scimitar, the teeth refused to relinquish their hold. So he dropped his garment, and leaving it there with the still pendant head of his father, he fled naked from the chamber. And even as Uldulla fled, the life departed from Yadar, and he saw and heard no more….

Dimly, from the depths of oblivion, Yadar beheld the flaring of remote lights, and heard the chanting of a far voice. It seemed that he swam upward from black seas toward the voice and the lights, and he saw as if through a thin, watery film the face of Uldulla standing above him, and the fuming of strange vessels in the chamber of Vacharn. And it seemed that Uldulla said to him: "Arise from death, and be obedient in all things to me the master."

So, in answer to the unholy rites and incantations of necromancy, Yadar arose to such life as was possible for a resurrected lich. And he walked again, with the black gore of his wound in a great clot on his shoulder and breast, and made reply to Uldulla in the fashion of the living dead. Vaguely, and as matters of no import, he remembered something of his death and the circumstances preceding it; and vainly, with filmed eyes, in the wrecked chamber, he looked for the sundered head and body of Vacharn, and for Vokal and the weasel-demon.

Then it seemed that Uldulla said to him: "Follow me;" and he went forth with the necromancer into the light of the red, swollen moon that had soared from the Black River upon Naat. There, on the fell before the mansion, was a vast heap of ashes where coals glowed and glared like living eyes in the moonlight. Uldulla stood in contemplation before the heap; and Yadar stood beside him, knowing not that he gazed on the burnt-out pyre of Vacharn and Vokal, which the dead slaves had built and fired at Uldulla's direction.

Then, with shrill, eerie wailings, a mighty wind came suddenly from the sea, and lifting all the ashes and sparks in a great, swirling cloud, it swept them upon Yadar and the necromancer. The twain could hardly stand against that wind, and their hair and beards and garments were filled with the leavings of the pyre, and both were blinded thereby. Then the wind went on, sweeping the cloud of ashes over the mansion and into its doorways and windows; and through all its apartments. And for many days thereafter, little swirls of ash rose up like phantoms under the feet of those who passed along the halls; and though there was a daily plying of besoms by the dead at Uldulla's injunction, it seemed that the place was never again wholly clean of those ashes….

Regarding Uldulla, there remains little enough to be told: for his lordship over the dead was a brief thing. Abiding always alone, except for those liches who attended him, and the ashes that still haunted the mansion, he became possessed by a weird melancholy that turned quickly toward madness. No longer could he conceive the aims and objects of life; and the languor of death rose up around him like a black, stealthy sea, full of soft murmurs and shadow-like arms that were fain to draw him doomward. Soon he came to envy the dead, and to deem their lot desirable above any other. So, carrying that scimitar he had used at the slaying of Vacharn, he went into his father's chamber, which he had not entered since the raising up of Prince Yadar. There, beside the sun-bright mirror of divinations, he disembowelled himself, and fell amid the dust and the cobwebs that had gathered heavily over all. And, since there was no other necromancer to bring him back even to a semblance of life, he lay rotting and undisturbed forever after.

But in the gardens of Vacharn the dead people still labored, heedless of Uldulla's passing; and they still kept the goats and cattle, and dived for pearls in the dark, torrent main, even as before.

And Yadar, who had been called from nothingness to a dim, crepuscular state of being, dwelt and toiled with the other liches. He remembered but vaguely the various events that were antecedent to his death; and the fiery days of his youth in Zyra were less than ashes. The promise made to him by the sons of Vacharn, and his hope of escaping with Dalili, had now lost their meaning; and he knew the death of Uldulla only as the vanishing of a shadow. Yet, with a ghostly yearning, he was still drawn to Dalili; and he followed her during the day, and felt a ghostly comfort in her nearness; and through the night-time he lay beside her, and she was a dim sweetness in his shadowy dreams. The quick despair that had racked him aforetime, and the long torments of desire and separation, were as things faded and forgot; and he shared with Dalili a shadowy love and a dim contentment.

THE TREADER OF THE DUST

...The olden wizards knew him, and named him Quachil Uttaus. Seldom is he revealed: for he dwelleth beyond the outermost circle, in the dark limbo of unsphered time and space. Dreadful is the word that calleth him, though the word be unspoken save in thought: for Quachil Uttaus is the ultimate corruption; and the instant of his coming is like the passage of many ages; and neither flesh nor stone may abide his treading, but all things crumble beneath it atom from atom. And for this, some have called him The Treader of the Dust.
                              —*The Testaments of Carnamagos.*

It was after interminable debate and argument with himself, after many attempts to exorcise the dim, bodiless legion of his fears, that John Sebastian returned to the house he had left so hurriedly. He had been absent only for three days; but even this was an interruption without precedent in the life of reclusion and study to which he had given himself completely following his inheritance of the old mansion together with a generous income. At no time would he have defined fully the reason of his flight: nevertheless, flight had seemed imperative. There was some horrible urgency that had driven him forth; but now, since he had determined to go back, the urgency was resolved into a matter of nerves overwrought by too close and prolonged application to his books. He had fancied certain things: but the fancies were patently absurd and altogether baseless.

Even if the phenomena that had perturbed him were not all imaginary, there must be some natural solution that had not occurred to his overheated mind at the time. The sudden yellowing of a newly purchased notebook, the crumbling of the sheets at their edges, were no doubt due to a latent imperfection of the paper; and the queer fading of his entries, which, almost overnight, had become faint as age-old writing, was clearly the result of cheap, faulty chemicals in the ink. The aspect of sheer, brittle, worm-hollowed antiquity which had manifested itself in certain articles of furniture, certain portions of the mansion, was no more than the sudden revealing of a covert disintegration that had gone on unnoticed by him in his sedulous application to dark but absorbing researches. And it was this same application, with its unbroken years of toil and confinement, which had brought about his premature aging; so that, looking into the mirror on the morn of his flight, he had been startled and shocked as if by the apparition of a withered mummy. As to the manservant, Timmers—well, Timmers had been old ever since he could remember. It was only the exaggeration of sick nerves that had lately found in Timmers a decrepitude so extreme that it might fall, without the intermediacy of death, at any moment, into the corruption of the grave.

Indeed, he could explain all that had troubled him without reference to the wild, remote lore, the forgotten demonologies and systems of magic into which he had delved. Those passages in *The Testaments of Carnamagos*, over which he had pondered with weird dismay, were relevant only to the horrors evoked by mad sorcerers in bygone aeons....

Sebastian, firm in such convictions, came back at sunset to his house. He did not tremble or falter as he crossed the pine-darkened grounds and ran quickly up the front steps. He fancied, but could not be sure, that there were fresh signs of dilapidation in the steps; and the house itself, when he approached it, had seemed to lean a little aslant, as if from some ruinous settling of the foundations: but this, he told himself, was an illusion wrought by the gathering twilight.

No lamps had been lit, but Sebastian was not unduly surprised by this, for he knew that Timmers, left to his own devices, was prone to dodder about in the gloom like a senescent owl, long after the proper time of lamplighting. Sebastian, on the other hand, had always been averse to darkness or even deep shadow; and of late the aversion had increased upon him. Invariably he turned on all the bulbs in the house as soon as the daylight began to fail. Now, muttering his irritation at Timmers' remissness, he pushed open the door and reached hurriedly for the hall-switch.

Because, perhaps, of a nervous agitation which he would not own to himself, he fumbled for several moments without finding the knob. The hall was strangely dark, and a glimmering from the ashen sunset, sifted between tall pines into the doorway behind him, was seemingly powerless to penetrate beyond its threshold. He could see nothing; it was as if the night of dead ages, creeping forth from hidden sepulchers, had laired in that hallway; and his nostrils, while he stood groping, were assailed by a dry pungency as of ancient dust, an odor as of corpses and coffins long indistinguishable in powdery decay.

At last he found the switch; but the illumination that responded was somehow dim and insufficient, and he seemed to detect a shadowy flickering, as if the circuit were at fault. However, it reassured him to see that the house, to all appearance, was very much as he had left it. Perhaps, unconsciously, he had feared to find the oaken panels crumbling away in riddled rottenness, the carpet falling into moth-eaten tatters; had apprehended the breaking through of rotted boards beneath his tread.

Where, he wondered now, was Timmers? The aged factotum, in spite of his growing senility, had always been quick to appear; and even if he had not heard his master enter, the switching on of the lights would have signalized Sebastian's return to him. But, though Sebastian listened with painful intentness, there was no creaking of the familiar tottery footsteps. Silence hung everywhere, like a funereal, unstirred arras.

No doubt, Sebastian thought, there was some commonplace explanation. Timmers had gone to the nearby village, perhaps to restock the larder, or in hope of receiving a letter from his master; and Sebastian had missed him on the way home from the station. Or perhaps the old man had fallen ill and was now lying helpless in his room. Filled with this latter thought, he went straight to Timmers' bedchamber, which was on the ground floor, at the back of the mansion. It was empty, and the bed was neatly made and had obviously not been occupied since the night before. With a suspiration of relief that seemed to lift a horrid incubus from his bosom, he decided that his first conjecture had been correct.

Now, pending the return of Timmers, he nerved himself to another act of inspection, and went forthwith into his study. He would not admit to himself precisely what it was that he had feared to see; but at first glance, the room was unchanged, and all things were as they had been at the time of his flurried departure. The confused and high-piled litter of manuscripts, volumes, notebooks on his writing-table had seemingly lain untouched by anything but his own hand; and his bookshelves, with their bizarre and terrific array of authorities on diabolism, necromancy, goety, on all the ridiculed or outlawed sciences, were undisturbed and intact. On the old lectern or reading-stand which he used for his heavier tomes, *The Testaments of Carnamagos*, in its covers of shagreen with hasps of human bone, lay open at the very page which had frightened him so unreasonably with its eldritch intimations.

Then, as he stepped forward between the reading-stand and the table, he perceived for the first time the inexplicable *dustiness* of everything. Dust lay everywhere: a fine grey dust like a powder of dead atoms. It had covered his manuscripts with a deep film, it had settled thickly upon the chairs, the lampshades, the volumes; and the rich poppylike reds and yellows of the Oriental rugs were bedimmed by its accumulation. It was as if many desolate years had passed through the chamber since his own departure, and had shaken from their shroud-like garments the dust of all ruined things. The mystery of it chilled Sebastian: for he knew that the room had been clean-swept only three days previous; and Timmers would have dusted the place each morning with meticulous care during his absence.

Now the dust rose up in a light, swirling cloud about him, it filled his nostrils with the same dry odor, as of fantastically ancient dissolution, that had met him in the hall. At the same moment he grew aware of a cold, gusty draft that had somehow entered the room. He thought that one of the windows must have been left open, but a glance assured him that they were shut, with tightly drawn blinds; and the door was closed behind him. The draft was light as the sighing of a phantom, but wherever it passed, the fine, weightless powder soared aloft, filling the air and settling again with utmost slowness. Sebastian felt a weird alarm, as if a wind had blown upon him from chartless dimensions, or through some hidden rift of ruin; and simultaneously he was seized by a paroxysm of prolonged and violent coughing.

He could not locate the source of the draft. But, as he moved restlessly about, his eye was caught by a low long mound of the grey dust, which had heretofore been hidden from view by the table. It lay beside the chair in which he usually sat while writing. Near the heap was the feather-duster used by Timmers in his daily round of housecleaning.

It seemed to Sebastian that the rigor of a great, lethal coldness had invaded all his being. He could not stir for several minutes, but stood peering down at the inexplicable mound. In the center of that mound he saw a vague depression, which might have been the mark of a very small footprint half erased by the gusts of air that had evidently taken much of the dust and scattered it about the chamber.

At last the power of motion returned to Sebastian. Without conscious recognition of the impulse that prompted him, he bent forward to pick up the feather-duster. But, even as his fingers touched it, the handle and the feathers crumbled into fine powder which, settling in a low pile, preserved vaguely the outlines of the original object!

A weakness came upon Sebastian, as if the burden of utter age and mortality had gathered crushingly on his shoulders between one instant and the next. There was a whirling of vertiginous shadows before his eyes in the lamplight, and he felt that he should swoon unless he sat down immediately. He put out his hand to reach the chair beside him—and the chair, at his touch, fell instantly into light, downward-sifting clouds of dust.

Afterwards—how long afterwards he could not tell—he found himself sitting in the high chair before the lectern on which *The Testaments of Carnamagos* lay open. Dimly he was surprised that the seat had not crumbled beneath him. Upon him, as once before, there was the urgency of swift, sudden flight from that accursed house: but it seemed that he had grown too old, too weary and feeble; and that nothing mattered greatly—not even the grisly doom which he apprehended.

Now, as he sat there in a state half terror, half stupor, his eyes were drawn to the wizard volume before him: the writings of that evil sage and seer, Carnamagos, which had been recovered a thousand years agone from some Graeco-Bactrian tomb, and transcribed by an apostate monk in the original Greek, in the blood of an incubus-begotten monster. In that volume were the chronicles of great sorcerers of old, and the histories of demons earthly and ultra-cosmic, and the veritable spells by which the demons could be called up and controlled and dismissed. Sebastian, a profound student of such lore, had long believed that the book was a mere medieval legend; and he had been startled as well as gratified when he found this copy on the shelves of a dealer in old manuscripts and incunabula. It was said that only two copies had ever existed, and that the other had been destroyed by the Spanish Inquisition early in the thirteenth century.

The light flickered as if ominous wings had flown across it; and Sebastian's eyes blurred with a gathering rheum as he read again that sinister, fatal passage which had served to provoke his shadowy fears:

"Though Quachil Uttaus cometh but rarely, it hath been well attested that his advent is not always in response to the spoken rune and the drawn pentacle.... Few wizards, indeed, would call upon a spirit so baleful.... But let it be understood that he who readeth to himself, in the silence of his chamber, the formula given hereunder, must incur a grave risk if in his heart there abide openly or hidden the least desire of death and annihilation. For it may be that Quachil Uttaus will come to him, bringing that doom which toucheth the body to eternal dust, and maketh the soul as a vapor forevermore dissolved. And the advent of Quachil Uttaus is foreknowable by certain tokens: for in the person of the evocator, and even perchance in those about him, will appear the signs of sudden age; and his house, and those belongings which he hath touched, will assume the marks of untimely decay and antiquity...."

Sebastian did not know that he was mumbling the sentences half aloud as he read them; that he was also mumbling the terrible incantation that followed.... His thoughts crawled as if through a chill and freezing medium. With a dull, ghastly certainty, he knew that Timmers had not gone to the village. He should have warned Timmers before leaving; he should have closed and locked *The Testaments of Carnamagos*... for Timmers, in his way, was something of a scholar and was not without curiosity concerning the occult studies of his master. Timmers was well able to read the Greek of Carnamagos... even that dire and soul-blasting formula to which Quachil Uttaus, demon of ultimate corruption, would respond from the outer void.... Too well Sebastian divined the origin of the grey dust, the reason of those mysterious crumblings....

Again he felt the impulse of flight: but his body was a dry dead incubus that refused to obey his volition. Anyway, he reflected, it was too late now, for the signs of doom had gathered about him and upon him.... Yet surely there had never been in his heart the least longing for death and destruction. He had wished only to pursue his delvings into the blacker mysteries that environed the mortal estate. And he had always been cautious, had never cared to meddle with magic circles and evocations of perilous presences. He had known that there were spirits of evil, spirits of wrath, perdition, annihilation: but never, of his own will, should he have summoned any of them from their night-bound abysms....

His lethargy and weakness seemed to increase: it was as if whole lustrums, whole decades of senescence had fallen upon him in the drawing of a breath. The thread of his thoughts was broken at intervals, and he recovered it with difficulty. His memories, even his fears, seemed to totter on the edge of some final forgetfulness. With dulled ears he heard a sound as of timbers breaking and falling somewhere in the house; with dimmed eyes like those of an ancient he saw the lights waver and go out beneath the swooping of a bat-black darkness.

It was as if the night of some crumbling catacomb had closed upon him. He felt at whiles the chill faint breathing of the draft that had troubled him before with its mystery; and again the dust rose up in his nostrils. Then he realized that the room was not wholly dark, for he could discern the dim outlines of the lectern before him. Surely no ray was admitted by the drawn window-blinds: yet somehow there was light. His eyes, lifting with enormous effort, saw for the first time that a rough, irregular gap had appeared in the room's outer wall, high up in the north corner. How long it had been there he could not know. Through it, a single star shone into the chamber, cold and remote as the eye of a demon glaring across intercosmic gulfs.

Out of that star—or from the spaces beyond it—a sudden beam of livid radiance, wan and deathly, was hurled like a spear upon Sebastian. Broad as a plank, unwavering, immovable, it seemed to transfix his very body and to form a bridge between himself and the worlds of unimagined darkness.

He was as one petrified by the gaze of the Gorgon. Then, through the aperture of ruin, there came something that glided stiffly and rapidly into the room toward him, along the beam. The wall seemed to crumble, the rift widened as it entered.

It was a figure no larger than a young child, but sere and shrivelled as some millennial mummy. Its hairless head, its unfeatured face, borne on a neck of skeleton thinness, were lined by a thousand reticulated wrinkles. The body was like that of some monstrous, withered abortion that had never drawn breath. The pipy arms, ending in bony claws, were outthrust as if ankylosed in the posture of an eternal dreadful groping. The legs, with feet like those of a pigmy Death, were drawn tightly together as though confined by the swathings of the tomb; nor was there any movement of striding or pacing. Upright and rigid, the horror floated swiftly down the wan, deathly grey beam toward Sebastian.

Now it was close upon him, its head level with his brow and its feet opposite his bosom. For a fleeting moment he knew that the horror had touched him with its outflung hands, with its starkly floating feet. It seemed to merge within him, to become one with his being. He felt that his veins were choked with dust, that his brain was crumbling cell by cell. Then he was no longer John Sebastian, but a universe of dead stars and worlds that fell eddying into darkness before the tremendous blowing of some ultrastellar wind....

The thing that immemorial wizards had named Quachil Uttaus was gone; and night and starlight had returned to that ruinous chamber. But nowhere was there any shadow of John Sebastian: only a low mound of dust on the floor beside the lecturn, bearing a vague depression like the imprint of a small foot... or of two feet that were pressed closely together....

THE BLACK ABBOT OF PUTHUUM

Let the grape yield for us its purple flame,
And rosy love put off its maidenhood:
By blackening moons, in lands without a name,
We slew the Incubus and all his brood.
                    —*Song of King Hoaraph's Bowmen*

Zobal the archer and Cushara the pike-bearer had poured many a libation to their friendship in the sanguine liquors of Yoros and the blood of the kingdom's enemies. In that long and lusty amity, broken only by such passing quarrels as concerned the division of a wineskin or the apportioning of a wench, they had served amid the soldiery of King Hoaraph for a strenuous decade. Savage warfare and wild, fantastic hazard had been their lot. The renown of their valor had drawn upon them, ultimately, the honor of Hoaraph's attention, and he had assigned them for duty among the picked warriors that guarded his palace in Faraad. And sometimes the twain were sent together on such missions as required no common hardihood and no disputable fealty to the king.

Now, in company with the eunuch Simban, chief purveyor to Hoaraph's well-replenished harem, Zobal and Cushara had gone on a tedious journey through the tract known as Izdrel, which clove the western part of Yoros asunder with its rusty-colored wedge of desolation. The king had sent them to learn if haply there abode any verity in certain travellers' tales, which concerned a young maiden of celestial beauty who had been seen among the pastoral peoples beyond Izdrel. Simban bore at his girdle a bag of gold coins with which, if the girl's pulchritude should be in any wise commensurate with the renown thereof, he was empowered to bargain for her purchase. The king had deemed that Zobal and Cushara should form an escort equal to all contingencies: for Izdrel was a land reputedly free of robbers, or, indeed, of any human inhabitants. Men said, however, that malign goblins, tall as giants and humped like camels, had oftentimes beset the wayfarers through Izdrel; that fair but ill-meaning lamiæ had lured them to an eldritch death. Simban, quaking corpulently in his saddle, rode with small willingness on that outward journey; but the archer and the pike-bearer, full of wholesome

145

skepticism, divided their bawdy jests equally between the timid eunuch and the elusive demons.

Without other mishap than the rupturing of a wineskin from the force of the new vintage it contained, they came to the verdurous pasture-lands beyond that dreary desert. Here, in low valleys that held the middle meanderings of the river Vos, cattle and dromedaries were kept by a tribe of herders who sent biannual tribute to Hoaraph from their teeming droves. Simban and his companions found the girl, who dwelt with her grandmother in a village beside the Vos; and even the eunuch acknowledged that their journey was well rewarded.

Cushara and Zobal, on their part, were instantly smitten by the charms of the maiden, whose name was Rubalsa. She was slender and of queenly height, and her skin was pale as the petals of white poppies; and the undulant blackness of her heavy hair was full of sullen copper gleamings beneath the sun. While Simban haggled shrilly with the crone-like grandmother, the warriors eyed Rubalsa with circumspect ardor and addressed to her such gallantries as they deemed discreet within hearing of the eunuch.

At last the bargain was driven and the price paid, to the sore depletion of Simban's money-bag. Simban was now eager to return to Faraad with his prize, and he seemed to have forgotten his fear of the haunted desert. Zobal and Cushara were routed from their dreams by the impatient eunuch before dawn; and the three departed with the still drowsy Rubalsa ere the village could awaken about them.

Noon, with its sun of candent copper in a blackish-blue zenith, found them far amid the rusty sands and iron-toothed ridges of Izdrel. The route they followed was little more than a footpath: for, though Izdrel was but thirty miles in width at that point, few travellers would dare those fiend-infested leagues; and most preferred an immensely circuitous road, used by the herders, that ran to the southward of that evil desolation, following the Vos nearly to its debouchment in the Indaskian Sea.

Cushara, splendid in his plate-armor of bronze, on a huge piebald mare with a cataphract of leather scaled with copper, led the cavalcade. Rubalsa, who wore the red homespun of the herders' women, followed on a black gelding with silk and silver harness, which Hoaraph had sent for her use. Close behind her came the watchful eunuch, gorgeous in particolored sendal, and mounted ponderously, with swollen saddle-bags all about him, on the grey ass of uncertain age which, through his fear of horses and camels, he insisted on riding at all times. In his hand he held the leading-rope of another ass which was nearly crushed to the ground by the wineskins, water-jugs and other provisions. Zobal guarded the rear, with unslung bow, slim and wiry in his suiting of light chain-mail, on a nervous red stallion that chafed incessantly at the rein. At his back he bore a quiver filled with arrows which the court-sorcerer, Amdok, had prepared with singular spells and dippings in doubtful fluids, for his possible use against demons. Zobal had accepted the arrows courteously but had satisfied himself later that their iron barbs were in no wise impaired by Amdok's treatment. A similarly ensorcelled pike had been offered by Amdok to Cushara, who had refused it bluffly, saying that his own well-tried weapon was equal to the spitting of any number of devils.

Because of Simban and the two asses, the party could make little speed. However, they hoped to cross the wilder and more desolate portion of Izdrel ere night. Simban, though he still eyed the dismal waste dubiously, was plainly more concerned with his precious charge than with the imagined imps and lamiæ. And Cushara and Zobal, both rapt in amorous reveries that centered about the luscious Rubalsa, gave only a perfunctory attention to their surroundings.

The girl had ridden all morning in demure silence. Now, suddenly, she cried out in a voice whose sweetness was made shrill by alarm. The others reined their mounts, and Simban babbled questions. To these Rubalsa replied by pointing toward the southern horizon, where, as her companions now saw, a peculiar pitch-black darkness had covered a great portion of the sky and hills, obliterating them wholly. This darkness, which seemed due neither to cloud nor sandstorm, extended itself in a crescent on either hand, and came swiftly toward the travellers. In the course of a minute or less, it had blotted the pathway before and behind them like a black mist; and the two arcs of shadow, racing northward, had flowed together, immuring the party in a circle. The darkness then became stationary, its walls no more than a hundred feet away on every side. Sheer, impenetrable, it surrounded the wayfarers, leaving above them a clear space from which the sun still glared down, remote and small and discolored, as if seen from the bottom of a deep pit.

"Ai! ai! ai!" howled Simban, cowering amid his saddle-bags. "I knew well that some devilry would overtake us."

At the same moment the two asses began to bray loudly, and the horses, with a frantic neighing and squealing, trembled beneath their riders. Only with much cruel spurring could Zobal force his stallion forward beside Cushara's mare.

"Mayhap it is only some pestilential mist," said Cushara.

"Never have I seen such mist," replied Zobal doubtfully. "And there are no vapors to be met with in Izdrel. Methinks it is like the smoke of the seven hells that men fable beneath Zothique."

"Shall we ride forward?" said Cushara. "I would learn whether or not a pike can penetrate that darkness."

Calling out some words of reassurance to Rubalsa, the twain sought to spur their mounts toward the murky wall. But, after a few swerving paces, the mare and the stallion balked wildly, sweating and snorting, and would go no farther. Cushara and Zobal dismounted and continued their advance on foot.

Not knowing the source or nature of the phenomenon with which they had to deal, the two approached it warily. Zobal nocked an arrow to his string, and Cushara held the great bronze-headed pike before him as if charging an embattled foe. Both were more and more puzzled by the murkiness, which did not recede before them in the fashion of fog, but maintained its opacity when they were close upon it.

Cushara was about to thrust his weapon into the wall. Then, without the least prelude, there arose in the darkness, seemingly just before him, a horrible multitudinous clamor as of drums, trumpets, cymbals, jangling armor, jarring voices, and mailed feet that tramped to and fro on the stony ground with a mighty clangor. As Cushara and Zobal drew back in amazement, the clamor swelled and spread, till it filled with a babel of warlike noises the whole circle of mysterious night that hemmed in the travellers.

"Verily, we are sore beset," shouted Cushara to his comrade as they went back to their horses. "It would seem that some king of the north has sent his myrmidons into Yoros."

"Yea," said Zobal…. "But it is strange that we saw them not ere the darkness came. And the darkness, surely, is no natural thing."

Before Cushara could make any rejoinder, the martial clashings and shoutings ceased abruptly. All about it seemed that there was a rattling of innumerable sistra, a hissing of countless huge serpents, a raucous hooting of ill-omened birds that had foregathered by thousands. To these indescribably hideous sounds, the horses now added a continual screaming, and the asses a more frenzied braying, above which the outcries of Rubalsa and Simban were scarce audible.

Cushara and Zobal sought vainly to pacify their mounts and comfort the madly frightened girl. It was plain that no army of mortal men had beleaguered them: for the noises still changed from instant to instant, and they heard a most evil howling, and a roaring as of hell-born beasts that deafened them with its volume.

Naught, however, was visible in the gloom, whose circle now began to move swiftly, without widening or contracting. To maintain their position in its center, the warriors and their charges were compelled to leave the path and to flee northwardly amid the harsh ridges and hollows. All around them the baleful noises continued, keeping, as it seemed, the same interval of distance.

The sun, slanting westward, no longer shone into that eerily moving pit, and a deep twilight enveloped the wanderers. Zobal and Cushara rode as closely beside Rubalsa as the rough ground permitted, straining their eyes constantly for any visible sign of the cohorts that seemed to encompass them. Both were filled with the darkest misgivings, for it had become all too manifest that supernatural powers were driving them astray in the untracked desert.

Moment by moment the gross darkness seemed to close in; and there was a palpable eddying and seething as of monstrous forms behind its curtain. The horses stumbled over boulders and out-croppings of ore-sharp stone, and the grievously burdened asses were compelled to put forth an unheard-of speed to keep pace with the ever-shifting circle that menaced them with its horrid clamor. Rubalsa had ceased her outcries, as if overcome by exhaustion or resignation to the horror of her plight; and the shrill screeches of the eunuch had subsided into a fearful wheezing and gasping.

Ever and anon, it seemed that great fiery eyes glared out of the gloom, floating close to earth or moving aloft at a gigantic height. Zobal began to shoot his enchanted arrows at these appearances, and the speeding of each bolt was hailed by an appalling outburst of Satanic laughters and ululations.

In such wise they went on, losing all measure of time and sense of orientation. The animals were galled and footsore. Simban was nigh dead from fright and fatigue; Rubalsa drooped in her saddle; and the warriors, awed and baffled by the predicament in which their weapons appeared useless, began to flag with a dull weariness.

"Never again shall I doubt the legendry of Izdrel," said Cushara gloomily.

"It is in my mind that we have not long either to doubt or believe," rejoined Zobal.

To add to their distress, the terrain grew rougher and steeper, and they climbed acclivitous hillsides and went down endlessly into drear valleys. Anon they came to a flat, open, pebbly space. There, all at once, it seemed that the pandemonium of evil noises drew back on every hand, receding and fading into faint, dubious whispers that died at a vast remove. Simultaneously, the circling night thinned out, and a few stars shone in the welkin, and the sharp-spined hills of the desert loomed starkly against a vermilion afterglow. The travellers paused and peered wonderingly at each other in a gloom that was no more than that of natural twilight.

"What new devilry is this?" asked Cushara, hardly daring to believe that the hellish leaguers had vanished.

"I know not," said the archer, who was staring into the dusk. "But here, mayhap, is one of the devils."

The others now saw that a muffled figure was approaching them, bearing a lit lantern made of some kind of translucent horn. At some distance behind the figure, lights appeared suddenly in a square dark mass which none of the party had discerned before. This mass was evidently a large building with many windows.

The figure, drawing near, was revealed by the dim yellowish lantern as a black man of immense girth and tallness, garbed in a voluminous robe of saffron such as was worn by certain monkish orders, and crowned with the two-horned purple hat of an abbot. He was indeed a singular and unlooked-for apparition: for if any monasteries existed amid the barren reaches of

Izdrel, they were hidden and unknown to the world. Zobal, however, searching his memory, recalled a vague tradition he had once heard concerning a chapter of negro monks who had flourished in Yoros many centuries ago. The chapter had long been extinct, and the very site of its monastery was forgotten. Nowadays there were few blacks anywhere in the kingdom, other than those who did duty as eunuchs guarding the seraglios of nobles and rich merchants.

The animals began to display a certain uneasiness at the stranger's approach.

"Who art thou?" challenged Cushara, his fingers tightening on the haft of his weapon.

The black man grinned capaciously, showing great rows of discolored teeth whose incisors were like those of a wild dog. His enormous unctuous jowls were creased by the grin into folds of amazing number and volume; and his eyes, deeply slanted and close together, seemed to wink perpetually in pouches that shook like ebon jellies. His nostrils flared prodigiously; his purple, blubbery lips drooled and quivered, and he licked them with a fat, red, salacious tongue before replying to Cushara's question.

"I am Ujuk, abbot of the monastery of Puthuum," he said, in a thick voice of such extraordinary volume that it appeared almost to issue from the earth under his feet. "Methinks the night has overtaken you far from the route of travellers. I bid you welcome to our hospitality."

"Aye, the night took us betimes," Cushara returned dryly. Neither he nor Zobal was reassured by the look of lust in the abbot's obscenely twinkling eyes as he peered at Rubalsa. Moreover, they had now noted the excessive and disagreeable length of the dark nails on his huge hands and bare, splayed feet: nails that were curving, three-inch talons, sharp as those of some beast or bird of prey.

It seemed, however, that Rubalsa and Simban were less abhorrently impressed, or had not noticed these details: for both made haste to acknowledge the abbot's proffer of hospitality and to urge acceptance upon the visibly reluctant warriors. To this urging, Zobal and Cushara yielded, both inwardly resolving to keep a close watch on all the actions and movements of the abbot of Puthuum.

Ujuk, holding the horn lantern aloft, conducted the travellers to that massive building whose lights they had discerned at no great distance. A ponderous gate of dark wood swung open silently at their approach, and they entered a spacious courtyard cobbled with worn, greasy-looking stones, and dimly illumined by torches in rusty iron sockets. Several monks appeared with startling suddenness before the travellers, who had thought the courtyard vacant at first glance. They were all of unusual bulk and stature, and their features possessed an extraordinary likeness to those of Ujuk, from whom, indeed, they could hardly have been distinguished save by the yellow cowls which they wore in lieu of the abbot's horned purple hat. The similarity extended even to their curved and talon-like nails of inordinate length. Their movements were phantasmally furtive and silent. Without speaking, they took charge of the horses and asses. Cushara and Zobal relinquished their mounts to the care of these doubtful hostlers with a reluctance which, apparently, was not shared by Rubalsa or the eunuch.

The monks also signified a willingness to relieve Cushara of his heavy pike and Zobal of his ironwood bow and half-emptied quiver of ensorcelled arrows. But at this the warriors balked, refusing to let the weapons pass from their possession.

Ujuk led them to an inner portal which gave admission to the refectory. It was a large, low room, lit by brazen lamps of antique workmanship, such as ghouls might have recovered from a desert-sunken tomb. The abbot, with ogre-like grinnings, besought his guests to take their place at a long massive table of ebony with chairs and benches of the same material.

When they had seated themselves, Ujuk sat down at the table's head. Immediately, four monks came in, bearing platters piled with spicily smoking viands, and deep earthen flagons full of a dark amber-brown liquor. And these monks, like those encountered in the courtyard, were gross ebon-black simulacra of their abbot, resembling him precisely in every feature and member. Zobal and Cushara were chary of tasting the liquor, which, from its odor, appeared to be an exceptionally potent kind of ale: for their doubts concerning Ujuk and his monastery grew graver every moment. Also, in spite of their hunger, they refrained from the food set before them, which consisted mainly of baked meats that neither could identify. Simban and Rubalsa, however, addressed themselves promptly to the meal with appetites sharpened by long fasting and the weird fatigues of the day.

The warriors observed that neither food nor drink had been placed before Ujuk, and they conjectured that he had already dined. To their growing disgust and anger, he sat lolling obesely, with lustful eyes upon Rubalsa in a stare broken only by the nictations that accompanied his perpetual grinning. This stare soon began to abash the girl, and then to alarm and frighten her. She ceased eating; and Simban, who had been deeply preoccupied till then with his supper, was plainly perturbed when he saw the flagging of her appetite. He seemed for the first time to notice the abbot's unmonastic leering, and showed his disapproval by sundry horrible grimaces. He also remarked pointedly, in a loud, piercing voice, that the girl was destined for the harem of King Hoaraph. But at this, Ujuk merely chuckled, as if Simban had uttered some exquisitely humorous jest.

Zobal and Cushara were hard put to repress their wrath, and both itched hotly for the fleshing of their weapons in the abbot's gross bulk. He, however, seemed to have taken Simban's hint, for he shifted his gaze from the girl. Instead, he began to eye the warriors with a curious and loathsome avidity, which they found little less insupportable than his ogling of Rubalsa. The well-nourished eunuch also came in for his share of Ujuk's regard, which seemed to have in it the hunger of a hyena gloating over his prospective prey.

Simban, obviously ill at ease, and somewhat frightened, now tried to carry on a conversation with the abbot, volunteering much information as to himself, his companions, and the adventures which had brought them to Puthuum. Ujuk seemed little surprised by this information; and Zobal and Cushara, who took no part in the conversation, became surer than ever that he was no true abbot.

"How far have we gone astray from the route to Faraad?" asked Simban.

"I do not consider that you have gone astray," rumbled Ujuk in his subterranean voice, "for your coming to Puthuum is most timely. We have few guests here, and we are loath to part with those who honor our hospitality."

"King Hoaraph will be impatient for our return with the girl," Simban quavered. "We must depart early tomorrow."

"Tomorrow is another matter," said Ujuk, in a tone half unctuous, half sinister. "Perhaps, by then, you will have forgotten this deplorable haste."

Little was said during the rest of the meal; and, indeed, little was drunk or eaten; for even Simban seemed to have lost his normally voracious appetite. Ujuk, still grinning as if at some uproarious jest known only to himself, was apparently not concerned with the urging of food upon his guests.

Certain of the monks came and went unbidden, removing the laden dishes, and as they departed, Zobal and Cushara perceived a strange thing: for no shadows were cast by the monks on the lamplit floor beside the moving adumbrations of the vessels they carried! From Ujuk, however, a heavy, misshapen umbrage fell and lay like a prone incubus beside his chair.

"Methinks we have come to a hatching-place of demons," whispered Zobal to Cushara. "We have fought many men, thou and I, but never such as wanted wholesome shadows."

"Aye," muttered the pike-bearer.... "But I like this abbot even less than his monks: though he alone is the caster of a shade."

Ujuk now rose from his seat, saying: "I trow that ye are all weary and would sleep betimes."

Rubalsa and Simban, who had both drunk a certain amount of the powerful ale of Puthuum, nodded a drowsy assent. Zobal and Cushara, noting their premature sleepiness, were glad they had declined the liquor.

The abbot led his guests along a corridor whose gloom was but little relieved by the flaring of torches in a strong draft that blew stealthily from an undetermined source, causing a rout of wild shadows to flitter beside the passers. On either hand there were cells with portals shut only by hangings of a coarse hempen fabric. The monks had all vanished, the cells were seemingly dark, and an air of age-old desolation pervaded the monastery, together with a smell as of mouldering bones piled in some secret catacomb.

Midway in the hall, Ujuk paused and held aside the arras of a doorway that differed in no wise from the rest. Within, a lamp burned, depending from an archaic chain of curiously linked and fretted metal. The room was bare but spacious, and a bed of ebony with opulent quiltings of an olden fashion stood by the farther wall under an open window. This chamber, the abbot indicated, was for the occupancy of Rubalsa; and he then offered to show the men and the eunuch their respective quarters.

Simban, seeming to wake all at once from his drowsiness, protested at the idea of being separated in such wise from his charge. As if Ujuk had been prepared for this, and had given orders accordingly, a monk appeared forthwith, bringing quilts which he laid on the flagged floor within the portals of Rubalsa's room. Simban stretched himself promptly on the improvised bed, and the warriors withdrew with Ujuk.

"Come," said the abbot, his wolfish teeth gleaming in the torchlight. "Ye will sleep soundly in the beds I have prepared."

Zobal and Cushara, however, had now assumed the position of guardsmen outside the doorway of Rubalsa's chamber. They told Ujuk curtly that they were responsible to King Hoaraph for the girl's safety and must watch over her at all times.

"I wish ye a pleasant vigil," said Ujuk, with a cachinnation like the laughter of hyenas in some underground tomb.

With his departure, it seemed that the black slumber of a dead antiquity settled upon all the building. Rubalsa and Simban, apparently, slept without stirring, for there was no sound from behind the hempen arras. The warriors spoke only in whispers, lest they should arouse the girl. Their weapons held ready for instant use, they watched the shadowy hall with a jealous vigilance: for they did not trust the quietude about them, being well assured that a host of foul cacodemons couched somewhere behind it, biding the time of assault.

Howbeit, nothing occurred to reconfirm them in such apprehensions. The draft that breathed furtively along the hall seemed to tell only of age-forgotten death and cyclic solitude. The two began to perceive signs of dilapidation in walls and floor that had heretofore escaped their notice. Eerie, phantastical thoughts came to them with insidious persuasion: it seemed that the building was a ruin that had lain uninhabited for a thousand years; that the black abbot Ujuk and his shadowless monks were mere imaginations, things that had never been; that the moving circle of darkness, the pandemonian voices, that had herded them toward Puthuum, were no more than a daymare whose memory was now fading in the fashion of dreams.

Thirst and hunger troubled them, for they had not eaten since early morn, and had snatched only a few hasty drafts of wine or water during the day. Both, however, began to feel the oncreeping of a sleepy hebetude which, under the circumstances, was most undesirable. They nodded, started and awoke recurrently to their peril. But still, like a siren voice in poppy-dreams, the silence seemed to tell them that all danger was a bygone thing, an illusion that belonged to yesterday.

Several hours passed, and the hall lightened with the rising of a late moon that shone through a window at its eastern end. Zobal, less bedrowsed than Cushara, was awakened to full awareness by a sudden commotion among the animals in the courtyard without. There were loud neighings that rose to a frenzied pitch, as if something had frightened the horses; and to these the asses began to add their heavy braying, till Cushara was also aroused.

"Make sure that thou drowsest not again," Zobal admonished the pike-bearer. "I shall go forth and inquire as to the cause of this tumult."

"'Tis a good thought," commended Cushara. "And while thou art gone, see to it that none has molested our provisions. And bring back with thee some apricots and cakes of sesame and a skin of ruby-red wine."

The monastery itself remained silent as Zobal went down the hall, his buskins of link-covered leather ringing faintly. At the hall's end an outer door stood open, and he passed through it into the courtyard. Even as he emerged, the animals ceased their clamor. He could see but dimly, for all the torches in the courtyard, save one, had burnt out or been extinguished; and the low gibbous moon had not yet climbed the wall. Nothing, to all appearance, was amiss: the two asses were standing quietly beside the mountainous piles of provisions and saddle-bags they had borne; the horses seemed to drowse amicably in a group. Zobal decided that perhaps there had been some temporary bickering between his stallion and Cushara's mare.

He went forward to make sure that there was no other cause of disturbance. Afterwards he turned to the wineskins, intending to refresh himself before rejoining Cushara with a supply of drinkables and comestibles. Hardly had he washed the dust of Izdrel from his throat with a long draught, when he heard an eerie, dry whispering whose source and distance he could not at once determine. Sometimes it seemed at his very ear, and then it ebbed away as if sinking into profound subterranean vaults. But the sound, though variable in this manner, never ceased entirely; and it seemed to shape itself into words that the listener almost understood: words that were fraught with the hopeless sorrow of a dead man who had sinned long ago, and had repented his sin through black sepulchral ages.

As he harkened to the sere anguish of that sound, the hair bristled on the archer's neck, and he knew such fear as he had never known in the thick of battle. And yet, at the same time, he was aware of deeper pity than the pain of dying comrades had ever aroused in his heart. And it seemed that the voice implored him for commiseration and succor, laying upon him a weird compulsion that he dared not disobey. He could not wholly comprehend the things that the whisperer besought him to do: but somehow he must ease that desolate anguish.

Still the whispering rose and fell; and Zobal forgot that he had left Cushara to a lone vigil beset with hellish dangers; forgot that the voice itself might well be only a device of demons to lure him astray. He began to search the courtyard, his keen ears alert for the source of the sound; and, after some dubitation, he decided that it issued from the ground in a corner opposite the gateway. Here, amid the cobbling, in the walls' angle, he found a large slab of syenite with a rusty metal ring in its center. He was quickly confirmed in his decision: for the whispering became louder and more articulate, and he thought that it said to him: "Lift the slab."

The archer grasped the rusty ring with both hands, and putting forth all his strength, he succeeded in tilting back the stone, albeit not without such exertion as made him feel that his very spine would crack. A dark opening was exposed, and from it surged a charnel stench so overpowering that Zobal turned his face away and was like to have vomited. But the whisper came with a sharp, woeful beseeching, out of the darkness below; and it said to him: "Descend."

Zobal wrenched from its socket the one torch that still burned in the courtyard. By its lurid flaring he saw a flight of worn steps that went down into the reeking sepulchral gloom; and resolutely he descended the steps, finding himself at their bottom in a hewn vault with deep shelves of stone on either hand. The shelves, running away into darkness, were piled with human bones and mummified bodies; and plainly the place was the catacomb of the monastery.

The whispering had ceased, and Zobal peered about him in bewilderment not unmixed with horror.

"I am here," resumed the dry, susurrous voice, issuing from amid the heaps of mortal remnants on the shelf close beside him. Startled, and feeling again that crisping of the hairs on his neck, Zobal held his torch to the low shelf as he looked for the speaker. In a narrow niche between stacks of disarticulated bones, he beheld a half-decayed corpse about whose long, attenuate limbs and hollow body there clung a few rotten shreds of yellow cloth. These, he thought, were the remnants of a robe such as was worn by the monks of Puthuum. Then, thrusting his torch into the niche, he discerned the lean, mummy-like head, on which mouldered a thing that had once been the horned hat of an abbot. The corpse was black as ebony, and plainly it was that of a great negro. It bore an aspect of incredible age, as if it had lain there for centuries: but from it came the odor of newly ripe corruption that had sickened Zobal when he lifted the slab of syenite.

As he stood staring down, it seemed to Zobal that the cadaver stirred a little, as if fain to rise from its recumbent posture; and he saw a gleaming as of eyeballs in the deep-shadowed sockets; and the dolorously curling lips were retracted still farther; and from between the bared teeth there issued that awful whispering which had drawn him into the catacomb.

"Listen closely," said the whispering. "There is much for me to tell thee, and much for thee to do when the telling is done.

"I am Uldor, the abbot of Puthuum. More than a thousand years ago I came with my monks to Yoros from Ilcar, the black empire of the north. The emperor of Ilcar had driven us forth, for our cult of celibacy, our worship of the maiden goddess Ojhal, were hateful to him. Here amid the desert of Izdrel we built our monastery and dwelt unmolested.

"We were many in number at first; but the years went by, and one by one the Brothers were laid in the catacomb we had delved for our resting-place. They died with none to replace them. I alone survived in the end: for I had won such sanctity as ensures longeval days, and had also become a master of the arts of sorcery. Time was a demon that I held at bay, like one who stands in a charmed circle. My powers were still hale and unimpaired; and I lived on as an anchorite in the monastery.

"At first the solitude was far from irksome to me, and I was wholly absorbed in my study of the arcana of nature. But after a time it seemed that such things no longer sufficed. I grew aware of my loneliness, and was much beset by the demons of the waste, who had troubled me little heretofore. Succubi, fair but baneful, lamiæ with the round soft bodies of women, came to tempt me in the drear vigils of the night.

"I resisted…. But there was one she-devil, more cunning than the others, who crept into my cell in the semblance of a girl I had loved long ago, ere yet I had taken the vow of Ojhal. To her I succumbed; and of that unholy union was born the half-human fiend, Ujuk, who has since called himself the abbot of Puthuum.

"After that sin, I wished to die…. And the wish was manifoldly strengthened when I beheld the progeny of the sin. Too greatly, however, had I offended Ojhal; and a frightful penance was decreed for me. I lived… and daily I was plagued and persecuted by the monster, Ujuk, who grew lustily in the manner of such offspring. But when Ujuk had gained his full stature, there came upon me such weakness and decrepitude as made me hopeful of death. Scarce could I stir in my impotence, and Ujuk, taking advantage of this, bore me in his horrid arms to the catacomb and laid me among the dead. Here I have remained ever since, dying and rotting eternally—and yet eternally alive. For almost a millennium I have suffered unsleepingly the dire anguish of repentance that brings no expiation.

"Through the powers of saintly and sorcerous vision that never left me, I was doomed to watch the foul deeds, the hell-dark iniquities of Ujuk. Wearing the guise of an abbot, endowed with strange infernal powers together with a kind of immortality, he has presided over Puthuum through the centuries. His enchantments have kept the monastery hidden… save from those that he wishes to draw within reach of his ghoulish hunger, his incubus-like desires. Men he devours; and women are made to serve his lust…. And still

I am condemned to see his turpitudes; and the seeing is my most grievous punishment."

The whisper sank away; and Zobal, who had listened in eldritch awe, as one who hears the speech of a dead man, was doubtful for a moment that Uldor still lived. Then the sere voice went on:

"Archer, I crave a boon from thee; and I offer in return a thing that will aid thee against Ujuk. In thy quiver thou bearest charmed arrows: and the wizardry of him that wrought them was good. Such arrows can slay the else-immortal powers of evil. They can slay Ujuk—and even such evil as endures in me and forbids me to die. Archer, grant me an arrow through the heart: and if that suffice not, an arrow through the right eye, and one through the left. And leave the arrows in their mark, for I deem that thou canst well spare so many. One alone is needed for Ujuk. As to the monks thou hast seen, I will tell thee a secret. They are twelve in number, but...."

Zobal would scarcely have believed the thing that Uldor now unfolded, if the events of the day had not left him beyond all incredulity. The abbot continued:

"When I am wholly dead, take thou the talisman which depends about my neck. The talisman is a touchstone that will dissolve such ill enchantments as have a material seeming, if applied thereto with the hand."

For the first time, Zobal perceived the talisman, which was an oval of plain grey stone lying upon Uldor's withered bosom on a chain of black silver.

"Make haste, O archer," the whispering implored.

Zobal had socketed his torch in the pile of mouldering bones beside Uldor. With a sense of mingled compulsion and reluctance, he drew an arrow from his quiver, notched it, and aimed unflinchingly down at Uldor's heart. The shaft went straightly and deeply into its mark; and Zobal waited. But anon from the retracted lips of the black abbot there issued a faint murmuring: "Archer, another arrow!"

Again the bow was drawn, and a shaft sped unerringly into the hollow orbit of Uldor's right eye. And again, after an interval, there came the almost inaudible pleading: "Archer, still another shaft."

Once more the bow of ironwood sang in the silent vault, and an arrow stood in the left eye of Uldor, quivering with the force of its propulsion. This time there was no whisper from the rotting lips: but Zobal heard a curious rustling, and a sigh as of lapsing sand. Beneath his gaze the black limbs and body crumbled swiftly, the face and head fell in, and the three arrows sagged awry, since there was naught now but a pile of dust and parting bones to hold them embedded.

Leaving the arrows as Uldor had enjoined him to do, Zobal groped for the grey talisman that was now buried amid those fallen relics. Finding it, he hung it carefully at his belt beside the long straight sword which he carried. Perhaps, he reflected, the thing might have its use ere the night was over.

Quickly he turned away and climbed the steps to the courtyard. A saffron-yellow and lopsided moon was soaring above the wall, and he knew by this that he had been absent overlong from his vigil with Cushara. All, however, seemed tranquil: the drowsing animals had not stirred; and the monastery was dark and soundless. Seizing a full wineskin and a bag containing such edibles as Cushara had asked him to bring, Zobal hurried back to the open hall.

Even as he passed into the building, the arras-like silence before him was burst asunder by a frightful hubbub. He distinguished amid the clamor the screaming of Rubalsa, the screeching of Simban, and the furious roaring of Cushara: but above these, as if to drown them all, an obscene laughter mounted continually, like the welling forth of dark subterrene waters thick and foul with the fats of corruption.

Zobal dropped the wineskin and the sack of comestibles, and raced forward, unslinging his bow as he went. The outcries of his companions continued, but he heard them faintly now above the damnable incubus-like laughter that swelled as if to fill the whole monastery. As he neared the space before Rubalsa's chamber, he saw Cushara beating with the haft of his pike at a blank wall in which there was no longer a hempen-curtained doorway! Behind the wall the screeching of Simban ceased in a gurgling moan like that of some butchered steer; but the girl's terror-sharpened cries still mounted through the smothering cachinnation.

"This wall was wrought by demons," raged the pike-bearer as he smote vainly at the smooth masonry. "I kept a faithful watch—but they built it behind me in a silence as of the dead. And a fouler work is being done in that chamber."

"Master thy frenzy," said Zobal, as he strove to regain the command of his own faculties amid the madness that threatened to overwhelm him. At that instant he recalled the oval grey touchstone of Uldor, which hung at his baldric from its black silver chain; and it came to him that the closed wall was perhaps an unreal enchantment against which the talisman might serve even as Uldor had said.

Quickly he took the touchstone in his fingers and held it to the blank surface where the doorway had been. Cushara looked on with an air of stupefaction, as if deeming the archer demented. But even as the talisman clicked faintly against it, the wall seemed to dissolve, leaving only a rude arras that fell away in tatters as if it too had been no more than a sorcerous illusion. The strange disintegration continued to spread, the whole partition melted away to a few worn blocks, and the gibbous moon shone in as the abbey of Puthuum crumbled silently to a gapped and roofless ruin!

All this had occurred in a few moments; but the warriors found no room for wonder. By the livid light of the moon, which peered down like the face of a worm-gnawed cadaver, they looked upon a scene so hideous that it caused them to forget all else. Before them, on a cracked floor from whose interstices grew desert grasses, the eunuch Simban lay sprawled in death. His raiment was torn to a hundred streamers, and blood bubbled darkly from his mangled throat. Even the leather pouches which he bore at his girdle had been ripped open, and gold coins, vials of medicine and other oddments were scattered around him.

Beyond, by the half-crumbled outer wall, Rubalsa lay in a litter of rotted cloth and woodwork which had been the gorgeously quilted ebon bed. She was trying to fend off with her lifted hands the enormously swollen shape that hung horizontally above her, as if levitated by the floating wing-like folds of its saffron robe. This shape the warriors recognized as the abbot Ujuk.

The overwelling laughter of the black incubus had ceased, and he turned upon the intruders a face contorted by diabolic lust and fury. His teeth clashed audibly, his eyes glowed in their pouches like beads of red-hot metal, as he withdrew from his position over the girl and loomed monstrously erect before her amid the ruins of the chamber.

Cushara rushed forward with leveled pike ere Zobal could fit one of his arrows to the string. But even as the pike-bearer crossed the sill, it seemed that the fouly bloated form of Ujuk multiplied itself in a dozen yellow-garmented shapes that surged to meet Cushara's onset. Appearing as if by some hellish legerdemain, the monks of Puthuum had mustered to assist their abbot.

Zobal cried out in warning, but the shapes were all about Cushara, dodging the thrusts of his weapon and clawing ferociously at his plate-armor with their terrific three-inch talons. Valiantly he fought them, only to go down after a little and disappear from sight as if whelmed by a pack of ravening hyenas.

Remembering the scarce-credible thing that Uldor had told him, Zobal wasted no arrows upon the monks. His bow ready, he waited for full sight of Ujuk beyond the seething rout that wrangled malignantly back and forth above the fallen pike-bearer. In an eddying of the pack he aimed swiftly at the looming incubus, who seemed wholly intent on that fiendish struggle, as if directing it in some wise without spoken word or ponderable gesture. Straight and true the arrow sped with an exultant singing; and good was the sorcery of Amdok, who had wrought it: for Ujuk reeled and went down, his horrid fingers tearing vainly at the shaft that was driven nigh to its fledging of eagle-quills in his body.

Now a strange thing occurred: for, as the incubus fell and writhed to and fro in his dying, the twelve monks all dropped away from Cushara, and lay tossing convulsively on the floor as if they were but shaken shadows of the thing that died. It seemed to Zobal that their forms grew dim and diaphanous, and he saw the cracks in the flagstones beyond them; and their writhings lessened with those of Ujuk; and when Ujuk lay still at last, the faint outlines of the figures vanished as though erased from earth and air. Naught remained but the noisome bulk of that fiend who had been the progeny of the abbot Uldor and the lamia. And the bulk shrank visibly from instant to instant beneath its sagging garments, and a smell of ripe corruption arose, as if all that was human in the hellish thing were rotting swiftly away.

Cushara had scrambled to his feet and was peering about in a stunned fashion. His heavy armor had saved him from the talons of his assailants; but the armor itself was scored from greaves to helmet with innumerable scratches.

"Whither have the monks gone?" he inquired. "Methought they were all about me an instant ago, like so many wild dogs worrying a fallen aurochs."

"The monks were but emanations of Ujuk," said Zobal. "They were mere phantasms, multiple eidola, that he sent forth and withdrew into himself at will; and they had no real existence apart from him. With Ujuk's death they have become less than shadows."

"Verily, such things are prodigious," opined the pike-bearer.

The warriors now turned their attention to Rubalsa, who had struggled to a sitting posture amid the downfallen wreckage of her bed. The tatters of rotten quilting which she clutched about her with shamefast fingers at their approach, served but little to conceal her well-rounded ivory nakedness. She wore an air of mingled fright and confusion, like a sleeper who has just awakened from some atrocious nightmare.

"Had the incubus harmed thee?" inquired Zobal anxiously. He was reassured by her faint, bewildered negative. Dropping his eyes before the piteous disarray of her girlish beauty, he felt in his heart a deeper enamorment than before, a passion touched with such tenderness as he had never known in the hot, brief loves of his hazard-haunted days. Eyeing Cushara covertly, he knew with dismay that this emotion was shared to the fullest by his comrade.

The warriors now withdrew to a little distance and turned their backs decorously while Rubalsa dressed.

"I deem," said Zobal in a low voice beyond overhearing of the girl, "that thou and I tonight have met and conquered such perils as were not contracted for in our service to Hoaraph. And I deem that we are of one mind concerning the maiden, and love her too dearly now to deliver her to the captious lust of a sated king. Therefore we cannot return to Faraad. If it please thee, we shall draw lots for the girl; and the loser will attend the winner as a true comrade till such time as we have made our way from Izdrel, and have crossed the border of some land lying beyond Hoaraph's rule."

To this Cushara agreed. When Rubalsa had finished her dressing, the two began to look about them for such objects as might serve in the proposed sortilege. Cushara would have tossed one of the gold coins, stamped with Hoaraph's image, which had rolled from Simban's torn money-bag. But Zobal shook his head at the suggestion, having espied certain items which he thought even more exquisitely appropriate than the coin. These objects were the talons of the incubus, whose corpse had now dwindled in size and was horribly decayed, with a hideous wrinkling of the whole head and an actual shortening of the members. In this process, the claws of hands and feet had all dropped away and were lying loose on the pavement. Removing his helmet, Zobal stooped down and placed within it the five hellish-looking talons of the right hand, among which that of the index finger was the longest.

He shook the helmet vigorously, as one shakes a dice-box, and there was a sharp clattering from the claws. Then he held the helmet out to Cushara, saying: "He who draws the forefinger talon shall take the girl."

Cushara put in his hand and withdrew it quickly, holding aloft the heavy thumbnail, which was shortest of all. Zobal drew the nail of the middle finger; and Cushara, at his second trial, brought forth the little finger's claw. Then, to the deep chagrin of the pike-bearer, Zobal produced the dearly coveted index talon.

Rubalsa, who had been watching this singular procedure with open curiosity, now said to the warriors: "What are ye doing?"

Zobal started to explain, but before he had finished, the girl cried out indignantly: "Neither of ye has consulted my preference in this matter." Then, pouting prettily, she turned away from the disconcerted archer and proceeded to fling her arms about the neck of Cushara.

THE DEATH OF ILALOTHA

Black Lord of bale and fear, master of all confusion!
By thee, thy prophet saith,
New power is given to wizards after death,
And witches in corruption draw forbidden breath
And weave such wild enchantment and illusion
As none but lamiæ may use;
And through thy grace the charneled corpses lose
Their horror, and nefandous loves are lighted
In noisome vaults long nighted;
And vampires make their sacrifice to thee—
Disgorging blood as if great urns had poured
Their bright vermilion hoard
About the washed and weltering sarcophagi.
                    —*Ludar's Litany to Thasaidon.*

According to the custom in old Tasuun, the obsequies of Ilalotha, lady-in-waiting to the self-widowed Queen Xantlicha, had formed an occasion of much merrymaking and prolonged festivity. For three days, on a bier of diverse-colored silks from the Orient, under a rose-hued canopy that might well have domed some nuptial couch, she had lain clad with gala garments amid the great feasting-hall of the royal palace in Miraab. About her, from morning dusk to sunset, from cool even to torridly glaring dawn, the feverish tide of the funeral orgies had surged and eddied without slackening. Nobles, court officials, guardsmen, scullions, astrologers, eunuchs, and all the high ladies, waiting women and female slaves of Xantlicha, had taken part in that prodigal debauchery which was believed to honor most fitly the deceased. Mad songs and obscene ditties were sung, and dancers whirled in vertiginous frenzy to the lascivious pleading of untirable lutes. Wines and liquors were poured torrentially from monstrous amphoras; the tables fumed with spicy meats piled in huge hummocks and forever replenished. The drinkers offered libation to Ilalotha, till the fabrics of her bier were stained to darker hues by the spilt vintages. On all sides around her, in attitudes of disorder or prone abandonment, lay those who had yielded to amorous license or the fullness of their potations. With half-shut eyes and lips slightly parted, in the rosy shadow cast by the catafalque, she wore no

163

aspect of death but seemed a sleeping empress who ruled impartially over the living and the dead. This appearance, together with a strange heightening of her natural beauty, was remarked by many: and some said that she seemed to await a lover's kiss rather than the kisses of the worm.

On the third evening, when the many-tongued brazen lamps were lit and the rites drew to their end, there returned to court the Lord Thulos, acknowledged lover of Queen Xantlicha, who had gone a week previous to visit his domain on the western border and had heard nothing of Ilalotha's death. Still unaware, he came into the hall at that hour when the saturnalia began to flag and the fallen revelers to outnumber those who still moved and drank and made riot.

He viewed the disordered hall with little surprise, for such scenes were familiar to him from childhood. Then, approaching the bier, he recognized its occupant with a certain startlement. Among the numerous ladies of Miraab who had drawn his libertine affections, Ilalotha had held sway longer than most; and, it was said, she had grieved more passionately over his defection than any other. She had been superseded a month before by Xantlicha, who had shown favor to Thulos in no ambiguous manner; and Thulos, perhaps, had abandoned her not without regret: for the role of lover to the queen, though advantageous and not wholly disagreeable, was somewhat precarious. Xantlicha, it was universally believed, had rid herself of the late King Archain by means of a tomb-discovered vial of poison that owed its peculiar subtlety and virulence to the art of ancient sorcerers. Following this act of disposal, she had taken many lovers, and those who failed to please her came invariably to ends no less violent than that of Archain. She was exigent, exorbitant, demanding a strict fidelity somewhat irksome to Thulos; who, pleading urgent affairs on his remote estate, had been glad enough of a week away from court.

Now, as he stood beside the dead woman, Thulos forgot the queen and bethought him of certain summer nights that had been honeyed by the fragrance of jasmine and the jasmine-white beauty of Ilalotha. Even less than the others could he believe her dead: for her present aspect differed in no wise from that which she had often assumed during their old intercourse. To please his whim, she had feigned the inertness and complaisance of slumber or death; and at such times he had loved her with an ardor undismayed by the pantherine vehemence with which, at other whiles, she was wont to reciprocate or invite his caresses.

Moment by moment, as if through the working of some powerful necromancy, there grew upon him a curious hallucination, and it seemed that he was again the lover of those lost nights, and had entered that bower in the palace gardens where Ilalotha waited him on a couch strewn with overblown petals, lying with bosom quiet as her face and hands. No longer was he aware of the crowded hall: the high-flaring lights, the wine-flushed faces had become a moon-bright parterre of drowsily nodding blossoms, and the voices of the courtiers were no more than a faint suspiration of wind amid cypress and jasmine. The warm, aphrodisiac perfumes of the June night welled about him; and again, as of old, it seemed that they arose from the person of Ilalotha no less than from the flowers. Prompted by intense desire, he stooped over and felt her cool arm stir involuntarily beneath his kiss.

Then, with the bewilderment of a sleep-walker awakened rudely, he heard a voice that hissed in his ear with soft venom: "Hast forgotten thyself, my Lord Thulos? Indeed, I wonder little, for many of my bawcocks deem that she is fairer in death than in life." And, turning from Ilalotha, while the weird spell dissolved from his senses, he found Xantlicha at his side. Her garments were disarrayed, her hair was unbound and dishevelled, and she reeled slightly, clutching him by the shoulder with sharp-nailed fingers. Her full, poppy-crimson lips were curled by a vixenish fury, and in her long-lidded yellow eyes there blazed the jealousy of an amorous cat.

Thulos, overwhelmed by a strange confusion, remembered but partially the enchantment to which he had succumbed; and he was unsure whether or not he had actually kissed Ilalotha and had felt her flesh quiver to his mouth. Verily, he thought, this thing could not have been, and a waking dream had momentarily seized him. But he was troubled by the words of Xantlicha and her anger, and by the half-furtive drunken laughters and ribald whispers that he heard passing among the people about the hall.

"Beware, my Thulos," the queen murmured, her strange anger seeming to subside; "for men say that she was a witch…."

"How did she die?" queried Thulos.

"From no other fever than that of love, it is rumored."

"Then, surely, she was no witch," Thulos argued with a lightness that was far from his thoughts and feelings; "for true sorcery should have found the cure."

"It was from love of thee," said Xantlicha darkly; "and, as all women know, thy heart is blacker and harder than black adamant. No witchcraft, however potent, could prevail thereon." Her mood, as she spoke, appeared to soften suddenly. "Thy absence has been long, my lord. Come to me at midnight: I will wait for thee in the south pavilion." Then, eyeing him sultrily for an instant from under drooped lids, and pinching his arm in such manner that her nails pierced through cloth and skin like a cat's talons, she turned from Thulos to hail certain of the harem-eunuchs.

Thulos, when the queen's attention was disengaged from him, ventured to look again at Ilalotha; pondering, meanwhile, the curious remarks of Xantlicha. He knew that Ilalotha, like many of the court-ladies, had dabbled in spells and philtres; but her witchcraft had never concerned him, since he felt no interest in other charms or enchantments than those with which nature had endowed the bodies of women. And it was quite impossible for him to believe that Ilalotha had died from a fatal passion: since, in his experience, passion was never fatal.

Indeed, as he regarded her with confused emotions, he was again beset by the impression that she had not died at all. There was no repetition of the weird, half-remembered hallucination of other time and place; but it seemed to him that she had stirred from her former position on the wine-stained bier, turning her face toward him a little, as a woman turns to an expected lover; that the arm he had kissed (either in dream or reality) was outstretched a little farther from her side.

Thulos bent nearer, fascinated by the mystery and drawn by a stranger attraction that he could not have named. Again, surely, he had dreamt or had been mistaken. But even as the doubt grew, it seemed that the bosom of Ilalotha stirred in faint respiration and he heard an almost inaudible but thrilling whisper: "Come to me at midnight. I will wait for thee... in the tomb."

At this instant there appeared beside the catafalque certain people in the sober and rusty raiment of sextons, who had entered the hall silently, un-perceived by Thulos or by any of the company. They carried among them a thin-walled sarcophagus of newly welded and burnished bronze. It was their office to remove the dead woman and bear her to the sepulchral vaults of her family, which were situated in the old necropolis lying somewhat to northward of the palace-gardens.

Thulos would have cried out to restrain them from their purpose; but his tongue clove tightly; nor could he move any of his members. Not knowing whether he slept or woke, he watched the people of the cemetery as they placed Ilalotha in the sarcophagus and bore her quickly from the hall, unfol-lowed and still unheeded by the drowsy bacchanalians. Only when the somber cortège had departed was he able to stir from his position by the empty bier. His thoughts were sluggish, and full of darkness and indecision. Smitten by an immense fatigue that was not unnatural after his daylong journey, he withdrew to his apartments and fell instantly into death-deep slumber.

Freeing itself gradually from the cypress-boughs, as if from the long, stretched fingers of witches, a waning and misshapen moon glared hori-zontally through the eastern window when Thulos awoke. By this token, he knew that the hour drew toward midnight, and recalled the assignation which Queen Xantlicha had made with him: an assignation which he could hardly break without incurring the queen's deadly displeasure. Also, with singular clearness, he recalled another rendezvous... at the same time but in a dif-ferent place. Those incidents and impressions of Ilalotha's funeral, which, at the time, had seemed so dubitable and dreamlike, returned to him with a profound conviction of reality, as if etched on his mind by some mordant chemistry of sleep... or the strengthening of some sorcerous charm. He felt that Ilalotha had indeed stirred on her bier and spoken to him; that the sextons had borne her still living to the tomb. Perhaps her supposed demise had been merely a sort of catalepsy; or else she had deliberately feigned death in a last effort to revive his passion. These thoughts awoke within him a raging fever of curiosity and desire; and he saw before him her pale, inert, luxurious beauty, presented as if by enchantment.

Direly distraught, he went down by the lampless stairs and hallways to the moonlit labyrinth of the gardens. He cursed the untimely exigence of Xantlicha. However, as he told himself, it was more than likely that the queen, continuing to imbibe the liquors of Tasuun, had long since reached a condition in which she would neither keep nor recall her appointment. This thought reassured him: in his queerly bemused mind, it soon became a certainty; and he did not hasten toward the south pavilion but strolled vaguely amid the wan and somber boscage.

More and more it seemed unlikely that any but himself was abroad: for the long, unlit wings of the palace sprawled as in vacant stupor; and in the gardens there were only dead shadows, and pools of still fragrance in which the winds had drowned. And over all, like a pale, monstrous poppy, the moon distilled her death-white slumber.

Thulos, no longer mindful of his rendezvous with Xantlicha, yielded without further reluctation to the urgence that drove him toward another goal…. Truly, it was no less than obligatory that he should visit the vaults and learn whether or not he had been deceived in his belief concerning Ilalotha. Perhaps, if he did not go, she would stifle in the shut sarcophagus, and her pretended death would quickly become an actuality. Again, as if spoken in the moonlight before him, he heard the words she had whispered, or seemed to whisper, from the bier: "Come to me at midnight… I will wait for thee… in the tomb."

With the quickening steps and pulses of one who fares to the warm, petal-sweet couch of an adored mistress, he left the palace-grounds by an unguarded northern postern and crossed the weedy common between the royal gardens and the old cemetery. Unchilled and undismayed, he entered those always-open portals of death, where ghoul-headed monsters of black marble, glaring with hideously pitted eyes, maintained their charnel postures before the crumbling pylons.

The very stillness of the low-bosomed graves, the rigor and pallor of the tall shafts, the deepness of bedded cypress shadows, the inviolacy of death by which all things were invested, served to heighten the singular excitement that had fired Thulos' blood. It was as if he had drunk a philtre spiced with mummia. All around him the mortuary silence seemed to burn and quiver with a thousand memories of Ilalotha, together with those expectations to which he had given as yet no formal image….

Once, with Ilalotha, he had visited the subterranean tomb of her ancestors;

and, recalling its situation clearly, he came without indirection to the low-arched and cedar-darkened entrance. Rank nettles and fetid fumitories, growing thickly about the seldom-used adit, were crushed down by the tread of those who had entered there before Thulos; and the rusty, iron-wrought door sagged heavily inward on its loose hinges. At his feet there lay an extinguished flambeau, dropped, no doubt, by one of the departing sextons. Seeing it, he realized that he had brought with him neither candle nor lanthorn for the exploration of the vaults, and found in that providential torch an auspicious omen.

Bearing the lit flambeau, he began his investigation. He gave no heed to the piled and dusty sarcophagi in the first reaches of the subterrane: for, during their past visit, Ilalotha had shown to him a niche at the innermost extreme, where, in due time, she herself would find sepulture among the members of that decaying line. Strangely, insidiously, like the breath of some vernal garden, the languid and luscious odor of jasmine swam to meet him through the musty air, amid the tiered presence of the dead; and it drew him to the sarcophagus that stood open between others tightly lidded. There he beheld Ilalotha, lying in the gay garments of her funeral, with half-shut eyes and half-parted lips; and upon her was the same weird and radiant beauty, the same voluptuous pallor and stillness, that had drawn Thulos with a necromantic charm.

"I knew that thou wouldst come, O Thulos," she murmured, stirring a little, as if involuntarily, beneath the deepening ardor of his kisses that passed quickly from throat to bosom....

The torch that had fallen from Thulos' hand expired in the thick dust....

Xantlicha, retiring to her chamber betimes, had slept illy. Perhaps she had drunk too much or too little of the dark, ardent vintages; perhaps her blood was fevered by the return of Thulos, and her jealousy still troubled by the hot kiss which he had laid on Ilalotha's arm during the obsequies. A restlessness was upon her; and she rose well before the hour of her meeting with Thulos, and stood at her chamber window seeking such coolness as the night air might afford.

The air, however, seemed heated as by the burning of hidden furnaces; her heart appeared to swell in her bosom and stifle her; and her unrest and agitation were increased rather than diminished by the spectacle of the moon-lulled gardens. She would have hurried forth to the tryst in the pavilion; but, despite her impatience, she thought it well to keep Thulos waiting. Leaning thus from her sill, she beheld Thulos when he passed amid the parterres and arbors below. She was struck by the unusual haste and intentness of his steps; and she wondered at their direction, which could bring him only to places remote from the rendezvous she had named. He disappeared from her sight in the cypress-lined alley that led to the north garden-gate; and her wonderment was soon mingled with alarm and anger when he did not return.

It was incomprehensible to Xantlicha that Thulos, or any man, would dare to forget the tryst in his normal senses; and seeking an explanation, she surmised that a baleful and potent sorcery was probably involved. Nor, in the light of certain incidents that she had observed, and much else that had been rumored, was it hard for her to identify the possible sorceress. Ilalotha, the queen knew, had loved Thulos to the point of frenzy, and had grieved inconsolably after his desertion of her. People said that she had wrought various ineffectual spells to bring him back; that she had vainly invoked demons and sacrificed to them, and had made futile invultuations and death-charms against Xantlicha. In the end, she had died of sheer chagrin and despair, or perhaps had slain herself with some undetected poison…. But, as was commonly believed in Tasuun, a witch dying thus, with unslaked desires and frustrate cantraips, could turn herself into a lamia or vampire and procure thereby the consummation of all her sorceries….

The queen shuddered, remembering these things; and all too well she surmised the destination of Thulos, and the danger to which he had gone forth if her suspicions were true. And, with the knowledge that she must face an equal danger, Xantlicha determined to follow him.

She made little preparation, for there was no time to waste; but took from beneath the silken cushions of her bed a small, straight-bladed dagger that she kept always within reach. The dagger had been anointed from point to hilt with such venom as was believed efficacious against either the living or the dead. Bearing it in her right hand, and carrying in the other a slot-eyed lanthorn that she might require later, Xantlicha stole swiftly from the palace.

The last lees of the evening's wine ebbed wholly from her brain, and dim, ghastly fears awoke, warning her like the voices of ancestral phantoms. But, firm in her determination, she followed the path taken by Thulos; the path taken earlier by those sextons who had borne Ilalotha to her place of sepulture. Hovering from tree to tree, the moon accompanied her like a worm-hollowed visage; and the gaunt cypresses, rearing stilly in their cerements of light, had assumed a rigid and funereal watch over that fatal way. The soft, quick patter of her cothurns, breaking the white silence, seemed to tear the filmy cobweb pall that withheld from her a world of spectral abominations. And more and more she recalled, of those legendries that concerned such beings as Ilalotha; and her heart was shaken within her: for she knew that she would meet no mortal woman but a thing raised up and inspirited by the seventh hell. But amid the chill of these horrors, the thought of Thulos in the lamia's arms was like a red brand that seared her bosom.

Now the necropolis yawned before Xantlicha, and her path entered the cavernous gloom of far-vaulted funereal trees, as if passing into monstrous and shadowy mouths that were tusked with white monuments. The air grew dank and noisome, as if filled with the breathings of open crypts. Here the queen faltered, for it seemed that black, unseen cacodemons rose all about her from the graveyard ground, towering higher than the shafts and boles, and standing in readiness to assail her if she went farther. Nevertheless, she came anon to the dark adit that she sought. Tremulously she lit the wick of the slot-eyed lanthorn; and, piercing the gross underground darkness before her with its bladed beam, she paused with ill-subdued terror and repugnance into that abode of the dead… and perchance of the Undead.

However, as she followed the first turnings of the catacomb, it seemed that she was to encounter nothing more abhorrent than charnel mould and century-sifted dust; nothing more formidable than the serried sarcophagi that lined the deeply hewn shelves of stone: sarcophagi that had stood silent and undisturbed ever since the time of their deposition…. Here, surely the slumber of all the dead was unbroken, and the nullity of death was inviolate….

Almost the queen doubted that Thulos had preceded her there; till, turning her light on the ground, she discerned the print of his poulaines, long-tipped and slender in the deep dust amid those footmarks left by the rudely shod sextons. And she saw that the footprints of Thulos pointed only in one direction, while those of the others plainly went and returned.

Then, at an undetermined distance in the shadows ahead, Xantlicha heard a sound in which the sick moaning of some amorous woman was blent with a snarling as of jackals over their meat. Her blood returned frozen upon her heart as she went onward step by slow step, clutching her dagger in a hand drawn sharply back, and holding the light high in advance. The sound grew louder and more distinct; and there came to her now a perfume as of flowers in some warm June night; but, as she still advanced, the perfume was blended with more and more of a smothering foulness such as she had never heretofore known, and was touched with the hot reeking of blood.

A few paces more, and Xantlicha stood as if a demon's arm had arrested her: for her lanthorn's light had found the inverted face and upper body of Thulos, hanging from the end of a burnished, newly wrought sarcophagus that occupied a scant interval between others green with rust. One of Thulos' hands clutched rigidly the rim of the sarcophagus, while the other hand, moving feebly, seemed to caress a shadowy shape that leaned above him with arms showing jasmine-white in the narrow beam, and dark fingers plunging into his bosom. His head and body seemed but an empty hull, and his hand hung skeleton-thin on the bronze rim, and his whole aspect was vein-drawn, as if he had lost more blood than was evident on his torn throat and face, and in his sodden raiment and dripping hair.

From the thing stooping above Thulos, there came ceaselessly that sound which was half moan and half snarl. And as Xantlicha stood in petrific fear and loathing, she seemed to hear from Thulos' lips an indistinct murmur, more of ecstasy than pain. The murmur ceased, and his head hung slacklier than before, so that the queen deemed him verily dead. At this she found such wrathful courage as enabled her to step nearer and raise the lanthorn higher: for, even amid her extreme panic, it came to her that by means of the wizard-poisoned dagger she might still haply slay the thing that had slain Thulos.

Waveringly the light crept aloft, disclosing inch by inch that infamy which Thulos had caressed in the darkness…. It crept even to the crimson-smeared wattles, and the fanged and ruddled orifice that was half mouth and half beak… till Xantlicha knew why the body of Thulos was a mere shrunken hull…. In what the queen saw, there remained nothing of Ilalotha except the white, voluptuous arms, and a vague outline of human breasts melting momently into breasts that were not human, like clay moulded by a demon sculptor. The arms too began to change and darken; and, as they changed, the dying hand of Thulos stirred again and fumbled with a caressing movement toward the horror. And the thing seemed to heed him not but withdrew its fingers from his bosom, and reached across him with members stretching enormously, as if to claw the queen or fondle her with its dribbling talons.

It was then that Xantlicha let fall the lanthorn and the dagger, and ran with shrill, endless shriekings and laughters of immitigable madness from the vault.

MOTHER OF TOADS

"**W**hy must you always hurry away, my little one?"

The voice of Mère Antoinette, the witch, was an amorous croaking. She ogled Pierre, the apothecary's young apprentice, with eyes full-orbed and unblinking as those of a toad. The folds beneath her chin swelled like the throat of some great batrachian. Her huge breasts, pale as frog-bellies, bulged from her torn gown as she leaned toward him.

Pierre Baudin, as usual, gave no answer; and she came closer, till he saw in the hollow of those breasts a moisture glistening like the dew of marshes… like the slime of some amphibian… a moisture that seemed always to linger there.

Her voice, raucously coaxing, persisted. "Stay awhile tonight, my pretty orphan. No one will miss you in the village. And your master will not mind." She pressed against him with shuddering folds of fat. With her short flat fingers, which gave almost the appearance of being webbed, she seized his hand and drew it to her bosom.

Pierre wrenched the hand away and drew back discreetly. Repelled, rather than abashed, he averted his eyes. The witch was more than twice his age, and her charms were too uncouth and unsavory to tempt him for an instant. Also, her repute was such as to have nullified the attractions of a younger and fairer sorceress. Her witchcraft had made her feared among the peasantry of that remote province, where belief in spells and philtres was still common. The people of Averoigne called her *La Mère des Crapauds,* Mother of Toads, a name given for more than one reason. Toads swarmed innumerably about her hut; they were said to be her familiars, and dark tales were told concerning their relationship to the sorceress, and the duties they performed at her bidding. Such tales were all the more readily believed because of those batrachian features that had always been remarked in her aspect.

The youth disliked her, even as he disliked the sluggish, abnormally large toads on which he had sometimes trodden in the dusk, upon the path between her hut and the village of Les Hiboux. He could hear some of these creatures croaking now; and it seemed, weirdly, that they uttered half-articulate echoes of the witch's words.

It would be dark soon, he reflected. The path along the marshes was not pleasant by night, and he felt doubly anxious to depart. Still without replying to Mère Antoinette's invitation, he reached for the black triangular vial she had set before him on her greasy table. The vial contained a philtre of curious potency which his master, Alain le Dindon, had sent him to procure. Le Dindon, the village apothecary, was wont to deal surreptitiously in certain dubious medicaments supplied by the witch; and Pierre had often gone on such errands to her osier-hidden hut.

The old apothecary, whose humor was rough and ribald, had sometimes rallied Pierre concerning Mère Antoinette's preference for him. "Some night, my lad, you will remain with her," he had said. "Be careful, or the big toad will crush you." Remembering this gibe, the boy flushed angrily as he turned to go.

"Stay," insisted Mère Antoinette. "The fog is cold on the marshes; and it thickens apace. I knew that you were coming, and I have mulled for you a goodly measure of the red wine of Ximes."

She removed the lid from an earthen pitcher and poured its steaming contents into a large cup. The purplish-red wine creamed delectably, and an odor of hot, delicious spices filled the hut, overpowering the less agreeable odors from the simmering cauldron, the half-dried newts, vipers, bat-wings and evil, nauseous herbs hanging on the walls, and the reek of the black candles of pitch and corpse-tallow that burned always, by noon or night, in that murky interior.

"I'll drink it," said Pierre, a little grudgingly. "That is, if it contains nothing of your own concoction."

" 'Tis naught but sound wine, four seasons old, with spices of Arabia," the sorceress croaked ingratiatingly. " 'Twill warm your stomach… and…" She added something inaudible as Pierre accepted the cup.

Before drinking, he inhaled the fumes of the beverage with some caution but was reassured by its pleasant smell. Surely it was innocent of any drug, any philtre brewed by the witch: for, to his knowledge, her preparations were all evil-smelling.

Still, as if warned by some premonition, he hesitated. Then he remembered that the sunset air was indeed chill; that mists had gathered furtively behind him as he came to Mère Antoinette's dwelling. The wine would fortify him for the dismal return walk to Les Hiboux. He quaffed it quickly and set down the cup.

"Truly, it is good wine," he declared. "But I must go now."

Even as he spoke, he felt in his stomach and veins the spreading warmth of the alcohol, of the spices... of something more ardent than these. It seemed that his voice was unreal and strange, falling as if from a height above him. The warmth grew, mounting within him like a golden flame fed by magic oils. His blood, a seething torrent, poured tumultuously and more tumultuously through his members.

There was a deep soft thundering in his ears, a rosy dazzlement in his eyes. Somehow the hut appeared to expand, to change luminously about him. He hardly recognized its squalid furnishings, its litter of baleful oddments, on which a torrid splendor was shed by the black candles, tipped with ruddy fire, that towered and swelled gigantically into the soft gloom. His blood burned as with the throbbing flame of the candles.

It came to him, for an instant, that all this was a questionable enchantment, a glamour wrought by the witch's wine. Fear was upon him and he wished to flee. Then, close beside him, he saw Mère Antoinette.

Briefly he marvelled at the change that had befallen her. Then fear and wonder were alike forgotten, together with his old repulsion. He knew why the magic warmth mounted ever higher and hotter within him; why his flesh glowed like the ruddy tapers.

The soiled skirt she had worn lay at her feet, and she stood naked as Lilith, the first witch. The lumpish limbs and body had grown voluptuous; the pale, thick-lipped mouth enticed him with a promise of ampler kisses than other mouths could yield. The pits of her short round arms, the concave of her ponderously drooping breasts, the heavy creases and swollen rondures of flanks and thighs, all were fraught with luxurious allurement.

"Do you like me now, my little one?" she questioned.

This time he did not draw away but met her with hot, questing hands when she pressed heavily against him. Her limbs were cool and moist; her breasts yielded like the turf-mounds above a bog. Her body was white and wholly hairless; but here and there he found curious roughnesses... like those on the skin of a toad... that somehow sharpened his desire instead of repelling it.

She was so huge that his fingers barely joined behind her. His two hands, together, were equal only to the cupping of a single breast. But the wine had filled his blood with a philterous ardor.

She led him to her couch beside the hearth where a great cauldron boiled mysteriously, sending up its fumes in strange-twining coils that suggested vague and obscene figures. The couch was rude and bare. But the flesh of the sorceress was like deep, luxurious cushions....

Pierre awoke in the ashy dawn, when the tall black tapers had dwindled down and had melted limply in their sockets. Sick and confused, he sought vainly to remember where he was or what he had done. Then, turning a little, he saw beside him on the couch a thing that was like some impossible monster of ill dreams: a toad-like form, large as a fat woman. Its limbs were somehow like a woman's arms and legs. Its pale, warty body pressed and bulged against him, and he felt the rounded softness of something that resembled a breast.

Nausea rose within him as memory of that delirious night returned. Most foully he had been beguiled by the witch, and had succumbed to her evil enchantments.

It seemed that an incubus smothered him, weighing upon all his limbs and body. He shut his eyes, that he might no longer behold the loathsome thing that was Mère Antoinette in her true semblance. Slowly, with prodigious effort, he drew himself away from the crushing nightmare shape. It did not stir or appear to waken; and he slid quickly from the couch.

Again, compelled by a noisome fascination, he peered at the thing on the couch—and saw only the gross form of Mère Antoinette. Perhaps his impression of a great toad beside him had been but an illusion, a half-dream that lingered after slumber. He lost something of his nightmarish horror; but his gorge still rose in a sick disgust, remembering the lewdness to which he had yielded.

Fearing that the witch might awaken at any moment and seek to detain him, he stole noiselessly from the hut. It was broad daylight, but a cold, hueless mist lay everywhere, shrouding the reedy marshes, and hanging like a ghostly curtain on the path he must follow to Les Hiboux. Moving and seething always, the mist seemed to reach toward him with intercepting fingers as he started homeward. He shivered at its touch, he bowed his head and drew his cloak closer around him.

Thicker and thicker the mist swirled, coiling, writhing endlessly, as if to bar Pierre's progress. He could discern the twisting, narrow path for only a few paces in advance. It was hard to find the familiar landmarks, hard to recognize the osiers and willows that loomed suddenly before him like grey phantoms and faded again into the white nothingness as he went onward. Never had he seen such fog: it was like the blinding, stifling fumes of a thousand witch-stirred cauldrons.

Though he was not altogether sure of his surroundings, Pierre thought that he had covered half the distance to the village. Then, all at once, he began to meet the toads. They were hidden by the mist till he came close upon them. Misshapen, unnaturally big and bloated, they squatted in his way on the little footpath or hopped sluggishly before him from the pallid gloom on either hand.

Several struck against his feet with a horrible and heavy flopping. He stepped unaware upon one of them, and slipped in the squashy noisomeness it had made, barely saving himself from a headlong fall on the bog's rim. Black, miry water gloomed close beside him as he staggered there.

Turning to regain his path, he crushed others of the toads to an abhorrent pulp under his feet. The marshy soil was alive with them. They flopped against him from the mist, striking his legs, his bosom, his very face with their clammy bodies. They rose up by scores like a devil-driven legion. It seemed that there was a malignance, an evil purpose in their movements, in the buffeting of their violent impact. He could make no progress on the swarming path, but lurched to and fro, slipping blindly, and shielding his face with lifted hands. He felt an eerie consternation, an eldritch horror. It was as if the nightmare of his awakening in the witch's hut had somehow returned upon him.

The toads came always from the direction of Les Hiboux, as if to drive him back toward Mère Antoinette's dwelling. They bounded against him like a monstrous hail, like missiles flung by unseen demons. The ground was covered by them, the air was filled with their hurtling bodies. Once, he nearly went down beneath them.

Their number seemed to increase, they pelted him in a noxious storm. He gave way before them, his courage broke, and he started to run at random, without knowing that he had left the safe path. Losing all thought of direction, in his frantic desire to escape from those impossible myriads, he plunged on amid the dim reeds and sedges, over ground that quivered gelatinously beneath him. Always at his heels he heard the soft, heavy flopping of the toads; and sometimes they rose up like a sudden wall to bar his way and turn him aside. More than once, they drove him back from the verge of hidden quagmires into which he would otherwise have fallen. It was as if they were herding him deliberately and concertedly to a destined goal.

Now, like the lifting of a dense curtain, the mist rolled away, and Pierre saw before him in a golden dazzle of morning sunshine the green, thick-growing osiers that surrounded Mère Antoinette's hut. The toads had all disappeared, though he could have sworn that hundreds of them were hopping close about him an instant previously. With a feeling of helpless fright and panic, he knew that he was still within the witch's toils; that the toads were indeed her familiars, as so many people believed them to be. They had prevented his escape, and had brought him back to the foul creature… whether woman, batrachian, or both… who was known as The Mother of Toads.

Pierre's sensations were those of one who sinks momently deeper into some black and bottomless quicksand. He saw the witch emerge from the hut and come toward him. Her thick fingers, with pale folds of skin between them like the beginnings of a web, were stretched and flattened on the steaming cup that she carried. A sudden gust of wind arose as if from nowhere, lifting the scanty skirts of Mère Antoinette about her fat thighs, and bearing to Pierre's nostrils the hot, familiar spices of the drugged wine.

"Why did you leave so hastily, my little one?" There was an amorous wheedling in the very tone of the witch's question. "I should not have let you go without another cup of the good red wine, mulled and spiced for the warming of your stomach…. See, I have prepared it for you… knowing that you would return."

She came very close to him as she spoke, leering and sidling, and held the cup toward his lips. Pierre grew dizzy with the strange fumes and turned his head away. It seemed that a paralyzing spell had seized his muscles, for the simple movement required an immense effort.

His mind, however, was still clear, and the sick revulsion of that nightmare dawn returned upon him. He saw again the great toad that had lain at his side when he awakened.

"I will not drink your wine," he said firmly. "You are a foul witch, and I loathe you. Let me go."

"Why do you loathe me?" croaked Mère Antoinette. "You loved me yester-night. I can give you all that other women give… and more."

"You are not a woman," said Pierre. "You are a big toad. I saw you in your true shape this morning. I'd rather drown in the marsh-waters than sleep with you again."

An indescribable change came upon the sorceress before Pierre had finished speaking. The leer slid from her thick and pallid features, leaving them blankly inhuman for an instant. Then her eyes bulged and goggled horribly, and her whole body appeared to swell as if inflated with venom.

"Go, then!" she spat with a guttural virulence. "But you will soon wish that you had stayed…."

The queer paralysis had lifted from Pierre's muscles. It was as if the injunction of the angry witch had served to revoke an insidious, half-woven spell. With no parting glance or word, Pierre turned from her and fled with long, hasty steps, almost running, on the path to Les Hiboux.

He had gone little more than a hundred paces when the fog began to return. It coiled shoreward in vast volumes from the marshes, it poured like smoke from the very ground at his feet. Almost instantly, the sun dimmed to a wan silver disk and disappeared. The blue heavens were lost in the pale and seething voidness overhead. The path before Pierre was blotted out till he seemed to walk on the sheer rim of a white abyss, that moved with him as he went.

Like the clammy arms of specters, with death-chill fingers that clutched and caressed, the weird mists drew closer still about Pierre. They thickened in his nostrils and throat, they dripped in a heavy dew from his garments. They choked him with the fetor of rank waters and putrescent ooze… and a stench as of liquefying corpses that had risen somewhere to the surface amid the fen.

Then, from the blank whiteness, the toads assailed Pierre in a surging, solid wave that towered above his head and swept him from the dim path with the force of falling seas as it descended. He went down, splashing and floundering, into water that swarmed with the numberless batrachians. Thick slime was in his mouth and nose as he struggled to regain his footing. The water, however, was only knee-deep, and the bottom, though slippery and oozy, supported him with little yielding when he stood erect.

He discerned indistinctly through the mist the nearby margin from which he had fallen. But his steps were weirdly and horribly hampered by the toad-seething waters when he strove to reach it. Inch by inch, with a hopeless panic deepening upon him, he fought toward the solid shore. The toads leaped and tumbled about him with a dizzying eddy-like motion. They swirled like a viscid undertow around his feet and shins. They swept and swelled in great loathsome undulations against his retarded knees.

However, he made slow and painful progress, till his outstretched fingers could almost grasp the wiry sedges that trailed from the low bank. Then, from that mist-bound shore, there fell and broke upon him a second deluge of those demoniac toads; and Pierre was borne helplessly backward into the filthy waters.

Held down by the piling and crawling masses, and drowning in nauseous darkness at the thick-oozed bottom, he clawed feebly at his assailants. For a moment, ere oblivion came, his fingers found among them the outlines of a monstrous form that was somehow toadlike... but large and heavy as a fat woman. At the last, it seemed to him that two enormous breasts were crushed closely down upon his face.

THE GARDEN OF ADOMPHA

Lord of the sultry, red parterres
And orchards sunned by hell's unsetting flame!
Amid thy garden blooms the Tree which bears
Unnumbered heads of demons for its fruit;
And, like a slithering serpent, runs the root
That is called Baaras;
And there the forky, pale mandragoras,
Self-torn from out the soil, go to and fro,
Calling upon thy name:
Till men new-damned will deem that devils pass,
Crying in wrathful frenzy and strange woe.

       —Ludar's Litany to Thasaidon

It was well known that Adompha, king of the wide orient isle of Sotar, possessed amid his far-stretching palace grounds a garden secret from all men except himself and the court magician, Dwerulas. The square-built granite walls of the garden, high and formidable as those of a prison, were plain for all to see, rearing above the stately beefwood and camphor trees, and broad plots of multi-colored blossoms. But nothing had ever been ascertained regarding its interior: for such care as it required was given only by the wizard beneath Adompha's direction; and the twain spoke thereof in deep riddles that none could interpret. The thick brazen door responded to a mechanism whose mystery they shared with none other; and the king and Dwerulas, whether separately or together, visited the garden only at those hours when others were not abroad. And none could verily boast that he had beheld even so much as the opening of the door.

Men said that the garden had been roofed over against the sun with great sheets of lead and copper, leaving no cranny through which the tiniest star could peer down. Some swore that the privacy of its masters during their visits was ensured by a lethean slumber which Dwerulas, through his magic art, was wont to lay at such times upon the whole vicinity.

A mystery so salient could hardly fail to provoke curiosity, and sundry different beliefs arose concerning the garden's nature. Some averred that it was filled with evil plants of nocturnal habit, that yielded their swift and mordant poisons for Adompha's use, along with more insidious and baleful essences employed by the warlock in the working of his enchantments. Such tales, it seemed, were perhaps not without authority: since, following the construction of the closed garden, there had been at the royal court numerous deaths attributable to poisoning, and disasters that were plainly the sendings of a wizard, together with the bodily vanishment of people whose mundane presence no longer pleased Adompha or Dwerulas.

Other tales, of a more extravagant kind, were whispered among the credulous. That legend of unnatural infamy, which had surrounded the king from childhood, assumed a more hideous tinge; and Dwerulas, who had reputedly been sold to the Archdemon before birth by his haggish mother, acquired a new blackness of renown as one exceeding all other sorcerers in the depth and starkness of his abandonment.

Waking from such slumber and such dreams as the juice of the black poppy had given him, King Adompha rose in the dead, stagnant hours between moonset and dawn. About him the palace lay hushed like a charnel-house, its occupants having yielded to their nightly sopor of wine, drugs and arrack. Around the palace, the gardens and the capital city of Loithé slept beneath the slow stars of windless southern heavens. At this time Adompha and Dwerulas were wont to visit the high-walled close with little fear of being followed or observed.

Adompha went forth, pausing but briefly to turn the covert eye of his black bronze lanthorn into the lampless chamber adjoining his own. The room had been occupied by Thuloneah, his favorite odalisque for the seldom-equalled period of eight nights; but he saw without surprise or disconcertion that the bed of disordered silks was now empty. By this, he felt sure that Dwerulas had preceded him to the garden. And he knew, moreover, that Dwerulas had not gone idly or unburdened.

The grounds of the palace, steeped everywhere in unbroken shadow, appeared to maintain that secrecy which the king preferred. He came to the shut brazen door in the blankly towering granite wall; emitting, as he approached it, a sharp sibilation like the hissing of a cobra. In response to the rising and falling of this sound, the door swung inwardly silently and closed silently behind him.

The garden, planted and tilled so privily, and sealed by its metal roof from the orbs of heaven, was illumined solely by a strange, fiery globe that hung in mid-air at the center. Adompha regarded this globe with awe, for its nature and purveyance were mysterious to him. Dwerulas claimed that it had risen from hell on a moonless midnight at his bidding, and was levitated by infernal power, and fed with the never-dying flames of that clime in which the fruits of Thasaidon swelled to unearthly size and enchanted savor. It gave forth a sanguine light, in which the garden swam and weltered as if seen through a luminous mist of blood. Even in the bleak nights of winter, the globe yielded a genial warmth; and it fell never from its weird suspension, though without palpable support; and beneath it the garden flourished balefully, lush and exuberant as some parterre of the nether circles.

Indeed, the growths of that garden were such as no terrestrial sun could have fostered, and Dwerulas said that their seed was of like origin with the globe. There were pale, bifurcated trunks that strained upward as if to disroot themselves from the ground, unfolding immense leaves like the dark and ribbed wings of dragons. There were amaranthine blossoms, broad as salvers, supported by arm-thick stems that trembled continually.... And there were many other weird plants, diverse as the seven hells, and having no common characteristics other than the scions which Dwerulas had grafted upon them here and there through his unnatural and necromantic art.

These scions were the various parts and members of human beings. Consummately, and with never-failing success, the magician had joined them to the half-vegetable, half-animate stocks, on which they lived and grew thereafter, drawing an ichor-like sap. Thus were preserved the carefully chosen souvenirs of a multitude of persons who had inspired Dwerulas and the king with distaste or ennui. On palmy boles, beneath feathery-tufted foliage, the heads of eunuchs hung in bunches, like enormous black drupes. A bare, leafless creeper was flowered with the ears of delinquent guardsmen. Misshapen cacti were fruited with the breasts of women, or foliated with their hair. Entire limbs or torsos had been united with monstrous trees. Some of the huge salver-like blossoms bore palpitating hearts, and certain smaller blooms were centered with eyes that still opened and closed amid their lashes. And there were other graftings, too obscene or repellent for narration.

Adompha went forward among the hybrid growths, which stirred and rustled at his approach. The heads appeared to crane toward him a little, the ears quivered, the breasts shuddered lightly, the eyes widened or narrowed as if watching his progress. These human remnants, he knew, lived only with the sluggish life of the plants, shared only in their sub-animal activity. He had regarded them with a curious and morbid aesthetic pleasure, had found in them the infallible attraction of things enormous and hypernatural. Now, for the first time, he passed among them with a languid interest. He began to apprehend that fatal hour when the garden, with all its novel thaumaturgies, would offer no longer a refuge from his inexorable ennui.

At the core of the strange pleasance, where a circular space was still vacant amid the crowding growths, Adompha came to a mound of loamy, fresh-dug earth. Beside it, wholly nude, and pale and supine as if in death, there lay the odalisque Thuloneah. Near her, various knives, and other implements, together with vials of liquid balsams and viscid gums that Dwerulas used in his grafting, had been emptied upon the ground from a leathern bag. A plant known as the *dedaim*, with a bulbous, pulpy, whitish-green bole from whose center rose and radiated several leafless reptilian boughs, dripped upon Thuloneah's bosom an occasional drop of yellowish-red ichor from incisions made in its smooth bark.

Behind the loamy mound, Dwerulas rose to view with the suddenness of a demon emerging from his subterrene lair. In his hands he held the spade with which he had just finished digging a deep and grave-like hole. Beside the regal stature and girth of Adompha, he seemed no more than a wizened dwarf. His aspect bore all the marks of immense age, as if dusty centuries had sered his flesh and sucked the blood from his veins. His eyes glowed in the bottom of pitlike orbits; his features were black and sunken as those of a long-dead corpse; his body was gnarled as some millennial desert cedar. He stooped incessantly so that his lank, knotty arms hung almost to the ground. Adompha marvelled, as always, at the well-nigh demoniac strength of those arms; marvelled that Dwerulas could have wielded the heavy shovel so expeditiously, could have carried to the garden on his back without human aid the burden of those victims whose members he had utilized in his experiments. The king had never demeaned himself to assist at such labors; but, after indicating from time to time the people whose disappearance would in no wise displease him, had done nothing more than watch and supervise the baroque gardening.

"Is she dead?" Adompha questioned, eyeing the luxurious limbs and body of Thuloneah without emotion.

"Nay," said Dwerulas, in a voice harsh as a rusty coffin-hinge, "but I have administered to her the drowsy and overpowering juice of the *dedaim*. Her heart beats impalpably, her blood flows with the sluggishness of that mingled ichor. She will not reawaken... save as a part of the garden's life, sharing its obscure sentience. I wait now your further instructions. What portion... or portions?..."

"Her hands were very deft," said Adompha, as if musing aloud, in reply to the half-uttered question. "They knew the subtle ways of love and were learned in all amorous arts. I would have you preserve her hands... but nothing else."

The singular and magical operation had been completed. The fair, slim, tapering hands of Thuloneah, severed cleanly at the wrists, were attached with little mark of suture to the pale and lopped extremities of the two topmost branches of the *dedaim*. In this process the magician had employed the gums of infernal plants, and had repeatedly invoked the curious powers of certain underground genii, as was his wont on such occasions. Now, as if in suppliance, the semi-vegetable arms reached out toward Adompha with their human hands. The king felt a revival of his old interest in Dwerulas' horticulture, a queer excitement woke within him before the mingled grotesquery and beauty of the grafted plant. At the same time there lived again in his flesh the subtle ardors of outworn nights... for the hands were filled with memories.

He had quite forgotten Thuloneah's body, lying close by with its maimed arms. Recalled from his reverie by the sudden movement of Dwerulas, he turned and saw the wizard stooping above the unconscious girl, who had not stirred during the whole course of the operation. Blood still flowed and puddled upon the dark earth from the stumps of her wrists. Dwerulas, with that unnatural vigor which informed all his movements, seized the odalisque in his pipy arms and swung her easily aloft. His air was that of a laborer resuming his unfinished task; but he seemed to hesitate before casting her into the hole that would serve as a grave; where, through seasons warmed and illumined by the hell-drawn globe, her hidden, decaying body would feed the roots of that anomalous plant which bore her own hands for scions. It was as if he were loath to relinquish his voluptuous burden. Adompha, watching him curiously, was aware as never before of the stark evil and turpitude that flowed like an overwhelming fetor from Dwerulas' hunched body and twisted limbs.

Deeply as he himself had gone into all manner of iniquities, the king felt a vague revulsion. Dwerulas reminded him of a loathsome insect that he had once surprised during its ghoulish activities. He remembered how he had crushed the insect with a stone... and remembering, he conceived one of those bold and sudden inspirations that had always impelled him to equally sudden action. He had not, he told himself, entered the garden with any such thought: but the opportunity was too urgent and too perfect to be overpassed. The wizard's back was turned to him for the nonce; the arms of the wizard were encumbered with their heavy and pulchritudinous load. Snatching up the iron spade, Adompha brought it down on the small, withered head of Dwerulas with a fair amount of warlike strength inherited from heroic and piratic ancestors. The dwarf, still carrying Thuloneah, toppled forward into the deep pit.

Poising the spade for a second blow if such should be necessary, the king waited; but there was neither sound nor movement from the grave. He felt a certain surprise at having overcome with such ease the formidable magician, of whose superhuman powers he was half convinced; a certain surprise, too, at his own temerity. Then, reassured by his triumph, the king bethought him that he might try an experiment of his own: since he believed himself to have mastered much of Dwerulas' peculiar skill and lore through observation. The head of Dwerulas would form a unique and suitable addition to one of the garden plants. However, upon peering into the pit, he was forced to relinquish this idea: for he saw that he had struck only too well and had reduced the sorcerer's head to a state in which it was useless for his experiment, since such graftings required a certain integrity of the human part or member.

Reflecting, not without disgust, on the unlooked-for frailty of the skulls of magicians, which were as easily squashed as emus' eggs, Adompha began to fill the pit with loam. The prone body of Dwerulas, the huddled form of

Thuloneah beneath it, sharing the same inertness, were soon covered from view by the soft and dissolving clods. The king, who had grown to fear Dwerulas in his heart, was aware of a distinct relief when he had tamped the grave down very firmly and had levelled it smoothly with the surrounding soil. He told himself that he had done well: for the magician's stock of learning had come latterly to include too many royal secrets; and power such as his, whether drawn from nature or from occult realms, was never quite compatible with the secure dominion and prolonged empire of kings.

II

At King Adompha's court and throughout the sea-bordering city of Loithé, the vanishment of Dwerulas became the cause of much speculation but little inquiry. There was a division of opinion as to whether Adompha or the fiend Thasaidon could be thanked for so salutary a riddance; and in consequence, the king of Sotar and the lord of the seven hells were both feared and respected as never before. Only the most redoubtable of men or demons could have made away with Dwerulas, who was said to have lived through a whole millennium, never sleeping for one night, and crowding all his hours with iniquities and sorceries of a sub-tartarean blackness.

Following the inhumation of Dwerulas, a dim sentiment of fear and horror, for which he could not altogether account, had prevented the king from revisiting the sealed garden. Smiling impassively at the wild rumors of the court, he continued his search for novel pleasures and violent or rare sensations. In this, however, he met with small success: it seemed that every path, even the most outré and tortuous, led only to the hidden precipice of boredom. Turning from strange loves and cruelties, from extravagant pomps and mad music; from the aphrodisiac censers of far-sought blossoms, the quaintly shapen breasts of exotic girls, he recalled with new longing those semi-animate floral forms that had been endowed by Dwerulas with the most provocative charms of women.

So, on a latter night, at an hour midway between moonfall and sunrise, when all the palace and the city of Loithé were plunged in sodden slumber, the king arose from beside his concubine and went forth to the garden that was now secret from all men excepting himself.

In answer to the cobra-like sibilation, which alone could actuate its cunning mechanism, the door opened to Adompha and closed behind him. Even as it closed, he grew aware that a singular change had come upon the garden during his absence. Burning with a bloodier light, a more torrid radiation, the mysterious air-hung globe glared down as if fanned by wrathful demons; and the plants, which had grown excessively in height, and were muffled and hooded with a heavier foliage than they had worn priorly, stood motionless amid an atmosphere that was like the heated breath of some crimson hell.

Adompha hesitated, doubtful of the meaning of these changes. For a moment he thought of Dwerulas, and recalled with a slight shiver certain unexplained prodigies and necromantic feats performed by the wizard.... But he had slain Dwerulas and had buried him with his own royal hands. The waxing heat and radiance of that globe, the excessive growth of the garden, were no doubt due to some uncontrolled natural process.

Held by a strong curiosity, the king inhaled the giddying perfumes that came to assail his nostrils. The light dazzled his eyes, filling them with queer, unheard-of colors; the heat smote upon him as if from a nether solstice of infernal summer. He thought that he heard voices, almost inaudible at first, but mounting anon to a half-articulate murmur that seduced his ear with unearthly sweetness. At the same time he seemed to behold amid the stirless vegetation, in flashing glimpses, the half-veiled limbs of dancing bayaderes: limbs that he could not identify with any of the graftings made by Dwerulas.

Drawn by the charm of mystery, and seized by a vague intoxication, the king went forward into the hell-born labyrinth. The plants recoiled gently when he neared them, and drew back on either side to permit his passage. As if in arboreal masquerade, they seemed to hide their human scions behind the mantles of their newly-grown leafage. Then, closing behind Adompha, they appeared to cast off their disguise, revealing wilder and more anomalous fusions than he had remembered. They changed about him from instant to instant like shapes of delirium, so that he was never quite sure how much of their semblance was tree and flower, how much was woman and man. By turns he beheld a swinging of convulsed foliage, a commotion of riotous limbs and bodies. Then, by some undiscerned transition, it seemed that they were no longer rooted in the ground but were moving about him on dim, fantastic feet, in ever-swiftening circles, like the dancers of some bewildering festival.

Around and around Adompha raced the forms that were both floral and human; till the dizzy madness of their motion swirled with an equal vertigo through his brain. He heard the soughing of a storm-driven forest, together with a clamoring of familiar voices that called him by name, that cursed or supplicated, mocked or exhorted, in myriad tones of warrior, councillor, slave, courtling, castrado or leman. Over all, the sanguine globe blazed down with an ever-brightening and more baleful effulgence, an ardor that became always more insupportable. It was as if the whole life of the garden turned and rose and flamed and swiftened ecstatically to some infernal culmination.

King Adompha had lost all memory of Dwerulas and his dark magic. In his senses burned the ardor of the hell-risen orb, and he seemed to share the delirious motion and ecstasy of those obscure shapes by which he was surrounded. A mad ichor mounted in his blood; before him hovered the vague images of pleasures he had never known or suspected: pleasures in which he would pass far beyond the ordained limits of mortal sensation.

Then, amid that whirling phantasmagoria, he heard the screeching of a voice that was harsh as some rusty hinge on the lifted lid of a sarcophagus. He could not understand the words: but, as if a spell of stillness had been uttered, the whole garden resumed immediately a hushed and hooded aspect. The king stood in a very stupor: for the voice had been that of Dwerulas! He looked about him wildly, bemazed and bewildered, seeing only the still plants with their mantling of profuse leafage. Before him towered a growth which he somehow recognized as the *dedaim*, though its bulb-shaped bole and elongated branches had put forth a matted-mass of dark, hairlike filaments.

Very slowly and gently, the two topmost branches of the *dedaim* descended till their tips were level with Adompha's face. The slender, tapering hands of Thuloneah emerged from their foliage and began to caress the king's cheeks with that loverlike adroitness which he still remembered. At the same moment, he saw the thick hairy matting fall apart upon the broad and flattish top of the *dedaim*'s bole; and from it, as if rearing from hunched shoulders, the small, wizened head of Dwerulas rose up to confront him....

Still gazing in vacuous horror at the crushed and blood-clotted cranium, at the features sered and blackened as if by centuries, at the eyes that glowed in dark pits like embers blown by demons, Adompha had the confused impression of a multitude of people that hurled themselves upon him from every side. There were no longer any trees in that garden of mad minglings and sorcerous transformations. About him in the fiery air swam faces that he recalled only too well: faces now contorted with malign rage, and the lethal lust of revenge. Through an irony which Dwerulas alone could have conceived, the soft fingers of Thuloneah continued to caress him, while he felt the clutching of numberless hands that tore all his garments into rags and shredded all his flesh with their nails.

THE GREAT GOD AWTO

(Class-room lecture given by the Most Honorable Erru Saggus, Professor of Hamurriquanean Archaeology at the World-University of Toshtush, on the 365th day of the year 5998.)

Males, females, androgynes and neuters of the class in archaeology, you have learned, from my previous lectures, all that is known or inferred concerning the crudely realistic art and literature of the ancient Hamurriquanes. With some difficulty, owing to the fragmentary nature of the extant remains, I have reconstructed for you their bizarre and hideous buildings, their rude mechanisms.

Also, you are now familiar with the unimaginably clumsy, corrupt and inefficient legal and economic systems that prevailed among them, together with the garblings of crass superstition and scant knowledge that bore the sacred names of the sciences. You have listened, not without amusement, to my account of their ridiculous amatory and social customs, and have heard with horror the unutterable tale of their addiction to all manner of violent crimes.

Today I shall speak regarding a matter that throws into even grosser relief the low-grade barbarism, the downright savagery, of this bloody and besotted people.

Needless to say, my lecture will concern their well-nigh universal cult of human sacrifice and self-immolation to the god Awto: a cult which many of my confreres have tried to associate with the worship of the Heendouan deity, Yokkurnudd, or Jukkernot. In this cult, the wild religious fanaticism of the Hamurriquanes, together with the national blood-lust for which they were notorious, found its most congenial and spacious outlet.

If we grant the much-disputed relationship between Awto and Yokkurnudd, it seems plain that the latter god was an extremely mild and refined variation of Awto, worshipped by a gentler and more advanced people. The rites done to Yokkurnudd were localized and occasional while the sacrifices required by Awto took place at all hours on every street and highway.

However, in the face of certain respected authorities, I am inclined to doubt if the two religions had much in common. Certainly nothing apart from the ritual usage of crushing wheels of ponderous earth-vehicles, such as you have seen in our museums among the exhumed relics of antiquity.

It is my fond hope that I shall eventually find evidence to confirm this doubt, and thus vindicate the Heendouans of the blackest charge that legend and archaeology have brought against them. I shall have made a worthy contribution to science if I can show that they were among the few ancient peoples who were never tainted by the diabolic cult of Awto originating in Hamurriqua.

Because of a religion so barbarous, it has sometimes been argued that the Hamurriquanean culture—if one can term it such—must have flourished at an earlier period in man's development than the Heendouan. However, in dealing with a realm of research that borders upon prehistory, such relative chronology can be left to theorists.

Excepting, of course, in our own superior modern civilization, human progress has been slow and uncertain, with many intercalated Dark Ages, many reversions to partial or total savagery. I believe that the Hamurriquanean epoch, whether prior to that of the Heendouans or contemporary with it, can well be classified as one of these Dark Ages.

To return to my main theme, the cult of Awto. It is doubtless well known to you that in recent years certain irresponsible so-called archaeologists, misled by a desire to create sensation at the cost of truth, have fathered the fantastic thesis that there never was any such god as Awto. They believe, or profess to believe, that the immolatory vehicles of the ancients, and the huge destruction of life and limb caused by their use, were quite without religious significance.

A premise so absurd could be maintained only by madmen or charlatans. I mention it merely that I may refute and dismiss it with all the contempt that it deserves.

Of course, I cannot deny the dubiousness of some of our archaeological deductions. Great difficulties have attended our researches in the continent-embracing deserts of Hamurriqua, where all food-supplies and water must be transported for thousands of miles.

The buildings and writings of the ancients, often made of the most ephemeral materials, lie deep in ever-drifting sands that no human foot has trod for millenniums. Therefore, it is small wonder that guesswork must sometimes fill the gaps of precise knowledge.

I can safely say, however, that few of our deductions are so completely proven, so solidly based, as those relating to the Awto cult. The evidence, though largely circumstantial, is overwhelming.

Like most religions, it would seem that this cult was obscure and shadowy in its origin. Legend and history have both lost the name of the first promulgator. The earliest cars of immolation were slow and clumsy, and the rite of sacrifice was perhaps rarely and furtively practiced in the beginning. There is no doubt, too, that the intended victims often escaped. Awto, at first, can hardly have inspired the universal fear and reverence of later epochs.

Certain scraps of Hamurriquanean printing, miraculously preserved in air-tight vaults and deciphered before they could crumble, have given us the names of two early prophets of Awto, Anriford and Dhodzh. These amassed fortunes from the credulity of their benighted followers. It was under the influence of these prophets that the dark and baleful religion spread by leaps and bounds, until no Hamurriquanean street or highway was safe from the thunderously rolling wheels of the sacrificial cars.

It is doubtful whether Awto, like most other savage and primordial deities, was ever represented by graven images. At least, no such images have been recovered in all our delvings. However, the rusty remains of the iron-built temples of Awto, called *grahges*, have been exhumed everywhere in immense numbers.

Strange vessels and metal implements of mysterious hieratic use have been found in the *grahges*, together with traces of oils by which the sacred vehicles were anointed, and the vehicles lie buried in far-spread, colossal scrapheaps. All this, however, throws little light on the deity himself.

It is probable that Awto, sometimes known as Mhotawr, was simply an abstract principle of death and destruction and was believed to manifest himself through the homicidal speed and fury of the fatal machines. His demented devotees flung themselves before these vehicles as before the embodiment of the god.

The power and influence of Awto's priesthood, as well as its numbers, must have been well nigh beyond estimation. The priesthood, it would seem, was divided into at least three orders:

The *mekniks*, or keepers of the *grahges*. The *shophurs*, who drove the sacred vehicles. And an order—whose special name has been lost—that served as guardians of innumerable wayside shrines. It was at these shrines where a mineral liquid called *ghas* used in the fuelling of the vehicles, was dispensed from crude and curious pumping mechanisms.

Several well-preserved mummies of *mekniks*, in sacerdotal raiment blackened by the sacred oils, have been recovered from *grahges* in the central Hamurriquanean deserts, where they were apparently buried by sudden sandstorms.

Chemical analysis of the oiled garments has so far failed to confirm a certain legendary belief current among the degenerate bushmen who form the scant remnant of Hamurriqua's teeming myriads. I refer to a belief that the oils used in anointing those ancient cars were often mixed with unctuous matters obtained from the bodies of their victims.

However, a usage so barbarous would have conformed well enough with the principles of the hideous cult. Further research may establish the old legend as a truth.

From the evidence we have unearthed, it is plain that the cult assumed enormous power and wide-spread proportions within a few decades of its inception. The awful apex was reached in little more than a century. In my opinion, it is no coincidence that the whole period of the Awto cult corresponded very closely with Hamurriqua's decline and ultimate downfall.

Some will consider my statements too definite, and will ask for the evidence above mentioned. In answer, I need only point to the condition of those skeletons exhumed by thousands from tombs and vaults dated according to the Hamurriquanean chronology.

Throughout the time-period we have assigned to the Awto cult there is a steady, accelerative increase of bone-fractures, often of the most horribly complicated nature. Toward the end, when the fearful cult was at its height, we find few skeletons that do not show at least one or two minor, if not major, breakages.

The shattered condition of these skeletons, often decapitated or wholly disarticulated, is almost beyond belief.

The rusty remains of the ancient vehicles bear similar witness. Built with an eye to ever greater speed and deadliness, they fall into types that show the ghastly growth and progress of the cult. The later types, found in prodigious numbers, are always more or less dented, broken, crumpled—often they are mere heaps of indescribably tangled wreckage.

Toward the end, it would seem that virtually the whole population must have belonged to the blood-mad priesthood. Going forth daily in the rituals of Awto, they must have turned their cars upon each other, hurtling together with the violence of projectiles. A universal mania for speed went hand in hand with a mania for homicide and suicide.

Picture, if you can, the ever-mounting horror of it all. The nation-wide madness of immolation. The carnivals of bloody holidays. The highways lined from coast to coast with crushed and dismembered sacrifices!

Can you wonder that this ancient people, their numbers decimated, their mentality sapped and bestialized by dire superstition, should have declined so rapidly? Should have fallen almost without a struggle before the hordes of the Orient?

Let history and archaeology draw the curtain. The moral is plain. But luckily, in our present state of high enlightenment, we have little need to fear the rise of any savage terror such as that which attended the worship of Awto.

Obituary item broadcast from Toshtush on the 1st day of the year 5999:

We are sorry to record the sudden death of Professor Erru Saggus, who had just delivered the last of his series of lectures on Hamurriquanean

Archaeology at the University of Toshtush.

Returning on the same afternoon to his home in the Himalayas, Professor Saggus was the victim of a most unfortunate accident. His stratosphere ship, one of the very newest and speediest models, collided within a few leagues of its destination with a ship driven by one Jar Ghoshtar, a chemistry student from the great College of Ustraleendia.

Both ships were annihilated by the impact, plunging earthward in a single flaming meteoric mass which ignited and destroyed an entire Himalayan village. Several hundred people are said to have burned to death in the resultant conflagration.

Such accidents are all too frequent nowadays, owing to the crowded condition of stratosphere traffic. We must deplore the recklessness of navigators who exceed the 950 mile speed limit. All who saw the recent accident bear witness that Erru Saggus and Jar Ghoshtar were both driving at a speed very much in excess of 1000 miles per hour.

While regretting this present-day mania for mere mileage, we cannot agree with certain ill-advised satirists who have tried to draw a parallel between the fatalities of modern traffic and the ancient rites of immolation to the god Awto.

Superstition is one thing, Science is another. Such archaeologists as Professor Saggus have proven to us that the worshippers of Awto were the victims of a dark and baleful error. It is unthinkable that such superstition will ever again prevail. With pride for our achievements, and full confidence in the future, we can number the most Honorable Professor Erru Saggus among the martyrs of Science.

STRANGE SHADOWS

Downing his thirteenth dry Martini, Gaylord Jones drew a complacent sigh and regarded the barroom floor with grave attention. He was drunk. He knew that he was drunk. With superb lucidity, he calculated the exact degree of his inebriation.

A great white light was pivoted in his brain. He could turn this light, instantly, on the most obscure corners of the nothingness called life. At last he was able to appreciate the absurd logic of the cosmos. It was all very simple. Nothing mattered in the least.

It was all very simple, and nothing mattered as long as one could keep himself sufficiently pickled. Ah, that was the problem. Reflecting long and deeply, Jones decided that just one more Martini would help to maintain his intoxication at the right stage.

He had, however, consumed three drinks in a row at this particular bar. The Martinis were well mixed. The bartender's manners were unexceptionable. But Jones felt that he should not play any favorites when it came to barrooms. There were so many others that deserved his patronage. In fact, there was one just around the corner on his homeward route.

"I wonder often what the vintners buy one-half so precious as the stuff they sell," he quoted, muttering to himself, as he descended carefully from his seat.

Jones prided himself on knowing his capacity. So far, he had never had the misfortune to overestimate it. He could carry one, two, three, even four more drinks if necessary, without deviating from the proverbial chalk line. Every night, for at least a month past, he had collected a full cargo at various alcoholic ports between his office and hotel. The stuff never hurt him. He had never been known to stagger or even wobble at any point along the route. His morning headaches, if any, were light and fleeting.

He stood up and looked at himself in the mirror behind the bar. Yes, he could hold his liquor. No casual observer would be able to tell that he had had three Martinis, let alone thirteen. His eyes were clear, his face no redder or paler than usual. He adjusted his tie neatly, bade the bartender a crisp goodnight, and started toward the door.

Of course, his locomotor faculties were under perfect control. He knew that they would not fail him as long as he observed due caution and didn't move too precipitately. His senses had never played him tricks either. But, as he crossed the long room, Jones received a curious impression. The room was empty except for a few late patrons at the bar or remote tables. Yet once, twice, thrice, it seemed to him that he had trodden on someone's heels. It was a baffling and disconcerting sensation, since, visibly, no one was in front of him or even near at hand. With some effort, each time, he checked himself from stumbling.

Jones went on, feeling slightly disturbed and annoyed. Again, as he approached the door, the mysterious sensation was repeated. It was as if his toes had collided with the heel of some stranger who preceded him down the room. This time, Jones nearly fell on his face before he could recover himself.

"Who the hell—" he started to mumble. But, as before, there was no one, nothing, against whom or which he could have tripped. Looking down, he could see only his own shadow, now stretching doorward in the light cast by the electric chandeliers.

Jones stood peering at the shadow with a vague but growing puzzlement. It was a funny sort of shadow, he thought. There must be something queer about the lights in that barroom. It didn't look like his own shadow, or, in fact, the shadow of any human being. He wasn't squeamish. He had never been a stickler for aesthetic propriety or any kind of propriety. But he felt a sense of actual shock when he began to consider the various things that were wrong with the shadow's outline.

Though he himself was correctly attired, there was no suggestion that the caster of the shadow wore either clothing, hat or shoes. Indeed, it hardly seemed to indicate any sort of creature that would wear clothing.

Jones thought of the gargoyles of Notre Dame. He thought of antique satyrs. He thought of goats and swine. The shadow was gargoylish, it was satyr-like. It was goatish and porcine—it was even worse. It was the adumbration of some shambling, obscene, pot-bellied monster, trying to stand upright like a man on its hind legs, and holding its forelegs a little away from the body on each hand.

Its edges were hairy as the silhouette of an ape. Appendages that were huge ears or horns rose above its swollen head. The rear shanks were bent at a bestial angle. Something like a tail depended between them. The four feet gave the appearance of hooves. The two lifted feet were visibly cloven.

Apart from these deformities of outline, the shadow possessed an unnatural thick blackness. It was like a pool of tar. Sometimes it seemed to swell upward from the floor, to take on a third dimension.

Sobriety had almost returned to Jones. But now the thirteen cumulative Martinis resumed their work. By one of those sudden shifts of a drunkard's mood, he began to forget his feelings of shock and perplexity. The shadow's very grotesquery began to amuse him.

"Must be another guy's shadow," he chuckled. "But what a guy!"

He stepped forward cautiously, holding out his right arm at a dead level and parting all the fingers of his right hand. The shadow moved with him. Its right fore-member rose and protruded at the angle of his arm. But still there was only the shadow of a cloven hoof where the shadows of five outspread fingers should have registered.

Jones shook his head bewilderedly. Maybe it was the lights, after all. There must be some explanation.

He stepped backward, maintaining a balance that had become slightly precarious. This time, the shadow did not follow his change of position. It lay as before, its hind hooves separated from his own nattily shod feet by an interval of light.

Jones felt a confused outrage. Here was a problem that defied the blazing white logic of alcohol. What could one make of a shadow that not only failed to reproduce its owner's periphery, but refused to follow all his movements?

To make matters worse, he saw that the shadow had now begun to display an activity of its own. Lurching and weaving while he stood stock still, it danced abominably from side to side on the floor, like the shadow of a drunken satyr. It capered and cavorted. It made vile gestures with its forelegs.

At this moment a patrolman, parched, no doubt, from his long evening vigil, entered the barroom. He was formidably tall and broad. Giving Jones the tail of a truculent eye, he passed on toward the bar without seeming to notice the outrageous behavior of Jones' errant shadow.

Behind the patrolman's bulk there trailed a shadow like that of some diminutive monkey. It appeared to cower at his heels. It seemed to scamper and scuttle behind the arrogant pomp of his advance. It was incredibly thin, wizened, puny-looking.

Jones rubbed his eyes. Here, perhaps, was something to reassure him. If his own shadow had gone screwy, the patrolman's was equally haywire.

This conclusion was instantly confirmed. The shadow that, by courtesy, Jones called his own, had ceased its indecorous caperings. It wheeled about suddenly and ran past him as if following the officer. At the same time the policeman's monkey-like shadow detached itself from its owner's heels and fled swiftly toward a remote corner of the room. Jones' shadow pursued it in great, goatish leaps, with gesticulations of obscene anger and menace.

The officer, quite oblivious of his loss, continued barward. Jones heard him order a beer.

Jones decided that he had lingered all too long in that particular drinking-place. Matters had grown slightly embarrassing, not to say compromising. Shadow or no shadow, he would speed his progress to the next bar. After two or three additional Martinis, he could manage well enough without a shadow. Good riddance, anyway. Let the policeman keep the damned thing in order if he could.

The street outside was well-lighted but almost empty of pedestrians. With a sense of urgency and compulsion, Jones hurried to the saloon around the corner. He avoided looking down at the pavement as he went.

Ordering three Martinis, he drank them down as fast as the bartender could mix and pour them. The result was all that he had hoped for. His feeling of cosmic detachment and independence returned to him. What was a shadow, anyway? The one cast by the bartender's hand and arm, moving over the bar, was not that of a normal human limb; but Jones refused to consider it. He could take his shadows or leave them.

He took three more drinks. His sense of alcoholic caution told him that it was now curfew-time. Promptly, though a little unsteadily, he began the last lap of his homeward journey.

Somewhere on the way, he perceived rather vaguely that his shadow had rejoined him. It was more monstrous than ever under the street-lamps—more obscene and unnatural. Then, suddenly, there were two shadows. This, however, was not surprising, since he had begun to see telephone-posts, lights, cars, hydrants, people, and other objects along his route all in duplicate.

He awoke the next morning with a dull headache and a confused impression that the scheme of things had somehow gone wrong. Just how or why it had gone wrong he could not remember at first. But he had had one or two drinks too many and had fallen asleep in his clothes on top of the bedding.

Groaning, he pulled himself from the bed and stood up groggily with his back to the bright sunlight that streamed in through his apartment windows. It seemed that something rose with him—a black, solid silhouette that stood erect for an instant in the air. Horribly startled, he saw the thing resolve itself into a shadow stretching across the floor. It was the gargoylish, goatish, satyrish, porcine shadow of the previous night.

It was something that neither sunlight nor lamplight, by any trick or distortion, could conceivably have wrought from Jones' head, limbs and body. In the bright glare, it was blacker, grosser, more hirsute than before. Curiously, it was broader and less elongated than a shadow should have been in the full early light.

It was like some foul incubus of legend—a separate entity that companioned him in place of his rightful shadow.

Jones felt thoroughly frightened. He was sober, with the profound, excessive sobriety of the morning after. He did not believe in the supernatural. Plainly, he had become the victim of a set of bizarre hallucinations, confined to one subject. Otherwise, his sensory perceptions were quite normal. Perhaps, without realizing it, he had been drinking too much and had developed a new kind of delirium tremens. He knew that alcoholism didn't always result in the seeing of mauve elephants and cerise reptiles.

Or maybe it was something else. There were all sorts of obscure mental diseases, symptomized by aberrant or deluded sense-perceptions. He knew little of such things, but knew that the possibilities were infinitely various and terrifying.

Averting his eyes from the shadow, he fled to his bathroom, where there was no direct sunlight. Even here he had the sensation of being accompanied. Again, as in the barroom, he seemed to stumble over the heels of some unseen person who had preceded him.

With nightmare difficulty he concentrated on the tasks of washing and shaving himself. A dreadful gulf had opened at his feet amid the solid reality of things.

A clock struck somewhere in the apartment-house, and Jones realized that he had overslept and must hurry to his office. There was no time for breakfast, even if he had not lacked the appetite.

Dogged by his weirdly altered shadow, he went out on the crowded street in the clear April morning. Embarrassment mingled with his sense of horror. It seemed that everyone must notice the black changeling that followed him like a wizard's familiar.

However, the early throng, hurrying intently to the day's work or pleasure, paid no more attention to Jones and his shadow than on any other morning. It was more and more obvious that he suffered from some sort of visual hallucination: for the people about him were apparently quite untroubled by the oddities which he perceived in their shadows as well as in his own.

Studying these shadows with a morbid fascination as they passed by on the walls and pavements, Jones well-nigh forgot the dark miscreation at his own heels. It was like looking at the shadows of some hellish menagerie. Among them all, there was none that corresponded to the visible physique of its owner. And now and then some person went by, like the legendary vampire, without appearing to cast a shadow at all.

Demure young girls were attended by adumbrations that might have been those of lascivious she-apes or coquetting sphinxes. A benign priest was followed by the shadow of some murderous devil. A rich and popular society matron was paired with the four-legged shadow of a humpbacked cow. Shadows like those of hyenas trotted behind respectable bankers and aldermen.

Jones noted that the shadows cast by inorganic objects, such as trees and buildings, had not shared in the change. But the shadows of animals bore as little likeness to their casters as those of men. Oddly, those of dogs and horses were often quasihuman, seeming to indicate a rise rather than a degradation in the scale of being.

Sometimes, as on the evening before, Jones witnessed the incredible behavior of shadows that moved and acted with complete detachment from their owners. He saw pantomimes that were grotesque, ludicrous, often indecent.

It was in the mental state of a man bewitched that he reached the office of his young but thriving insurance business. Miss Owens, the rather mature typist, was already settled at her machine. She raised her well-plucked eyebrows at his lateness.

Jones noted mechanically that his business partner, Caleb Johnson, was even later than himself. A moment afterwards, Johnson entered. He was heavy-set, darkly florid, older than Jones. As usual, he looked like the aftermath of a season of misspent nights. The rings under his eyes were strongly marked as those of a raccoon's tail. Miss Owens did not appear to notice his entrance, but bent closer above her machine.

Johnson grunted by way of greeting. It was a one-syllable, Anglo-Saxon grunt. He went to his desk, which was opposite Miss Owens'. The office settled to its daily routine.

Jones, trying to control his whirling wits and fix them on his work, was thankful for the diffused light at that hour. Somehow, he succeeded in applying himself to a pile of letters, and even dictated a few replies. Several clients came in. There were some new applicants for fire and accident insurance. It reassured Jones a little, to find that he could talk and answer questions without betraying the incoherence of his thoughts.

Part of the morning went by. At times the mad mystery that troubled him receded to the margin of consciousness. It was too unreal, too much like the phantasms of dreams. But he would go easy on drinking in the future. No doubt the hallucinations would wear off when he had freed his system from any residue of alcohol. Perhaps his nerves were already righting themselves and he wouldn't see any more crazy shadows.

At that moment he happened to look over toward Johnson and Miss Owens. The rays of the sun in its transit had now entered the broad plate-glass window, spreading obliquely across them both and casting their shadows on the floor.

Jones, who was no prude, almost blushed at the outlines formed by Miss Owens' shadow. It showed a figure that was not only outrageously unclothed but betrayed proclivities more suitable to a witches' Sabbat than a modern business office. It moved forward in an unseemly fashion while Miss Owens remained seated. It met the shadow cast by Johnson... which, without going into detail, was hardly that of a respectable business man....

Miss Owens, looking up from her Remington, intercepted Jones' eye. His expression seemed to startle her. A natural flush deepened her brunette rouge.

"Is anything wrong, Mr. Jones?" she queried.

Johnson also looked up from the account book in which he was making entries. He too appeared startled. His heavy-lidded eyes became speculative.

"Nothing is wrong, as far as I know," said Jones, shamefacedly, averting his eyes from the shadows. He had begun to wonder about something. Johnson was a married man with two half-grown children. But there had been hints.... More than once, Jones had met him with Miss Owens after business hours. Neither of them had seemed particularly pleased by such meetings. Of course, it wasn't Jones' affair what they did. He was not interested. What did interest him now was the behavior of the shadows. After all, was there at times some hidden relevance, some bearing upon reality, in the phenomena that he had regarded as baseless hallucinations? The thought was far from pleasant in one sense. But he decided to keep his eyes and his mind open.

Jones had lunched with more semblance of appetite than he had believed possible. The day drew on toward five o'clock. The lowering sun filled a westward window with its yellow blaze. Johnson stood up to trim and light a cigar. His strong black shadow was flung on the gold-lit door of the company's big iron safe in the corner beyond.

The shadow, Jones noted, was not engaged in the same action as its owner. There was nothing like the shadow of a cigar in its outthrust hand. The black fingers seemed trying to manipulate the dial on the safe's door. They moved deftly, spelling out the combination that opened the safe. Then they made the movement of fingers that draw back a heavy hinged object. The shadow moved forward, stooping and partly disappearing. It returned and stood erect. Its fingers carried something. The shadow of the other hand became visible. Jones realized, with a sort of startlement, that Johnson's shadow was counting a roll of shadowy bills. The roll was apparently thrust into its pocket, and the shadow went through the pantomime of closing the safe.

All this had set Jones to thinking again. He had heard, vaguely, that Johnson gambled—either on stocks or horses, he couldn't remember which. And Johnson was the firm's bookkeeper. Jones had never paid much attention to the bookkeeping, apart from noting cursorily that the accounts always seemed to balance.

Was it possible that Johnson had been using, or meant to use, the firm's money for irregular purposes? Large sums were often kept in the safe. Offhand, Jones thought that there must be more than a thousand dollars on hand at present.

Oh, well, maybe it was preferable to think that excess cocktails had endowed him with a new brand of heeby-jeebies. It would be better than believing that Johnson was a possible embezzler.

That evening he visited a doctor instead of making the usual round of barrooms.

The doctor frowned very learnedly as Jones described his strange affliction. He took Jones' pulse and temperature, tested his knee-jerk and other reflexes, flashed a light into his eyes, looked at his tongue.

"You haven't any fever, and there's no sign of d.t.," he reassured finally. "Your nerves seem to be sound though jumpy. I don't think you're likely to go insane—at least not for some time. Probably it's your eyes. You'd better see a good oculist tomorrow. In the meanwhile I'll prescribe a sedative for your nervousness. Of course you ought to ease up on liquor—maybe the alcohol is affecting your eyesight."

Jones hardly heard the doctor's advice. He had been studying the doctor's shadow, flung across an expensive rug by a tall and powerful floor-lamp. It was the least human and most unpleasant of all the shadows he had yet seen. It had the contours and the posture of a ghoul stooping over a ripe carrion.

After leaving the doctor's office, Jones remembered that he had a fiancée. He had not seen her for a week. She did not approve of Martinis—at least not in such quantities as Jones had been collecting nightly for the past month. Luckily—unless he collected them in her company—she was unable to tell whether he had had two drinks or a dozen. He was very fond of Marcia. Her quaint ideas about temperance weren't too much of a drawback. And anyway he was going to be temperate himself till he got rid of the shadows. It *would* be something to tell Marcia.

On second thought he decided to leave out the shadow part. She would think he had the heeby-jeebies.

Marcia Dorer was a tall blonde, slender almost to thinness. She gave Jones a brief kiss. Sometimes her kisses made him feel slightly refrigerated. This was one of the times.

"Well, where have you been keeping yourself?" she asked. There was a sub-acid undertone in her soprano. "In front of all the bars in town, I suppose?"

"Not today," said Jones gravely. "I haven't had a drink since last night. In fact, I have decided to quit drinking."

"Oh, I'm glad," she cooed, "if you really mean it. I know liquor can't be good for you—at least, not so much of it. They say it does things to your insides."

She pecked him again, lightly, between cheek and lips. Just at that moment Jones thought to look at their shadows on the parlor wall. What would Marcia's shadow be like?

In spite of the queer phenomena he had already seen, Jones was unpleasantly surprised, even shocked. He hardly knew what he had expected, but certainly it wasn't anything like this.

To begin with, there were three shadows on the wall. One was Jones', porcine, satyr-like as usual. In spite of his physical proximity to Marcia, it stood far apart from hers.

Marcia's shadow he could not clearly distinguish from the third one, since, with its back turned to Jones', it was united with the other in a close embrace. It resembled Marcia only in being a shadow of a female. The other shadow was plainly male. It lifted a grossly swollen, bearded profile above the head of its companion. It was not a refined-looking shadow. Neither was Marcia's.

Marcia had never embraced him like that, thought Jones. He felt disgusted; but after all, he couldn't be jealous of an unidentified shadow.

Somehow, it was not a very successful evening. Jones turned his eyes away from the wall and refrained from looking at it again. But he could not forget the shadows. Marcia chattered without seeming to notice his preoccupation; but there was something perfunctory in her chatter, as if she too were preoccupied.

"I guess you'd better go, darling," she said at last. "Do you mind? I didn't sleep well, and I'm tired tonight."

Jones looked at his wrist-watch. It was only twenty minutes past nine.

"Oh, all right," he assented, feeling a vague relief. He kissed her and went out, seeing with the tail of his eye that the third shadow was still in the room. It was still on the parlor wall, with Marcia's shadow in its arms.

Halfway down the block, beside a lamp-post, Jones passed Bertie Filmore. The two nodded. They knew and liked each other very slightly. Jones peered down at Filmore's shadow on the sidewalk as he went by. Filmore was a floorwalker in a department store—a slim, sleek youth who neither drank, smoked nor indulged in any known vice. He attended the Methodist church every Sunday morning and Wednesday evening. Jones felt a profane and cynical curiosity as to what his shadow would look like.

The adumbration that he saw was shortened by the nearby lamp. But its profile was unmistakably the gross, bearded profile of the third shadow on Marcia's wall! It bore no resemblance to Filmore.

"What the hell!" thought Jones, very disagreeably startled. "Is there something in this?"

He slackened his pace and glanced back at Filmore's receding figure. Filmore sauntered on as if out for an airing, without special objective, and did not turn to look back at Jones. He went in at the entrance of Marcia's home.

"So that's why she wanted me to leave early," Jones mused. It was all plain to him now... plain as the clinching shadows. Marcia had expected Filmore. The shadows weren't all katzen-jammer, not by a jugful.

His pride was hurt. He had known that Marcia was acquainted with the fellow. But it was a shock to think that Filmore had displaced him in her affections. In Jones' estimation, the fellow was a cross between a Sunday school teacher and a tailor's dummy. No color or character to him.

Chewing the cud of his bitterness, Jones hesitated at several barroom doors. Perhaps he would see worse shadows if he killed another row of Martinis. Or… maybe he wouldn't. What the hell….

He went into the next bar without hesitating.

The morning brought him a headache worthy of the bender to which twenty—or was it twenty-one—more or less expert mixologists had contributed.

He reached his office an hour behind time. Surprisingly, Miss Owens, who had always been punctual, was not in evidence. Less surprisingly, Johnson was not there either. He often came late.

Jones was in no mood for work. He felt as if all the town clocks were striking twelve in his head. Moreover, he had a heart which, if not broken, was deeply cracked. And there was still the nerve-wracking problem of those strangely distorted and often misplaced shadows.

He kept seeing in his mind the shadows on Marcia's wall. They nauseated him… or perhaps his stomach was slightly upset from more than the due quota of Martinis. Then, as many minutes went by and neither Miss Owens nor Johnson appeared, he recalled the queer shadow-play in his office of the previous afternoon. Why in hell hadn't he thought of that before? Perhaps—

His unsteady fingers spun the combination of the safe, drew back the door. Cash, negotiable bonds, a few checks that had come in too late for banking—all were gone. Johnson must have returned to the office that night. Or perhaps he had cleared out the safe before leaving in the late afternoon. Both he and Miss Owens had stayed after Jones' departure. They often did that, and Jones hadn't thought much about it since both were busy with unfinished work.

Jones felt paralyzed. One thing was clear, however: Johnson's shadow had forewarned him with its pantomime of opening the safe, removing and counting money. It had betrayed its owner's intention beforehand. If he had watched and waited, Jones could no doubt have caught his partner in the act. But he had felt so doubtful about the meaning of the shadows, and his main thought when he left the office had been to see a doctor. Later, the discovery of Marcia's deceit had upset him, made him forget all else.

The telephone broke into his reflections with its jangling. A shrill female voice questioned him hysterically. It was Mrs. Johnson. "Is Caleb there? Have you seen Caleb?"

"No. I haven't seen him since yesterday."

"Oh, I'm so worried, Mr. Jones. Caleb didn't come home last night but phoned that he was working very late at the office. Said he might not get in till after midnight. He hadn't come in when I fell asleep; and he wasn't here this morning. I've been trying to get the office for the past hour."

"I was late myself," said Jones. "I'll tell Johnson to call you when he comes. Maybe he had to go out of town suddenly." He did not like the task of telling Mrs. Johnson that her husband had embezzled the firm's cash and had probably eloped with the typist.

"I'm going to call the police," shrilled Mrs. Johnson. "Something dreadful must have happened to Caleb."

Jones kept remembering that other shadow-scene in his office which had made him almost blush. More as a matter of form than anything else, he rang up the apartment house at which Miss Owens roomed. She had returned there as usual the previous evening but had left immediately with a valise, saying that she was called away by the sudden death of an aunt and would not be back for several days.

Well, that was that. Jones had lost a good typist, together with more cash than he could afford to lose. As to Johnson—well, the fellow had been no great asset as a partner. Jones, who had no head for figures, had been glad to delegate the bookkeeping to him. But he could have hired a good accountant at far less expense.

There was nothing to do but put the matter in the hands of the police. Jones had reached again for the receiver, when the mailman entered, bringing several letters and a tiny registered package.

The package was addressed to Jones in Marcia's neat and somewhat prim handwriting. One of the letters bore the same hand. Jones signed for the package and broke the letter open as soon as the mailman had gone. It read:

> Dear Gaylord,
> I am returning your ring. I have felt for some time past that I am not the right girl to make you happy. Another man, of whom I am very fond, wishes to marry me. I hope you will find someone better suited to you than I should be.
>
> Always yours,
Marcia

Jones put the little package aside without opening it. His thoughts were bitter. Marcia must have written to him and mailed the package early that morning. Filmore, of course, was the other man. Probably he had proposed to her the night before, after Jones had passed him on the street.

Jones could definitely add a sweetheart to his other losses. And he had gained, it seemed, a peculiar gift for seeing shadows that did not correspond to their owners' physical outlines... which did not always duplicate their movements... shadows that were sometimes revelatory of hidden intentions, prophetic of future actions.

It seemed, then, that he possessed a sort of clairvoyance. But he had never believed in such things. What good was it doing him anyway?

After he phoned the police about Johnson, he would call it a day and gather enough drinks to dissolve the very substance of reality into a shadow.

THE ENCHANTRESS OF SYLAIRE

"Why, you big ninny! I could never marry you," declared the demoiselle Dorothée, only daughter of the Sieur des Flêches. Her lips pouted at Anselme like two ripe berries. Her voice was honey—but honey filled with bee-stings.

"You are not so ill-looking. And your manners are fair. But I wish I had a mirror that could show you to yourself for the fool that you really are."

"Why?" queried Anselme, hurt and puzzled.

"Because you are just an addle-headed dreamer, poring over books like a monk. You care for nothing but silly old romances and legends. People say that you even write verses. It is lucky that you are at least the second son of the Comte du Framboisier—for you will never be anything more than that."

"But you loved me a little yesterday," said Anselme, bitterly. "A woman finds nothing good in the man she has ceased to love."

"Dolt! Donkey!" cried Dorothée, tossing her blonde ringlets in pettish arrogance. "If you were not all that I have said, you would never remind me of yesterday. Go, idiot—and do not return."

Anselme, the hermit, had slept little, tossing distractedly on his hard, narrow pallet. His blood, it seemed, had been fevered by the sultriness of the summer night.

Then, too, the natural heat of youth had contributed to his unease. He had not wanted to think of women—a certain woman in particular. But, after thirteen months of solitude, in the heart of the wild woodland of Averoigne, he was still far from forgetting. Crueler even than her taunts was the remembered beauty of Dorothée des Flêches: the full-ripened mouth, the round arms and slender waist, the breast and hips that had not yet acquired their amplest curves.

Dreams had thronged the few short intervals of slumber, bringing other visitants, fair but nameless, about his couch.

He arose at sundawn, weary but restless. Perhaps he would find refreshment by bathing, as he had often done, in a pool fed from the river Isoile and hidden among alder and willow thickets. The water, deliciously cool at that hour, would assuage his feverishness.

His eyes burned and smarted in the morning's gold glare when he emerged from the hut of wattled osier withes. His thoughts wandered, still full of the night's disorder. Had he been wise, after all, to quit the world, to leave his friends and family, and seclude himself because of a girl's unkindness? He could not deceive himself into thinking that he had become a hermit through any aspiration toward sainthood, such as had sustained the old anchorites. By dwelling so much alone, was he not merely aggravating the malady he had sought to cure?

Perhaps, it occurred to him belatedly, he was proving himself the ineffectual dreamer, the idle fool that Dorothée had accused him of being. It was weakness to let himself be soured by a disappointment.

Walking with downcast eyes, he came unaware to the thickets that fringed the pool. He parted the young willows without lifting his gaze, and was about to cast off his garments. But at that instant, the nearby sound of splashing water startled him from his abstraction.

With some dismay, Anselme realized that the pool was already occupied. To his further consternation, the occupant was a woman. Standing near to the center, where the pool deepened, she stirred the water with her hands till it rose and rippled against the base of her bosom. Her pale wet skin glistened like white rose petals dipped in dew.

Anselme's dismay turned to curiosity and then to unwilling delight. He told himself that he wanted to withdraw but feared to frighten the bather by a sudden movement. Stooping with her clear profile and her shapely left shoulder toward him, she had not perceived his presence.

A woman, young and beautiful, was the last sight he had wished to see. Nevertheless, he could not turn his eyes away. The woman was a stranger to him, and he felt sure that she was no girl of the village or countryside. She was lovely as any châtelaine of the great castles of Averoigne. And yet surely no lady or demoiselle would bathe unattended in a forest pool.

Thick-curling chestnut hair, bound by a light silver fillet, billowed over her shoulders and burned to red, living gold where the sun-rays searched it out through the foliage. Hung about her neck, a light golden chain seemed to reflect the lusters of her hair, dancing between her breasts as she played with the ripples.

The hermit stood watching her like a man caught in webs of sudden sorcery. His youth mounted within him, in response to her beauty's evocation.

Seeming to tire of her play, she turned her back and began to move toward the opposite shore, where, as Anselme now noticed, a pile of feminine garments lay in charming disorder on the grass. Step by step she rose up from the shoaling water, revealing hips and thighs like those of an antique Venus.

Then, beyond her, he saw that a huge wolf, appearing furtively as a shadow from the thicket, had stationed itself beside the heap of clothing. Anselme had never seen such a wolf before. He remembered the tales of werewolves, that were believed to infest that ancient wood, and his alarm was touched instantly with the fear which only preternatural things can arouse. The beast was strangely colored, its fur being a glossy bluish-black. It was far larger than the common grey wolves of the forest. Crouching inscrutably, half hidden in the sedges, it seemed to await the woman as she waded shoreward.

Another moment, thought Anselme, and she would perceive her danger, would scream and turn in terror. But still she went on, her head bent forward as if in serene meditation.

"Beware the wolf!" he shouted, his voice strangely loud and seeming to break a magic stillness. Even as the words left his lips, the wolf trotted away and disappeared behind the thickets toward the great elder forest of oaks and beeches. The woman smiled over her shoulder at Anselme, turning a short oval face with slightly slanted eyes and lips red as pomegranate flowers. Apparently she was neither frightened by the wolf nor embarrassed by Anselme's presence.

"There is nothing to fear," she said, in a voice like the pouring of warm honey. "One wolf, or two, will hardly attack me."

"But perhaps there are others lurking about," persisted Anselme. "And there are worse dangers than wolves for one who wanders alone and unattended through the forest of Averoigne. When you have dressed, with your permission I shall attend you safely to your home, whether it be near or far."

"My home lies near enough in one sense, and far enough in another," returned the lady, cryptically. "But you may accompany me there if you wish."

She turned to the pile of garments, and Anselme went a few paces away among the alders and busied himself by cutting a stout cudgel for weapon against wild beasts or other adversaries. A strange but delightful agitation possessed him, and he nearly nicked his fingers several times with the knife. The misogyny that had driven him to a woodland hermitage began to appear slightly immature, even juvenile. He had let himself be wounded too deeply and too long by the injustice of a pert child.

By the time Anselme finished cutting his cudgel, the lady had completed her toilet. She came to meet him, swaying like a lamia. A bodice of vernal green velvet, baring the upper slopes of her breasts, clung tightly about her as a lover's embrace. A purple velvet gown, flowered with pale azure and crimson, moulded itself to the sinuous outlines of her hips and legs. Her slender feet were enclosed in fine soft leather buskins, scarlet-dyed, with tips curling pertly upward. The fashion of her garments, though oddly antique, confirmed Anselme in his belief that she was a person of no common rank.

Her raiment revealed, rather than concealed, the attributes of her femininity. Her manner yielded—but it also withheld.

Anselme bowed before her with a courtly grace that belied his rough country garb.

"Ah! I can see that you have not always been a hermit," she said, with soft mockery in her voice.

"You know me, then," said Anselme.

"I know many things. I am Séphora, the enchantress. It is unlikely that you have heard of me, for I dwell apart, in a place that none can find—unless I permit them to find it."

"I know little of enchantment," admitted Anselme. "But I can believe that you are an enchantress."

For some minutes they had followed a little used path that serpentined through the antique wood. It was a path the hermit had never come upon before in all his wanderings. Lithe saplings and low-grown boughs of huge beeches pressed closely upon it. Anselme, holding them aside for his companion, came often in thrilling contact with her shoulder and arm. Often she swayed against him, as if losing her balance on the rough ground. Her weight was a delightful burden, too soon relinquished. His pulses coursed tumultuously and would not quiet themselves again.

Anselme had quite forgotten his eremitic resolves. His blood and his curiosity were excited more and more. He ventured various gallantries, to which Séphora gave provocative replies. His questions, however, she answered with elusive vagueness. He could learn nothing, could decide nothing, about her. Even her age puzzled him: at one moment he thought her a young girl, the next, a mature woman.

Several times, as they went on, he caught glimpses of black fur beneath the low, shadowy foliage. He felt sure that the strange black wolf he had seen by the pool was accompanying them with a furtive surveillance. But somehow his sense of alarm was dulled by the enchantment that had fallen upon him.

Now the path steepened, climbing a densely wooded hill. The trees thinned to straggly, stunted pines, encircling a brown, open moorland as the tonsure encircles a monk's crown. The moor was studded with Druidic monoliths, dating from ages prior to the Roman occupation of Averoigne. Almost at its center, there towered a massive cromlech, consisting of two upright slabs that supported a third like the lintel of a door. The path ran straight to the cromlech.

"This is the portal of my domain," said Séphora, as they neared it. "I grow faint with fatigue. You must take me in your arms and carry me through the ancient doorway."

Anselme obeyed very willingly. Her cheeks paled, her eyelids fluttered and fell as he lifted her. For a moment he thought that she had fainted; but her arms crept warm and clinging around his neck.

Dizzy with the sudden vehemence of his emotion, he carried her through the cromlech. As he went, his lips wandered across her eyelids and passed deliriously to the soft red flame of her lips and the rose pallor of her throat. Once more she seemed to faint, beneath his fervor.

His limbs melted and a fiery blindness filled his eyes. The earth seemed to yield beneath them like an elastic couch as he and Séphora sank down.

Lifting his head, Anselme looked about him with swiftly growing bewilderment. He had carried Séphora only a few paces—and yet the grass on which they lay was not the sparse and sun-dried grass of the moor, but was deep, verdant and filled with tiny vernal blossoms! Oaks and beeches, huger even than those of the familiar forest, loomed umbrageously on every hand with masses of new, golden-green leafage, where he had thought to see the open upland. Looking back, he saw that the grey, lichened slabs of the cromlech itself alone remained of that former landscape.

Even the sun had changed its position. It had hung at Anselme's left, still fairly low in the east, when he and Séphora had reached the moorland. But now, shining with amber rays through a rift in the forest, it had almost touched the horizon on his right.

He recalled that Séphora had told him she was an enchantress. Here, indeed, was proof of sorcery! He eyed her with curious doubts and misgivings.

"Be not alarmed," said Séphora, with a honeyed smile of reassurance. "I told you that the cromlech was the doorway to my domain. We are now in a land lying outside of time and space as you have hitherto known them. The very seasons are different here. But there is no sorcery involved, except that of the great ancient Druids, who knew the secret of this hidden realm and reared those mighty slabs for a portal between the worlds. If you should weary of me, you can pass back at any time through the doorway. —But I hope that you have not tired of me so soon."

Anselme, though still bewildered, was relieved by this information. He proceeded to prove that the hope expressed by Séphora was well-founded.

Indeed, he proved it so lengthily and in such detail that the sun had fallen below the horizon before Séphora could draw a full breath and speak again.

"The air grows chill," she said, pressing against him and shivering lightly. "But my home is close at hand."

They came in the twilight to a high round tower among trees and grass-grown mounds.

"Ages ago," announced Séphora, "there was a great castle here. Now the tower alone remains, and I am its châtelaine, the last of my family. The tower and the lands about it are named Sylaire."

Tall dim tapers lit the interior, which was hung with rich arrases, vaguely and strangely pictured. Aged, corpse-pale servants in antique garb went to and fro with the furtiveness of specters, setting wines and foods before the enchantress and her guest in a broad hall. The wines were of rare flavor and immense age, the foods were curiously spiced. Anselme ate and drank copiously. It was all like some fantastic dream, and he accepted his surroundings as a dreamer does, untroubled by their strangeness.

The wines were potent, drugging his senses into warm oblivion. Even stronger was the inebriation of Séphora's nearness.

However, Anselme was a little startled when the huge black wolf he had seen that morning entered the hall and fawned like a dog at the feet of his hostess.

"You see, he is quite tame," she said, tossing the wolf bits of meat from her plate. "Often I let him come and go in the tower; and sometimes he attends me when I go forth from Sylaire."

"He is a fierce-looking beast," Anselme observed doubtfully.

It seemed that the wolf understood the words, for he bared his teeth at Anselme, with a preternaturally deep growl. Spots of red fire glowed in his somber eyes, like coals fanned by devils in dark pits.

"Go away, Malachie," commanded the enchantress, sharply. The wolf obeyed her, slinking from the hall with a malign backward glance at Anselme.

"He does not like you," said Séphora. "That, however, is perhaps not surprising."

Anselme, bemused with wine and love, forgot to inquire the meaning of her last words.

Morning came too soon, with upward-slanting beams that fired the tree-tops around the tower.

"You must leave me for awhile," said Séphora, after they had breakfasted. "I have neglected my magic of late—and there are matters into which I should inquire."

Bending prettily, she kissed the palms of his hands. Then, with backward glances and smiles, she retired to a room at the tower's top beside her bed-chamber. Here, she had told Anselme, her grimoires and potions and other appurtenances of magic were kept.

During her absence, Anselme decided to go out and explore the woodland about the tower. Mindful of the black wolf, whose tameness he did not trust despite Séphora's reassurances, he took with him the cudgel he had cut that previous day in the thickets near the Isoile.

There were paths everywhere, all leading to fresh loveliness. Truly, Sylaire was a region of enchantment. Drawn by the dreamy golden light, and the breeze laden with the freshness of spring flowers, Anselme wandered on from glade to glade.

He came to a grassy hollow, where a tiny spring bubbled from beneath mossed boulders. He seated himself on one of the boulders, musing on the strange happiness that had entered his life so unexpectedly. It was like one of the old romances, the tales of glamour and fantasy, that he had loved to read. Smiling, he remembered the gibes with which Dorothée des Flèches had expressed her disapproval of his taste for such reading matter. What, he wondered, would Dorothée think now? At any rate, she would hardly care—

His reflections were interrupted. There was a rustling of leaves, and the black wolf emerged from the boscage in front of him, whining as if to attract his attention. The beast had somehow lost his appearance of fierceness.

Curious, and a little alarmed, Anselme watched in wonder while the wolf began to uproot with his paws certain plants that somewhat resembled wild garlic. These he devoured with palpable eagerness.

Anselme's mouth gaped at the thing which ensued. One moment the wolf was before him. Then, where the wolf had been, there rose up the figure of a man, lean, powerful, with blue-black hair and beard, and darkly flaming eyes. The hair grew almost to his brows, the beard nearly to his lower eyelashes. His arms, legs, shoulders and chest were matted with bristles.

"Be assured that I mean you no harm," said the man. "I am Malachie du Marais, a sorcerer, and the one-time lover of Séphora. Tiring of me, and fearing my wizardry, she turned me into a werewolf by giving me secretly the waters of a certain pool that lies amid this enchanted domain of Sylaire. The pool is cursed from old time with the infection of lycanthropy—and Séphora has added her spells to its power. I can throw off the wolf shape for a little while during the dark of the moon. At other times I can regain my human form, though only for a few minutes, by eating the root that you saw me dig and devour. The root is very scarce."

Anselme felt that the sorceries of Sylaire were more complicated than he had hitherto imagined. But amid his bewilderment he was unable to trust the weird being before him. He had heard many tales of werewolves, who were reputedly common in medieval France. Their ferocity, people said, was that of demons rather than of mere brutes.

"Allow me to warn you of the grave danger in which you stand," continued Malachie du Marais. "You were rash to let yourself be enticed by Séphora. If you are wise, you will leave the purlieus of Sylaire with all possible dispatch. The land is old in evil and sorcery, and all who dwell within it are ancient as the land, and are equally accursed. The servants of Séphora, who waited upon you yestereve, are vampires that sleep by day in the tower vaults and come forth only by night. They go out through the Druid portal, to prey on the people of Averoigne."

He paused as if to emphasize the words that followed. His eyes glittered balefully, and his deep voice assumed a hissing undertone. "Séphora herself is an ancient lamia, well-nigh immortal, who feeds on the vital forces of young men. She has had many lovers throughout the ages—and I must deplore, even though I cannot specify, their ultimate fate. The youth and beauty that she retains are illusions. If you could see Séphora as she really is, you would recoil in revulsion, cured of your perilous love. You would see her—unthinkably old, and hideous with infamies."

"But how can such things be?" queried Anselme. "Truly, I cannot believe you."

Malachie shrugged his hairy shoulders. "At least I have warned you. But the wolf-change approaches, and I must go. If you will come to me later, in my abode which lies a mile to the westward of Séphora's tower, perhaps I can convince you that my statements are the truth. In the meanwhile, ask yourself if you have seen any mirrors, such as a beautiful young woman would use, in Séphora's chamber. Vampires and lamias are afraid of mirrors—for a good reason."

Anselme went back to the tower with a troubled mind. What Malachie had told him was incredible. Yet there was the matter of Séphora's servants. He had hardly noticed their absence that morning—and yet he had not seen them since the previous eve—and he could not remember any mirrors among Séphora's various feminine belongings.

He found Séphora awaiting him in the tower's lower hall. One glance at the utter sweetness of her womanhood, and he felt ashamed of the doubts with which Malachie had inspired him.

Séphora's blue-grey eyes questioned him, deep and tender as those of some pagan goddess of love. Reserving no detail, he told her of his meeting with the werewolf.

"Ah! I did well to trust my intuitions," she said. "Last night, when the black wolf growled and glowered at you, it occurred to me that he was perhaps becoming more dangerous than I had realized. This morning, in my chamber of magic, I made use of my clairvoyant powers—and I learned much. Indeed, I have been careless. Malachie has become a menace to my security. Also, he hates you, and would destroy our happiness."

"Is it true, then," questioned Anselme, "that he was your lover, and that you turned him into a werewolf?"

"He was my lover—long, long ago. But the werewolf form was his own choice, assumed out of evil curiosity by drinking from the pool of which he told you. He has regretted it since, for the wolf shape, while giving him certain powers of harm, in reality limits his actions and his sorceries. He wishes to return to human shape, and if he succeeds, will become doubly dangerous to us both.

"I should have watched him well—for now I find that he has stolen from me the recipe of antidote to the werewolf waters. My clairvoyance tells me that he has already brewed the antidote, in the brief intervals of humanity regained by chewing a certain root. When he drinks the potion, as I think that he means to do before long, he will regain human form—permanently. He waits only for the dark of the moon, when the werewolf spell is at its weakest."

"But why should Malachie hate me?" asked Anselme. "And how can I help you against him?"

"That first question is slightly stupid, my dear. Of course, he is jealous of you. As for helping me—well, I have thought of a good trick to play on Malachie."

She produced a small purple glass vial, triangular in shape, from the folds of her bodice.

"This vial," she told him, "is filled with the water of the werewolf pool. Through my clairvoyant vision, I learned that Malachie keeps his newly brewed potion in a vial of similar size, shape and color. If you can go to his den and substitute one vial for the other without detection, I believe that the results will be quite amusing."

"Indeed, I will go," Anselme assured her.

"The present should be a favorable time," said Séphora. "It is now within an hour of noon; and Malachie often hunts at this time. If you should find him in his den, or he should return while you are there, you can say that you came in response to his invitation."

She gave Anselme careful instructions that would enable him to find the werewolf's den without delay. Also, she gave him a sword, saying that the blade had been tempered to the chanting of magic spells that made it effective against such beings as Malachie. "The wolf's temper has grown uncertain," she warned. "If he should attack you, your alder stick would prove a poor weapon."

It was easy to locate the den, for well-used paths ran toward it with little deviation. The place was the mounded remnant of a tower that had crumbled down into grassy earth and mossy blocks. The entrance had once been a lofty doorway: now it was only a hole, such as a large animal would make in leaving and returning to its burrow.

Anselme hesitated before the hole. "Are you there, Malachie du Marais?" he shouted. There was no answer, no sound of movement from within. Anselme shouted once more. At last, stooping on hands and knees, he entered the den.

Light poured through several apertures, latticed with wandering treeroots, where the mound had fallen in from above. The place was a cavern rather than a room. It stank with carrion remnants into whose nature Anselme did not inquire too closely. The ground was littered with bones, broken stems and leaves of plants, and shattered or rusted vessels of alchemic use. A verdigris-eaten kettle hung from a tripod above ashes and ends of charred faggots. Rain-sodden grimoires lay mouldering in rusty metal covers. The three-legged ruin of a table was propped against the wall. It was covered with a medley of oddments, among which Anselme discerned a purple vial resembling the one given him by Séphora.

In one corner was a litter of dead grass. The strong, rank odor of a wild beast mingled with the carrion stench.

Anselme looked about and listened cautiously. Then, without delay, he substituted Séphora's vial for the one on Malachie's table. The stolen vial he placed under his jerkin.

There was a padding of feet at the cavern's entrance. Anselme turned—to confront the black wolf. The beast came toward him, crouching tensely as if about to spring, with eyes glaring like crimson coals of Avernus. Anselme's fingers dropped to the hilt of the enchanted sword that Séphora had given him.

The wolf's eyes followed his fingers. It seemed that he recognized the sword. He turned from Anselme, and began to chew some roots of the garlic-like plant, which he had doubtless collected to make possible those operations which he could hardly have carried on in wolfish form.

This time, the transformation was not complete. The head, arms and body of Malachie du Marais rose up again before Anselme; but the legs were the hind legs of a monstrous wolf. He was like some bestial hybrid of antique legend.

"Your visit honors me," he said, half snarling, with suspicion in his eyes and voice. "Few have cared to enter my poor abode, and I am grateful to you. In recognition of your kindness, I shall make you a present."

With the padding movements of a wolf, he went over to the ruinous table and groped amid the confused oddments with which it was covered. He drew out an oblong silver mirror, brightly burnished, with jewelled handle, such as a great lady or damsel might own. This he offered to Anselme.

"I give you the mirror of Reality," he announced. "In it, all things are reflected according to their true nature. The illusions of enchantment cannot deceive it. You disbelieved me when I warned you against Séphora. But if you hold this mirror to her face and observe the reflection, you will see that her beauty, like everything else in Sylaire, is a hollow lie—the mask of ancient horror and corruption. If you doubt me, hold the mirror to my face—now: for I, too, am part of the land's immemorial evil."

Anselme took the silver oblong and obeyed Malachie's injunction. A moment, and his nerveless fingers almost dropped the mirror. He had seen reflected within it a face that the sepulcher should have hidden long ago. . . .

The horror of that sight had shaken him so deeply that he could not afterwards recall the circumstances of his departure from the werewolf's lair. He had kept the werewolf's gift; but more than once he had been prompted to throw it away. He tried to tell himself that what he had seen was merely the result of some wizard trick. He refused to believe that any mirror would reveal Séphora as anything but the young and lovely sweetheart whose kisses were still warm on his lips.

All such matters, however, were driven from Anselme's mind by the situation that he found when he re-entered the tower hall. Three visitors had arrived during his absence. They stood fronting Séphora, who, with a tranquil smile on her lips, was apparently trying to explain something to them. Anselme recognized the visitors with much amazement, not untouched with consternation.

One of them was Dorothée des Flèches, clad in a trim traveling habit. The others were two serving men of her father, armed with longbows, quivers of arrows, broadswords and daggers. In spite of this array of weapons, they did not look any too comfortable or at home. But Dorothée seemed to have retained her usual matter-of-fact assurance.

"What are you doing in this queer place, Anselme?" she cried. "And who is this woman, this châtelaine of Sylaire, as she calls herself?"

Anselme felt that she would hardly understand any answer that he could give to either query. He looked at Séphora, then back at Dorothée. Séphora was the essence of all the beauty and romance that he had ever craved. How could he have fancied himself in love with Dorothée, how could he have spent thirteen months in a hermitage because of her coldness and changeability? She was pretty enough, with the common bodily charms of youth. But she was stupid, wanting in imagination—prosy already in the flush of her girlhood as a middle-aged housewife. Small wonder that she had failed to understand him.

"What brings you here?" he countered. "I had not thought to see you again."

"I missed you, Anselme," she sighed. "People said that you had left the world because of your love for me, and had become a hermit. At last I came to seek you. But you had disappeared. Some hunters had seen you pass yesterday with a strange woman, across the moor of Druid stones. They said you had both vanished beyond the cromlech, fading as if in air. Today I followed you with my father's serving men. We found ourselves in this strange region, of which no one has ever heard. And now this woman—"

The sentence was interrupted by a mad howling that filled the room with eldritch echoes. The black wolf, with jaws foaming and slavering, broke in through the door that had been opened to admit Séphora's visitors. Dorothée des Flèches began to scream as he dashed straight toward her, seeming to single her out for the first victim of his rabid fury.

Something, it was plain, had maddened him. Perhaps the water of the werewolf pool, substituted for the antidote, had served to redouble the original curse of lycanthropy.

The two serving men, bristling with their arsenal of weapons, stood like effigies. Anselme drew the sword given him by the enchantress, and leaped forward between Dorothée and the wolf. He raised his weapon, which was straight-bladed, and suitable for stabbing. The mad werewolf sprang as if hurled from a catapult, and his red, open gorge was spitted on the outthrust point. Anselme's hand was jarred on the sword-hilt, and the shock drove him backward. The wolf fell threshing at Anselme's feet. His jaws had clenched on the blade. The point protruded beyond the stiff bristles of his neck.

Anselme tugged vainly at the sword. Then the black-furred body ceased to thresh—and the blade came easily. It had been withdrawn from the sagging mouth of the dead ancient sorcerer, Malachie du Marais, which lay before Anselme on the flagstones. The sorcerer's face was now the face that Anselme had seen in the mirror, when he had held it up at Malachie's injunction.

"You have saved me! How wonderful!" cried Dorothée. Anselme saw that she had started toward him with outthrust arms. A moment more, and the situation would become embarrassing.

He recalled the mirror, which he had kept under his jerkin, together with the vial he had stolen from Malachie du Marais. What, he wondered, would Dorothée see in its burnished depths?

He drew the mirror forth swiftly and held it to her face as she advanced upon him. What she beheld in the mirror he never knew but the effect was startling. Dorothée gasped, and her eyes dilated in manifest horror. Then, covering her eyes with her hands, as if to shut out some ghastly vision, she ran shrieking from the hall. The serving men followed her. The celerity of their movements made it plain that they were not sorry to leave this dubious lair of wizards and witches.

Séphora began to laugh softly. Anselme found himself chuckling. For awhile they abandoned themselves to uproarious mirth. Then Séphora sobered.

"I know why Malachie gave you the mirror," she said. "Do you not wish to see my reflection in it?"

Anselme realized that he still held the mirror in his hand. Without answering Séphora, he went over to the nearest window, which looked down on a deep pit lined with bushes, that had been part of an ancient, half-filled moat. He hurled the silver oblong into the pit.

"I am content with what my eyes tell me, without the aid of any mirror," he declared. "Now let us pass to other matters, which have been interrupted too long."

Again the clinging deliciousness of Séphora was in his arms, and her fruit-soft mouth was crushed beneath his hungry lips.

The strongest of all enchantments held them in its golden circle.

Double Cosmos

It is for the reader to decide how much importance can be attached to the manuscript left by Bernard Meecham. Doubtless few will consider it anything more than a record of delirium induced by the strange drug that Meecham had compounded. Even from this standpoint the record possesses a certain medical interest: for it throws a startling light on the possibilities of human sensation. And if one accepts Meecham's experiences at his own valuation, it will be seen that the veil of a new and heretofore unsuspected world has been lifted.

Meecham, a brilliant young chemist, had made from the beginning a special study of narcotic drugs. He had been freed by an ample inheritance from the necessity of commercializing his knowledge and his talents, and was thus able to give his whole time to the specialty which absorbed him so deeply. A recluse, he was incommunicative regarding the aim of his researches; and the revolutionary theory he had conceived was not known to his colleagues. This theory, as well as the outcome of his experiments, he confided only to the manuscript written and dated shortly before his unexplained disappearance. The manuscript was found lying on his laboratory desk. It is now published in accord with a brief, unaddressed note of instructions also left behind by Meecham.

The Manuscript

Even in my childhood, I began to suspect that the world about us was perhaps only the curtain of hidden things. The suspicion was born following my recovery from an attack of scarlet fever attended by intervals of delirium. In that delirium, recalled dimly afterwards, I had seemed to live in a monstrous world peopled by strange misshapen beings whose actions were fraught with terror and menace; or, when not menacing, were wholly cryptic and unearthly. This realm of shadow had seemed no less real than the world perceived by my normal senses; and during my convalescence I believed that it still existed somewhere beyond the corners of the familiar room; and I feared that its horrible spectres might reappear at any moment.

My nightly dreams, which were often very strange and vivid, also served to confirm my intuition of other spheres and secret aspects of the known world. Each night it seemed to me that I stepped across the border of an actual land lying conterminous with the lands of day, but accessible only in sleep.

Such beliefs, whether pure fantasy or fantasy mingled with an obscure truth are no doubt more or less common to imaginative children. However, as my faculties matured, I did not wholly dismiss them but was led into speculations concerning the enigmas of human perception and the workings of the sense-mechanism. It soon occurred to me that the five classified senses were very poor and doubtful channels for the cognition of reality; in fact, that their testimony regarding the nature of our surroundings might well be partially or wholly erroneous. The fact that all so-called sane and normal people, possessed of sight, hearing and the other senses, agreed substantially in their impressions of outward phenomena, might prove only the existence of common flaws or limitations in the sensory apparatus of the species. The thing called reality, perhaps, was merely a communal hallucination; and certainly, as science itself had tended to prove, man could lay claim to no finality of perception. The imagery discerned by the human eye was not that beheld by the multi-faceted eye of an insect; the colors that man saw were not perceived by the bird. Where, then, was actuality?

Inevitably, following this line of thought, I became interested in the effect of drugs, especially those narcotics which modify sensation so profoundly and in such varied and fantastic ways. I read with absorption such books as De Quincey's *Opium-Eater, The Artificial Paradises* of Charles Baudelaire, and the almost forgotten *Hashish-Eater* of Fitzhugh Ludlow. This literary interest soon led me to study the chemistry of narcotics as well as their physiological action. Herein, I felt, were profound mysteries and a clue to secrets which none had yet unraveled.

Thus began the ten years of research and experiment which have left me a nerve-shaken wreck at twenty-nine. The earlier stages I must summarize briefly, for little enough time remains in which to record that inconceivably awesome discovery on which I stumbled in the end.

My laboratory was equipped with the finest and subtlest apparatus, and I procured for analysis all narcotic drugs familiar to modern chemistry, together with certain others found by explorers in remote savage regions. Opium and all its derivatives, the extract of hashish and the dried plant itself—mescal, atropine, peyote, kava—these and numerous others were the subjects of my experimentation. From the very first I had conceived an inkling of a strange and seemingly unauthorized theory; and to prove the theory it was necessary to study the effect of drugs on my own sensory system. Also, I was compelled to invent an incredibly delicate photo-electric device, a graph for the tracing and registration of obscure neural impulses.

My theory was, that the visions, the so-called hallucinations induced by drugs, were not due to a mere derangement of the sensory nerves, but sprang from the excitation of some new and undeveloped sense. This sense, though more complex and esoteric than the others, was akin to sight; and I suspected that its organ was one of the glands, probably the pineal. I did not disregard the function of growth-regulation assigned to the pineal gland by endocrinologists, but merely surmised a secondary function wholly latent under the conditions of everyday life.

Under the terrific stimulus of drugs, this third eye was partially awakened, affording distorted, broken glimpses of that larger reality which the outward senses failed to mirror. Through it, perhaps, one could behold dimensions higher than the three to which our perceptions were limited. Small reliance, however, could be placed on the testimony of the organ; for I felt sure that no known drug was powerful enough to rouse it into full consciousness. It was like the untaught eye of a newborn babe, which beholds its surroundings without any true perception of the form, distance, perspective and relationship of objects. Thus the mad variety, the wavering, ever-shifting fantasy, of narcotic visions; thus their alternations and minglings of horror, splendor, grotesquery, obscurity. Yet through them infinite vistas of untold realms were shadowed darkly upon the mind of man.

I shall say only that I succeeded in demonstrating, through the graphic device that I had invented, the direct influence of narcotics on the pineal gland, and the temporary activating of that gland as a sort of optic organ. The reactions recorded by this instrument while I was enduring the effect of hashish were unusually strong, and markedly similar to those which the graph had detected in the human eye during the reception of sight-images. Thus was confirmed my thesis of an objective world behind the teeming phantasmagoria evoked by drugs.

It remained now to invent or compound a drug sufficiently potent to stimulate the new eye into full and mature awareness of this hidden world. I shall not record here the details of my many trials and failures with complicated mixtures of strange alkaloids. Nor shall I record the elements of the composite super-drug through which I attained eventual success at the cost of a fatally shattered nervous system—or perhaps something worse. I do not wish others to pay the price that I have paid.

My first sensations under the new drug were similar to those induced by a strong dose of *Cannabis indica*. There was the same protraction of the time-sense, by which mere minutes were stretched out into ages; and the same spatial expansion, by which my laboratory walls appeared to recede to an immense distance, and my own body, as well as the familiar objects

222 • Clark Ashton Smith

about me, extended themselves to prodigious height and length. The legs of my chair were tall as the famed sequoias. My hand and arm, reaching up to make sure that the graph was correctly adjusted on my forehead over the pineal gland, seemed to scale a gulf like that of some profound canyon. A carboy loomed like a giant monument.

All this was familiar to me, and I felt somewhat disappointed. Was the new compound a failure, like the others?

I closed my eyes, as I had often done before, to shut out any ordinary sight-impressions that might obscure the vision of the third optic. Certain details disappeared and others were added but the imagery on which I peered remained fundamentally the same. Then, gradually, there was a change, and the scene before me divided itself into what I can only describe as two different planes or levels, distinct from each other as water and land.

The first plane was composed of my immediate surroundings, the laboratory and its fixtures, which had now become transparent as if permeated by some sort of radio-active light. My own body shared in this transparency, but, together with all the objects around me, retained clearly separate outlines.

Beyond this immediate plane was the second, in which everything seemed to possess a comparative solidity and opaqueness. I gazed on a medley of strange-angled forms that might have materialized from a geometrician's nightmare. These forms were immense, complicated, mysterious. Then, slowly, I perceived that they were an apparent extension of the forms in my own plane, thus accounting for my original impression that everything about me had stretched itself out to inordinate length and distance.

It is hard to describe exactly what I saw, since my vision doubtless included an extra dimension. My limbs and body, my chair, the tables, shelves, bottles and littered chemical apparatus, all seemed to protract themselves at incredibly oblique angles into the medley of super-Euclidean shapes that crowded the new world. My eyes, like those of an infant learning to see, gradually began to distinguish detail and establish proportion and perspective where all had seemed meaninglessly blurred and chaotic at first glance.

My attention centered itself on a figure that seemed to correspond to my own. This figure, seated on a vaguely chair-like structure, was of colossal size. It presented a hundred strange facets, convexities, concavities. However, I made out the various parts equivalent to human head, torso, arms and legs. The figure appeared to sit facing me, for there was a multi-angled suggestion of eyes, mouth and other features in the immensely proportioned head.

Was this, I wondered, a living entity like myself? If so, what was my relationship to this being in a world never before penetrated by human vision?

At length a very simple experiment occurred to me. Slowly and with some effort—since the drug's influence entailed a slight loss of muscular control—I raised my right arm until it was level with the shoulder. Simultaneously and with the same slowness, the being before me raised the member that corresponded to a *left* arm. It was as if I were watching my own prodigiously magnified and distorted image in some strange mirror. Perhaps, in peering from one plane, from one dimension to another, there was the same apparent reversal that a reflection would present.

Now I rose to my feet and began to walk around the laboratory, tottering a little at first from that loss of control I have mentioned. The other-dimensional figure also rose and walked, with the same shaky and uncertain steps. I picked up a beaker. The entity took in his hand a baroquely shaped vessel and raised it aloft. From sheer weakness, the beaker slipped from my fingers, crashing into many fragments. The vessel held by the being dropped at the same moment, and its shards littered that otherworld floor.

It seemed that every movement I made was duplicated in perfect synchronism by this amazing *alter ego*.

An obvious but startling question now occurred to me. I went over to the table and took up the graduated bottle in which I kept my supply of the new drug. I measured out a fifth of the amount I had already taken, feeling that it would be reasonably safe to add this much to the dose. Dissolving the powder in a little water, I swallowed it.

Using vessels of more complex geometric form, the being in that other laboratory reproduced my every motion.

Was he too an experimenter, seeking to pierce the manifold veils of the cosmos? Did he see me, I wondered? Was he experiencing a revelation similar in kind to the one I experienced? Was he performing the acts that I performed, to test the correspondence that existed between us? Did all the objects, entities, causes and effects of his world possess their counterparts in mine?

Perhaps, I thought, the relation between the worlds was one of cause and effect. But if so, which world was primary, which secondary? Did my actions determine those of that alien self? Or did his determine mine?

I felt that my new visual sense was being sharpened by the small additional dose of the drug I had taken. The details of the strange dimension grew clearer, more distinct. Hitherto it had all been colorless, like the grey tones of a photograph. Now I began to distinguish hues that were quite indescribable, since they did not belong to the known spectrum.

Feeling a little light-headed, I went over and stretched myself on a couch that I had placed in the laboratory for use during my experiments. Synchronously, the being in that other laboratory reclined on a vast, many-cubed object that corresponded to the couch in mine.

We lay facing each other, motionless. At length the vision blurred, becoming once more chaotic and distorted. Finally it faded, leaving only the familiar details of the room about me.

During my next experiment, I risked going out on the street while the drug's influence was at its height. Step by step, as I went, the vision changed with the shifting scene about me; and step by step I was accompanied in the vision by that being whom I had grown to regard as an other-cosmic self.

It was a double city that I beheld—the city of our own world, traversed by autos, by street-cars, by throngs of pedestrians—and a city of that alien plane, with vehicles, people, buildings, all corresponding to ours in movement or position, but vaster and more complex in their geometric forms.

Absorbed in that astounding revelation, I forgot the danger to which I was exposed. An auto, driven slowly, struck me with its fender as I stepped from the sidewalk at a crossing. As I fell, I saw that my visioned companion had been struck by one of the vehicles in his city, and was also falling.

I had sustained no injuries apart from a few slight bruises. Passersby helped me to my feet, while, in that other city, pedestrians performed the same service for my strange double.

I repeated the experiment under varying conditions, in city and country. Always I saw my ultra-dimensional double, in an equivalent situation, duplicating my actions. It seemed that there was no person, animal, plant, machine, building, landscape, in our world which did not have its counterpart in the other. All happenings occurred coincidentally in the two spheres.

Then came the astounding change. I had deferred taking the drug for some days, realizing that my health had suffered too heavily from its use and that death might soon follow if I persisted in further experiments. During that time I had experienced some strange mental states, which I could not recall clearly afterwards. Also, there had been several odd lapses of consciousness, lasting for several hours, which were always preceded by mental confusion and a preoccupation with thoughts remote from my usual trend. In particular, there would come to me the thought of an absolute vacuum, between the worlds, apart from time and place. Through superior, godlike will-power, it seemed to me, a being might enter this vacuum and thus insulate himself from the cosmic laws that would otherwise control his destiny. Such insulation seemed desirable to me, and I would find myself willing it intently just as consciousness deserted me. Thus alone could I divorce my actions from those of the otherworld being, and escape the doom which menaced us both through repeated use of the powerful compound drug.

Feeling still too weak and ill to go out, I made the next experiment with the drug in my laboratory, lying on the couch. The drug acted as usual, the vision clarifying itself till I saw once more the vessels and furniture of that alien laboratory beyond my own. But, to my amazement, the vast, many-cubed couch, on which I had thought to see a reclining figure, was vacant! I looked everywhere about the place, but in vain, for the companion of my visions.

Then, for the first time in my use of the super-drug, I experienced the sensation of hearing. A voice began to speak, low, toneless, coming from no direction—and yet from all directions. Sometimes I thought it spoke in my own brain, rather than from any point in space. It said:

"Can you hear me? I am Abernarda Chameechamach, your twin in the four-dimensioned cosmos you have visioned."

"Yes, I can hear you," I replied. "Where are you?" Whether I spoke aloud, or merely thought the words, I am not sure.

"I have isolated myself in the vacuum of super-space," was the answer. "It is the only way in which I can break the rapport between our existences—which must be broken if I am to escape the death that threatens you. In this vacuum, all laws and all forces are inoperative, except those of thought and will. I can will myself into the vacuum and out of it again. My thoughts can pass to your world and become audible to you in your present state under the influence of the drug."

"But how can you do these things independently of me?" I asked.

"Because my will and my brain are superior to yours, though otherwise identical with them. Our worlds are twin, as you have realized; but mine, which has one more dimension than yours, is the primary one, the world of causes. Yours is the secondary world of effects. It was I who invented the super-drug, in my efforts to stimulate a new sense that would reveal cosmic reality. Your invention of it was the result of mine, just as your existence is the result of my existence. I alone of the people in this world, through the drug, have learned that there is a secondary sphere; and you alone, in yours, have visioned the primary sphere. *My knowledge, through a law of the higher dimension, enables me to act now upon the secondary world through thought alone.* Insulating myself in this vacuum, I have willed that you should per-form actions from whose necessity I myself am exempt. Several times the only result was a loss of consciousness on your part, corresponding to my stay in the vacuum. But now I have triumphed. You have taken the drug, while I stand aloof between the worlds, invisible, and apart from the chain of cause and effect."

"Since you have not used the drug," I asked, "how is it that you are conscious of me? Can you see me?"

"No, I cannot see you. But I am aware of you through a sense not dependent upon the drug: a sense that my very knowledge of your existence enables me to use. It is part of my superior mind power. I do not intend to use the drug again; but I wish that you shall continue to use it."

"Why?" I queried.

"Because you will soon die from the effects of such use. I, abstaining, will escape death. Such a thing, I believe, has never before happened in the history of the double cosmos. Death, in your world, like birth and everything else, has always been the concomitant of a like happening in mine. What the outcome will be, I am not quite sure. But, by breaking the nexus between us, and outliving you, it may be that I shall never die."

"But is my death possible without yours?" I questioned.

"I think that it is. It will result from the continuation of actions that would also cause my death, if I did not choose to interrupt them in myself. When your death approaches, I shall enter the vacuum again, where no cosmic cause or consequence can follow me. Thus I shall be doubly safe."

For several hours past, I have been writing this account at my laboratory desk. Whatever happens to me—whether death or something stranger than death—a record of my incredible experiences will at least remain when I am gone.

Since my conversation with the being who calls himself Abernarda Chameechamach, I have tried to abstain wholly from the super-drug and have several times delayed yielding to the impulse that makes me continue its use. I find myself wishing, *willing* intensely that Abernarda Chameechamach should take the drug while I refrain, and should perish in my stead.

During my few recent experiments with the drug, I have seen only the empty laboratory of my trans-dimensional twin. Apparently, on each occasion, that being has absented himself in super-space. He has not spoken to me again.

However, I have a strange feeling that I am closer to him than at any time during our mutual visions or our one conversation. My physical enfeeblement has progressed pace by pace with a remarkable strengthening and enlargement of my mental faculties. It seems, indescribably, that another dimension has been added to my mind. I feel myself the possessor of senses beyond the normal five and the one activated by the drug. I believe that the powers of Abernarda Chameechamach, though directed against me, have to some extent passed into me through a cosmic law that not even he is able to abrogate from his station beyond time and place. There is a balance that must right itself, even though temporarily disturbed by the unknown forces of a four-dimensioned mind.

His very volition has transferred itself to me, and has turned back against him, though I am subject to him in ways already indicated. I am possessed by the image of the cosmic vacuum in which he isolates himself. More and more I feel in myself the desire, the will and the power to project myself bodily into the vacuum, and thus escape the chain of consequences that began with the discovery of the super-drug.

What, I wonder, will happen if I should escape in this manner before the drug kills me? What will happen to me, and to Abernarda Chameechamach, if we should meet face to face in that void between the worlds of our double cosmos?

Will the meeting mean annihilation for us both? Will we survive as two entities—or a single entity? I can only wait and conjecture.

Does that other also doubt and wonder while he waits?

Are there two of us—or is there only one?

NEMESIS OF THE UNFINISHED

The authentic talent of Francis La Porte, fiction-writer, was allied with an industry no less than prodigious. Unfortunately, he was self-critical to an excessive degree. Dissatisfaction, morbid and meticulous, kept him from finishing more than one manuscript out of a dozen. Though editors importuned him for stories and bought readily the few that he submitted, Francis could seldom outdistance the wolf by a full running jump.

He had left hundreds of stories in various stages of incompletion, clipped together with the double or triple carbons that he was always careful to make. Many ran to the size of novelettes or novels; some existed only as a few beginning paragraphs. Often he had written several variant versions, carried to more or less length. There were also countless synopses of tales attempted or unbegun.

They crammed the drawers of his desk to overflowing, they bulged and towered in insecure piles from the boxes that were stacked along the walls of his study. These voluminous abortions were the labor of a lifetime.

Most of them were eldritch tales of horror and death, of wizardry and diabolism. Their pages teemed with spectres and cadavers, with ghouls and *loups-garous* and poltergeists.

Often they haunted La Porte like a bad conscience. Sometimes they seemed to talk to him and reproach him with ghostly whispers in the dark hours before dawn. He would fall asleep vowing to complete one or more of them without further procrastination.

In spite of such resolutions, the dust still thickened on the piled reams. A new day would always bring Francis an idea for a new plot. Occasionally he would complete one of his shorter and simpler tales, and would receive in due time a small check from *Outlandish Stories* or *Eerie Narratives*. Then he would indulge in one of his rare debauches of food and wine, and his brain would fume with wild inspirations that he was seldom able to recall afterwards.

Though he did not suspect, La Porte was in the position of a necromancer who has called up spirits from the deep without knowing how to control or dismiss them.

He had fallen asleep one night after absorbing nearly a half-gallon of cheap claret, bought from the proceeds of a recent sale. His slumber was heavy but brief. It seemed that a vague commotion, in which he distinguished articulate voices, had awakened him. Puzzled, and still confused by his potations, he listened intently for some moments but the noises had ceased. Then suddenly there was a sound like the light rustling of paper. Then a louder noise as if great masses of paper were sliding and shifting. Then conversation, as if a crowd of people were talking all at once. It was an unintelligible babel, and he could determine nothing except that the noises came from the direction of his workroom.

La Porte's spine began to tingle as he sat up in bed. The sounds were eerie and mysterious as anything that he had ever imagined in his tales of nocturnal terror. It seemed now that he was overhearing some bizarre and sinister dialogue, in which voices of unhuman timbre replied to others that were apparently human. Once or twice he caught his own name uttered in strange gibbering tones, somehow fraught with the sense of inimical conspiracy.

La Porte sprang out of bed. Lighting an oil-lamp and going into his study, he peered into every corner but saw only the stacks of overpiled manuscripts. Apparently the piles were undisturbed but he seemed to see them through a thick haze. At the same time he began to choke and cough. Going closer to inspect the manuscripts, he perceived that the accumulated dust of months and years had been shaken from their massed reams.

He searched the room repeatedly but found no further sign of invasion either human or supernatural. Perhaps some sudden gust had performed the mysterious office of dusting the paper piles. But the windows were all closed, and the night outside was windless. He returned to bed: but sleep refused to visit him again.

There was no repetition of the rustlings and voices that had seemed to awaken him. He began to wonder if he had been the victim of some distempered dream inspired by the evening's wine. Finally he convinced himself that this was the only credible explanation.

The next morning, moved by an unwonted impulse, La Porte selected a manuscript at random from the heaps of unfinished material. It was entitled *Incomplete Sorceries,* and dealt with a man who had achieved partial power over demons and elementals, but was still seeking certain lost formulæ that were requisite to full masterdom. La Porte had abandoned the tale through indecision regarding the alternate solutions of the sorcerer's problem suggested by his all too fertile fancy. He sat down at the typewriter, determined that he would finish the story to his satisfaction.

For once, he did not hesitate over variant wordings or divergencies of plot-development. It all seemed miraculously clear to him, and he wrote steadily through the forenoon and afternoon and evening. At midnight he ended the last paragraph, in which, after many perils and tribulations, the sorcerer stood triumphant amid his infrangible circles, compelling the dread kings of the four infernal quarters to serve his least whim.

La Porte felt that he had seldom written so well. The story should bring him a substantial check, as well as the acclaim of his many faithful but impatient admirers. He would send it out in the morning mail after a few possible re-touchings. A new title was manifestly required by the denouement: he would think of one easily after a night's sleep.

He had almost forgotten the queer dream that had followed his recent bac-chanal. Again he slept deeply, but not too soundly. At intervals some portion of his brain, emerging numbly from oblivion, seemed to hear the recurrent clatter of his old Remington in the next room. Drugged with fatigue, he did not awaken fully to the strangeness of the sound under such circumstances but accepted it without question as one accepts the unexplained vagaries of dreamland.

After his meager breakfast La Porte began to reread *Incomplete Sorceries,* with his pencil poised for errors of typing or minor revisions. He found nothing to change in the first few pages, written months before, and has-tened over their familiar incidents to the point at which he had begun his continuation of the sorcerer's vicissitudes. Here he paused in astonishment, for he could not remember writing a single sentence of the freshly typed paragraphs! The astonishment became stupefaction as he went on: the plot, the incidents, the whole trend of development, were alien to what he had conceived and set down.

It was as if some demon-guided hand had reversed and perverted the story. Pandemonium, and the lords of Pandemonium, prevailed throughout. The sorcerer, with all his formulæ, was a mere pawn moved hither and thither at their will, in a monstrous game for supremacy over souls and planets and galaxies. The very style was foreign to La Porte's usual manner: it was studded with strange archaisms and neologisms; it burned with phrases like hellish gems; it blazed and vapored with images that were like censers of evil before Satanic altars.

More than once, La Porte wanted to drop the horribly transfigured tale. But a baleful fascination, mingling with his dumbfoundment and incredulity, held him to the end where the hapless necromancer was crushed into pulp beneath the ponderous grimoires he had collected in his lifelong search for mastery. It was only then that La Porte could lay down the manuscript. His fingers trembled as if they had touched the coils of some deadly serpent.

Tormenting his brain for some tenable explanation, he recalled the dreamlike clattering of the Remington that he had seemed to hear in slumber. Was it possible that he had risen from his bed and had rewritten the story in a somnambulistic state? Was it the work of some spectral or demoniac hand? Unmistakably the typing had been done on his own machine: several slightly blurred letters and punctuation-marks occurred throughout the entire manuscript.

The mystery disturbed him beyond measure. He had never found in himself the least tendency to sleepwalking or to trance states of any kind. Though the supernatural was, so to speak, his literary stock-in-trade, his reason refused to accept the ideas of an extrahuman agency.

Unable to resolve the problem, La Porte tried to busy himself with the beginning of a new tale. But concentration was impossible, since he could not dismiss the unanswered riddle from his thoughts for a moment.

Abandoning all further effort to work, he left the house with hurried steps, as if driven by the spurs of an incubus.

It was many hours later that La Porte wandered homeward rather unsteadily by the rays of a cloud-strangled moon. Forgetting his usual economy, he had consumed numberless brandies at a village bar. He did not care for the people who frequented such places; but somehow he had been reluctant to leave. Never before had he been loath to face the solitude of his cabin, peopled only with books and manuscripts, with unwritten and half-written fantasies.

Still dimly troubled by the mystery that had driven him forth, he fell across the unmade bed without undressing or even lighting a lamp, and slid into drunken slumber.

Wild dreams came to visit him anon. Weird voices shrieked and muttered in his ears, indistinct but nightmarish figures milled around him like the dancers of some demonian Sabbat. Amid the voices that seemed to conspire against his peace and safety, he heard the incessant click and rattle of a typewriter. There was a clacking as of drawers opened and shut without cessation, a multitudinous rustling as of paper slithering from place to place in unaccountable sibilant movement.

La Porte awoke from endless repetitions of this dream—to find that the noises still continued. Again, as on a former occasion, he sprang from bed, lit his lamp, and entered the workroom from which the sounds and voices appeared to come.

Still dazed with sleep and inebriation, his eyes beheld a vast chamber whose roof and walls receded beyond the illumination of the lamp he carried in shaking fingers. Amid this chamber his manuscripts rose in massive piles, multiplied and magnified as if by the black sorcery of hashish. They seemed to loom above him with topless tiers, lost in the reaches of some Avernian vault.

On the desk at the room's center his Remington, operated as if by some unseen entity, ran and clattered with infernal speed. Black lines appeared momently on the sheet that emerged rapidly from the roller.

The floor was covered with other sheets, lying singly or in heaps, that slid and rustled about the chamber in mysterious perpetual agitation. The air was filled with the eerie gibberings and whispers that had haunted La Porte's dreams and awakened him. They came, it seemed, from nowhere and everywhere—from the scattered pages on the floor, from the typewriter desk, from the tiered boxes and reams that beetled into nightmare vastness, and from the apparent vacancy of space itself.

La Porte felt on his face the breathing of terrible powers, of eldritch and forbidden things, as he stood in hesitant stupor on the threshold. A wind sprang up, he knew not whence, winding and wreathing about him in icy serpentine volumes. He thought that the room grew vaster, that the floor heaved and tilted at strange impossible angles, that the towers and battlements of swollen manuscripts leaned toward him in perilous inclination.

The weird wind strengthened and swiftened, sweeping up the numberless loose sheets in a wild storm, and extinguishing the lamp that he held in his nerveless hand. Darkness fell—a darkness of vertigo and delirium, into which La Porte was hurled resistlessly, falling through endless gulfs, battling with countless evil things that swooped upon him from all directions, and hearing a thunder as of loosened avalanches....

Neighbors, noticing the absence of smoke from La Porte's chimney, and missing him on the road to the village, became sufficiently alarmed to investigate after the third day. Opening the unlocked outer door, they saw the littered paper, mingled with fragments of a shattered kerosene lamp, that overflowed the threshold of his workroom.

Ream upon ream of paper almost filled the room itself: a mountain of heaped and dishevelled manuscripts covering the one chair and desk and typewriter with its high-piled summit. They found Francis La Porte lying in a convulsed posture beneath the pile. In his rigid hands, upthrust protectively before his face, were clutched the sheets of several thick manuscripts, torn and ripped asunder as if in some violent struggle. Other sheets, torn to confetti-like pieces, strewed his upturned body. Still others were locked in a tetanic rigor between his bared teeth.

THE MASTER OF THE CRABS

I remember that I grumbled a little when Mior Lumivix awakened me. The past evening had been a tedious one with its unpleasant familiar vigil, during which I had nodded often. From sunfall till the setting of Scorpio, which occurred well after midnight at that season, it had been my duty to tend the gradual inspissation of a decoction of scarabs, much favored by Mior Lumivix in the compounding of his most requested love-potions. He had warned me often that this liquor must be thickened neither too slowly nor too rapidly, by maintaining an even fire in the athanor, and had cursed me more than once for spoiling it. Therefore I did not yield to my drowsiness till the decoction was safely decanted and strained thrice through the sieve of perforated shark-skin.

Taciturn beyond his wont, the Master had retired early to his chamber. I knew that something troubled him; but was too tired for overmuch conjecture, and had not dared to question him.

It seemed that I had not slept for more than the period of a few pulse-beats—and here was the Master thrusting the yellow-slotted eye of his lantern into my face and dragging me from the pallet. I knew that I should not sleep again that night: for the Master wore his one-horned hat, and his cloak was girdled tightly about him, with the ancient arthame depending from the girdle in its shagreen sheath that time and the hands of many magicians had blackened.

"Abortion fathered by a sloth!" he cried. "Suckling of a sow that has eaten mandragora! Would you slumber till doomsday? We must hurry: I have learned that Sarcand has procured the chart of Omvor and has gone forth alone to the wharves. No doubt he means to embark in quest of the temple-treasure. We must follow quickly for much time has already been lost."

I rose now without further demur and dressed myself expeditiously, knowing well the urgency of this matter. Sarcand, who had but lately come to the city of Mirouane, had already made himself the most formidable of all my master's competitors. It was said that he was native to Naat, amid the somber western ocean, having been begotten by a sorcerer of that isle on a woman of the black cannibals who dwell beyond its middle mountains. He combined his mother's savage nature with the dark necromantic craft of his father; and, moreover, had acquired much dubious knowledge and repute in his travels through orient kingdoms before settling in Mirouane.

The fabulous chart of Omvor, dating from lost ages, was a thing that many generations of wizards had dreamt to find. Omvor, an ancient pirate still renowned, had performed successfully a feat of impious rashness. Sailing up a closely guarded estuary by night with his small crew disguised as priests in stolen temple-barges, he had looted the fane of the Moon-God in Faraad and had carried away many of its virgins, together with gems, gold, altar-vessels, talismans, phylacteries and books of eldritch elder magic. These books were the gravest loss of all, since even the priests had never dared to copy them. They were unique and irreplaceable, containing the erudition of buried aeons.

Omvor's feat had given rise to many legends. He and his crew and the ravished virgins, in two small brigantines, had vanished ultimately amid the western seas. It was believed that they had been caught by the Black River, that terrible ocean-stream which pours with an irresistible swiftening beyond Naat to the world's end. But before that final voyage, Omvor had lightened his vessels of the looted treasure and had made a chart on which the location of its hiding-place was indicated. This chart he had given to a former comrade who had grown too old for voyaging.

No man had ever found the treasure. But it was said that the chart still existed throughout the centuries, hidden somewhere no less securely than the loot of the Moon-God's temple. Of late there were rumors that some sailor, inheriting it from his fathers, had brought the map to Mirouane. Mior Lumivix, through agents both human and preterhuman, had tried vainly to trace the sailor; knowing that Sarcand and the other wizards of the city were also seeking him.

This much was known to me; and the Master told me more while, at his bidding, I collected hastily such provisions as were needed for a voyage of several days.

"I have watched Sarcand like an osprey watching its nest," he said. "My familiars told me that he had found the chart's owner, and had hired some thief to steal it; but they could tell me little else. Even the eyes of my devil-cat, peering through his windows, were baffled by the cuttle-fish darkness with which his magic surrounds him at will.

"Tonight I did a dangerous thing, since there was no other way. Drinking the juice of the purple *dedaim*, which induces profound trance, I projected my ka into his elemental-guarded chamber. The elementals knew my presence, they gathered about me in shapes of fire and shadow, menacing me unspeakably.

They opposed me, they drove me forth… but I had seen—enough."

The Master paused, bidding me gird myself with a consecrated magic sword, similar to his own but of less antiquity, which he had never before allowed me to wear. By this time I had gathered together the required provision of food and drink, storing it in a strong fish-net that I could carry easily over my shoulder by the handle. The net was one that we used mainly for catching certain sea-reptiles, from which Mior Lumivix extracted a venom possessing unique virtue.

It was not till we had locked all the portals, and had plunged into the dark seaward-winding streets, that the Master resumed his account:

"A man was leaving Sarcand's chamber at the moment of my entrance. I saw him briefly, ere the black arras parted and closed; but I shall know him again. He was young and plump, with powerful sinews under the plumpness, with slanted squinting eyes in a girlish face and the swart yellow skin of a man from the southern isles. He wore the short breeks and ankle-topping boots of a mariner, being otherwise naked.

"Sarcand was sitting with his back half-turned, holding an unrolled sheet of papyrus, yellow as the sailor's face, to that evil, four-horned lamp which he feeds with cobras' oil. The lamp glared like a ghoul's eye. But I looked over his shoulder… long enough… before his demons could hurry me from the room. The papyrus was indeed the chart of Omvor. It was stiff with age, and stained with blood and sea-water. But its title and purpose and appellations were still legible, though inscribed in an archaic script that few can read nowadays.

"It showed the western shore of the continent Zothique, and the seas beyond. An isle lying due westward from Mirouane was indicated as the burial-place of the treasure. It was named the Island of Crabs on the chart: but plainly it is none other than the one now called Iribos which, though seldom visited, lies at a distance of only two days' voyaging. There are no other islands within a hundred leagues, either north or south, excepting a few desolate rocks and small atolls."

Urging me to greater haste, Mior Lumivix continued:

"I woke too tardily from the swoon induced by the *dedaim*. A lesser adept would never have awakened at all.

"My familiars warned me that Sarcand had left his house a full hour ago. He was prepared for a journey, and went wharfward. But we will overtake him. I think that he will go without companions to Iribos, desiring to keep the treasure wholly secret. He is indeed strong and terrible, but his demons are of a kind that cannot cross water, being entirely earthbound. He has left them behind with the moiety of his magic. Have no fear for the outcome."

The wharves were still and almost deserted, except for a few sleeping sailors who had succumbed to the rank wine and arrack of the taverns. Under the late moon, that had curved and sharpened to a slim scimitar, we unmoored our boat and pushed away, the Master holding the tiller, while I bent my shoulders to the broad-bladed oars. Thus we threaded the huddled maze of far-gathered ships, of xebecs and galleys, of river-barges and scows and feluccas, that thronged that immemorial harbor. The sluggish air, hardly stirring our tall lateen sail, was pregnant with sea-smells, with the reek of laden fishing-boats and the spices of exotic cargoes. None hailed us; and we heard only the calling of watchmen on shadowy decks, proclaiming the hour in outlandish tongues.

Our boat, though small and open, was stoutly built of orient beef-wood. Sharply prowed and deeply keeled, with high bulwarks, it had proven itself seaworthy even in tempests such as were not to be apprehended at this season.

Blowing over Mirouane, from fields and orchards and desert kingdoms, a wind freshened behind us as we cleared the harbor. It stiffened, till the sail bellied like a dragon's wing. The furrows of foam curved high beside our sharp prow, as we followed Capricornus down the west.

Far out on the waters before us, in the dim moonlight, something seemed to move, to dance and waver like a phantom. Perhaps it was Sarcand's boat… or another's. Doubtless the Master also saw it; but he said only:

"You may sleep now."

So I, Manthar the apprentice, composed myself to slumber, while Mior Lumivix steered on, and the starry hooves and horns of the Goat sank seaward.

The sun was high above our stern when I awakened. The wind still blew, strong and favorable, driving us into the west with unabated speed. We had passed beyond sight of the shore-line of Zothique. The sky was void of clouds, the sea vacant of any sail, unrolling before us like a vast scroll of somber azure, lined only with the shifting and fading foam-crests.

The day went by, ebbing beyond the still-empty horizon; and night overtook us like the heaven-blotting purple sail of a god, sewn with the Signs and planets. The night too went over, and a second dawn.

All this time, without sleeping, the Master had steered the boat, with eyes peering implacably westward like those of an ocean-hawk; and I wondered greatly at his endurance. Now for awhile he slept, sitting upright at the helm. But it seemed that his eyes were still vigilant behind their lids; and his hand still held the rudder straight, without slackening.

In a few hours the Master opened his eyes; but hardly stirred from the posture he maintained throughout.

He had spoken little during our voyage. I did not question him, knowing that he would tell me whatever was needful at the due time. But I was full of curiosities; and was not without fear and doubt regarding Sarcand, whose rumored necromancies might well have dismayed others than a mere novice.

I could surmise nothing of the Master's thoughts, except that they concerned dark and esoteric matters.

Having slept for the third time since our embarkment, I was roused by the Master crying loudly. In the dimness of the third dawn, an island towered before us, impending with jagged cliffs and jutting crags, and barring the sea for several leagues to northward and southward. It was shaped somewhat like a monster, facing north. Its head was a high-horned promontory, dipping a great griffin-like beak in the ocean.

"This is Iribos," the Master told me. "The sea is strong about it, with strange tides and perilous currents. There are no landing-places on this side, and we must not venture too close. We must round the northern headland. There is a small cove amid the western cliffs, entered only through a sea-cavern. It is there that the treasure lies."

We tacked northward slowly and deviously against the wind, at a distance of three or four bow-shots from the island. All our sea-craft was required to make progress: for the wind strengthened wildly, as if swollen by the breath of devils. Above its howling we heard the surf's clamor upon those monstrous rocks that rose bare and gaunt from cerements of foam.

"The isle is unpeopled," said Mior Lumivix. "It is shunned by sailors and even by the sea-fowl. Men say that the curse of the maritime gods was laid upon it long ago, forbidding it to any but the creatures of the submarine deep. Its coves and caverns are haunted by crabs and octopi… and perhaps by stranger things."

We sailed on in a tedious serpentine course, beaten back at times or borne perilously shoreward by the shifting gusts that opposed us like evil demons. The sun climbed in the orient, shining starkly down on the desolation of crags and scarps that was Iribos.

Still we tacked and veered; and I seemed to sense the beginning of a strange unease in the Master. But of this, if such there was, his manner betrayed no sign.

It was almost noon when we rounded at last the long beak of the northern promontory. There, when we turned southerly, the wind fell in a weird still-ness, and the sea was miraculously calmed as if by wizard oils. Our sail hung limp and useless above mirror-like waters, in which it seemed that the boat's reflected image and ours, unbroken, moveless, might float forever amid the unchanging reflection of the monster-shapen isle. We both began to ply the broad oars; but even thus the boat crawled with a singular slowness.

I observed the isle strictly as we passed along, noting several inlets where, to all appearance, a vessel could have landed readily.

"There is much danger here," said Mior Lumivix, without elucidating his statement.

Again, as we continued, the cliffs became a wall that was broken only by rifts and chasms. They were crowned in places by a sparse, funereal-colored vegetation that hardly served to soften their formidable aspect. High up in the clefted rocks, where it seemed that no natural tide or tempest could have flung them, I observed the scattered spars and timbers of antique vessels.

"Row closer," enjoined the Master. "We are nearing the cavern that leads to the hidden inlet."

Even as we veered landward through the crystalline calm, there was a sudden seething and riffling about us, as if some monster had risen beneath. The boat began to shoot with plummet-like speed toward the cliffs, the sea foaming and streaming all around as though some kraken were dragging us to its caverned lair. Borne like a leaf on a cataract, we toiled vainly with straining oars against the ineluctable current.

Heaving higher momentarily, the cliffs seemed to shear the heavens above us, unscalable, without ledge or foothold. Then, in the sheer wall, appeared the low, broad arch of a cavern-mouth that we had not discerned heretofore, toward which the boat was drawn with dreadful swiftness.

"It is the entrance!" cried the Master. "But some wizard tide has flooded it."

We shipped our useless oars and crouched down behind the thwarts as we neared the opening: for it seemed that the lowness of the arch would afford bare passage to our high-built prow. There was no time to unstep the mast, which broke instantly like a reed as we raced on without slackening into blind torrential darkness.

Half-stunned, and striving to extricate myself from the fallen, spar-weighted sail, I felt the chillness of water splashing about me and knew that the boat was filling and sinking. A moment more, and the water was in my ears and eyes and nostrils: but even as I sank and drowned there was still the sense of swift onward motion. Then it seemed dimly that arms were around me in the strangling darkness; and I rose suddenly, choking and gasping and spewing, into sunlight.

When I had rid my lungs of the brine and regained my senses more fully, I found that Mior Lumivix and I were floating in a small haven, shaped like a half-moon, and surrounded by crags and pinnacles of sullen-colored rock. Close by, in a sheer, straight wall, was the inner mouth of the cavern through which the mysterious current had carried us, with faint ripples spreading around it and fading away into water smooth and green as a platter of jade. Opposite, on the haven's farther side, was the long curve of a shelving beach strewn with boulders and driftwood. A boat resembling ours, with an unshipped mast and a furled sail the color of fresh blood, was moored to the beach. Near it, from the shoaling water, protruded the broken-off mast of another boat, whose sunken outlines we discerned obscurely. Two objects which we took for human figures were lying half in and half out of the shallows a little farther along the strand. At that distance we could hardly know whether they were living men or cadavers. Their contours were half-hidden by what seemed a curious sort of brownish-yellow drapery that trailed away amid the rocks, appearing to move and shift and waver incessantly.

"There is mystery here," said Mior Lumivix in a low voice. "We must proceed with care and circumspection."

We swam ashore at the near end of the beach, where it narrowed like the tip of a crescent moon to meet the sea-wall. Taking his arthame from its sheath the Master wiped it dry with the hem of his cloak, bidding me do likewise with my own weapon lest the brine corrode it. Then, hiding the wizard blades beneath our raiment, we followed the broadening beach toward the moored boat and the two reclining figures.

"This is indeed the place of Omvor's chart," observed the Master. "The boat with the blood-red sail belongs to Sarcand. No doubt he has found the cave, which lies hidden somewhere among the rocks. But who are these others? I do not think that they came with Sarcand."

As we neared the figures, the appearance of a yellowish-brown drapery that covered them resolved itself in its true nature. It consisted of a great number of crabs who were crawling over their half-submerged bodies and running to and fro behind a heap of immense boulders.

We went forward and stooped over the bodies, from which the crabs were busily detaching morsels of bloody flesh. One of the bodies lay on its face; the other stared with half-eaten features at the sun. Their skin, or what remained of it, was a swarthy yellow. Both were clad in short purple breeks and sailor's boots, being otherwise naked.

"What hellishness is this?" inquired the Master. "These men are but newly dead—and already the crabs rend them. Such creatures are wont to wait for the softening of decomposition. And look—they do not even devour the morsels they have torn, but bear them away."

This indeed was true, for I saw now that a constant procession of crabs departed from the bodies, each carrying a shred of flesh, to vanish beyond the rocks; while another procession came, or perhaps returned, with empty pincers.

"I think," said Mior Lumivix, "that the man with the upturned face is the sailor that I saw leaving Sarcand's room; the thief who had stolen the chart for Sarcand from its owner."

In my horror and disgust I had picked up a fragment of rock and was about to crush some of the hideously laden crabs as they crawled away from the corpses.

"Nay," the Master stayed me, "let us follow them."

Rounding the great heap of boulders, we saw that the twofold procession entered, and emerged from, the mouth of a cavern that had heretofore been hidden from view.

With hands tightening on the hilts of our arthames, we went cautiously and circumspectly toward the cavern and paused a little short of its entrance.

From this vantage, however, nothing was visible within except the lines of crawling crabs.

"Enter!" cried a sonorous voice that seemed to prolong and repeat the word in far-receding reverberations, like the voice of a ghoul echoing in some profound sepulchral vault.

The voice was that of the sorcerer Sarcand. The Master looked at me, with whole volumes of warning in his narrowed eyes, and we entered the cavern.

The place was high-domed and of indeterminable extent. Light was afforded by a great rift in the vault above, through which, at this hour, the direct rays of the sun slanted in, falling goldenly on the cavern's foreground and tipping with light the great fangs of stalactites and stalagmites in the gloom beyond. At one side was a pool of water, fed by a thin rill from a spring that dripped somewhere in the darkness.

With the shafted splendor shining full upon him, Sarcand reposed half-sitting, half-recumbent, with his back against an open chest of age-darkened bronze. His huge ebon-black body, powerfully muscled though inclining toward corpulence, was nude except for a necklace of rubies, each the size of a plover's egg, that depended about his throat. His crimson sarong, strangely tattered, bared his legs as they lay outstretched amid the cavern's rubble. The right leg had manifestly been broken somewhere below the knee, for it was rudely bound with splints of driftwood and strips torn from the sarong.

Sarcand's cloak of lazuli-colored silk was outspread beside him. It was strewn with graven gems and amulets, with gold coins and jewel-crusted altar-vessels, that flashed and glittered amid volumens of parchments and papyrus. A book with black metal covers lay open as if newly put aside, showing illuminations drawn in fiery ancient inks.

Beside the book, within reach of Sarcand's fingers, was a mound of raw and bloody shreds. Over the cloak, over the coins and scrolls and jewels, crawled the incoming line of crabs, each of which added its torn-off morsel to the mound and then crept on to join the outgoing column.

I could well believe the tales regarding Sarcand's ancestry. Indeed, it seemed that he favored his mother entirely: for his hair and features as well as his skin were those of the negro cannibals of Naat as I had seen them depicted in travellers' drawings. He fronted us inscrutably, his arms crossed on his bosom. I noticed a great emerald shining darkly on the index finger of his right hand.

"I knew that you would follow me," he said, "even as I knew that the thief and his companion would follow. All of you have thought to slay me and take the treasure. It is true that I have suffered an injury: a fragment of loosened rock fell from the cavern-roof, breaking my leg as I bent over to inspect the treasures in the opened chest. I must lie here till the bone has knit. In the meanwhile I am well armed... and well served and guarded."

"We came to take the treasure," replied Mior Lumivix directly. "I had thought to slay you, but only in fair combat, man to man and wizard to wizard, with none but my neophyte Manthar and the rocks of Iribos for witness."

"Aye, and your neophyte is also armed with an arthame. However, it matters little. I shall feast on your liver, Mior Lumivix, and wax stronger by such power of sorcery as was yours."

This the Master appeared to disregard.

"What foulness have you conjured now?" he inquired sharply, pointing to the crabs who were still depositing their morsels on the grisly mound.

Sarcand held aloft the hand on whose index finger gleamed the immense emerald, set, as we now perceived, in a ring that was wrought with the tentacles of a kraken clasping the orb-like gem.

"I found this ring amid the treasure," he boasted. "It was closed in a cylinder of unknown metal, together with a scroll that informed me of the ring's uses and its mighty magic. It is the signet-ring of Basatan, the sea-god. He who looks long and deeply into the emerald may behold distant scenes and happenings at will. He who wears the ring can exert control over the winds and currents of the sea and over the sea's creatures, by describing certain signs in air with his finger."

While Sarcand spoke it seemed that the green jewel brightened and darkened and deepened strangely, like a tiny window with all the sea's mystery and immensity lying beyond. Enthralled and entranced, I forgot the circumstances of our situation: for the jewel swelled upon my vision, blotting from view the black fingers of Sarcand, with a swirling as of tides and of shadowy fins and tentacles far down in its glimmering greenness.

"Beware, Manthar," the Master murmured in my ear. "We face a dreadful magic, and must retain the command of all our faculties. Avert your eyes from the emerald."

I obeyed the dimly heard whisper. The vision dwindled away, vanishing swiftly, and the form and features of Sarcand returned. His lubber lips were curved in a broad sardonic grin, showing his strong white teeth that were pointed like those of a shark. He dropped the huge hand that wore the signet of Basatan, plunging it into the chest behind him and bringing it forth filled with many-tinted gems, with pearls, opals, sapphires, bloodstones, diamonds, chatoyants. These he let dribble in a flashing rill from his fingers, as he resumed his peroration:

"I preceded you to Iribos by many hours. It was known to me that the outer cavern could be entered safely only at low tide, with an unstepped mast.

"Perhaps you have already inferred whatever else I might tell you. At any rate the knowledge will perish with you very shortly.

"After learning the uses of the ring I was able to watch the seas around Iribos in the jewel. Lying here with my shattered leg, I saw the approach of the thief and his fellow. I called up the sea-current by which their boat was drawn into the flooded cavern, sinking swiftly. They would have swum ashore: but at my command the crabs in the haven drew them under and drowned them; letting the tide beach their corpses later.... That cursed thief! I had paid him well for the stolen chart, which he was too ignorant to read, suspecting only that it concerned a treasure-trove....

"Still later I trapped you in the same fashion, after delaying you awhile with contrary winds and an adverse calm. I have preserved you, however, for another doom than drowning."

The voice of the necromancer sank away in profound echoes, leaving a silence fraught with insufferable suspense. It seemed that we stood amid the gaping of undiscovered gulfs, in a place of awful darkness, lit only by the eyes of Sarcand and the ring's talismanic jewel.

The spell that had fallen upon me was broken by the cold ironic tones of the Master:

"Sarcand, there is another sorcery that you have not mentioned."

Sarcand's laughter was like the sound of a mounting surf. "I follow the custom of my mother's people; and the crabs serve me with that which I require, summoned and constrained by the sea-god's ring."

So saying, he raised his hand and described a peculiar sign with the index finger, on which the ring flashed like a circling orb. The double column of crabs suspended their crawling for a moment. Then, moved as if by a single impulse, they began to scuttle toward us, while others appeared from the cavern's entrance and from its inner recesses to swell their rapidly growing numbers. They surged upon us with a speed beyond belief, assailing our ankles and shins with their knife-sharp pincers as if animated by demons. I stooped over, striking and thrusting with my arthame; but the few that I crushed in this manner were replaced by scores; while others, catching the hem of my cloak, began to climb it from behind and weigh it down. Thus encumbered, I lost my footing on the slippery ground and fell backward amid the scuttling multitude.

Lying there while the crabs poured over me like a seething wave, I saw the Master shed his burdened cloak and cast it aside. Then, while the spell-drawn army still besieged him, climbing upon each other's backs and scaling his very knees and thighs, he hurled his arthame with a strange circular motion at the upraised arm of Sarcand. Straightly the blade flew, revolving like a disk of brightness; and the hand of the black necromancer was sundered cleanly at the wrist, and the ring flashed on its index finger like a falling star as it fell groundward.

Blood spouted in a fountain from the handless wrist, while Sarcand sat as in a stupor, maintaining for a brief instant the gesture of his conjuration. Then the arm dropped to his side and the blood rilled out upon the littered cloak, spreading swiftly amid the gems and coins and volumens, and staining the mound of crab-deposited morsels. As if the arm's movement had been another signal, the crabs fell away from the Master and myself and swarmed in a long, innumerable tide toward Sarcand. They covered his legs, they climbed his great torso, they scrambled for place on his escaladed shoulders. He tore them away with his one hand, roaring terrible curses and imprecations that rolled in countless echoes throughout the cavern. But the crabs still assailed him as if driven by some demoniac frenzy; and blood trickled forth more and more copiously from the small wounds they had made, to suffuse their pincers and streak their shells with broadening rillets of crimson.

It seemed that long hours went by while the Master and I stood watching. At last the prostrate thing that was Sarcand had ceased to heave and toss under the living shroud that enswathed it. Only the splint-bound leg and the lopped-off hand with the ring of Basatan remained untouched by the loathsomely busied crabs.

"Faugh!" the Master exclaimed. "He left his devils behind when he came here; but he found others…. It is time that we went out for a walk in the sun. Manthar, my good lubberly apprentice, I would have you build a fire of driftwood on the beach. Pile on the fuel without sparing, to make a bed of coals deep and hot and red as the hearth of hell, in which to roast us a dozen crabs. But be careful to choose the ones that have come freshly from the sea."

MORTHYLLA

In Umbri, City of the Delta, the lights blazed with a garish brilliance after the setting of that sun which was now a coal-red decadent star, grown old beyond chronicle, beyond legend. Most brilliant, most garish of all were the lights that illumed the house of the aging poet Famurza, whose Anacreontic songs had brought him the riches that he disbursed in orgies for his friends and sycophants. Here, in porticoes, halls and chambers the cressets were thick as stars in a cloudless vault. It seemed that Famurza wished to dissipate all shadows, except those in arrased alcoves set apart for the fitful amours of his guests.

For the kindling of such amours there were wines, cordials, aphrodisiacs. There were meats and fruits that swelled the flaccid pulses. There were strange exotic drugs that aroused and prolonged pleasure. There were curious statuettes in half-veiled niches; and wall-panels painted with bestial loves, or loves human or superhuman. There were hired singers of all sexes, who sang ditties diversely erotic; and dancers whose contortions were calculated to restore the outworn sense when all else had failed.

But to all such incitants Valzain, pupil of Famurza, and renowned both as poet and voluptuary, was insensible.

With indifference turning toward disgust, a half-emptied cup in his hand, he watched from a corner the gala throng that eddied past him, and averted his eyes involuntarily from certain couples who were too shameless or drunken to seek the shadows of privacy for their dalliance. A sudden satiety had claimed him. He felt himself strangely withdrawn from the morass of wine and flesh into which, not long before, he had still plunged with delight. He seemed as one who stands on an alien shore, beyond waters of deepening separation.

"What ails you, Valzain? Has a vampire sucked your blood?" It was Famurza, flushed, grey-haired, slightly corpulent, who stood at his elbow. Laying an

245

affectionate hand on Valzain's shoulder, he hoisted aloft with the other that fescenninely graven quart goblet from which he was wont to drink only wine, eschewing the drugged and violent liquors often preferred by the sybarites of Umbri.

"Is it biliousness? Or unrequited love? We have cures here for both. You have only to name your medicine."

"There is no medicine for what ails me," countered Valzain. "As for love, I have ceased to care whether it be requited or unrequited. I can taste only the dregs in every cup. And tedium lurks at the middle of all kisses."

"Truly, yours is a melancholy case." There was concern in Famurza's voice. "I have been reading some of your late verses. You write only of tombs and yew-trees, of maggots and phantoms and disembodied loves. Such stuff gives me the colic. I need at least a half-gallon of honest vine-juice after each poem."

"Though I did not know it till lately," admitted Valzain, "there is in me a curiosity toward the unseen, a longing for things beyond the material world."

Famurza shook his head commiserately. "Though I have attained to more than twice your years, I am still content with what I see and hear and touch. Good juicy meats, women, wine, the songs of full-throated singers, are enough for me."

"In the dreams of slumber," mused Valzain, "I have clasped succubi who were more than flesh, have known delights too keen for the waking body to sustain. Do such dreams have any source, outside the earth-born brain itself? I would give much to find that source, if it exists. In the meanwhile there is nothing for me but despair."

"So young—and yet so exhausted! Well, if you're tired of women, and want phantoms instead, I might venture a suggestion. Do you know the old necropolis, lying midway between Umbri and Psiom—a matter of perhaps three miles from here? The goatherds say that a lamia haunts it—the spirit of the princess Morthylla, who died several centuries ago and was interred in a mausoleum that still stands, overtowering the lesser tombs. Why not go forth tonight and visit the necropolis? It should suit your mood better than my house. And perhaps Morthylla will appear to you. But don't blame me if you return with a nibbled throat—or fail to return at all. After all those years the lamia is still avid for human lovers; and she might well take a fancy to you."

"Of course, I know the place," said Valzain…. "But I think you are jesting."

Famurza shrugged his shoulders and moved on amid the revelers. A laughing dancer, blonde-limbed and lissom, came up to Valzain and threw a noose of plaited flowers about his neck, claiming him as her captive. He broke the noose gently, and gave the girl a tepid kiss that caused her to make wry faces. Unobtrusively but quickly, before others of the merry-makers could try to entice him, he left the house of Famurza.

Without impulses, other than that of an urgent desire for solitude, he turned his steps toward the suburbs, avoiding the neighborhood of taverns and lupanars, where the populace thronged. Music, laughter, snatches of songs, followed him from lighted mansions where symposia were held nightly by the city's richer denizens. But he met few roisterers on the streets: it was too late for the gathering, too early for the dispersal, of guests at such symposia.

Now the lights thinned out, with ever-widening intervals between, and the streets grew shadowy with that ancient night which pressed about Umbri, and would wholly quench its defiant galaxies of lamp-bright windows with the darkening of Zothique's senescent sun. Of such things, and of death's encircling mystery, were the musings of Valzain as he plunged into the outer darkness that he found grateful to his glare-wearied eyes.

Grateful too was the silence of the field-bordered road that he pursued for awhile without realizing its direction. Then, at some landmark familiar despite the gloom, it came to him that the road was the one which ran from Umbri to Psiom, that sister city of the Delta; the road beside whose middle meanderings was situated the long-disused necropolis to which Famurza had ironically directed him.

Truly, he thought, the earthy-minded Famurza had somehow plumbed the need that lay at the bottom of his disenchantment with all sensory pleasures. It would be good to visit, to sojourn for an hour or so, in that city whose people had long passed beyond the lusts of mortality, beyond satiety and disillusion.

A moon, swelling from the crescent toward the half, arose behind him as he reached the foot of the low-mounded hill on which the cemetery lay. He left the paved road, and began to ascend the slope, half-covered with stunted gorse, at whose summit the glimmering marbles were discernible. It was without path, other than the broken trails made by goats and their herders. Dim, lengthened and attenuate, his shadow went before him like a ghostly guide. In his fantasy it seemed to him that he climbed the gently sloping bosom of a giantess, studded afar with pale gems that were tombstones and mausoleums. He caught himself wondering, amid this poetic whimsy, whether the giantess was dead, or merely slept.

Gaining the flat expansive ground of the summit, where dwarfish dying yews disputed with leafless briars the intervals of slabs blotched with lichen, he recalled the tale that Famurza had mentioned, anent the lamia who was said to haunt the necropolis. Famurza, he knew well, was no believer in such legendry, and had meant only to mock his funereal mood. Yet, as a poet will, he began to play with the fancy of some presence, immortal, lovely and evil, that dwelt amid the antique marbles and would respond to the evocation of one who, without positive belief, had longed vainly for visions from beyond mortality.

Through headstone aisles of moon-touched solitude, he came to a lofty mausoleum, still standing with few signs of ruin at the cemetery's center. Beneath it, he had been told, were extensive vaults housing the mummies of an extinct royal family that had ruled over the twin cities Umbri and Psiom in former centuries. The princess Morthylla had belonged to this family.

To his startlement a woman, or what appeared to be such, was sitting on a fallen shaft beside the mausoleum. He could not see her distinctly; the tomb's shadow still enveloped her from the shoulders downward. The face alone, glimmering wanly, was lifted to the rising moon. Its profile was such as he had seen on antique coins.

"Who are you?" he asked, with a curiosity that overpowered his courtesy.

"I am the lamia Morthylla," she replied, in a voice that left behind it a faint and elusive vibration like that of some briefly sounded harp. "Beware me—for my kisses are forbidden to those who would remain numbered among the living."

Valzain was startled by this answer that echoed his fantasies. Yet reason told him that the apparition was no spirit of the tombs but a living woman who knew the legend of Morthylla and wished to amuse herself by teasing him. And yet what woman would venture alone and at night to a place so desolate and eerie?

Most credibly, she was a wanton who had come out to keep a rendezvous amid the tombs. There were, he knew, certain perverse debauchees who required sepulchral surroundings and furnishings for the titillation of their desires.

"Perhaps you are waiting for some one," he suggested. "I do not wish to intrude, if such is the case."

"I wait only for him who is destined to come. And I have waited long, having had no lover for two hundred years. Remain, if you wish: there is no one to fear but me."

Despite the rational surmises he had formed, there crept along Valzain's spine the thrill of one who, without fully believing, suspects the presence of a thing beyond nature…. Yet surely it was all a game—a game that he too could play for the beguilement of his ennui.

"I came here hoping to meet you," he declared. "I am weary of mortal women, tired of every pleasure—tired even of poetry."

"I, too, am bored," she said, simply.

The moon had climbed higher, shining on the dress of antique mode that the woman wore. It was cut closely at waist and hips and bosom, with voluminous downward folds. Valzain had seen such costumes only in old drawings. The princess Morthylla, dead for three centuries, might well have worn a similar dress.

Whoever she might be, he thought, the woman was strangely beautiful, with a touch of quaintness in the heavily coiled hair whose color he could not decide in the moonlight. There was a sweetness about her mouth, a shadow of fatigue or sadness beneath her eyes. At the right corner of her lips he discerned a small mole.

Valzain's meeting with the self-named Morthylla was repeated nightly while the moon swelled like the rounding breast of a titaness and fell away once more to hollowness and senescence. Always she awaited him by the same mausoleum—which, she declared, was her dwelling-place. And always she dismissed him when the east turned ashen with dawn, saying that she was a creature of the night.

Skeptical at first, he thought of her as a person with macabre leanings and fantasies akin to his own, with whom he was carrying on a flirtation of singular charm. Yet about her he could find no hint of the worldliness that he suspected: no seeming knowledge of present things, but a weird familiarity with the past and the lamia's legend. More and more she seemed a nocturnal being, intimate only with shadow and solitude.

Her eyes, her lips, appeared to withhold secrets forgotten and forbidden. In her vague, ambiguous answers to his questions, he read meanings that thrilled him with hope and fear.

"I have dreamed of life," she told him cryptically. "And I have dreamed also of death. Now, perhaps there is another dream—into which you have entered."

"I, too, would dream," said Valzain.

Night after night his disgust and weariness sloughed away from him, in a fascination fed by the spectral milieu, the environing silence of the dead, his withdrawal and separation from the carnal, garish city. By degrees, by alternations of unbelief and belief, he came to accept her as the actual lamia. The hunger that he sensed in her could be only the lamia's hunger; her beauty that of a being no longer human. It was like a dreamer's acceptance of things fantastic elsewhere than in sleep.

Together with his belief, there grew his love for her. The desires he had thought dead revived within him, wilder, more importunate.

She seemed to love him in return. Yet she betrayed no sign of the lamia's legendary nature, eluding his embrace, refusing him the kisses for which he begged.

"Sometime, perhaps," she conceded. "But first you must know me for what I am, must love me without illusion."

"Kill me with your lips, devour me as you are said to have devoured other lovers," beseeched Valzain.

"Can you not wait?" Her smile was sweet—and tantalizing. "I do not wish your death so soon, for I love you too well. Is it not sweet to keep our tryst among the sepulchers? Have I not beguiled you from your boredom? Must you end it all?"

250 • CLARK ASHTON SMITH

The next night he besought her again, imploring with all his ardor and eloquence the denied consummation.

She mocked him: "Perhaps I am merely a bodiless phantom, a spirit without substance. Perhaps you have dreamed me. Would you risk an awakening from the dream?"

Valzain stepped toward her, stretching out his arms in a passionate gesture. She drew back, saying:

"What if I should turn to ashes and moonlight at your touch? You would regret then your rash insistence."

"You are the immortal lamia," avowed Valzain. "My senses tell me that you are no phantom, no disembodied spirit. But for me you have turned all else to shadow."

"Yes, I am real enough in my fashion," she granted, laughing softly. Then suddenly she leaned toward him and her lips touched his throat. He felt their moist warmth a moment—and felt the sharp sting of her teeth that barely pierced his skin, withdrawing instantly. Before he could clasp her she eluded him again.

"It is the only kiss permitted to us at present," she cried, and fled swiftly with soundless footfalls among the gleams and shadows of the sepulchers.

On the following afternoon a matter of urgent and unwelcome business called Valzain to the neighboring city of Psiom: a brief journey, but one that he seldom took.

He passed the ancient necropolis, longing for that nocturnal hour when he could hasten once more to a meeting with Morthylla. Her poignant kiss, which had drawn a few drops of blood, had left him greatly fevered and distraught. He, like that place of tombs, was haunted; and the haunting went with him into Psiom.

He had finished his business, the borrowing of a sum of money from a usurer. Standing at the usurer's door, with that slightly obnoxious but necessary person beside him, he saw a woman passing on the street.

Her features, though not her dress, were those of Morthylla; and there was even the same tiny mole at one corner of her mouth. No phantom of the cemetery could have startled or dismayed him more profoundly.

"Who is that woman?" he asked the money-lender. "Do you know her?"

"Her name is Beldith. She is well-known in Psiom, being rich in her own right and having had numerous lovers. I've had a little business with her, though she owes me nothing at present. Should you care to meet her? I can easily introduce you."

"Yes, I should like to meet her," agreed Valzain. "She looks strangely like someone that I knew a long time ago."

The usurer peered slyly at the poet. "She might not make too easy a conquest. It is said of late that she has withdrawn herself from the pleasures of the city. Some have seen her going out at night toward the old necropolis, or returning from it in the early dawn. Strange tastes, I'd say, for one who is little more than a harlot. But perhaps she goes out to meet some eccentric lover."

"Direct me to her house," Valzain requested. "I shall not need you to introduce me."

"As you like." The money-lender shrugged, looking a little disappointed. "It's not far, anyway."

Valzain found the house quickly. The woman Beldith was alone. She met him with a wistful and troubled smile that left no doubt of her identity.

"I perceive that you have learned the truth," she said. "I had meant to tell you soon, for the deception could not have gone on much longer. Will you not forgive me?"

"I forgive you," returned Valzain sadly. "But why did you deceive me?"

"Because you desired it. A woman tries to please the man whom she loves; and in all love there is more or less deception.

"Like you, Valzain, I had grown tired of pleasure. And I sought the solitude of the necropolis, so remote from carnal things. You too came, seeking solitude and peace—or some unearthly spectre. I recognized you at once. And I had read your poems. Knowing Morthylla's legend, I thought to play a game with you. Playing it, I grew to love you.... Valzain, you loved me as the lamia. Can you not now love me for myself?"

"It cannot be," averred the poet. "I fear to repeat the disappointment I have found in other women. Yet at least I am grateful for the hours you gave me. They were the best I have known—even though I have loved something that did not, and could not, exist. Farewell, Morthylla. Farewell, Beldith."

When he had gone, Beldith stretched herself face downward among the cushions of her couch. She wept a little; and the tears made a dampness that quickly dried. Later she arose briskly enough and went about her household business.

After a time she returned to the loves and revelries of Psiom. Perhaps, in the end, she found such peace as may be given to those who have grown too old for pleasure.

But for Valzain there was no peace, no balm for this last and most bitter of disillusionments. Nor could he return to the carnalities of his former life. So it was that he finally slew himself, stabbing his throat to its deepest vein with a keen knife in the same spot which the false lamia's teeth had bitten, drawing a little blood.

After his death, he forgot that he had died; forgot the immediate past with all its happenings and circumstances.

Following his talk with Famurza, he had gone forth from Famurza's house and from the city of Umbri and had taken the road that passed the abandoned cemetery. Seized by an impulse to visit it, he had climbed the slope toward the marbles under a swelling moon that rose behind him.

Gaining the flat, expansive ground of the summit, where dwarfish dying yews disputed with leafless briars the intervals of slabs blotched with lichen, he recalled the tale that Famurza had mentioned, anent the lamia who was said to haunt the necropolis. Famurza, he knew well, was no believer in such legendry, and had meant only to mock his funereal mood. Yet, as a poet will, he began to play with the thought of some presence, immortal, lovely and evil, that dwelt amid the antique marbles and would respond to the evocation of one who, without positive belief, had longed vainly for visions from beyond mortality.

Through headstone aisles of moon-touched solitude, he came to a lofty mausoleum, still standing with few signs of ruin at the cemetery's center. Beneath it, he had been told, were extensive vaults housing the mummies of an extinct royal family that had ruled over the twin cities Umbri and Psiom in former centuries. The princess Morthylla had belonged to this family.

To his startlement a woman, or what appeared to be such, was sitting on a fallen shaft beside the mausoleum. He could not see her distinctly; the tomb's shadow still enveloped her from the shoulders downward. The face alone, glimmering wanly, was lifted to the rising moon. Its profile was such as he had seen on antique coins.

"Who are you?" he asked, with a curiosity that overpowered his courtesy.

"I am the lamia Morthylla," she replied.

SCHIZOID CREATOR

In the private laboratory which his practice as a psychiatrist had enabled him to build, equip and maintain, Dr. Carlos Moreno had completed certain preparations that were hardly in accord with the teachings of modern science. For these preparations he had drawn instruction from old grimoires, bequeathed by ancestors who had incurred the fatherly wrath of the Spanish Inquisition. According to a rather scurrilous family legend, other ancestors had been numbered among the Inquisitors.

At the end of the long room he had cleared the cluttered floor of its equipment, leaving only an immense globe of crystal glass that suggested an aquarium. About the globe he had traced with a consecrated knife, the sorcerers' arthame, a circle inscribed with pentagrams and the various Hebrew names of the Deity. Also, at a distance of several feet, a smaller circle, similarly inscribed.

Wearing a seamless and sleeveless robe of black, he stood now within the smaller, protective circle. Upon his breast and forehead was bound the Double Triangle, wrought perfectly from several metals. A silver lamp, engraved with the same sign, afforded the sole light, shining on a stand beside him. Aloes, camphor and storax burned in censers set about him on the floor. In his right hand he held the arthame; in his left, a hazel staff with a core of magnetized iron.

Like Dr. Faustus, Moreno designed an evocation of the Devil. But not, however, for the same purpose that had inspired Faustus.

Pondering long and gravely on the painful mysteries of the cosmos, the discrepancy of good and evil, Moreno had at last conceived an explanation that was startlingly simple.

There could, he reasoned, be only one Creator, God, who was or had been primarily benignant. Yet all the evidence pointed to the co-existence of an evil creative principle, a Satan. God, then, must be a split or dual personality, a sort of Jekyll and Hyde, manifesting sometimes as the Devil.

This duality, Moreno argued, must be a form of what is commonly called schizophrenia. He had a profound belief in the efficacy of shock treatment for such disorders. If God, in his aspect as the Devil, could be suitably confined and subjected to treatment, a cure might result. The confused problems of the universe would then resolve themselves under a sane and no longer semi-diabolic Deity.

The glass globe, specially constructed at great expense, contained at one side electrical apparatus of Moreno's own devising. The machine, far more complex than the portable apparatus used in electric shock treatment, could release a voltage powerful enough to electrocute simultaneously all the inmates of a state prison. Moreno considered that no lesser force could effect the shock necessary for the cure of a supernatural personage.

He had memorized an ancient spell for the calling up of the Devil and his confinement within a bottle. The globe would do admirably for the aforesaid bottle.

The spell was a bastard mixture of Greek, Hebrew and Latin. Its exact meaning seemed doubtful. It was filled with such terms as Eloha, Tetragrammaton, Kis, Elijon, Elohim, Saday and Zevaoth, the names of God. The word Bifrons recurred several times. This was no doubt one of the Devil's numerous names. But there could be only one Devil.

Moreno disregarded as childish those old demonologies that peopled Hell with a multitude of evil spirits, having each his own name, rank and office.

All, then, was in readiness. In a firm, sonorous voice which might have been that of a priest chanting the Mass, he began to recite the incantation.

When the summons came, Bifrons was busily engaged in amorous dalliance with the she-imp Foti. Like Janus, he was two-faced; and he possessed multiple members. Since Foti herself was somewhat peculiarly formed, their love-making was quite complicated.

Bifrons began to withdraw his members from about the she-imp, explaining, "Some damned sorcerer has gotten hold of that ancient spell containing my name. It's the first time in two hundred years. But I'll have to go."

"Hurry back," enjoined Foti, pouting with her four lips, two of which were located in her abdomen. "If you don't you may find me otherwise occupied."

The air sizzled behind Bifrons in his exit from the infernal regions.

Dr. Moreno felt surprised and even appalled when he saw the being that his incantation had called up in the globe. He had scarcely known what to expect, and had paid little attention to old pictures and descriptions of the Devil, seeing in them only the dementia of medieval superstition. But the teratology of this creature seemed incredible.

The two faces of Bifrons bloated alternately against the globe's interior; and his arms, legs, body and numerous other parts squirmed and flattened themselves convulsively in a furious effort to escape. But through the thickness of the glass, or the power of the surrounding circle, Bifrons was bottled up as helplessly as any djinn imprisoned by Solomon. He resigned himself presently and began to relax, floating awhile in mid-air, and finally seating himself on Moreno's electrical machine. As if feeling more at home, he looped some of his parts around the various pairs of forceps, ending in electrodes, that projected from the huge and intricate device.

"What the devil do you want?" he bellowed. The glass muffled his voice, which was still sufficiently audible. His tones bespoke anger and resentment.

"I want the Devil," said Moreno. "And I presume that you are he."

"*The* Devil?" queried Bifrons. "It's true that I'm *a* devil. But I'm not the Old Man himself. There are many thousands of us, as you should know if you've read the demonologists. I'm no infernal prince but merely a subordinate, though with special powers of my own. Again, what do you want? Money? Women? A Senatorship? The Presidency of your cock-eyed republic? Name it, and I'll grant the wish. I'm in a hellish hurry to get out of here."

"You can't fool me. I know that you are the Devil—the only one in the universe. And I don't want any of your gifts. All I want is to cure you."

Bifrons was startled. "Cure me? Of what? Say, what kind of a sorcerer are you anyway?"

"I'm not a sorcerer but a psychiatrist. My name is Dr. Moreno. My hope and intention is to cure you of being the Devil."

This madhouse doctor must be crazy himself, thought Bifrons. He cogitated. The trend of his cogitations was betrayed only by a sardonic one-sided twist of his left-hand mouth.

"All right, I'm the Devil," he agreed finally. "But let's get this over with. What do you mean to do with me?"

"Subject you to shock treatment," announced the doctor. "A very special high-voltage treatment. It should be the best thing for schizophrenia like yours."

"Schizo-what?" roared Bifrons. "Do you think I'm a lunatic?"

"Let me explain. I am using the term schizophrenia in its literal sense, meaning split personality—not as commonly applied to several types of psychic disintegration or regression. I think that you are really a sick Deity. Your illness consists in being Satan part of the time. A genuine case of dual and alternating egos. The Satanic self dominates at present, otherwise I shouldn't have been able to call you up. But we'll soon remedy all that."

The demon thought it well to conceal his consternation. He must get back to Hell as soon as possible and make a report. Satan, he felt, would be interested in Dr. Moreno.

"Get on with your treatment," he enjoined. "What is it, anyway?"

"Electricity."

Bifrons assumed an expression of double-faced dismay. "That's a highly dangerous and destructive force. Do you wish to annihilate me?"

"The result should be different in your case," said the doctor in his most soothing professional voice. "Are you ready?"

Bifrons gave a bicephalic nod. Moreno stepped cautiously from the circle and went over to a panel of switches and levers set in the laboratory wall. Watching the demon closely, he began to manipulate one of the levers.

The numerous forceps of the machine, on which Bifrons had so conveniently seated himself, closed themselves on various parts of his anatomy, applying their electrodes to his skin. A pair, hitherto concealed, sprang forth and seized his temples tightly.

Moreno grasped a switch firmly and turned on the full voltage. Then, still cautious, he returned to the protective circle.

A shower of sparks and short blue bolts issued from the machine within the globe. In spite of the many forceps that had tightened upon him, Bifrons writhed and tossed like a harpooned octopus. Smoke seemed to pour from his head, body and members, muffling the apparatus that held him captive. Soon a dark-brown cloud, seething and swelling, had filled the globe's interior, concealing everything from view. The cloud was something that Bifrons could emit at will, like the fluid of a cuttle-fish.

As a matter of fact, since his nature was itself electrical, he had absorbed the terrific voltage with merely a mild discomfort. The dark cloud was a necessary screen for the tactics that he now intended to use.

Perhaps, Moreno thought, the treatment had been sufficiently prolonged. He could repeat it if necessary. Emerging once more from his magic shelter, he turned off the switch and reversed the lever that had served to manipulate the forceps. Once again he went back to the circle.

After an interval of silence there issued from the clouded globe a voice which had no resemblance to that of Bifrons. It was both thunderous and mellow. To Moreno's inexperienced ear, it sounded like the Voice that spoke to Moses on the mountain.

"I am cured," it announced. "You have restored Me to My Divinity, O wise and beneficent doctor. Pronounce the formula of release and let Me go. Hell is henceforth abolished, together with all evil, sin and disease. The Devil is dead. God alone exists. And God is good."

Moreno was enraptured, believing that he had realized so quickly his fondest professional hope. Scarcely knowing what he did, he uttered the formula that served to release an imprisoned spirit.

Afterwards he asked, "Now will You reveal Yourself to me? I would behold You in all Your glory."

"It cannot be," the Voice thundered. "My glory would blast your eyes forever.

Therefore the cloud with which I have surrounded myself."

A moment later the globe burst asunder in flying fragments, like some gigantic bottle of new champagne. The released cloud, billowing vastly and voluminously, seemed to overspread the whole laboratory in an instant. Bifrons, raging behind it but still invisible, proceeded to wreck all of Moreno's equipment like a dozen baboons gone berserk. Tray-laden tables were overturned and smashed into splinters, shelves were pulled down with a crashing of countless vials and carboys. Coiled tubings were twisted and bent and ripped apart, heavily insulated wires snapped like twine. The old volumes of magic, piled in a corner, sprang into flame and burned to ashes in a few seconds. A violent wind, coming as if from nowhere, took up the ashes and scattered them throughout the room.

Moreno, protected by the circle, alone escaped the demon's wrath. He crouched at the circle's center, cowering and gibbering, while the cloud passed away through windows from which every pane had been broken.

Several of his colleagues, coming to consult him that evening, found him still crouching on the wreckage-littered floor. He did not seem to recognize them, and had obviously become deranged. His mouthings appeared to indicate a sort of theological mania.

The colleagues held an impromptu consultation of their own. As a result, Moreno was removed gently but forcibly to the same type of institution as that to which he had committed so many of his patients. His friends and fellow-psychiatrists deplored the interruption, perhaps the ending, of an illustrious career.

The wrecking of the laboratory remained a mystery. Had there been an explosion caused by one of Moreno's experiments? Had the doctor himself destroyed his equipment in a state of violent mania? Or—should the occurrence be classified as an act of God?

Fuming at the interruption of his tryst with Foti, Bifrons nevertheless thought it incumbent upon himself to report at once to Satan when he returned to the nether realms.

He found the Master of that picturesque region occupied in caressing a half-flayed girl. The flaying had been done to render the caresses more intimate and more exquisitely agonizing.

Satan listened gravely to the demon's account of Dr. Moreno. His tapering artistic fingers, with long-pointed nails of polished jet, ceased their occupation; and a furrow appeared like a black triangle between his luminous marble brows.

"This is all very interesting—and rather unfortunate," he said. "However, you have acted with admirable aplomb and presence of mind. The situation should be well under control as long as Moreno remains in the madhouse where you and his colleagues have landed him."

He paused, and his fingers resumed in an absent-minded fashion their gentle raking of his victim's lumbar regions.

"Of course, as you understand, Moreno was quite mad from the start. But lunatics with a speculative bent can sometimes stumble overly close to certain guarded cosmic secrets and there are spells which even *I* must answer and obey... not to mention the Unspeakable Name, the Shem-hamphorash, which coerces and compels Jehovah. After he recovers from his present state of shock, Moreno might be adjudged sane—and released to continue his researches and experiments.

"Such an eventuation must be forestalled permanently. My good Bifrons, you must return immediately to earth and watch over him. I have full trust in your abilities, and I confer upon you plenipotentiary powers. All I ask is, that you keep this doctor well bedeviled and legally insane until the hour of his death."

When Bifrons departed, Satan summoned his chief lieutenants before him in the halls of Pandemonium.

"I am going away for awhile," he told them. "There are certain obligations of a pressing nature that call me—and I must not neglect them too long. In my absence, I consign the management of Hell to your competent hands."

Bowing reversely, Gorson, Goap, Zimimar and Amaimon, lords of the four quarters, went out one after one, leaving their prince alone.

When they had gone, he descended from his globed throne and passed through many corridors and by many upward-winding stairs to the small postern door of Hell.

The door swung open without touch of any visible hand. A long white robe seemed to weave itself swiftly from the air about Satan's form. His infernal attributes withered and dropped away. And the long white beard of the Elohim sprouted and flowed down over his bosom as he stepped across the sill into Heaven.

Monsters in the Night

The change occurred before he could divest himself of more than his coat and scarf. He had only to step out of the shoes, to shed the socks with two backward kicks, and shuffle off the trousers from his lean hind-legs and belly. But he was still deep-chested after the change, and his shirt was harder to loosen. His hackles rose with rage as he slewed his head around and tore it away with hasty fangs in a flurry of falling buttons and rags. Tossing off the last irksome ribbons, he regretted his haste. Always heretofore he had been careful in regard to small details. The shirt was monogrammed. He must remember to collect all the tatters later. He could stuff them in his pockets, and wear the coat buttoned closely on his way home, when he had changed back.

Hunger snarled within him, mounting from belly to throat, from throat to mouth. It seemed that he had not eaten for a month—for a month of months. Raw butcher's meat was never fresh enough: it had known the coldness of death and refrigeration, and had lost all vital essence. Long ago there had been other meals, warm, and sauced with still-spurting blood. But now the thin memory merely served to exasperate his ravening.

Chaos raced within his brain. Inconsequently, for an instant, he recalled the first warning of his malady, preceding even the distaste for cooked meat: the aversion, the allergy, to silver forks and spoons. It had soon extended to other objects of the same metal. He had cringed even from the touch of coinage, had been forced to use paper and to refuse change. Steel, too, was a substance unfriendly to beings like him; and the time came when he could abide it little more than silver.

What made him think of such matters now, setting his teeth on edge with repugnance, choking him with something worse than nausea?

The hunger returned, demanding swift appeasement. With clumsy pads he pushed his discarded raiment under the shrubbery, hiding it from the heavy-jowled moon that peered down like a glutted vampire. It was the moon that drew the tides of madness in his blood, and compelled the bestial metamorphosis. But it must not betray to any chance passer the garments he would need later, when he returned to human semblance after the night's hunting.

The night was warm and windless, and the woodland seemed to hold its breath apprehending the presence of such as he. There were, he knew, other monsters abroad in that year of the Twenty-first Century. The vampire still survived, subtler and deadlier, protected by man's incredulity. And he himself was not the only lycanthrope: his brothers and sisters ranged unchallenged, preferring the darker urban jungles; while he, being country-bred, still kept the ancient ways. Moreover there were monsters unknown as yet to myth and superstition. But these too were mostly haunters of cities. He had no wish to meet any of them. And of such meeting, surely, there was small likelihood.

He followed a crooked lane, reconnoitered previously. It was too narrow for cars and it soon became a mere path. At the path's forking he ensconced himself in the shadow of a broad, mistletoe-blotted oak. The path was used by certain late pedestrians who lived even farther out from town. One of them might come along at any moment.

Whimpering a little, with the hunger of a starved hound, he waited. He was a monster that nature had made, ready to obey nature's first commandment: *Thou shalt kill and eat.* He was a thing of terror… a fable whispered around prehistoric cavern-fires… a miscegenation allied by later myth to the powers of hell and sorcery. But in no sense was he akin to those monsters beyond nature, the spawn of a new and blacker magic, who killed without hunger and without malevolence.

He had only minutes to wait, before his tensing ears caught the far-off vibration of footsteps. The steps came rapidly nearer, seeming to tell him much as they came. They were firm and resilient, tireless and rhythmic, telling of youth or of full maturity untouched by age. They told, surely, of a worthwhile prey; of prime lean meat and vital, abundant blood.

There was a slight froth on the lips of the one who waited. He had ceased to whimper. From pads to jaws, from hackles to tail, he grew taut for the anticipated leap.

The path ahead was heavily shadowed. Dimly, moving fast, the walker appeared in the shadows. He seemed to be all that the watcher had surmised from the sound of his footsteps. He was tall and well-shouldered, swinging with a lithe sureness, a precision of powerful tendon and muscle. His head was a faceless blur in the gloom. He was hatless, clad in dark coat and trousers such as anyone might wear. His steps rang with the assurance of one who has nothing to fear, and has never dreamt of the crouching creatures of darkness.

Now he was almost abreast of the watcher's covert. The watcher could wait no longer but sprang from his ambush of shadow, towering high upon the stranger as his hind-paws left the ground. His rush was irresistible, as always. The stranger toppled backward, sprawling and helpless, as others had done, and the assailant bent to the bare throat that gleamed more enticingly than that of a siren.

It was a strategy that had never failed… until now….

The shock, the consternation, had hurled him away from that prostrate figure and had forced him back upon teetering haunches. It was the shock, perhaps, that had caused him to change again, swiftly, resuming human shape before his hour. As the change began, he spat out several broken lupine fangs; and then he was spitting human teeth.

The stranger rose to his feet, seemingly unshaken and undismayed. He came forward in a rift of revealing moonlight, stooping to a half-crouch, and flexing his beryllium-steel fingers enameled with flesh-pink.

"Who—what—are you?" quavered the werewolf.

The stranger did not bother to answer as he advanced, every synapse of the computing brain transmitting the conditioned message, translated into simplest binary terms, "Dangerous. Not human. *Kill!*"

PHOENIX

R odis and Hilar had climbed from their natal caverns to the top chamber
of the high observatory tower. Pressed close together, for warmth as
well as love, they stood at an eastern window looking forth on hills
and valleys dim with perennial starlight. They had come up to watch the
rising of the sun: that sun which they had never seen except as an orb of
blackness, occluding the zodiacal stars in its course from horizon to horizon.

Thus their ancestors had seen it for millenniums. By some freak of cosmic
law, unforeseen, and inexplicable to astronomers and physicists, the sun's
cooling had been comparatively sudden, and the earth had not suffered the
long-drawn complete desiccation of such planets as Mercury and Mars. Rivers, lakes, seas, had frozen solid; and the air itself had congealed, all in a term
of years historic rather than geologic. Millions of the earth's inhabitants had
perished, trapped by the glacial ice, the centigrade cold. The rest, armed with
all the resources of science, had found time to entrench themselves against
the cosmic night in a world of ramified caverns, dug by atomic excavators
far below the surface.

Here, by the light of artificial orbs, and the heat drawn from the planet's
still-molten depths, life went on much as it had done in the outer world.
Trees, fruits, grasses, grains, vegetables, were grown in isotope-stimulated
soil or hydroponic gardens, affording food, renewing a breathable atmosphere. Domestic animals were kept; and birds flew; and insects crawled or
fluttered. The rays considered necessary for life and health were afforded by
the sunbright lamps that shone eternally in all the caverns.

Little of the old science was lost; but, on the other hand, there was now
little advance. Existence had become the conserving of a fire menaced by inexorable night. Generation by generation a mysterious sterility had lessened
the numbers of the race from millions to a few thousands. As time went on,

a similar sterility began to affect animals; and even plants no longer flourished with their first abundance. No biologist could determine the cause with certainty.

Perhaps man, as well as other terrestrial life-forms, was past his prime, and had begun to undergo collectively the inevitable senility that comes to the individual. Or perhaps, having been a surface-dweller throughout most of his evolution, he was inadaptable to the cribbed and prisoned life, the caverned light and air; and was dying slowly from the deprivation of things he had almost forgotten.

Indeed, the world that had once flourished beneath a living sun was little more than a legend now, a tradition preserved by art and literature and history. Its beetling Babelian cities, its fecund hills and plains, were swathed impenetrably in snow and ice and solidified air. No living man had gazed upon it, except from the night-bound towers maintained as observatories.

Still, however, the dreams of men were often lit by primordial memories, in which the sun shone on rippling waters and waving trees and grass. And their waking hours were sometimes touched by an undying nostalgia for the lost earth. . . .

Alarmed by the prospect of racial extinction, the most able and brilliant savants had conceived a project that was seemingly no less desperate than fantastic. The plan, if executed, might lead to failure or even to the planet's destruction. But all the necessary steps had now been taken toward its launching.

It was of this plan that Rodis and Hilar spoke, standing clasped in each other's arms, as they waited for the rising of the dead sun.

"And you must go?" said Rodis, with averted eyes and voice that quavered a little.

"Of course. It is a duty and an honor. I am regarded as the foremost of the younger atomicists. The actual placing and timing of the bombs will devolve largely upon me."

"But—are you sure of success? There are so many risks, Hilar." The girl shuddered, clasping her lover with convulsive tightness.

"We are not sure of anything," Hilar admitted. "But, granting that our calculations are correct, the multiple charges of fissionable materials, including more than half the solar elements, should start chain-reactions that will restore the sun to its former incandescence. Of course, the explosion may be too sudden and too violent, involving the nearer planets in the formation of a nova. But we do not believe that this will happen—since an explosion of such magnitude would require instant disruption of *all* the sun's elements. Such disruption should not occur without a starter for each separate atomic structure. Science has never been able to break down all the known elements. If it had been, the earth itself would undoubtedly have suffered destruction in the old atomic wars."

Hilar paused, and his eyes dilated, kindling with a visionary fire.

"How glorious," he went on, "to use for a purpose of cosmic renovation the deadly projectiles designed by our forefathers only to blast and destroy. Stored in sealed caverns, they have not been used since man abandoned the earth's surface so many millenniums ago. Nor have the old space-ships been used either. . . . An interstellar drive was never perfected; and our voyagings were always limited to the other worlds of our own system—none of which was inhabited, or inhabitable. Since the sun's cooling and darkening, there has been no object in visiting any of them. But the ships too were stored away. And the newest and speediest one, powered with anti-gravity magnets, has been made ready for our voyage to the sun."

Rodis listened silently, with an awe that seemed to have subdued her misgivings, while Hilar continued to speak of the tremendous project upon which he, with six other chosen technicians, was about to embark. In the meanwhile, the black sun rose slowly into heavens thronged with the cold ironic blazing of innumerable stars, among which no planet shone. It blotted out the sting of the Scorpion, poised at that hour above the eastern hills. It was smaller but nearer than the igneous orb of history and legend. In its center, like a Cyclopean eye, there burned a single spot of dusky red fire, believed to mark the eruption of some immense volcano amid the measureless and cinder-blackened landscape.

To one standing in the ice-bound valley below the observatory, it would have seemed that the tower's litten window was a yellow eye that stared back from the dead earth to that crimson eye of the dead sun.

"Soon," said Hilar, "you will climb to this chamber—and see the morning that none has seen for a century of centuries. The thick ice will thaw from the peaks and valleys, running in streams to re-molten lakes and oceans. The liquified air will rise in clouds and vapors, touched with the spectrum-tinted splendor of the light. Again, across earth, will blow the winds of the four quarters; and grass and flowers will grow, and trees burgeon from tiny saplings. And man, the dweller in closed caves and abysses, will return to his proper heritage."

"How wonderful it all sounds," murmured Rodis. "But... you will come back to me?"

"I will come back to you... in the sunlight," said Hilar.

II

The space-vessel *Phosphor* lay in a huge cavern beneath that region which had once been known as the Atlas Mountains. The cavern's mile-thick roof had been partly blasted away by atomic disintegrators. A great circular shaft slanted upward to the surface, forming a mouth in the mountain-side through which the stars of the Zodiac were visible. The prow of the *Phosphor* pointed at the stars.

All was now ready for its launching. A score of dignitaries and savants, looking like strange ungainly monsters in suits and helmets worn against the spatial cold that had invaded the cavern, were present for the occasion. Hilar and his six companions had already gone aboard the *Phosphor* and had closed its air-locks.

Inscrutable and silent behind their metalloid helmets, the watchers waited. There was no ceremony, no speaking or waving of farewells; nothing to indicate that a world's destiny impended on the mission of the vessel.

Like mouths of fire-belching dragons the stern-rockets flared, and the *Phosphor*, like a wingless bird, soared upward through the great shaft and vanished.

Hilar, gazing through a rear port, saw for a few moments the lamp-bright window of that tower in which he had stood so recently with Rodis. The window was a golden spark that swirled downward in abysses of devouring night—and was extinguished. Behind it, he knew, his beloved stood watching the *Phosphor*'s departure. It was a symbol, he mused… a symbol of life, of memory… of the suns themselves… of all things that flash briefly and fall into oblivion.

But such thoughts, he felt, should be dismissed. They were unworthy of one whom his fellows had appointed as a light-bringer, a Prometheus who should re-kindle the dead sun and re-lumine the dark world.

There were no days, only hours of eternal starlight, to measure the time in which they sped outward through the void. The rockets, used for initial propulsion, no longer flamed astern; and the vessel flew in darkness except for the gleaming Argus eyes of its ports, drawn now by the mighty gravitational drag of the blind sun.

Test-flights had been considered unnecessary for the *Phosphor*. All its machinery was in perfect condition; and the mechanics involved were simple and easily mastered. None of its crew had ever been in extraterrestrial space before; but all were well-trained in astronomy, mathematics, and the various techniques essential to a voyage between worlds. There were two navigators; one rocket-engineer; and two engineers who would operate the powerful generators, charged with a negative magnetism reverse to that of gravity, with which they hoped to approach, circumnavigate, and eventually depart in safety from an orb enormously heavier than the system's ten planets merged into one. Hilar and his assistant, Han Joas, completed the personnel. Their sole task was the timing, landing, and distribution of the bombs.

All were descendants of a mixed race with Latin, Semitic, Hamitic, and negroid ancestry: a race that had dwelt, before the sun's cooling, in countries south of the Mediterranean, where the former deserts had been rendered fertile by a vast irrigation-system of lakes and canals.

This mixture, after so many centuries of cavern life, had produced a characteristically slender, well-knit type, of short or medium stature and pale olive complexion. The features were often of negroid softness; the general physique marked by a delicacy verging upon decadence.

To an extent surprising, in view of the vast intermediate eras of historic and geographic change, this people had preserved many pre-atomic traditions and even something of the old classic Mediterranean cultures. Their language bore distinct traces of Latin, Greek, Spanish and Arabic.

Remnants of other peoples, those of sub-equatorial Asia and America, had survived the universal glaciation by burrowing underground. Radio communication had been maintained with these peoples till within fairly recent times, and had then ceased. It was believed that they had died out, or had retrograded into savagery, losing the civilization to which they had once attained.

Hour after hour, intervaled only by sleep and eating, the *Phosphor* sped onward through the black unvarying void. To Hilar, it seemed at times that they flew merely through a darker and vaster cavern whose remote walls were spangled by the stars as if by radiant orbs. He had thought to feel the overwhelming vertigo of unbottomed and undirectioned space. Instead, there was a weird sense of circumscription by the ambient night and emptiness, together with a sense of cyclic repetition, as if all that was happening had happened many times before and must recur often through endless future kalpas.

Had he and his companions gone forth in former cycles to the relighting of former perished suns? Would they go forth again, to rekindle suns that would flame and die in some posterior universe? Had there always been, would there always be, a Rodis who awaited his return?

Of these thoughts he spoke only to Han Joas, who shared something of his innate mysticism and his trend toward cosmic speculation. But mostly the two talked of the mysteries of the atom and its typhonic powers, and discussed the problems with which they would shortly be confronted.

The ship carried several hundred disruption-bombs, many of untried potency: the unused heritage of ancient wars that had left chasmal scars and lethal radio-active areas, some a thousand miles or more in extent, for the planetary glaciers to cover. There were bombs of iron, calcium, sodium, helium, hydrogen, sulphur, potassium, magnesium, copper, chromium, strontium, barium, zinc: elements that had all been anciently revealed in the solar spectrum. Even at the apex of their madness, the warring nations had wisely refrained from employing more than a few such bombs at any one time. Chain-reactions had sometimes been started; but, fortunately, had died out.

Hilar and Han Joas hoped to distribute the bombs at intervals over the sun's entire circumference; preferably in large deposits of the same elements as those of which they were composed. The vessel was equipped with radar apparatus by which the various elements could be detected and located. The bombs would be timed to explode with as much simultaneity as possible. If all went well, the *Phosphor* would have fulfilled its mission and traveled most of the return distance to earth before the explosions occurred.

It had been conjectured that the sun's interior was composed of still-molten magma, covered by a relatively thin crust: a seething flux of matter that manifested itself in volcanic activities. Only one of the volcanoes was visible from earth to the naked eye; but numerous others had been revealed to telescopic study. Now, as the *Phosphor* drew near to its destination, these others flamed out on the huge, slowly rotating orb that had darkened a fourth of the ecliptic and had blotted Libra, Scorpio and Sagittarius wholly from view.

For a long time it had seemed to hang above the voyagers. Now, suddenly, as if through some prodigious legerdemain, it lay beneath them: a monstrous, ever-broadening disk of ebon, eyed with fiery craters, veined and spotted and blotched with unknown pallid radio-actives. It was like the buckler of some macrocosmic giant of the night, who had entrenched himself in the abyss lying between the worlds.

The *Phosphor* plunged toward it like a steel splinter drawn by some tremendous lodestone.

Each member of the crew had been trained beforehand for the part he was to play; and everything had been timed with the utmost precision. Sybal and Samac, the engineers of the anti-gravity magnets, began to manipulate the switches that would build up resistance to the solar drag. The generators, bulking to the height of three men, with induction-coils that suggested some colossal Laocoön, could draw from cosmic space a negative force capable of counteracting many earth-gravities. In past ages they had defied easily the pull of Jupiter; and the ship had even coasted as near to the blazing sun as its insulation and refrigeration systems would safely permit. Therefore it seemed reasonable to expect that the voyagers could accomplish their purpose of approaching closely to the darkened globe, of circling it, and pulling away when the disruption-charges had all been planted.

A dull, subsonic vibration, felt rather than heard, began to emanate from the magnets. It shook the vessel, ached in the voyagers' tissues. Intently, with anxiety unbetrayed by their impassive features, they watched the slow, gradual building-up of power shown by gauge-dials on which giant needles crept like horologic hands, registering the reversed gravities one after one, till a drag equivalent to that of fifteen earths had been neutralized. The clamp of the solar gravitation, drawing them on with projectile-like velocity, crushing them to their seats with relentless increase of weight, was loosened. The needles crept on… more slowly now… to sixteen… to seventeen… and stopped. The *Phosphor*'s fall had been retarded but not arrested. And the switches stood at their last notch.

Sybal spoke, in answer to the unuttered questions of his companions.

"Something is wrong. Perhaps there has been some unforeseen deterioration of the coils, in whose composition strange and complex alloys were used. Some of the elements may have been unstable—or have developed instability through age. Or perhaps there is some interfering force, born of the sun's decay. At any rate, it is impossible to build more power toward the twenty-seven anti-gravities we will require close to the solar surface."

Samac added: "The decelerative jets will increase our resistance to nineteen anti-gravities. It will still be far from enough, even at our present distance."

"How much time have we?" inquired Hilar, turning to the navigators, Calaf and Caramod.

The two conferred and calculated.

"By using the decelerative jets, it will be two hours before we reach the sun," announced Calaf finally.

As if his announcement had been an order, Eibano, the jet-engineer, promptly jerked the levers that fired to full power the reversing rockets banked in the Phosphor's nose and sides. There was a slight further deceleration of their descent, a further lightening of the grievous weight that oppressed them. But the Phosphor still plunged irreversibly sunward.

Hilar and Han Joas exchanged a glance of understanding and agreement. They rose stiffly from their seats, and moved heavily toward the magazine, occupying fully half the ship's interior, in which the hundreds of disruption-bombs were racked. It was unnecessary to announce their purpose; and no one spoke either in approval or demur.

Hilar opened the magazine's door; and he and Han Joas paused on the threshold, looking back. They saw for the last time the faces of their fellow-voyagers, expressing no other emotion than resignation, vignetted, as it were, on the verge of destruction. Then they entered the magazine, closing its door behind them.

They set to work methodically, moving back to back along a narrow aisle between the racks in which the immense ovoid bombs were piled in strict order according to their respective elements. Because of various coordinated dials and switches involved, it was a matter of minutes to prepare a single bomb for explosion. Therefore, Hilar and Han Joas, in the time at their disposal, could do no more than set the timing and detonating mechanism of one bomb of each element. A great chronometer, ticking at the magazine's farther end, enabled them to accomplish this task with precision. The bombs were thus timed to explode simultaneously, detonating the others through chain-reaction, at the moment when the Phosphor should touch the sun's surface.

The solar pull, strengthening momently as the Phosphor fell to its doom, had now made their movements slow and difficult. It would, they feared, immobilize them before they could finish preparing a second series of bombs for detonation. Laboriously, beneath the burden of a weight already trebled, they made their way to seats that faced a reflector in which the external cosmos was imaged.

It was an awesome and stupendous scene on which they gazed. The sun's globe had broadened vastly, filling the nether heavens. Half-seen, a dim unhorizoned landscape, fitfully lit by the crimson far-sundered flares of volcanoes, by bluish zones and patches of strange radio-active minerals, it deepened beneath them abysmally, disclosing mountains that would have made the Himalayas seem like hillocks, revealing chasms that might have engulfed asteroids and planets.

At the center of this Cyclopean landscape burned the great volcano that had been called Hephaestus by astronomers. It was the same volcano watched by Hilar and Rodis from the observatory window. Tongues of flame a hundred miles in length arose and licked skyward from a crater that seemed the mouth of some ultramundane hell.

Hilar and Han Joas no longer heard the chronometer's portentous ticking, and had no eyes for the watching of its ominous hands. Such watching was needless now: there was nothing more to be done, and nothing before them but eternity. They measured their descent by the broadening of the dim solar plain, the leaping into salience of new mountains, the deepening of new chasms and gulfs in the globe that had now lost all semblance of a sphere.

It was plain now that the *Phosphor* would fall directly into the flaming and yawning crater of Hephaestus. Faster and faster it plunged, heavier grew the piled chains of gravity that giants could not have lifted....

At the very last, the reflector on which Hilar and Han Joas peered was filled entirely by the tongued volcanic fires that enveloped the *Phosphor*.

Then, without eyes to see or ears to apprehend, they were part of the pyre from which the sun, like a Phoenix, was reborn.

III

Rodis, climbing to the tower, after a period of fitful sleep and troublous dreams, saw from its window the rising of the rekindled orb.

It dazzled her, though its glory was half-dimmed by rainbow-colored mists that fumed from the icy mountain-tops. It was a sight filled with marvel and with portent. Thin rills of downward threading water had already begun to fret the glacial armor on slopes and scarps; and later they would swell to cataracts, laying bare the buried soil and stone. Vapors, that seemed to flow and fluctuate on renascent winds, swam sunward from lakes of congealed air at the valley's bottom. It was a visible resumption of the elemental life and activity so long suspended in hibernal night. Even through the tower's insulating walls, Rodis felt the solar warmth that later would awaken the seeds and spores of plants that had lain dormant for cycles.

Her heart was stirred to wonder by the spectacle. But beneath the wonder was a great numbness and a sadness like unmelting ice. Hilar, she knew, would never return to her—except as a ray of the light, a spark of the vital heat, that he had helped to relumine. For the nonce, there was irony rather than comfort in the memory of his promise: "I will come back to you—in the sunlight."

THE THEFT OF THE
THIRTY-NINE GIRDLES

Vixeela, daughter of beauty and doom!
Thy name, an invocation, calls to light
Dead moons, and draws from overdated night
The rosy-bosomed specter of delight.
Like some delaying sunset, brave with gold,
The glamours and the perils shared of old
Outsoar the shrunken empire of the mould.

—Lament for Vixeela

L et it be said, as a preamble to this tale, that I have robbed no man who
was not in some way a robber of others. In all my long and arduous
career, I, Satampra Zeiros of Uzuldaroum, sometimes known as the
master-thief, have endeavored to serve merely as an agent in the rightful
re-distribution of wealth. The adventure I have now to relate was no excep-
tion: though, as it happened in the outcome, my own pecuniary profits were
indeed meager, not to say trifling.

Age is upon me now; and sitting at that leisure which I have earned through
hazards many and multiform, I drink the wines that are heartening to age.
To me, as I sip, return memories of splendid loot and brave nefarious enterprise. Before me shine the outpoured sackfuls of *djals* or *pazoors*, removed so
dexterously from the coffers of iniquitous merchants and money-lenders. I
dream of rubies redder than the blood that was shed for them; of sapphires
bluer than depths of glacial ice; of emeralds greener than the jungle in spring.
I recall the escalade of pronged balconies; the climbing of terraces and towers guarded by men or monsters; the sacking of altars beneath the eyes of
malign idols or sentinel serpents.

Often I think of Vixeela, my one true love and the most adroit and courageous of my companions in burglary. She has long since gone to the bourn
of all good thieves and comrades; and I have mourned her sincerely these
many years. But still dear is the memory of our amorous or adventurous
nights and the feats we performed together. Of such feats, perhaps the most
signal and audacious was the theft of the thirty-nine girdles.

These were the golden and jewelled chastity girdles, worn by the virgins consecrated to the moon-god Leniqua, whose temple had stood from immemorial time in the suburbs of Uzuldaroum. The virgins were always thirty-nine in number. They were chosen for their youth and beauty, and retired from service to the god at the age of thirty-one.

The girdles were padlocked with the toughest bronze and their keys retained by the high-priest who, on certain nights, rented them at a high price to the richer gallants of the city. It will thus be seen that the virginity of the priestesses was nominal; but its frequent and repeated sale was regarded as a meritorious act of sacrifice to the god.

Vixeela herself had at one time been numbered among the virgins; but had fled from the temple and from Uzuldaroum several years before the sacerdotal age of release from her bondage. She would tell me little of her life in the temple; and I surmised that she had found small pleasure in the religious prostitution, and had chafed at the confinement entailed by it. After her flight she had suffered many hardships and vicissitudes in the cities of the south; of these, too, she spoke but sparingly, as one who dreads the reviving of painful recollections.

She had returned to Uzuldaroum a few months prior to our first meeting. Being now a little over age, and having dyed her russet-blonde hair to a raven black, she had no great fear of recognition and punishment by the priests of Leniqua. As was their custom, they had promptly replaced her loss with another and younger virgin; and would have small interest now in one so long delinquent.

At the time of our foregathering, Vixeela had already committed various petty larcenies; but, being unskilled, she had failed to finish any but the easier and simpler ones, and had grown quite thin from starvation. She was still attractive; and her keenness of wit and quickness in learning soon endeared her to me. She was small and agile and could climb like a lemur. I soon found her help invaluable, since she could climb through windows and other apertures impassable to my greater bulk.

We had consummated several lucrative burglaries, when the thought of entering Leniqua's temple and making away with the costly girdles occurred to me. The problems offered, and the difficulties to be overcome, appeared at first sight little less than fantastic. But such obstacles have always challenged my acumen and have never daunted me.

Firstly, there was the problem of entrance without detection and serious mayhem at the hands of the sickle-armed eunuchs who guarded Leniqua's fane on all sides with baleful and incorruptible vigilance. Luckily, during her term of temple service, Vixeela had learned of a subterranean adit, long disused but, she believed, still passable. This entrance was through a tunnel, the continuation of a natural cavern located somewhere in the woods behind Uzuldaroum. It had been used almost universally by the virgin's visitors in former ages. But the visitors now entered openly by the temple's main doors or by posterns little less public: a sign, perhaps, that religious sentiment had deepened or that modesty had declined. Vixeela had never seen the cavern herself; but she knew its approximate location. The temple's inner adit was closed only by a flagstone, easily levitated from below or above, behind the image of Leniqua in the great nave.

Secondly, there was the selection of a proper time, when the women's girdles had been unlocked and laid aside. Here again Vixeela was invaluable, since she knew the nights on which the rented keys were most in demand. These were known as nights of sacrifice, greater or lesser, the chief one being at the moon's full. All the women were then in repeated request.

Since, however, the fane on such occasions would be crowded with people, the priests, the virgins and their clients, a seemingly insurmountable difficulty remained. How were we to collect and make away with the girdles in the presence of so many persons? This, I must admit, baffled me.

Plainly, we must find some way in which the temple could be evacuated, or its occupants rendered unconscious or otherwise incapable during the period needed for our nefarious operations.

I thought of a certain soporific drug, easily and quickly vaporized, which I had used on more than one occasion to put the inmates of a house asleep. Unfortunately the drug was limited in its range and would not penetrate to all the chambers and alcoves of a large edifice like the temple. Moreover it was necessary to wait for a full half hour, with doors or windows opened, till the fumes were dissipated: otherwise the robbers would be overcome together with their victims.

There was also the pollen of a rare jungle lily, which, if cast in a man's face, would induce a temporary paralysis. This too I rejected: there were too many persons to be dealt with, and the pollen could hardly be obtained in sufficient quantities.

At last I decided to consult the magician and alchemist, Veezi Phenquor, who, possessing furnaces and melting-pots, had often served me as the converter of stolen gold and silver work into ingots or other safely unrecognizable forms. Though skeptical of his powers as a magician, I regarded Veezi Phenquor as a skilled pharmacist and toxicologist. Having always on hand a supply of strange and deadly medicaments, he might well be able to provide something that would facilitate our project.

We found Veezi Phenquor decanting one of his more noisome concoctions from a still bubbling and steaming kettle into vials of stout stoneware. By the smell I judged that it must be something of special potency: the exudations of a pole-cat would have been innocuous in comparison. In his absorption he did not notice our presence until the entire contents of the kettle had been decanted and the vials tightly stoppered and sealed with a blackish gum.

"That," he observed with unctuous complacency, "is a love-philtre that would inflame a nursing infant or resurrect the powers of a dying nonagenarian. Do you—?"

"No," I said emphatically. "We require nothing of the sort. What we need at the moment is something quite different." In a few terse words I went on to outline the problem, adding:

"If you can help us, I am sure you will find the melting-down of the golden girdles a congenial task. As usual, you will receive a third of the profits."

Veezi Phenquor creased his bearded face into a half-lubricious, half-sardonic smile.

"The proposition is a pleasant one from all angles. We will free the temple-girls from incumbrances which they must find uncomfortable, not to say burdensome; and will turn the irksome gems and metal to a worthier purpose—notably, our own enrichment." As if by way of afterthought, he added:

"It happens that I can supply you with a most unusual preparation, warranted to empty the temple of all its occupants in a very short time."

Going to a cobwebbed corner, he took down from a high shelf an abdominous jar of uncolored glass filled with a fine grey powder and brought it to the light.

"I will now," he said, "explain to you the singular properties of this powder and the way in which it must be used. It is truly a triumph of chemistry, and more devastating than a plague."

We were astounded by what he told us. Then we began to laugh.

"It is to be hoped," I said, "that none of your spells and cantraips are involved."

Veezi Phenquor assumed the expression of one whose feelings have been deeply injured.

"I assure you," he protested, "that the effects of the powder, though extraordinary, are not beyond nature."

After a moment's meditation he continued: "I believe that I can further your plan in other ways. After the abstraction of the girdles, there will be the problem of transporting undetected such heavy merchandise across a city which, by that time, may well have been aroused by the horrendous crime and busily patrolled by constabulary. I have a plan...."

We hailed with approval the ingenious scheme outlined by Veezi Phenquor. After we had discussed and settled to our satisfaction the various details, the alchemist brought out certain liquors that proved more palatable than anything of his we had yet sampled. We then returned to our lodgings, I carrying in my cloak the jar of powder, for which Veezi Phenquor generously refused to accept payment. We were filled with the rosiest anticipations of success, together with a modicum of distilled palm-wine.

Discreetly, we refrained from our usual activities during the nights that intervened before the next full moon. And we kept closely to our lodgings, hoping that the police, who had long suspected us of numerous peccadilloes, would believe that we had either quitted the city or retired from burglary.

A little before midnight, on the evening of the full moon, Veezi Phenquor knocked discreetly at our door—a triple knock as had been agreed.

Like ourselves, he was heavily cloaked in peasant's homespun.

"I have procured the cart of a vegetable seller from the country," he said. "It is loaded with seasonable produce and drawn by two small asses. I have concealed it in the woods, as near to the cave-adit of Leniqua's temple as the overgrown road will permit. Also, I have reconnoitered the cave itself.

"Our success will depend on the utter confusion created. If we are not seen to enter or depart by the rear adit, in all likelihood no one will remember its existence. The priests will be searching elsewhere.

"Having removed the girdles and concealed them under our load of farm produce, we will then wait till the hour before dawn when, with other vegetable and fruit dealers, we will enter the city."

Keeping as far as we could from the public places, where most of the police were gathered around taverns and the cheaper lupanars, we circled across Uzuldaroum and found, at some distance from Leniqua's fane, a road that ran countryward. The jungle soon grew denser and the houses fewer. No one saw us when we turned into a side-road overhung with leaning palms and closed in by thickening brush. After many devious turnings, we came to the ass-drawn cart, so cleverly screened from view that even I could detect its presence only by the pungent aroma of certain root-vegetables and the smell of fresh-fallen dung. Those asses were well-trained for the use of thieves: there was no braying to betray their presence.

We groped on, over hunching roots and between clustered boles that made the rest of the way impassable for a cart. I should have missed the cave; but Veezi Phenquor, pausing, stooped before a low hillock to part the matted creepers, showing a black and bouldered aperture large enough to admit a man on hands and knees.

Lighting the torches we had brought along, we crawled into the cave, Veezi going first. Luckily, due to the rainless season, the cave was dry and our clothing suffered only earth-stains such as would be proper to agricultural workers.

The cave narrowed where piles of debris had fallen from the roof. I, with my width and girth, was hard put to squeeze through in places. We had gone an undetermined distance when Veezi stopped and stood erect before a wall of smooth masonry in which shadowy steps mounted.

Vixeela slipped past him and went up the steps. I followed. The fingers of her free hand were gliding over a large flat flagstone that filled the stair-head. The stone began to tilt noiselessly upward. Vixeela blew out her torch and laid it on the top step while the gap widened, permitting a dim, flickering light to pour down from beyond. She peered cautiously over the top of the flag, which became fully uptilted by its hidden mechanism, and then climbed through motioning us to follow.

We stood in the shadow of a broad pillar at one side of the back part of Leniqua's temple. No priest, woman or visitor was in sight but we heard a confused humming of voices at some vague remove. Leniqua's image, presenting its reverend rear, sat on a high dais in the center of the nave. Altar-fires, golden, blue and green, flamed spasmodically before the god, making his shadow writhe on the floor and against the rear wall like a delirious giant in a dance of copulation with an unseen partner.

Vixeela found and manipulated the spring that caused the flagstone to sink back as part of a level floor. Then the three of us stole forward, keeping in the god's wavering shadow. The nave was still vacant but noise came more audibly from open doorways at one side, resolving itself into gay cries and hysterical laughters.

"Now," whispered Veezi Phenquor.

I drew from a side-pocket the vial he had given us and pried away the wax with a sharp knife. The cork, half-rotten with age, was easily removed. I poured the vial's contents on the back bottom step of Leniqua's dais—a pale stream that quivered and undulated with uncanny life and luster as it fell in the god's shadow. When the vial was empty I ignited the heap of powder.

It burned instantly with a clear, high-leaping flame. Immediately, it seemed, the air was full of surging phantoms—a soundless, multitudinous explosion, beating upon us, blasting our nostrils with charnel fetors till we reeled before it, choking and strangling. There was, however, no sense of material impact from the hideous forms that seemed to melt over and through us, rushing in all directions, as if every atom of the burning powder had released a separate ghost.

Hastily we covered our noses with the squares of thick cloth that Veezi had warned us to bring for this purpose. Something of our usual aplomb returned and we moved forward through the seething rout. Lascivious blue cadavers intertwined around us. Miscegenations of women and tigers arched over us. Monsters double-headed and triple-tailed, goblins and ghouls rose obliquely to the far ceiling or rolled and melted to other and more nameless apparitions in lower air. Green sea-things, like unions of drowned men and octopi, coiled and dribbled with dank slime along the floor.

Then we heard the cries of fright from the temple's inmates and visitors and began to meet naked men and women who rushed frantically through that army of beleaguering phantoms toward the exits. Those who encountered us face to face recoiled as if we too were shapes of intolerable horror.

The naked men were mostly young. After them came middle-aged merchants and aldermen, bald and pot-bellied, some clad in under-garments, some in snatched-up cloaks too short to cover them below the hips. Women, lean, fat or buxom, tumbled screaming for the outer doors. None of them, we saw with approbation, had retained her chastity girdle.

Lastly came the temple-guards and priests, with mouths like gaping squares of terror, emitting shrill cries. All of the guards had dropped their sickles. They passed us, blindly disregarding our presence, and ran after the rest. The host of powder-born specters soon shrouded them from view.

Satisfied that the temple was now empty of its inmates and clients, we turned our attention to the first corridor. The doors of the separate rooms were all open. We divided our labors, taking each a room, and removing from disordered beds and garment-littered floors the cast-off girdles of gold and gems. We met at the corridor's end, where our collected loot was thrust into the strong thin sack I had carried under my cloak. Many of the phantoms still lingered, achieving new and ghastlier fusions, dropping their members upon us as they began to diswreathe.

Soon we had searched all the rooms apportioned to the women. My sack was full, and I had counted thirty-eight girdles at the end of the third corridor. One girdle was still missing; but Vixeela's sharp eyes caught the gleam of an emerald-studded buckle protruding from under the dissolving legs of a hairy satyr-like ghost on a pile of male garments in the corner. She snatched up the girdle and carried it in her hand hence-forward.

We hurried back to Leniqua's nave, believing it to be vacant of all human occupants by now. To our disconcertion the High-Priest, whose name Vixeela knew as Marquanos, was standing before the altar, striking blows with a long phallic rod of bronze, his insignia of office, at certain apparitions that remained floating in the air.

Marquanos rushed toward us with a harsh cry as we neared him, dealing a blow at Vixeela that would have brained her if she had not slipped agilely to one side. The High-Priest staggered, nearly losing his balance. Before he could turn upon her again, Vixeela brought down on his tonsured head the heavy chastity girdle she bore in her right hand. Marquanos toppled like a slaughtered ox beneath the pole-ax of the butcher, and lay prostrate, writhing a little. Blood ran in rills from the serrated imprint of the great jewels on his scalp. Whether he was dead or still living, we did not pause to ascertain.

We made our exit without delay. After the fright they had received, there was small likelihood that any of the temple's denizens would venture to return for some hours. The movable slab fell smoothly back into place behind us. We hurried along the underground passage, I carrying the sack and the others preceding me in order to drag it through straitened places and over piles of rubble when I was forced to set it down. We reached the creeper-hung entrance without incident. There we paused awhile before emerging into the moon-streaked woods, and listened cautiously to cries that diminished with distance. Apparently no one had thought of the rear adit or had even realized that there was any such human motive as robbery behind the invasion of terrifying specters.

Reassured, we came forth from the cavern and found our way back to the hidden cart and its drowsing asses. We threw enough of the fruits and vegetables into the brush to make a deep cavity in the cart's center, in which our sackful of loot was then deposited and covered over from sight. Then, settling ourselves on the grassy ground, we waited for the hour before dawn. Around us, after awhile, we heard the furtive slithering and scampering of small animals that devoured the comestibles we had cast away.

If any of us slept, it was, so to speak, with one eye and one ear. We rose in the horizontal sifting of the last moonbeams and long eastward-running shadows of early twilight.

Leading our asses, we approached the highway and stopped behind the brush while an early cart creaked by. Silence ensued, and we broke from the wood and resumed our journey cityward before other carts came in sight.

In our return through outlying streets we met only a few early passers, who gave us no second glance. Reaching the neighborhood of Veezi Phenquor's house, we consigned the cart to his care and watched him turn into the courtyard unchallenged and seemingly unobserved by others than ourselves. He was, I reflected, well supplied with roots and fruits....

We kept closely to our lodgings for two days. It seemed unwise to remind the police of our presence in Uzuldaroum by any public appearance. On the evening of the second day our food-supply ran short and we sallied out in our rural costumes to a nearby market which we had never before patronized.

Returning, we found evidence that Veezi Phenquor had paid us a visit during our absence, in spite of the fact that all the doors and windows had been, and still were, carefully locked. A small cube of gold reposed on the table, serving as paper-weight for a scribbled note.

The note read: "My esteemed friends and companions: After removing the various gems, I have melted down all the gold into ingots, and am leaving one of them as a token of my great regard. Unfortunately, I have learned that I am being watched by the police, and am leaving Uzuldaroum under circumstances of haste and secrecy, taking the other ingots and all the jewels in the ass-drawn cart, covered up by the vegetables I have providentially kept, even though they are slightly stale by now. I expect to make a long journey, in a direction which I cannot specify—a journey well beyond the jurisdiction of our local police, and one on which I trust you will not be perspicacious enough to follow me. I shall need the remainder of our loot for my expenses, et cetera. Good luck in all your future ventures.

Respectfully,

Veezi Phenquor.

"POSTSCRIPT: You too are being watched, and I advise you to quit the city with all feasible expedition. Marquanos, in spite of a well-cracked mazzard from Vixeela's blow, recovered full consciousness late yesterday. He recognized in Vixeela a former temple-girl through the trained dexterity of her movements. He has not been able to identify her; but a thorough and secret search is being made, and other girls have already been put to the thumb-screw and toe-screw by Leniqua's priests.

"You and I, my dear Satampra, have already been listed, though not yet identified, as possible accomplices of the girl. A man of your conspicuous height and bulk is being sought. The Powder of the Fetid Apparitions, some traces of which were found on Leniqua's dais, has already been analyzed. Unluckily, it has been used before, both by myself and other alchemists.

I hope you will escape—on other paths than the one I am planning to follow."

Symposium of the Gorgon

At the third cup I penetrate the Great Way;
A full gallon—Nature and I are one.

—*Li Po*

I do not remember where or with whom the evening had begun. Nor can I recall what vintages, brews and distillations I had mingled by the way. In those nights of an alcoholically flaming youth, I was likely to start anywhere, drink anything and end up almost anywhere else than at the port of embarkation.

It was therefore with interest but with little surprise that I found myself among the guests at the symposium in the Gorgon's hall. Do not ask me how I got there: I am still a bit vague about it myself. It would be useless to tell you, even if I could, unless you are one of the rare few elected for similar adventures. And if you are one of these, the telling would be needless.

Liquor brings oblivion to most; but to certain others, enfranchisement from time and space, the awareness of Tao, of all that is or has ever been or will ever be. By liquor I mean of course the true essence poured from the *Dive Bouteille*. But, on occasion, any bottle can be divine.

Just why, at that particular time, after what must have been a round of mundane barrooms, I should have entered the mythologic palace of Medusa, is a matter hardly apparent but determined, no doubt, by the arcanic and inflexible logic of alcohol. The night had been foggy, not to say wet; and on such nights one is prone to stray into the unlikeliest places. It was not the first time I had gotten a little mixed up in regard to the Einsteinian continuum.

Having read Bulfinch and other mythologists, I had small difficulty in orienting myself to the situation. At the moment of my entrance into the spacious early Grecian hall, I was stopped by a slave-girl attired only in three garlands of roses arranged to display and enhance her charms. This girl presented me with a brightly polished silver mirror, the rim and handle of which were twined appropriately with graven serpents. She also gave me a capacious wine-cup of unglazed clay. In a low voice, in the purest Greek of pre-Euripidean drama, she told me the mirror's purpose. The cup I could fill as often as I pleased, or was able, at a fountain of yellow wine in the foreground, rilling from the open mouth of a marble sea nymph that rose from amidst its bubbling ripples.

Thus forewarned, I kept my eyes on the mirror, which reflected the room before me with admirable clearness. I saw that my fellow-guests—at least any who possessed hands—had also been considerately equipped with mirrors, in which they could look with safety at their hostess whenever politeness required.

Medusa sat in a high-armed chair at the hall's center, weeping constant tears that could not dim the terrible brightness of her eyes. Her tonsure of curling serpents writhed and lifted incessantly. On each arm of the chair perched a woman-headed, woman-breasted fowl that I recognized as a harpy. In other chairs, the two sisters of Medusa sat immobile with lowered eyes.

All three were draining frequent cups served with averted eyes by the slave-girls, but showed no sign of intoxication.

There seemed to be a lot of statuary about the place: men, women, dogs, goats and other animals as well as birds. These, the first slave-girl whispered as she passed me, consisted of the various unwary victims turned to stone by the Gorgon's glance. In a whisper lower still, she added that the fatal visit of Perseus, coming to behead Medusa, was momentarily expected.

I felt that it was high time for a drink, and moved forward to the verge of the vinous pool. A number of ducks and swans, standing unsteadily about it with wine-splashed plumage, dipped their beaks in the fluid and tilted their heads back with obvious relish. They hissed at me viciously as I stepped among them. I slipped on their wet droppings and plunged hastily into the pool, but still retained the cup and the mirror as well as my footing. The fluid was quite shallow. Amid the loud quacking of the startled birds and the giggling of several golden-tressed sirens and russet-haired Nereids who sat on the farther edge, stirring the pool to luminous ripples with their cod-like tails, I stepped forward, splashing ankle-deep, to the marble sea-girl and lifted my cup to the yellow stream that issued from her grinning mouth. The cup filled instantly and slopped over, drenching my shirt-front. I drained it at a gulp. The wine was strong and good, though tasting heavily of resin like other antique vintages.

Before I could raise the cup for a second draft, it seemed that a flash of lightning, together with a violent wind, leapt horizontally across the hall from the open doorway. My face was fanned as if by the passing of a god. Forgetting the danger, I raised my eyes toward Medusa, over whom the lightning hovered an instant and swung back with the movement of a weapon about to strike.

I remembered my mythology. It was indeed the sword of Perseus, who wore Mercury's winged shoes and the helmet loaned by Hades which made him invisible. (Why the sword alone should be perceptible to sight, no myth-maker has explained.) The sword fell, and the head of Medusa sprang from her seated body and rolled in a spatter of blood across the floor and into the pool where I stood petrified. It was a moment of pandemonium. The ducks and geese scattered, quacking, honking madly, and the sirens and Nereids fled shrieking. They dropped their mirrors as they went. The head sank with a great splash, then rose to the surface. I caught a sidelong flick of one dreadful agonized eye—the left—as the head rolled over and soared from the water, its snaky locks caught in an unseen armored grip by the pursuing demigod. Then Perseus and his victim were gone, with a last lightning flash of the sword, through the doorway where the nymphs had vanished.

I climbed from the reddening pool, too dazed to wonder why I still retained power of movement after meeting the Gorgon's eye. The slave-girls had disappeared. The trunk of Medusa had fallen forward from its chair, upon which the harpies still perched, voiding their excrement into the empty seat as into a toilet, with bursts of shrill laughter.

Beside Medusa stood a beautiful winged white horse, dabbled from hoofs to mane with the blood that still ran from the fallen monster's neck. I knew that it must be Pegasus, born of her decapitation according to myth.

Pegasus pranced lightly toward me, neighing in excellent Greek:

"We must go. The decrees of the gods have been fulfilled. I see that you are a stranger from another time and space. I will take you wherever you wish to go, or as near to it as possible."

Pegasus kneeled and I mounted him bareback, since he had been born without saddle or reins.

"Cling tightly to my mane. I will not unhorse you," he promised, "whatever the speed or altitude of our journey."

He trotted out through the doorway, spread his shining wings on an orient dawn, and took off toward the reddening cirrus clouds. I turned my head a little later. An ocean lay behind us, far down, with raging billows turned to mere ripples by distance. The lands of morning gleamed before us.

"To what period of time, and what region?" asked Pegasus above the rhyth-mic drumming of his wings.

"I came from a country known as America, in the 20th century A.D.," I replied, raising my voice to reach his ears through the thunder.

Pegasus bridled and almost stopped in mid-flight.

"My prophetic insight forbids me to oblige you. I cannot visit the century, and, in particular, the country, that you name. Any poets who are born there must do without me—must hoist themselves to inspiration by their own bootstraps, rather than by the steed of the Muses. If I ventured to land there, I should be impounded at once and my wings clipped. Later they would sell me for horse meat."

"You underrate their commercial acumen," I said. "They'd put you in a side-show and charge a stiff entrance fee. You're well known, in a way. Your name and picture are on sideboards at many gas-stations. A synonym for speed if nothing else.

"Anyway, there is little inducement for me to return. I have been trying to drink myself out of it for years and decades. Why go back, after escaping? Why end up, as I will sooner or later, at the highly expensive mercy of doctors, hospitals and undertakers?"

"You are certainly sensible, will you indicate a place and period more to your liking?"

I mused awhile, reviewing all I could remember of both history and geography.

"Well," I decided at last, "some South Sea island might do, before the discovery by Captain Cook and the coming of the missionaries."

Pegasus began to accelerate his flight. Day and darkness shuttled by, sun, moon and stars were streaks above, and the regions below were blurred by inconceivable speed, so that I could not distinguish fertile from desert, land from water. We must have circled the earth innumerable times, through the birth and death of millenniums.

Gradually the speed of the winged horse decelerated. A cloudless sun became stable overhead. A balmy subtropic sea, full of green islands, rolled softly on all sides to the horizon.

Pegasus made an easy landing on the nearest island, and I slipped dizzily from his back.

"Good luck," he neighed. Then, stretching his wings once more, he soared toward the sun and disappeared with the suddenness of a time-machine.

Feeling that Pegasus had abandoned me in a rather summary fashion, I peered about at my surroundings. At first sight I had been left in an uninhabited isle, on a coral reef lined with untrodden grass and rimmed with pandanus and breadfruit trees.

Presently the foliage stirred and several natives crept forth. They were elaborately tattooed and armed with wooden clubs studded with sharks' teeth. Judging from their gestures of fear and wonder, they had never seen a white man or a horse of any color, winged or unwinged. They dropped their clubs as they neared me, and pointed questioning fingers, a trifle shaky, at the skies where Pegasus had vanished.

"Think nothing of it," I said in my suavest and most reassuring tones. Remembering a vague religious upbringing, I made the sign of benediction.

The savages grinned shyly, displaying an array of filed teeth only less formidable than the sharks' incisors and molars that decorated their clubs. Plainly they were losing their fear and making me welcome to the island. Their eyes appraised me with inscrutable blandness, like those of innocent children who expect someone to feed them.

I am penciling this account in a small notebook found in one of my pockets.

Three weeks have passed since Pegasus left me among the cannibals. They have treated me well and have fattened me with all the abundance that the isle affords. With taro and roast pig, with breadfruit, coconuts, guavas, and many unknown delicious vegetables. I feel like a Thanksgiving turkey.

How do I know they are cannibals? By human bones, hair, skin, piled or strewn about as animal remnants are in the neighborhood of slaughter-houses. Apparently they have moved their feasting places only when the bones got too thick. Bones of men, women, children, mixed with those of birds, pigs and small four-footed creatures. An untidy lot, even for anthropophagi.

The island is of small extent, perhaps no more than a mile in width by two in length. I have not learned its name and am uncertain to which of the many far-flung archipelagos it belongs. But I have picked up a few words of the soft, many-vowelled language—mainly the names of foodstuffs.

They have domiciled me in a clean enough hut, which I occupy alone. None of the women, who are comely enough and quite friendly, has offered to share it with me. Perhaps this is for therapeutic reasons—perhaps they fear I might lose weight if I were to indulge in amorous activity. Anyway, I am relieved. All women are cannibalistic, even if they don't literally tear the meat from one's bones. They devour time, money, attention, and give treachery in return. I have long learned to avoid them. Long ago my devotion to drink became single-hearted. Liquor at least has been faithful to me. It requires no eloquence, no flattery, no blandishments. To me, at least, it makes no false promises.

I wish Pegasus would return and carry me off again. Truly I made a chuckle-headed choice in selecting one of the South Sea isles. I am weaponless; and I don't swim very well. The natives could overtake me quickly if I stole one of their outrigger canoes. I never was much good at boating even in my college days. Barring a miracle, I am destined to line the gizzards of these savages.

The last few days they have allowed me all the palm-wine I can drink. Perhaps they believe it will improve the flavor. I swig it frequently and lie on my back staring at the bright blue skies where only parrots and sea-birds pass. I cannot get drunk and delirious enough to imagine that any of them is the winged horse. And I curse them in five languages, in English, Greek, French, Spanish, Latin, because they cannot be mistaken for Pegasus. Perhaps, if I had plenty of high-proof Scotch and Bourbon, I could walk out of this particular time-plexus into something quite different... as I did from modern New York into the ancient palace of Medusa.

Another entry, which I hardly expected to make. I don't know the day, the month, the year, the century. But according to the belief of these misguided islanders—and mine—it was pot-day. They brought out the pot at mid-morning: a huge vessel of blackening battered bronze inscribed around the sides with Chinese characters. It must have been left here by some far-strayed or storm-wrecked junk. I don't like to conjecture the fate of the crew, if any survived and came ashore. Being boiled in their own cooking-pot must have been a curious irony.

To get back to my tale. The natives had set out huge quantities of palm-wine in crude earthen vessels, and they and I were getting ginned up as fast as we could. I wanted a share of the funeral feast, even if I was slated to afford the *pièce-de-résistance*.

Presently there was a lot of jabbering and gesticulating. The chief, a big burly ruffian, was giving orders. A number of the natives scattered into the woods, and some returned with vessels full of spring-water which they emptied into the pot, while others piled dry grass and well-seasoned fagots around its base. A fire was started with flint and an old piece of metal which looked like the broken-off end of a Chinese sword-blade. It was probably a relic of the same junk that had provided the pot.

I hoped that the user had broken it only after laying out a long file of cannibals.

In a rather futile effort to raise my spirits, I began to sing the *Marseillaise*, and followed it with *Lulu* and various other bawdies. Presently the water was bubbling, and the cooks turned their attention to me. They seized me, stripped off my ragged clothes, and trussed me up adroitly, knees to chest and arms doubled at the sides, with some sort of tough vegetable fiber. Then, singing what was doubtless a cannibal chantey, they picked me up and heaved me into the pot, where I landed with a splash, and settled more or less upright in a sitting position.

At least, I had thought they would knock me on the head beforehand rather than boil me like a live lobster.

In my natural fright and confusion it took me some moments to realize that the water, which had seemed scalding hot, was in reality no warmer to the epidermis than my usual morning tub. In fact it was quite agreeable. Judging by the violence with which it bubbled beneath my chin, it was not likely to grow much hotter.

This anomaly of sensation puzzled me mightily. By all rights I should be suffering agonies. Then, like a flash of lightning, I remembered the passing sidelong flick of Medusa's left eye and the apparent lack of effect at the time. Her glance had in no way *petrified* me—but in some strange fashion it must have *toughened* my skin, which was now impervious to the normal effects of heat; and perhaps also to other phenomena. Perhaps, to cause the mythic petrification, it was necessary to sustain the regard of both the Gorgon's eyes.

These things are mysteries. Anyway, it was as if I had been given a flexible asbestos hide. But, curiously enough, my keenness of touch was unimpaired.

Through the veering smoke I saw that the cooks were coming back, laden with baskets of vegetables. They were all getting drunker; and the chief was the drunkest. He lurched about, waving his war-club, while the others emptied their baskets into the kettle. Only then did they perceive that things had not proceeded according to culinary rules. Their eyes grew rounder and they yelled with surprise to see me grinning at them from amidst the steaming ebullient contents. One of the cooks made a pass at my throat with a stone knife—and the knife broke in the middle. Then the chief stepped forward, shouting ferociously, and hoisted his toothed war-club.

I ducked under water and to one side. The club descended, making a huge splash—and missed me. Judging from their outcries, some of the cooks must have been scalded by the flying water. The chief fared worse. Over-balanced by that mighty stroke, he lurched against the pot, which careened heavily, spilling much of the contents. Using my weight repeatedly against the side, I managed to overthrow the vessel, and rolled out in a torrent of water, smoke and vegetables.

The chief, yowling from what must have been third-degree burns, was trying to extricate himself from the brands and embers into which he had fallen. Limping, he got to his feet after several vain attempts and staggered away. The other cooks, and the expectant feasters, had already decamped. I had the field to myself.

Looking around, I noticed the broken-off sword which had been used in striking fire, and levered myself in its direction. Holding it clumsily, I contrived to work my wrist-fetters against the edge. The blade was still fairly sharp and I soon had my hands free. After that, it was no trick to untruss my legs.

The wine had worn off but there were many unemptied pots of it still around. I collected two or three, and put some of the spilled vegetables to roast amid the glowing coals. Then, waiting comfortably for the cannibals' return, I began to laugh.

I was washing down a well-baked taro root with the second pot of wine when the first of them crawled out of the woods and fell prostrate before me. I learned afterwards that they were deprecating my anger and were very sorry they had not recognized me as a god.

They have christened me in their own tongue. *The-One-who-cannot-be-cooked.*

I wish that Pegasus would return.

THE DART OF RASASFA

J on Montrose and his wife Mildred were passing Belaran, a sun obscured to earth-astronomers by a small dense nebula many million
miles beyond Alpha Centauri. The sun's existence had been discovered
nine years previous by an expedition which had gone by to remoter spatial
objectives. Jon and Mildred were the only crew of the space-flier *Daedalus,* in
which they had left Earth two years before, and were making their maximum
speed of several light-years a week by atomic power.

In their reflectors Belaran, a white sun similar to our own, displayed a
system of seven worlds. The tint was unusual—most suns in proximity to
nebulae were blue or red. They were nearest to the fourth world when the
trouble began—a sudden and violent veering toward the planet, which lay to
starboard. Jon's quick inspection showed that the steering apparatus was in
good order. Some obscure magnetic force, not classified by their instruments,
was drawing them downward to the unknown world, which soon revealed
a conformation of plains and mountains below. The plains broadened, the
mountains leapt upward with tops and slopes that assumed color and sharp
definitude.

"Gods! we're going to crash!" Jon cried. He and Mildred watched helplessly as the vessel slanted past the high peaks with no visible snow and a
lichen-like purplish vegetation. They dipped into a long steep ravine showing
threads of water or other liquid at the bottom, and then landed on a sort
of shelf, their prow plunging into soil and rocks deeply enough to hold the
ship from sliding further.

Stunned and shaken by the impact, the voyagers soon regained full consciousness. They had held instinctively to the steering seat, but were bruised
and bleeding in places. No bones seemed to be broken. The engines were
silent. Air blowing in their faces drew their attention to the manhole in the

slanted wall. It had been forced half open, and their atmosphere was tempered by a cool fresh breeze from outside which seemed to have no deleterious effects but was perhaps a little higher in oxygen than that to which they were accustomed.

Jon examined the atomic engines. They had been turned off automatically by a breakage in the rod which connected them with the steering-gear. The rod was made of carborundum and zysturium, the last-named a new element found on the moon and certain outer planets. How it had been broken, unless flawed, was a mystery: the alloy was harder than diamond.

Unless the break could be mended, they would be powerless to resume their journey. Jon cursed in a low but vehement voice, remembering that they had neglected to bring along any spare parts, and wondering if the local landscape would afford the required materials. If so, they had a furnace for smelting and fusing and could mend the rod, even if rather crudely.

He told Mildred the problem, adding: "There's nothing to do but get out and hunt. Otherwise we'll be stuck here till the Second Coming—of Christ, Beelzebub, or what have you."

He packed a knapsack with food and a thermos bottle of coffee, and gave it to Mildred. Then, carrying slung from his shoulders a pick and shovel and a complicated new instrument for detecting all known minerals and elements up to a depth of ten or more feet, he forced the manhole lid open enough to climb out and descend to the ledge on a crazily slanted ladder. His wife followed, having strapped the knapsack about her neck.

They could now see much of the surrounding terrain. Far in the distance of the flat country below, towers or tall buildings glimmered. At their feet a series of rough projections in the stone made feasible their descent to the stream-bed where liquid pools and cascades gurgled between steep walls partly mantled with lichen or other short growth of the order of ice-plants.

They climbed down to the stream-bed, testing each of the salients carefully before trusting their full weight upon it. The pools were indistinguishable from common water at close view but might contain poisonous elements. They did not pause to test it but stepped across the stream and began to ascend the opposite side, stopping many times to try the detection instrument, which showed only minerals and metals of ordinary kind, including traces of gold, silver, iron, and mercury.

By slow degrees they worked diagonally toward the plain, crossing several ridges and streams, one of the latter a cataract which they had to circumnavigate laboriously. At last, on a downward slope, they found evidence of carborundum; and, not far away, a small deposit of zysturium. Jon started to dig. He had gone down about five feet and had struck the carborundum, Mildred stooping over him, when an interruption occurred. A heavy net of some clinging ropy material dropped over their heads and tightened. Beyond the meshes a group of incredible beings, reptile-headed but upright, bluish in color, with two hands and feet, were standing above them, holding the long handle of the net. One of these beings carried a sharp-pointed spear with which he touched them in turn, pricking through their clothes between the meshes. Unconsciousness quickly followed a spreading numbness at the touch of the spear.

Mildred awoke in a dungeon-like roofed enclosure, lit sparsely by small globes in the walls which had the look of staring violescent eyes. She was lying on a low couch of some soft and colorless material. Beside her on the floor was a flattish bowl containing, she conjectured, some sort of food-stuff. Still dazed and sick, she did not feel tempted to taste it. Anyway, the odor was not appetizing: it suggested stale fish.

She raised herself dizzily on her elbow. The floor seemed to reel, the lights in the walls to dance. Around a corner, swaying with the room's apparent motion, walked three of the bluish reptile-headed beings. One of them strapped an apparatus like an electrode to her forehead and held the other end to his own. She noticed for the first time that his hands were four-fingered. She heard in her brain a weird buzzing which began to shape itself into sounds that she could not recognize as words until after an interval. Presently she surmised that the sounds were a telepathic attempt at translation into English from a radically different tongue, in which many letters were hissed rather than spoken. Certain words were well-nigh unpronounceable by the human mouth-structure.

Mildred made out: "To temple you must go where waits Rasasfa... to sacrifice other person not yourself. Will result for us much benefit... much learning."

The sounds changed, becoming more rapid and less distinct, with a tone of stern command. Perhaps a hypnotic suggestion was being administered. At any rate she could not remember its nature or import when the being withdrew the instrument.

Her captors drew her upright. Their clammy touch made her shudder. Mildred's arms were supported while a reptile mask, not blue but whitish, was fastened over her face. She became aware for the first time that she had been quite naked, when a short pale dress was draped around her. Then they led her from the room through an open doorway and up several flights of coiling stairs and along endless dim corridors.

Somewhere the hilt of a stained, blackish, upward-pointing knife was placed in her hand, and her fingers were clasped tightly around it by cold reptile pressure. She could not recall why, or for what purpose, she was to use it. But a strong sense of predestination was upon her, and a feeling that she would be enlightened in due time.

Light opened before her at a turn in the corridor. She was led through a high broad doorway into a vast edifice where a reptile being, taller than any she had yet seen, stood before an open alcove which gave forth a golden glimmering. The alcove's entrance looked like a huge broad keyhole. The being held in his hand a sickle-butted dart. The walls of the alcove behind him seemed inlaid with oblique oblongs of yellow mosaic, and the floor was partly littered with unnamable objects.

Mildred was half-pushed, half-carried, and made to stand on an indented pedestal at the right hand of the armed entity. She faced a deeply bowing congregation of reptilians in the nave, which appeared lit by sunlight between pillars at the rear.

Still bewildered, she perceived that a man had entered at the left and had paused in front of the dart-bearer. For a while she failed to realize that the man was Jon: his features seemed blurred with the faces of others she had known, had liked or disliked in former years. An impulse of sudden hatred made her raise the black knife, and she was about to fling it toward him.

She never knew what checked her. Perhaps the hypnotic command implanted in her mind had suddenly been reversed. She paused, while the dart-bearer lifted his weapon and hurled it violently at Jon, piercing his shirt at the side as he dodged agilely with muscles trained by a multitude of tasks.

Something (perhaps a remaining part of the hypnosis) told her that the dart-bearer was Rasasfa, priest of an ultra-planetary sect. She leapt from the pedestal and stabbed him deeply in the side. Almost simultaneously, in his convulsive struggles, he scratched her breast with the dart-point before he dropped.

Jon and Mildred both underwent a strange hallucination, identical in all details, which they could never afterward forget. They had the sense of falling immeasurably, plunging through uncharted depths and dimensions, to hang insecurely poised on the verge of an alien hell, from which pointed flames, obscenely writhing monsters, dragon-like creatures with several heads and bodies, reached upward around their feet and sometimes over-towered them, breathing a fetid stench. Not the least horror was Rasasfa, standing close at hand, and thrusting with his dart at the monsters. And they, in turn, seemed to assail him with a special menace and venom, looming far up and lengthening fantastically into the skyless vault. He paid no attention to the humans, appearing oblivious of their presence.

At last the lurid glow, like ashen embers, dimmed in the depths. The figures grew vaporous, and broke up like wind-blown clouds, trailing and mingling and finally vanishing. Jon and Mildred stood alone on the precipice, which tottered and fell apart.

They awoke in the nave. The crowd had vanished. The reptile had dropped his dart but was still writhing. Pierced in a vital part by Mildred's knife, he was dying very slowly, as snakes die.

They found their way from the temple, meeting no one. Jon had picked up the dart and carried it. The sun had abandoned the skies, leaving a multitude of stars, among which hung the nebula. Using a small pocket-compass, of which his captors had not deprived him, they left the city. The place lay entirely dark and silent, as if deserted by its inhabitants; and quitting its narrow, tortuous streets, they returned toward the mountains. They surmised that the slaying of Rasasfa had wrought profound terror. Doubtless the people had believed him a supernatural or immortal being.

They traveled across a semi-desert land. The sun finally rose, and leaned over them, warm until evening. They followed the compass toward a magnetic pole in what they liked to believe was the north. The air was very cold at night, and they slept a few hours in each other's arms.

Fearing pursuit, they peered often backward at the city, which sank gradually on the horizon. Presently they found the tracks of the reptile people going city-ward from the mountains, often deeply printed because of the weight of the unconscious humans whom they carried. No doubt there were other cities in this world; but Jon and Mildred were glad to forgo any curiosity concerning them. Their one experience had been enough for several lifetimes.

They had suffered severely from thirst and hunger during that outward trip. There had been a few brackish pools from which they drank sparingly, hoping that the contents were rain-water; and a few bushes bearing a sourish red fruit of which they ate a small amount.

Late in the second afternoon the footsteps led them to the hollow in which Jon had been digging when they were captured by the falling net. Their tools and sacks and thermos lay where they had left them, their captors plainly thinking these appurtenances of no particular account. They saw with relief that the space-flier still occupied its shelf above.

The coffee was still warm in the thermos. They gulped some of it down eagerly. Then Jon resumed his digging while Mildred remained on the ridge watching the remote city, which seemed to waver and flicker like a mirage. Jon had filled one of the sacks with crude carborundum and was beginning to uncover the zysturium when Mildred cried out in warning. Hastily he climbed the ridge beside her, taking with him the dart-weapon and a pistol snatched from his pack.

A half dozen of the reptile men, climbing noiselessly, were hard upon them. All were armed with darts. They paused uncertainly when Jon brandished Rasasfa's weapon, as if realizing its weird powers and superiority to their own. Then they resumed their advance. Jon dropped two of them with the pistol, which was a sort of flame-thrower, and short-ranged. The others fell back and concealed themselves behind boulders. They had estimated closely the range of the flame-thrower.

"Take over while I get some of the zysturium," Jon instructed, giving Mildred the pistol. She obeyed, while Jon finished laying bare the needed element and partly filled his other sack. He attached the tools and sacks to his shoulder-band, and telling Mildred to follow, began his escalade toward the space-flier.

It was a close race, especially in rounding the cataract. He heard the snap and hiss of the pistol and Mildred's cry of triumph as at least one of their pursuers fell back.

At length, half blinded by sweat, with heart and lungs heaving stertorously, he was climbing the flier's ladder. Pushing his loads through the manhole, he hung at one side, and made sure that Mildred preceded him, snatching the pistol from her hand as she went past. One of the reptile-men had started to mount the ladder, but dropped into the ravine when Jon fired. Jon went through the manhole and made fast the outer and inner lids.

They worked on their repairs for much of that night, hearing the baffled cries of the reptiles and the futile crash of their weapons against the hull and windows.

The furnaces had done their fusing, and the rod was welded and left to cool.

At earliest morning they took off and regained the outer skies.

APPENDIX ONE:
STORY NOTES

Abbreviations Used:

AHT Arkham House Transcripts: a set of transcriptions and excerpts from the letters of H. P. Lovecraft prepared by Donald Wandrei and August Derleth after Lovecraft's death in preparation for what would be five volumes of *Selected Letters* (Sauk City, WI: Arkham House, 1965–1976).

AWD August W. Derleth (1909–1971), Wisconsin novelist, *Weird Tales* author, and co-founder of Arkham House.

AY *The Abominations of Yondo* (Sauk City, WI: Arkham House, 1960).

BB *The Black Book of Clark Ashton Smith* (Sauk City, WI: Arkham House, 1979).

BL Bancroft Library, University of California at Berkeley.

CAS Clark Ashton Smith (1893–1961).

DAW Donald A. Wandrei (1908–1987), poet, *Weird Tales* writer and co-founder of Arkham House.

DS *The Door to Saturn: The Collected Fantasies of Clark Ashton Smith, Volume Two.* Ed. Scott Connors and Ron Hilger (San Francisco: Night Shade Books, 2007).

EOD *Emperor of Dreams: A Clark Ashton Smith Bio-Bibliography* by Donald Sidney-Fryer et al. (West Kingston, RI: Donald M. Grant, 1978).

ES *The End of the Story: The Collected Fantasies of Clark Ashton Smith, Volume One.* Ed. Scott Connors and Ron Hilger (San Francisco: Night Shade Books, 2006).

FFT *The Freedom of Fantastic Things.* Ed. Scott Connors (New York: Hippocampus Press, 2006).

F&SF *The Magazine of Fantasy & Science Fiction*, a digest magazine founded in 1949 by Anthony Boucher and Robert Mills.

FW Farnsworth Wright (1888–1940), editor of *Weird Tales* from 1924 to 1940.

GL *Genius Loci and Other Tales* (Sauk City, WI: Arkham House, 1948).

HPL Howard Phillips Lovecraft (1890–1937), informal leader of a circle of writers for *Weird Tales* and related magazines, and probably the leading exponent of weird fiction in the twentieth century.

JHL Clark Ashton Smith Papers and H. P. Lovecraft Collection, John Hay Library, Brown University.

LL *Letters to H. P. Lovecraft.* Ed. Steve Behrends (West Warwick, RI: Necronomicon Press, 1987).

LW *Lost Worlds* (Sauk City, WI: Arkham House, 1944).

ME *The Maze of the Enchanter: The Collected Fantasies of Clark Ashton Smith, Volume Four.* Ed. Scott Connors and Ron Hilger (San Francisco: Night Shade Books, 2009).

MHS Donald Wandrei Papers, Minnesota Historical Society.

OD *Other Dimensions* (Sauk City, WI: Arkham House, 1970).

OST *Out of Space and Time* (Sauk City, WI: Arkham House, 1942).

PD *Planets and Dimensions: Collected Essays.* Ed. Charles K. Wolfe (Baltimore: Mirage Press, 1973).

PP *Poems in Prose* (Sauk City, WI: Arkham House, 1965).

RA *A Rendezvous in Averoigne* (Sauk City, WI: Arkham House, 1988).

RHB Robert H. Barlow (1918–1951), correspondent and collector of manuscripts of CAS, HPL, and other *WT* writers.

SHSW August Derleth Papers, State Historical Society of Wisconsin Library.

SL *Selected Letters of Clark Ashton Smith.* Ed. David E. Schultz and Scott Connors (Sauk City, WI: Arkham House, 2003).

SS *Strange Shadows: The Uncollected Fiction and Essays of Clark Ashton Smith.* Ed. Steve Behrends with Donald Sidney-Fryer and Rah Hoffman (Westport, CT: Greenwood Press, 1989).

ST *Strange Tales of Mystery and Terror*, a pulp edited by Harry Bates in competition with *WT*.

TSS *Tales of Science and Sorcery* (Sauk City, WI: Arkham House, 1964).

VA *A Vintage from Atlantis: The Collected Fantasies of Clark Ashton Smith, Volume Three.* Ed. Scott Connors and Ron Hilger (San Francisco: Night Shade Books, 2007).

WS *Wonder Stories*, a pulp published by Hugo Gernsback and edited first by David Lasser and then Charles D. Hornig.

WT *Weird Tales*, Smith's primary market for fiction, edited by FW (1924–1940) and later Dorothy McIlwraith (1940–1954).

The Dark Age

When Clark Ashton Smith wrote "The Dark Age," he intended to submit it to the Clayton *Astounding*, which had changed its policy to include a few occult-type stories.[1] It was finished by May 2, 1933, when he described the story as "my lousiest in many moons, largely, no doubt, because of the non-fantastic plot, which failed to engage my interest at any point. The one redeeming feature is the final paragraph, which takes a sly, underhanded crack at the benefits (?) of science."[2] We have not been able to locate any letter of rejection for this story, so it is not known if it was rejected under the auspices of the dying Clayton regime at *Astounding* or by the incoming editorial team of F. Orlin Tremaine and Desmond Hall that had already accepted "The Demon of the Flower" for the December 1933 issue.

Hugo Gernsback sold *Wonder Stories* to Leo Margulies' Better Publications on February 21, 1936. Mort Weisinger, who would later edit *Superman* during the so-called Silver Age of comics, took over from Charles D. Hornig as editor.[3] It is not known if Smith was invited to contribute or if he just sent in the typescript on his own initiative, but CAS wrote to Virgil Finlay that "The sale of a pseudo-science short to *Thrilling Wonder Stories* at $55.00 [*along with the sale of a carving*] brings my September [*1937*] income to $62.50! If such sales continue, I shall become a bloated plutocrat!"[4] "The Dark Age" appeared in *Thrilling Wonder Stories* for April 1938. This appearance was accompanied by a brief essay by Smith entitled "The Decline of Civilisation":

> "The Dark Age" was written to illustrate how easily scientific knowledge and its resultant inventions could be lost to the human race following the complete breakdown of a mechanistic civilization such as the present one. The tale seems far from fantastic or impossible; and I have tried to bring out several points and to emphasize the part played by mere chance and by personal emotions and reactions.
>
> I have shown the old knowledge conserved by a select few, the Custodians, who, in the beginning, are forced to isolate themselves completely because of the hostility displayed by the barbarians. Through habit, the isolation becomes permanent even when it is no longer necessary; and with the sole exception of Atullos, who has been expelled from the laboratory-fortress by his fellows, none of the Custodians tries to help the benighted people about them.
>
> In the end, through human passion, prejudice, misunderstanding, the Custodians perish with all their lore; and the night of the Dark Age is complete. The reader will note certain ironic ifs and might-have-beens in the tale. Other points that I have stressed are the immense, well-nigh insuperable difficulties met by Atullos in his attempt to reconstruct, amid primitive conditions, a few of the lost inventions for the benefit of the savages; and the total frustration of Torquane's studies and experiments through mere inability to read the books left by his dead father.
>
> Also I have shown how a chemical, such as gunpowder, might be used by one who had learned its effects but was wholly ignorant of its origin and nature.[5]

Smith would later collect the tale in *AY*. The current text is based upon an undated typescript among the Clark Ashton Smith Papers held by the John Hay Library of Brown University.

1. See *ME* pp. 317–318.
2. CAS, letter to AWD, May 2, 1933 (ms, SHSW).
3. See Mike Ashley and Robert A. W. Lowndes, *The Gernsback Days: A Study of the Evolution of Modern Science Fiction from 1911 to 1936* (Holicong, PA: Wildside Press, 2004): 249–250.
4. CAS, letter to Virgil Finlay, September 27, 1937 (*SL* 317).
5. *PD* 55.

The Death of Malygris

When Smith completed "The Death of Malygris," he mentioned to a fan correspondent that it contained "much genuine occultism and folk-lore,"[1] as can be seen from the following story idea found in the *Black Book*:

> Malygris, in death, lies incorrupt in his black tower and still tyrannizes over Susran. Maranapion, his enemy, a rival sorcerer, instigated by the king of Poseidonis, undertakes to free the land from his spell. Employing the invultuation principle [*the insertion of pins into a wax figure in order to bring harm to the person symbolized by the figure*], he makes an image of Malygris from synthetic flesh, and causes the image to rot, thus producing a corresponding decay in Malygris himself. Afterwards, Maranapion, invading the black tower to exult over the decay of his ancient foe, is cursed by the rotting corpse, and begins while still alive to putrefy in the same fashion as the dead man. The companions of Maranapion flee, leaving him in the tower with Malygris.[2]

When Farnsworth Wright rejected "The Death of Malygris," the words were by now all too familiar to Smith: "This seems more like a prose poem than a story; and we have learned from experience that our readers do not take to this type of story when it is more than three or four pages long. It is a beautiful thing, however, and the rhythmic prose fairly sings at times, but I don't think the average reader would care for it at all." He added this rather unhelpful piece of encouragement: "I think you would have something very, very fine if you would write this narrative to blank or rimed verse, but I don't know where you would find a market for it."[3] August Derleth commiserated with Smith, adding that Wright "gives me a godawful pain every once in a while. Makes me feel definitely homicidal."[4]

H. P. Lovecraft thought very highly of the story. He wrote to Robert Bloch that "Klarkash-Ton's 'Malygris' is splendid—& it is just like the capricious Brother Farnsworth to turn down a thing like that! The thing is pure poetry in places—indeed, the Dunsanian style suits C.A.S. more than it does me."[5] He called the story "a gorgeous bit of onyx & ebony prose-poetry in which the crawling menace advances as to the sound of evil flutes & crotala."[6]

After Wright accepted "The Flower-Women" upon resubmission, Smith decided to "try him again with 'The Death of Malygris,' a better tale than 'The F.W.' There is no excuse for his not accepting it."[7] Wright not only accepted "The Death of Malygris," but he commissioned Smith to draw an illustration for it as well. When this appeared in the April 1934 issue, Smith wrote to Lovecraft that he was "inclined to think it the best of my W.T. illustrations so far."[8] Robert E. Howard wrote to Smith after the tale's publication that "the Malygris story came up to expectations splendidly. In some ways I liked the illustration even better than that of 'The Charnel God,' though both were fine."[9] "The Death of Malygris" appears in both *LW* and *RA*. The current text is based upon an undated carbon copy at JHL.

1. CAS, letter to Lester Anderson, June 20, 1933 (ms, private collection).
2. *BB* 15.
3. FW, letter to CAS, May 16, 1933 (ms, JHL).
4. AWD, letter to CAS, May 27, 1933 (ms, JHL).
5. HPL, letter to Robert Bloch, June 9, 1933 (in *Letters to Robert Bloch*, Ed. S. T. Joshi and David E. Schultz [West Warwick, RI: Necronomicon Press, 1993]: p. 20).
6. HPL, letter to CAS, June 14, 1933 (ms, JHL).
7. CAS, letter to AWD, July 12, 1933 (*SL* 211).
8. CAS, letter to HPL, c. late January 1934 (*SL* 247).
9. Robert E. Howard, letter to CAS, May 21, 1934 (*Collected Letters of Robert E. Howard 1933–1936*, Ed. Rob Roehm [Robert E. Howard Foundation Press, 2008]: p. 208).

THE TOMB-SPAWN

A plot synopsis for this story may be found in the *Black Book* under the title of "The Tomb of Ossaru":

A desert-buried tomb in Yoros where a strange being from an alien world was interred by the wizard he had served and was surrounded by an inner zone of enchantment rendering him incorruptible, and an outer zone causing instant death and decay in any who might intrude. Two merchants, travelling through Yoros, are pursued by robbers, and take refuge in a ruined building. The pavement gives way beneath them—and they [are] precipitated into the Tomb of Ossaru. One falls in the inner zone beside the seated incorruptible monster—and the other in the outer zone. While the first, in horror, is watching the decay of his companion, Ossaru awakes and proceeds to devour him.[1]

Smith submitted the story to Wright under the title "The Tomb in the Desert" in July 1933;[2] since he submitted the story to *Astounding*, it would appear that Wright rejected it.[3] CAS wrote to Lovecraft that *Astounding* held on to the typescript for a month but ultimately returned it, then announced later in the same letter its acceptance by Wright under the current title.[4]

Since Smith prepared a new typescript under the new title, he apparently rewrote the story, but the extent of the revision is not apparent since the only manuscript or typescript to survive is an incomplete (missing the final page) carbon of the version published in *Weird Tales* (May 1934); a copy of the *WT* appearance was consulted for the text from the missing page. Some idea may be found in a letter to Derleth wherein he remarked "Glad you liked 'The Tomb-Spawn.' That little tale certainly cost me enough work, so it ought to be good."[5] Smith received thirty-five dollars for "The Tomb-Spawn,"[6] which was posthumously collected in *TSS*.

1. *BB* item 13.
2. CAS, letter to AWD, July 23, 1933 (*SL* 213).
3. CAS, letter to AWD, September 2, 1933 (*SL* 223).
4. CAS, letter to HPL, c. mid-October 1933 (*SL* 228).
5. CAS, letter to AWD, June 4, 1934 (ms, SHSW).
6. *WT*, letter to CAS, November 30, 1934 (ms, JHL).

THE WITCHCRAFT OF ULUA

Steve Behrends calls this "the first of Clark Ashton Smith's short stories to be rejected for publication because of an erotic tone or content,"[1] although as we have noted earlier that dubious distinction belongs to "The Disinterment of Venus."[2] CAS called the story, the first version of which was completed on August 22, 1933, "an erotic nightmare, and deals with a youth who had spurned a young witch and was bedevilled by her with various disagreeable sendings. He found amorous corpses in his bed, and was persecuted by peculiar succubi."[3]

Smith complained to August Derleth that Wright rejected the story "saying that it is a sex story and therefore unsuitable for W.T. Perhaps he is right; though erotic imagery was employed in the tale merely to achieve a more varied sensation of weirdness. The net result is surely macabre rather than risqué. I am enclosing the ms. and would appreciate your opinion. Also, if you can think of any possible market you might mention it. I can think of none...."[4] CAS denied any risqué intent, telling H. P. Lovecraft that he "was aiming mainly at weirdness; and whatever erotic imagery the tale contained was intended to be subordinate to its macabre qualities. Mere bawdiness is a bore, as far as I am concerned." He noted the irony of Wright's rejection: "Ye gods—when you consider the current cover of the magazine!"[5] (referring to the usual nude by artist Margaret Brundage, this one a lesbian whipping scene illustrating Robert E. Howard's "The Slithering Shadow").

Lovecraft, who had suffered more from Wright's rejections than any other writer, expressed his support and outrage: "Damn Satrap Pharnabazus for rejecting 'Ulua'! He certainly is a pip for consistency—to howl about excessive eroticism after deliberately adopting a policy of ha'penny satyr-tickling in his damn cover-designs... a policy which amusingly causes his more subservient writers (not excluding the illustrious Quinn &—at times—even the sanguinary Two-Gun Bob) to go miles out of their way to drag in a costumeless wench! But then—consistency & Brother Farny never were very close associates."[6] E. Hoffmann Price took a contrary position, asking "Hellsfire, must we have castrated wizards, and fair witches who have been very thoughtfully provided with a zone of anaesthesia reaching from... well, from there to there?"[7]

Smith next tried submitting "Ulua" to Astounding after revising the temptation scene, although he explicitly denied this to Derleth.[8] Earlier CAS told Derleth that he would not rewrite the story for resubmission to Weird Tales, adding "As to the so-called sexiness, it would not interest me to write a story dealing with anything so banal, hackneyed and limited as this type of theme is likely to be. Too many writers are doing it to death at the present time; and I have ended by revolting literarily against the whole business, and am prepared to maintain that a little Victorian reticence, combined with Puritan restraint, would harm nobody."[9] After the story was returned by Astounding, Smith, who was now more and more occupied with the care of his mother, now recuperating with a scalded foot, capitulated and submitted a third revised version to Wright, who accepted it on October 26, 1933 and offered thirty-three dollars.[10] He admitted to Derleth that he had "toned down the temptation scene a little," adding that "In the new version, Ulua teases the hero and twits him for his backwardness, instead of proffering her charms so flamboyantly. On the whole, it seems an improvement."[11]

Lovecraft read "The Witchcraft of Ulua" in typescript after its first rejection. He offered Smith his customary encouragement, calling it "a powerful piece—with intimations of horror & loathesomeness which do not soon leave the imagination. The style & atmosphere are admirable—prose-poetry in every line!"[12] He said much the same to Robert H. Barlow, adding "It has some terrific images."[13] (However, while commenting on the February 1934 issue of Weird Tales in which "Ulua" was published, HPL rated it "average."[14])

Despite the frustrations of rejection and revision, Smith was proud of "Ulua." He wrote to Barlow "I feel that it is well-written; and it gives a certain variant note to my series of tales dealing with Zothique."[15] Later, noting the uncharacteristically moralistic stance of the story, Smith told the same correspondent "You are damned well right about aretology—the word itself is marked obsolete in my Webster, which is of no recent date either. If I'm not careful, the latter-day bigots of phallicism will lock me up in the Iron Maiden for such anaphrodisiacs as Ulua! By the way, don't undervalue this tale; I wouldn't have had the originality to write it a few years back."[16]

The current text follows the lead of Steve Behrends, who based the text used in Necronomicon Press's *Unexpurgated Clark Ashton Smith* series upon the carbon of the version ultimately published by *Weird Tales*, but replacing the published temptation scene with the version submitted to *Astounding*. We concur in his judgment that the writing in this version was not done under duress and that it represents an improvement over the original. The first and third versions may be found in Appendix 2. Smith originally wanted to include "The Witchcraft of Ulua" in his third Arkham House collection, *GL*, but space restrictions pushed it back to his fourth, *AY*. We have made slightly different word choices in establishing a text. All typescripts may be found among Smith's papers at the John Hay Library of Brown University.

1. Steve Behrends, "Foreword" in *The Witchcraft of Ulua*, by Clark Ashton Smith (West Warwick, RI: Necronomicon Press, 1988): 5.
2. See *ME* 291–292.
3. CAS, letter to DAW, August 6, 1933 (*SL* 217).
4. CAS, letter to AWD, August 29, 1933 (*SL* 219).
5. CAS, letter to HPL, c. September 1, 1933 (*LL* 40).
6. HPL, letter to CAS, September 11, 1933 (ms, JHL).
7. E. Hoffmann Price, letter to CAS, undated (ms, JHL).
8. CAS, letter to Derleth, September 26, 1933 (*SL* 223).
9. CAS, letter to Derleth, September 14, 1933 (*SL* 220).
10. FW, letter to CAS, October 2, 1933 (ms, JHL).
11. CAS, letter to AWD, November 6, 1933 (ms, SHSW).
12. HPL, letter to CAS, November 13, 1933 (AHT).
13. HPL, letter to RHB, November 13, 1934 (in *O Fortunate Floridian: H. P. Lovecraft's Letters to R. H. Barlow* [Tampa, FL: University of Tampa Press, 2007]: p. 86).
14. HPL, letter to Robert Bloch, February 2, 1934 (in *Letters to Robert Bloch*, Ed. S. T. Joshi and David E. Schultz [West Warwick, RI: Necronomicon Press, 1993]: p. 47).
15. CAS, letter to RHB, October 4, 1933 (ms, JHL).
16. CAS, letter to RHB, December 5, 1933.

THE COMING OF THE WHITE WORM

Clark Ashton Smith probably had more fun writing "The Coming of the White Worm" than he did any other of his stories; he also probably experienced more frustration in getting it into print, and his remuneration was minimal at best. He announced the story in a postcard to H. P. Lovecraft: "I am doing the 'IX Chapter of Eibon' at present—a start on that much-requested cycle of occult elder lore!"[1] It appears that the impetus behind the story was the increasing number of readers who wanted to read more from such eldritch but imaginary tomes as the *Necronomicon* (Lovecraft), the *Book of Eibon* (Smith), or von Junzt's *Nameless Cults* (Howard), numbers which swelled after the July 1933 issue of *Weird Tales* ran no fewer than three stories referring to such fonts of dark lore.[2] Smith described its composition in a letter to August Derleth:

> It is hard to do, like most of my tales, because of the peculiar and carefully maintained style and tone-colour, which involves rejection of many words, images and locutions that might ordinarily be employed in writing. The story takes its text from a saying of the prophet Lith: "There is one that inhabits the place of utter cold, and One that respireth where none other may draw breath. In the days to come He shall issue forth among the isles and cities of men, and shall bring with Him as a white doom the wind that slumbereth in His dwelling".[3]

Smith completed the story on September 15, 1933 and submitted it to *Weird Tales*. Farnsworth Wright's letter of rejection sounded an all-too-familiar theme: "I enjoyed reading 'The Coming of the White Worm,' but I fear that we cannot use it. It would occupy eleven or twelve pages in Weird Tales, and many of our readers, I fear, would object strongly to reading a prose poem as long as this."[4]

Lovecraft's reactions to Smith's stories are often as entertaining as the story itself, and his reaction after reading "The Coming of the White Worm" is a case in point: "Nggrrrhh... what a revelation! Thank God you spared your readers the worst & most paralysing hints—such as the secret of Yikilth's origin, the reason why it bore certain shapes not of this planet, & the history of Rlim Shaikorth before he oozed down to the solar system & the earth through the void from _____ [HPL's underscore].... but I must not utter that name at which you, & Gaspard du Nord, & Eibon himself grew silent! Altogether, this is a stupendous fragment of primal horror & cosmic suggestion; & I shall call down the curses of Azathoth Itself if that ass Pharnabazus does not print it."[5] The story was next submitted to *Astounding*, which kept it for some time but ultimately returned it. CAS vented his frustrations to Derleth when he noted that "[Desmond] Hall, the sub-editor of that triply xxxed Astounding, deigned to drop me a line about their new policy following the rejection of the S-G with a blank, when he returned The White Worm after holding it for more than a month. I dare say one of these tales would have been bought if it hadn't been for such laboratory-minded donkeys as [Forrest J.] Ackerman. Of course, the lower type of 'fan' is always the most vociferous. A dozen such birds, I dare say, can change the policy of a magazine."[6]

Smith apparently gave the story to William L. Crawford for use in his semi-prozine *Unusual Stories*. Crawford, like many of his contemporaries, harbored a prejudice against weird stories (as witnessed by the contemporary exchange in the *Fantasy Fan*'s "Boiling Point" column discussed in earlier volumes[7]), but CAS felt that he was more open minded than many: "I should judge that his prejudice against weirdness applies largely to stuff dealing with stock superstitions. He seems to class work such as mine and Lovecraft's as 'pure fantasy.'"[8] Crawford had been given stories by Lovecraft and by Robert E. Howard, which he ran in *Marvel Tales*, a sister magazine that was slanted more to the fantastic. The Summer 1935 issue of *Marvel Tales* contains an announcement that "The Coming of the White Worm" would appear in the next issue, which never appeared.

"The Coming of the White Worm" appears to have remained in limbo until late 1938. It was at this time that Smith received a letter from an unexpected source: John W. Campbell:

> It has been a good many months since you appeared in Astounding, largely, I believe, because you have felt that fantasy wasn't too welcome here, and science didn't fit your style.
>
> At any rate, I hope there has been no other reason. For recently, readers have shown a definite and growing interest in fantasy, and I'd like very much to see some of your newer work. I'd like particularly the type that involves human reactions, fairly normal human characters against a background that is fantastic, or involved in some tangled action that is not explained or explainable, perhaps, but still is real to the characters.
>
> The kind I'd like to see would involve the humanness of the stories I've been trying to get in Astounding during the past year... but against a background of pure fantasy rather than science.[9]

Campbell was actually soliciting contributions for *Unknown*. Smith sent him "The Coming of the White Worm," which received the following response: "This story does not involve the inter-relations of human beings in an atmosphere of fantasy. It is the latter type that I would rather see from you. This material is so entirely without human reactions that I am afraid it would be unsuitable for Unknown."[10] If Smith had been following what Campbell was doing in *Astounding*, he would not have been greatly surprised by the rejection. Nonetheless, he would still try later on to write something that Campbell might find acceptable. It is a shame that CAS did not submit a rewritten version of "The Voyage of King Euvoran" to Campbell. E. Hoffmann Price, Smith's friend and collaborator, describes in his memoirs how he preferred Smith's stories "because he presented credible human beings more frequently than did [HPL and Robert E. Howard].... In Averoigne and in such tales as 'The Voyage of King Euvoran,' he portrayed human beings, not two dimensional and unconvincing simulacra which all too often rode unsteadily on a 'mood'."[11] (We would suggest that Campbell might also have found "The Last Hieroglyph" to his tastes had Wright not already published it.) Smith at his best was probably capable of writing a story that would pass muster with Campbell, but by the time *Unknown* arrived on the scene he was finding that his heart was no longer in fiction writing, but more in the writing of poetry, his first love, and in the carving of his marvelously outré figurines from native minerals found at a quarry owned by his uncle, Edwin C. Gaylord.

Farnsworth Wright wrote to Smith on November 23, 1938: "Since we are using your story, 'The Double Shadow', in our February issue, we are left without any manuscripts of yours on hand. This should not be."[12] By this time myriad rejections of his best work, ignorant criticisms by hostile science fiction fans, the loss of Lovecraft, his most appreciative reader, and the deaths of his parents, which removed the captives to fortune that motivated much of his story production, had taken their toll, and Smith had not completed a new story since July 1937. He had already placed slightly revised versions of two stories from *The Double Shadow and Other Fantasies* with Wright, and 1939 would see the publication of two more from that collection. Although no correspondence exists, it appears that Wright capitulated and accepted a pruned-down version of "The Coming of the White Worm." But once again Smith played fortune's fool.

Late in 1938 *Weird Tales* was purchased by a New York businessman, William J. Delaney, who already published the highly successful pulp *Short Stories*. Delaney relocated the operation to New York City. Wright was kept on as editor and made the move, but was let go with the March 1940 issue. An interview with Delaney appeared in a fanzine at the time of Wright's dismissal that boded ill for Smith. After promising that *Weird Tales* would continue to publish "all types of weird and fantasy fiction," the interview went on to add:

> There is one rule, however: Weird Tales does not want stories which center about sheer repulsiveness, stories which leave an impression not to be described by any other word than "nasty". This is not to imply that the "grim" story, or the tale which leaves the reader gasping at the verge of the unknown, is eliminated. Mr. Delaney believes that the story which leaves a sickish feeling in the reader is not truly weird and has no place in Weird Tales.... And, finally, stories wherein the characters are continually talking in French, German,

Latin, etc. will be frowned upon, as well as stories wherein the reader
must constantly consult an unabridged dictionary.[13]

The interviewer was Robert A. W. Lowndes, who shed some light on this
in a letter published years later:

> Delaney, who was a pleasant and cultured man, was very fond of
> weird stories, but he was also a strict Catholic.... He also found
> some of the Clark Ashton Smith stories on the 'disgusting' side and
> told me that he had returned one that Wright had in his inventory
> when he left. It was about a monstrous worm which, when attacked
> and pierced, shed forth rivers of slime. Later in 1940, when Donald
> A. Wollheim was starting Stirring Science Stories, Smith sent him
> "The Coming of the White Worm" and Don used it. When I read it,
> there was no doubt that this was the story Delaney had been talking
> about.... Concerned about the magazine's slipping circulation, he
> felt that the "more esoteric" type of story was a handicap, so this
> was mostly cut out.[14]

Smith wrote a letter around the time of Wright's dismissal that listed *Weird Tales'*
remaining inventory of his material at two stories and four poems.[15] Only one
story, "The Enchantress of Sylaire" (*Weird Tales* July 1941) appeared between the
date of that letter and the acceptance of Smith's next *WT* story, "The Epiphany of
Death," early in 1942,[16] so it would appear that one story was returned.

Further corroboration of these events may be found in the memoirs of
E. Hoffmann Price, which illustrate just how frustrated and upset Smith
was with magazine publishing. When Price visited him early in 1940, Smith
presented him with the typescripts of two unpublished stories, "The House
of the Monoceros" and "Dawn of Discord," and told Price to do whatever
he wanted with them: "Scrap the god-damn things if after all you don't like
them. The less I hear of them—." Price interpreted this to mean that Smith
realized "his stories did not fit into the publisher's new pattern. Clark, fed
up with adverse criticism or outright rejection, rejected the rejector, and
gave me the scripts."[17]

"The Coming of the White Worm" was finally published in *Stirring Science
Stories'* April 1941 issue. The story was placed by Donald A. Wollheim acting
as Smith's agent,[18] but according to Harry Warner Jr. *Stirring Science Stories*
was a non-paying market that relied upon donations.[19] It was reprinted in
the Canadian pulp *Uncanny Tales* that November, but by that time wartime
restrictions prevented publishers from paying American writers.[20] "The
Coming of the White Worm" was collected, in its pruned form, in both *LW*
and *RA*. The original version was first published in *SS*. The current text is
based upon the original typescript of the first version at the JHL.

1. CAS, postcard to HPL postmarked August 28, 1933 (ms, private collection).
2. See CAS's letter to AWD, July 12, 1933 (*SL* 211): "I have… recently received a letter from some reader who was struck by the numerous references to The Book of Eibon in that issue, and wanted to know where he could procure this rare work!" The stories were "The Dreams in the Witch-House" by H. P. Lovecraft; "The Horror in the Museum" by Hazel Heald (actually ghost-written by HPL); and Smith's own "Ubbo-Sathla."
3. CAS, letter to AWD, August 29, 1933 (*SL* 219).
4. FW, letter to CAS, September 29, 1933 (ms, JHL).
5. HPL, letter to CAS, October 3, 1933 (ms, JHL).
6. CAS, letter to AWD, November 17th, 1933 (ms, SHSW).
7. See *ME* p. 298. See also Scott Connors and Ron Hilger, "The Non-Human Equation." In *Star Changes*, by Clark Ashton Smith. Ed. Scott Connors and Ron Hilger (Seattle, WA: Darkside Press, 2005): pp. 17–18.
8. CAS, letter to AWD, October 19, 1933 (*SL* 232).
9. John W. Campbell, letter to CAS, October 27, 1938 (ms, JHL).
10. John W. Campbell, letter to CAS, April 7, 1939 (ms, private collection).
11. E. Hoffmann Price, *Book of the Dead. Friends of Yesteryear: Fictioneers & Others (Memories of the Pulp Era)*. Ed. Peter Ruber (Sauk City, WI: Arkham House, 2001): p. 125.
12. Farnsworth Wright, letter to CAS, November 23, 1938 (ms, JHL).
13. "Weird Tales Stays Weird." *Science Fiction Weekly* (March 24, 1940): 1.
14. Robert A. W. Lowndes, "Letters." *Weird Tales Collector* No. 5 (1979): 31.
15. CAS, letter to Margaret and Ray St. Clair, February 22, 1940 (*SL* 328).
16. Dorothy McIlwraith, letter to CAS, February 24, 1942 (ms, JHL).
17. Price, *Book of the Dead,* pp. 112–113. Price dates this encounter to 1939, but in a letter quoted in Steve Behrends, "The Price-Smith Collaborations" (*Crypt of Cthulhu* No. 26 [Hallowmas 1986]: 32) he places the date as 1940. "House of the Monoceros" was published as "The Old Gods Eat" (*Spicy Mystery Stories* February 1941); "Dawn of Discord" (Spicy Mystery Stories October 1940). Price paid Smith half of the proceeds for these stories. Science fiction writer Jack Williamson joined Price in this visit. He described Smith at this meeting as "defeated and pathetic" (*Wonder's Child: My Life in Science Fiction* [New York: Bluejay Books, 1984], p. 127).
18. See CAS, letter to AWD, November 6, 1944 (ms, SHSW).
19. Harry Warner, Jr. *All Our Yesterdays* (Chicago: Advent, 1969): 79–80.
20. Ibid., p. 164.

THE SEVEN GEASES

Smith's next story, "The Seven Geases," was completed on October 1, 1933. It may have been inspired in part by the circumstances surrounding the tale immediately preceding it, "The Coming of the White Worm." One of the readers who had requested to read more from the *Book of Eibon* was William Lumley (1880–1960), an eccentric correspondent of Lovecraft's who asserted that HPL, CAS, and their associates were "genuine agents of unseen Powers in distributing hints too dark & profound for human conception or comprehension. We may *think* we're writing fiction, & may even (absurd thought!) disbelieve what we write, but at bottom we are telling the truth in spite of ourselves—serving unwittingly as mouthpieces of Tsathoggua, Crom, Cthulhu, & other pleasant Outside gentry."[1] Lovecraft was quite fond of Lumley in spite of these eccentric views, and revised his story "The Diary of Alonzo Typer" (*Weird Tales* February 1938). Smith found Lumley to be quite the "rara avis, and I wish sincerely that there were more like him in this world of servile conformity to twentieth century skepticism and materialism! More power to such glorious heresy as that which he avows. I, for one, would hardly want the task of disproving his belief—even if I could disprove them. I must write him again before long."[2]

In his response to Smith's letter, Lovecraft seized upon these remarks to launch a defense of scientific materialism and skepticism:

> As for the Lumleys & Summers's of this world versus the Einsteins, Jeans's, de Sitters, Bohrs, & Heisenbergs—I must confess that I am essentially on the side of prose & science! It is true that we can form no conception of ultimate reality, or of the limitless gulfs of cosmic space beyond a trifling radius, but it is also true that we have a fair working estimate of the phenomena within our own small radius. We may not know what—if anything, as is highly unlikely—the phenomena *mean,* but we do know what to expect within the circle of our experience. No matter what the constitution of the larger cosmos is, certain occurrences come inevitably & regularly, whilst other alleged occurrences—stories of which were invented in primitive times to explain unknown things now conclusively explained otherwise—can never be shewn to happen.[3]

Smith replied that "Of course, it would seem that the arguments of material science are pretty cogent. Perhaps it is only my innate romanticism that makes me at least hopeful that the Jeans and Einsteins have overlooked something. If ever I have the leisure and opportunity, I intend some first-hand investigation of obscure phenomena. Enough inexplicable things have happened in my own experience to make me wonder."[4] Confronted with Lovecraft's "thoroughly modern disdain" for the otherworldly, one wonders if Ralibar Vooz doesn't represent Smith's true rebuttal.

The *Black Book* contains a plot synopsis under the title of "The Geas of Yzduggor." It reads:

> Yzduggor, wizard and hermit of the black Eiglophian Mts., is intruded upon during one of his experiments in evocation by an optimate from Commoriom who has gone forth with certain followers to hunt the alpine monsters known as the Voormis. Yzduggor, exceedingly wroth at the interruption, puts upon the optimate, Vooth Raluorn, a most terrible and ludicrous and demoniacal geas.[5]

The entry following it concerns "The spider-god, Atlach-Nacha, who weaves his webs across a Cimmerian gulf that has no other bridges."[6] Smith incorporated this note into the story as well.

Smith described the story's conception and composition in a letter to Lovecraft: "I am now midway in 'The Seven Geases,' another of the Hyperborean series. The demon of irony wants to have a hand in this yarn; but I am trying to achieve horror in some of the episodes even if not in the tout ensemble."[7] Its completion presented Smith with a dilemma: "Tsathoggua alone knows what I can do with it. Bates, who liked 'The Door to Saturn' so well, would have grabbed it in all likelihood; but I don't believe that the other fantasy editors have any sense of humour. It seems hard to think that the new *Astounding* editors could have: one of them, I understand, has just graduated from the editing of love story and confession magazines!"[8] (Smith did not mention *Weird Tales* as a possibility, doubtless due to the succession of rejections documented in earlier notes.) *Astounding Stories* held on to the story for a month before finally rejecting it without comment.

Wright also rejected the story, saying that it was "very interesting, especially on account of the dry humour, but lacked plot…. No heroine, no cross-complications, no triumph over obstacles; merely, as W. so wittily puts it, 'one geas after another'."[9] "But damn that ass Pharnabazus for turning down the 'Seven Geases,'" wrote Lovecraft. "This silly worship of artificial 'plot'—an element which I believe to be not only unnecessary but even intrinsically inartistic—certainly gets me seeing red."[10] Wright followed his by now familiar pattern: a month later he wrote that:

> I submitted the word 'geas' to Dr. Frank H. Vizetelly, editor-in-chief of the Standard Dictionary, and got the following reply: "The Celtic or Gaelic term *geas* is to be found in Gaelic dictionaries with the meaning 'charm, sorcery, enchantment,' and with the subordinate meaning 'oath and adjuration or religious vow.' In the latter senses it is used in expressions that translated would become 'I solemnly charge you.' Of the two Gaelic dictionaries on the Lexiconographer's shelves, only one shows the formation of plurals, and gives the plural of *geas* as *geasan*. The word is entirely Celtic, and until modern times has not appeared in the works of English writers."

I think I would like another look at "The Seven Geases," if you have not already placed it elsewhere.[11]

Smith received only seventy dollars for the story instead of the seventy-five dollars it should have received at the standard rate of one cent a word he usually received from *Weird Tales*, which did nothing to ease his increasing frustrations with editors.[12] Wright also used a drawing of Tsathoggua that Smith had shown him as an illustration when the story appeared in the October 1934 issue. He told Robert Barlow that "I am rather partial to ['The Seven Geases'] myself. These grotesque and elaborate ironies come all too naturally to me."[13] It was included in *LW* and *RA*. The current text is based upon a carbon copy of the original typescript deposited at JHL.

CAS refers to "the antehuman sorcerer Haon-Dor" in the story. This character first appeared in an uncompleted story called "The House of Haon-Dor" that Smith had started in June or July 1933 but then set aside. A synopsis appears in the *Black Book* (item 18) and the unfinished story was included in *SS*. A contemporary story of black magic, "The House of Haon-Dor" has little relationship to "The Seven Geases."

An event occurred during the writing of "The Seven Geases" that would have enormous repercussions for Smith and his parents. Sometime early in October 1933, Mary Frances "Fanny" Gaylord Smith, CAS's mother, accidentally knocked over a pot of hot tea and badly scalded her foot, and "this unfortunate accident has thrown another monkey wrench into my literary programme. I am doctor, nurse, chief dish-washer and god knows what."[14]

1. HPL, letter to CAS, October 3, 1933 (ms, JHL).
2. CAS, letter to HPL, c. late September 1933 (*LL* 41).
3. HPL, letter to CAS, October 22, 1933 (AHT).
4. CAS, letter to HPL, c. early November 1933 (*SL* 236).
5. *BB* item 33. Item 20 is also obviously germane: "Geas (pronounced gesh or gass) a Celtic tabu, or compulsion or injunction laid on a person in some such form as 'I place you under heavy geas, to do so and so.' —Celtic plural, *geases*." Smith came across the word in James Branch Cabell's novel *Figures of Earth* (see letter to RHB, October 25, 1933 [*SL* 233]).
6. *BB* item 33a.
7. CAS, letter to HPL, c. late September 1933 (*SL* 226).
8. CAS, letter to AWD, October 4, 1933 (ms, SHSW).
9. CAS, letter to AWD, November 17, 1933 (ms, SHSW).
10. HPL, letter to CAS, November 29, 1933 (ms, JHL).
11. FW, letter to CAS, December 1, 1933 (ms, JHL).
12. CAS, letter to AWD, December 31, 1933 (ms, SHSW).
13. CAS, letter to RHB, December 30, 1933 (ms, JHL).
14. CAS, letter to RHB, October 25, 1933 (*SL* 234).

THE CHAIN OF AFORGOMON

Although Clark Ashton Smith began "The Chain of Aforgomon" in April 1933, he did not complete the story until sometime early in 1934. The synopsis for the tale in the *Black Book*, which was originally to be called "The Curse of the Time-God," reads:

> John Millwarp, novelist, is found dead in his room under circumstances of shocking and inexplicable mystery. His body, beneath the unmarked clothing, is charred in concentric circles, as if by rings of fire, and a strange symbol is clearly branded on his forehead. His literary executor, taking charge of his manuscripts, finds among them a sort of diary, in which Millwarp tells of his growing addiction to a rare drug, which had caused him to remember scenes from former lives, and had finally revived the recollection of an avatar in a world that had antedated the earth. In this life, Millwarp had been the high priest of the Time-God, Aforgonis, and through his love for a dead woman, and his use of a temporal necromancy, had committed blasphemy against the logic of the god. He is punished with fiery tortures by his fellow-priests, and is doomed by Aforgonis to remember, at some far date of the future in another world, the circumstances of his offense, and to perish through the memory of the tortures.[1]

His description of its composition in a letter to Derleth gives some idea as to why the story was so difficult to complete:

> I have nearly finished the long-deferred "Chain of Aforgomon"—a most infernal chore, since the original inspiration seems to have gone cold, leaving the tale immalleable as chilled iron. Anyway, it is a devilishly hard yarn to write: the problem being to create any illusion of reality in an episode that occurs like a dream within a dream. Through the use of a rare Oriental drug, the hero remembers a former life, in a world antedating the earth, when he had been a priest of the time-god Aforgomon. After the death of his sweet-heart, he had committed a weird temporal necromancy by evoking, with all its circumstances, *one hour* of the preceding autumn when he and his love had been happy together. This *repetition* of a past hour was enough to set incalculable disorder in all the workings of the cosmos henceforward; and it constituted blasphemy against the sacred logic of time, which was a cult in this world. The remainder of the tale deals with the strange doom, involving the entire sequence of his future lives, which the priest brought upon himself by this necromancy. You will realize the difficulty of treatment.[2]

Smith's diminishing inspiration may be tracked not only to his ongoing frustrations with editorial capriciousness, but also to sheer physical exhaustion: his mother, Mary Frances "Fanny" Gaylord Smith, was severely injured when she upset a pot of tea on her foot and scalded it that October, which required Smith to take over as caregiver for her and his father, whose health was never that robust to begin with. He announced that it was finished on January 21, 1934 "after nearly finishing me," but he had "little hope that Wright will buy it."[3] Wright did reject it, complaining that the story sagged toward the end; Smith proffered to Derleth that "Personally, I'd say that the sagging, if there is much, occurs in the middle."[4] Wright did accept it after some revision, and it was published in the December 1935 issue.

The theme of reincarnation, and the image of a chain of incarnations stretching into infinity, occurs early in Smith's work. In "The Star-Treader" (1912) we find these lines:

> Through years reversed and lit again
> I followed that unending chain
> Wherein the suns are links of light;
> Retraced through lineal, ordered spheres
> The twisting of the threads of years
> In weavings wrought of noon and night;
> Through stars and deeps I watched the dream unroll,
> Those folds that form the raiment of the soul.[4]

The circumstances of John Milwarp's death recall the death of Smith's associate, Boutwell Dunlap (1877–1930), who died suddenly under murky circumstances in his rooms at the Graystone Hotel in San Francisco on December 22, 1930.[5] Dunlap was an attorney and historian who helped promote Smith's first book in 1912. Since Dunlap had attempted to hog all the credit for Smith's discovery, earning a rebuke from no less than Ambrose Bierce himself, Smith may not have been too well disposed toward Dunlap.[6]

Stefan Dziemianowicz has pointed out that the plot of "The Chain of Aforgomon" is similar to that of Universal Pictures' 1931 film *The Mummy* (dir. Karl Freund, starring Boris Karloff). According to a March 15, 1933 letter to Robert H. Barlow, Smith missed seeing *The Mummy* when it came to Auburn.[7]

When Smith included "The Chain of Aforgomon" in his first Arkham House collection, *OST*, he received a nice fan letter from Hannes Bok, the well-regarded artist and pulp illustrator who drew the dust jacket. Bok singled out the story for special praise, writing that "I think that THE CHAIN OF AFORGOMON is one of the most terrific things I've ever read. Most stories of 'unspeakable' blasphemies leave me cold, but here was a blasphemy which somehow convinced me. Yipes!"[8] The story was also included in *RA*.

The current text is based upon a carbon copy at JHL.

1. *BB* item 17.
2. CAS, letter to AWD, January 10, 1934 (ms, SHSW).
3. CAS, letter to AWD, January 21, 1934 (ms, SHSW).
4. CAS, "The Star-Treader." In *The Abyss Triumphant: The Complete Poetry and Translations Volume I*. Ed. S. T. Joshi and David E. Schultz (New York: Hippocampus Press, 2008): p. 71.
5. See "Boutwell Dunlap, Noted California Historian, Dies," *San Francisco Examiner* (December 23, 1930): 1; "Boutwell Dunlap Services Monday," *Auburn Journal* (January 1, 1931): 1.
6. See Scott Connors, "Who Discovered Clark Ashton Smith?" *Lost Worlds* No. 1 (2004): 25–34.
7. CAS, letter to RHB, March 15, 1933 (ms, JHL).
8. Hannes Bok, letter to CAS, undated but sent with AWD's letter dated August 13, 1942 (ms, JHL).

THE PRIMAL CITY

H. P. Lovecraft had described several of his recent dreams to Clark Ashton Smith, which drew forth the following account:

> My own recent dreams have been pretty tame; but in the past I have had some that were memorable. One that comes to mind was fraught with all the supernatural horror of antique myth: I was standing somewhere on a bleak, terrible plain, while past me and over me, with appalling demonic speed and paces and voices of thunder, there swept a vast array of cloudy, titanic Shapes. One of these, as it went by, pealed out the sonorous words "Eiton euclarion", which I somehow took to be the name of the cloudy entity or one of its fellows.[1]

(Smith was later to clarify that he was still a boy when he had this dream.)[2]
In his return letter Lovecraft wrote that "Your unusual dreams are tremendously interesting, & much fuller of genuine, unhackneyed strangeness than any of mine. *Eiton euclarion!* Of what festering horror in space-time's makeup have you had a veiled intimation?"[3] Smith jotted down a story idea that stemmed from this dream in the *Black Book* under the title "The Cloud-People:" "A remote mountain-region, with lost cities and treasure, deserted by human beings, but guarded by strange clouds that take the forms of men, animals, or demons."[4] The story was underway during the second half of January 1934, and ready for submission to *Weird Tales* by February 5, 1934.[5] At first Smith titled the story "The Cloud-Things," then "The Clouds," and finally "The Primal City." Wright rejected the story as "lacking 'plot'," of which CAS had elsewhere said "Few of

my stories… exhibit what is known in pulpdom as 'plot'."[6] Smith accordingly rewrote the story in March 1934 and resubmitted it, only to meet with rejection yet again. "The nameless spawn of Yub & Yoth!" wrote Lovecraft upon reading Wright's second rejection letter. "No wonder his damn'd magazine never prints anything worth reading except by accident! 'The Clouds' is *magnificent*—one of the most potent and moving things I've read in recent years. A breathless menace hangs over the scene from the first, & the doom—when it comes—is *really adequate*."[7] Lovecraft urged Smith to give the story to *The Fantasy Fan* if Wright did not finally accept it. This never happened, so the story first saw print in the November 1934 issue of Hornig's fanzine, which was appropriately a special "Clark Ashton Smith" issue.

F. Orlin Tremaine was replaced as editor of *Astounding Stories* late in 1938. He edited another science fiction magazine, *Comet Stories*, and Smith sold him a pruned version of "The Primal City" for the December 1940 issue. The copy editor at *Comet Stories* changed Smith's text in a number of places; one particularly egregious example is the change of the line "Their swiftness was that of mountain-sweeping winds" to "Their swiftness was that of powered aircraft." When Smith was assembling *GL*, he did not have a carbon but instead sent to Derleth tear sheets with handwritten corrections. Presented with a choice between the version published in *The Fantasy Fan* or that in *Comet Stories*, he went with the "more concise… and therefore preferable" *Comet Stories* version.[8] Both versions of this story have their strong points. The text included here represents a merger of the two versions that uses the typescript of the original version as a starting point. (Many of his later changes were written in pencil on this typescript.) However, the revisions in parts of the *Comet Stories* version are less poetic and imaginative, leading us to conclude these changes were done to achieve a sale.

1. CAS, letter to HPL, c. mid-October 1933 (*SL* 228).
2. CAS, "Excerpts from *The Black Book*." *The Acolyte* (Spring 1944). In *BB* p. 78.
3. HPL, letter to CAS, October 22, 1933 (AHT).
4. *BB* item 29.
5. See CAS, letter to AWD, January 21, 1934 (ms, SHSW); CAS, letter to AWD, February 5, 1934 (ms, SHSW).
6. CAS, letter to HPL, c. early November 1933 (*SL* 236).
7. Lovecraft's comments are written on Wright's March 23, 1934 letter to Smith (see Roy A. Squires' Catalog 8, item 123).
8. CAS, letter to AWD, February 7, 1947 (ms, SHSW).

XEETHRA

Clark Ashton Smith's heart-wrenching treatment of the Faust theme was completed on March 21, 1934, but like most of his stories the idea came to him much earlier. "The Traveller" (see Appendix 3), one of the prose poems in *Ebony and Crystal*, tells of a poor pilgrim who, when asked what it is he is searching for, replies "forevermore I seek the city and the land of my former home." A story idea may be found in the *Black Book* under that title:

> A young goatherd of Zothique, leading his charges in a wild, mountainous region, who enters an unexplored cave giving on a strange underworld of beautiful, sinister trees laden with strange fruits. This region is an outlying part of the subterrene realms of Thasaidon, and the boy Xeethra is frightened back to the entrance by a glimpse of fearful demoniac entities and monsters that roam through the frightful groves. He steals, however, certain of the fruits, and devours one of them. Afterwards, a madness comes over him, and he imagines that he is no longer Xeethra, but the prince of a great land beyond the mountains. He goes forth to regain his empire, and finds only a desert tract with ruinous cities where outcasts and lepers mock him in his madness. In his despair an emissary of Thasaidon comes to him, and reveals the truth, that the eating of the fruit has awakened in him the memory of a long-past life when he was indeed the ruler of this vanished empire. In return for his sworn fealty to the god of Evil, Xeethra is promised a necromantic revival of all the grandeur of his former incarnation which he shall retain *as long as he decrees it.* He accepts the bond; and, reliving his past life, he forgets the existence as Xeethra and the compact with Thasaidon; and, finding again the ennui and emptiness of power, he wishes himself a simple goat-herd. Thereupon the whole vision vanishes, and he is again the boy Xeethra, lost among lepers and pariahs in a ruined city, and remembers confusedly a strange dream, unable to forget the dream, regretting its lost splendour; a creature half-mad thenceforward, and wholly accursed.[1]

The reader who is familiar with Smith's life cannot help but wonder if Smith was recalling the acclaim he experienced as a youth when the San Francisco newspapers hailed him as the Boy Keats of the Sierras only to see his work fall out of critical favor. Smith was not one to wallow in self pity, but he certainly displayed a rather biting sense of ironic detachment that would have made Ambrose Bierce proud.

Smith fleshed out the above synopsis with additional details:

> The emissary appears before him like a pillar of shadow growing up from the earth into gigantic semi-human form. At the very end this being comes to him again, and Xeethra cries out, saying *take my soul in fulfillment of the bond.* But the emissary tells him mockingly that his soul is already part of the empery of Thasaidon.[2]

These entries in the *Black Book* appear several entries ahead of the one for "The Colossus of Ylourgne," which was completed on May 1, 1932. Smith first mentions the story in correspondence at the end of August 1933, when he mentions that "With the completion of two more tales, 'Xeethra,' and 'The Madness of Chronomage,' I will have a series totalling about 60,000 words, all dealing with the future continent of Zothique."[3] He also used an excerpt from the "Song of Xeethra" as a heading to "The Dark Eidolon," which was completed near the end of 1932.

Smith submitted "Xeethra" to *Weird Tales*, but it "was bowed politely from the palace of Pharnaces [*Farnsworth Wright*]" on the grounds that "it was more of a prose poem than a story," the same complaint that he had made about "The Death of Malygris" and "The Coming of the White Worm." These continued rejections did nothing to boost Smith's confidence in his work: "I'm afraid Wright is more than right in thinking that the casual reader is purblind and even hostile toward literature of a poetic cast. And poetry itself, in this country… has fallen into the hands of a lot of literary gangsters."[4]

Faced with the mounting costs of caring for his ailing parents, combined with the loss of incomes from his mother's magazine sales,[5] selling his stories became more important to Smith than any aesthetic aspirations he may have harbored earlier. As he described it, Smith "did a little topiary work on the verbiage, cutting it down from 8000 to 6800 words, and bringing out some of the 'points' a little more explicitly."[6] Wright accepted this version, paying sixty-eight dollars.[7] "Xeethra" was published in the December 1934 issue of *Weird Tales*, and was collected in *LW* and *RA*.

There are obvious similarities between "Xeethra" and H. P. Lovecraft's story "The Quest of Iranon" (first published in the July/August 1935 issue of *The Galleon*). Smith read the story in manuscript in July 1930.[8] The chief difference between the stories is that Iranon's quest was a fool's folly, and Xeethra found his kingdom and lost it again because of a tragic flaw.

The text of "Xeethra" was first restored by Steve Behrends as part of the *Unexpurgated Clark Ashton Smith* series published by Marc A. Michaud's Necronomicon Press. Like Mr. Behrends, we compared the top copy of the typescript of the first version, which Barlow bound together with several other Smith typescripts and donated to the Bancroft Library of the University of California at Berkeley, with the carbon of the published version among Smith's papers at JHL. We have restored more of the text from the first version that seemed to us to be richer than that of the published version.

1. *BB* item 34.
2. *BB* item 34a.
3. CAS, letter to AWD, August 29, 1933.
4. CAS, letter to AWD, April 4, 1934.
5. Mrs. Smith sold magazine subscriptions door-to-door to help support the fam-

ily. See Violet Heyer, "Letter." In *One Hundred Years of Klarkash-Ton*, Ed. Ronald Hilger (Averon Press, 1996): pp. 20–22.

6. CAS, letter to AWD, June 28, 1934 (ms, SHSW).
7. *WT*, letter to CAS, October 25, 1935 (ms, JHL).
8. See HPL, letter to CAS, July 18, 1930.

THE LAST HIEROGLYPH

Clark Ashton Smith first mentioned "The Last Hieroglyph" in a letter to August Derleth in March 1934:

> I have conceived a whale of a weird notion for a story to be called either The Last Hieroglyph or, In the Book of Agoma. It concerns a strange volume of hieroglyphic writings that belonged to a mysterious archimage. When he wished, he could bring one or more of the hieroglyphs to life in the forms that they represented, and could send them forth to do his bidding. In the story, a certain minor wizard enters the tower in which the book is kept—and is turned into a hieroglyph on the half-finished open page of the great volume.[1]

The first version of this story was completed on April 7, 1934. Farnsworth Wright rejected it "with the usual comment that he had enjoyed it and admired it personally. But he feared the c.r. [*casual reader*] would find it rather meaningless. He must have a bright lot of readers, if that is true." Smith's growing frustration showed itself when he added "Well, if I ever become any crazier than I am and have been, Wright's criticism and rejections will certainly be one of the contributing causes."[2]

Smith revised the story, changing the title to "In the Book of Vergama," and resubmitted it. Wright rejected it a second time, explaining that "Beautiful though many of its passages are, yet there is so little plot, and the motivation seems so inadequate, that I am afraid it would disappoint many of our readers who expect almost perfection itself from you."[3] Looking over the twice-rejected manuscript, CAS allowed that "It is possible that the tale is a little overwrought; and I may, eventually, cut out the portions about the merman and the salamander"[4] and solicited the opinions of Lovecraft and Robert Barlow. However, after completing a third revision, he informed Barlow that "You & Theobaldus [*nickname for HPL*] will be glad to know that I am not curtailing the Vergama story. On the contrary, I have done a longer version, detailing efforts of Nushain to sidestep his guides and evade the destiny that will turn him into a cipher. The guides, ironically, twit him with a lack of faith in his own horoscopic vaticinations! Vergama also waxes sardonic."[5] The third time *did* prove the charm, as Smith wrote to Derleth "Wright took my revision of 'The Last Hieroglyph.' I added about 2000 words to the tale and, I think, improved it considerably."[6]

Smith's correspondents were pleased with the results of all his efforts. Robert E. Howard mentioned that he "very much enjoyed" the story.[7] E. Hoffmann Price told him that it:

> has a strange charm... a certain humanity—I mean, the character and his two attendants have an appealing realness which gives force to the picture. The bungling, guessing astrologer, sometimes charlatan, sometimes (and perhaps coincidentally) giving a good prediction; he's in a way a symbol of all endeavour. And his doom seems rather a fulfillment, not a punishment. For all its outré adornments, the story has a homely, human touch which persistently hold its own.[8]

CAS wrote to Barlow that the story would "form the concluding item of my Zothique series, if this series should ever appear between book-covers."[9]

Wright included "The Last Hieroglyph" in the April 1935 issue of *Weird Tales*. Smith received sixty dollars.[10] It was included in *OST* and *RA*. A carbon copy of the published version from Smith's papers at JHL was used to establish the current text.

One of the first anthologies to mine the rich resources of such pulps as *Weird Tales, Unknown Worlds,* and *Astounding Stories* was *The Other Worlds: 25 Modern Stories of Mystery and Imagination,* edited by Phil Stong (1899–1957), a journalist and novelist who is best known for writing *State Fair,* the basis for the Rodgers and Hammerstein musical of the same name. Stong did not include a story by Smith, but the anthology does contain the following mention of "The Last Hieroglyph": "Clark Ashton Smith is another fantasy writer, a very popular one, who frequently has excellent and original ideas and then casts them into a precious style that does not fit them. Only, his idol is not Poe but Lord Dunsany. Smith's story of the magician [sic] who becomes an item of a cosmic manuscript is excellent, but there are too many Byzantine words."[11] It was undoubtedly Smith's encounters with sentiments such as these that inspired him when he composed two aphorisms that he published in his poetry collection *Spells and Philtres.* The first states that "The modern intolerance toward what is called 'painted speech,' toward 'the grand manner,' springs too often from the instinctive resentment inspired in vulgar minds by all that savors of loftiness, exaltation, nobility, sublimity and aristocracy." The second expresses the realization that "It is a ghastly but tenable proposition that the world is now ruled by the insane, whose increasing plurality will, in a few generations, make probable the incarceration of all sane people born among them."[12]

1. CAS, letter to AWD, March 18, 1934 (ms, SHSW).
2. CAS, letter to AWD, April 17, 1934 (ms, SHSW).
3. FW, letter to CAS, April 25, 1934 (ms, JHL).

4. CAS, letter to RHB, April 30, 1934 (ms, JHL).

5. CAS, letter to RHB, May 18, 1934 (ms, JHL).

6. CAS, letter to AWD, June 4, 1934 (ms, SHSW).

7. Robert E, Howard, letter to CAS, July 23, 1935 (*Collected Letters of Robert E. Howard 1933–1936*, Ed. Rob Roehm [Robert E. Howard Foundation Press, 2008]: p. 366).

8. E. Hoffmann Price, letter to CAS, September 13, 1942 (ms, JHL).

9. CAS, letter to RHB, May 21, 1934 (*SL* 255).

10. *WT*, letter to CAS, March 31, 1936 (ms, JHL).

11. Phil Stong, "Note to Part III," in *The Other Worlds: 25 Modern Stories of Mystery and Imagination* (New York: Garden City Publishing Co., 1941), pp. 330–331.

12. CAS, "Epigrams and Apothegms." *Spells and Philtres* (Sauk City, WI: Arkham House, 1958): pp. 53, 54.

NECROMANCY IN NAAT

As discussed in the preceding note, "The Last Hieroglyph" was intended to be the final story of Zothique. However, Smith's "benign, maleficent daemon" still had tales to tell of the last continent, and the first version of "Necromancy in Naat" was completed on February 6, 1935. Little survives concerning its composition or genesis. CAS told Donald Wandrei that he had "turned out several weirds, including 'The Treader of the Dust,' 'Necromancy in Naat' and 'The Black Abbot of Puthuum.'... The last quarter of Necromancy in Naat, however, will have to be rewritten according to the specifications of the satrap (Damn!!....******)"[1] Wright's letter of rejection apparently has not survived, so the exact nature of his objections are not known, but in a letter dated February 11, 1935 he acknowledges the receipt of a "new last page" for the story "and will get at the reading of that tale within a day or two."[2] Since this occurs *before* Smith's letter telling of its rejection, we can only speculate that either the last page somehow was lost or Smith decided to change the last page and sent it along. CAS spent the period between March 4 and March 25 rewriting the story, according to his notations on the typescript of the original version, and wrote to H. P. Lovecraft that "Naat" was one of several stories recently accepted by Wright.[3] "Necromancy in Naat" appeared in the July 1933 issue of *Weird Tales*, where it was accompanied by another Virgil Finlay illustration, where it tied with Robert E. Howard's "Red Nails" as the most popular story in the issue.[4] Smith was paid seventy-three dollars for the story.[5] Smith included "Necromancy in Naat" in *LW*, and it was later included in *RA*.

Smith wrote to August Derleth that "'Necromancy in Naat' seems the best of my more recently published weirds; though Wright forced me to mutilate the ending."[6] CAS cut the story by thirteen hundred words, eliminating much descriptive material. The biggest change that Smith made was to eliminate suggestions that Yadar and Dalili were proving Andrew Marvell wrong.[7] Thanks to an anonymous private collector who generously provided us with a copy of the original version, we have been able to restore most of these cuts, leaving those changes that we thought Smith made out of choice, not compulsion, most notably the beautiful words with which the story ends.

1. CAS, letter to DAW, February 28, 1935 (*SL* 261).
2. FW, letter to CAS, February 11, 1935 (ms, JHL).
3. CAS, postcard to HPL, April 5, 1935 (ms, private collection).
4. See "The Eyrie," *Weird Tales* (October 1936), p. 384.
5. *WT*, letter to CAS, March 29, 1937 (ms, JHL).
6. CAS, letter to AWD, April 13, 1937 (*CSL* 287).
7. See Marvell's poem "To His Coy Mistress:" "The grave's a fine and private place/ But none, I think, do there embrace."

THE TREADER OF THE DUST

Clark Ashton Smith's story "Xeethra" is prefaced by a quotation from an imaginary book entitled *The Testaments of Carnamagos*. This addition to the library of eldritch tomes stocked by the imaginations of H. P. Lovecraft's circle of writers was first mentioned in Smith's never-completed novel *The Infernal Star*. Smith went into much greater detail concerning the book and its disturbing history in "The Treader of the Dust," which he completed on February 15, 1935. Wright surprised Smith "by taking 'The Treader of the Dust' offhand, without revision or re-submission."[1] In his letter of acceptance, in which he offered Smith thirty dollars for the story, Wright told Smith that "I thought at first, while I was reading the story, that it would have a solution something like that given in 'An Inhabitant of Carcosa' by Ambrose Bierce, but I was all wet in that surmise."[2] "The Treader of the Dust" appeared in the August 1935 issue of *Weird Tales*. Smith included it in *LW*. The text is based upon that of a typescript deposited in Smith's papers at JHL.

1. CAS, letter to DAW, February 28. 1935 (*SL* 261).
2. FW, letter to CAS, February 22, 1935 (ms, JHL).

THE BLACK ABBOT OF PUTHUUM

"The Black Abbot of Puthuum" is one of three stories that Clark Ashton Smith submitted to *Weird Tales* in February 1935, but, like "Necromancy in Naat," it was rejected by editor Farnsworth Wright.[1] The idea for the story, another tale of Zothique, dates back to 1932 or earlier since the story was outlined in the *Black Book* several entries before that for "The Colossus of Ylourgne" (see note for "Xeethra"):

Two guardsmen and a palace-eunuch, bringing a purchased girl to the king of Yoros, find themselves lost among the enchantments of a strange desert. The enchantments lead them to a weird monastery inhabited by twelve black monks all of whom exactly resemble their superior, who is distinguished from them only by his garb. In the night, one of the guardsmen, wakeful and suspicious, steals from the chamber to which he and his fellow have been assigned. Wandering about the monastery, he stumbles on an altar to the dark demon, Thasaidon, and apprehends that the monks are devil-worshippers. Upon the altar are charred fragments of flesh and bone. Stealing back toward his room, the guardsman hears an outcry from the room where the girl sleeps, guarded by the eunuch. Rushing in, he meets the fleeing eunuch, whose eyes are wide with terror... In the gloom, above the girl's bed, he sees a vague monstrous incubus about to settle upon her. The thing seems to float on black voluminous wings. He attacks it with his sword, and the incubus resolves itself into the black abbot. Then the figure seems to multiply before his eyes and the chamber is suddenly filled with the monks, who drag down the guardsman. His companion, who is an archer, enters at this moment and shoots at the abbot (standing apart from the melee) an arrows [sic] that had been dipped in the mummia of a saint, and was therefore fatal to sorcerers or demons. It is his last arrow, the others having been discharged at desert phantoms. It slays the abbot and the twelve monks vanish. The abbot's body decays immediately, in a non-human fashion, and its long finger-nails slough away from the putrefying mass. One of the guardsmen puts the nails into his helmet, and he and his fellow draw lots for the girl. (The eunuch's throat had been ripped open by the abbot.)[2]

While writing the story Smith added a comic subplot that revealed how the girl, Rubalsa, had been stolen at birth by the nomads, and included another character who turned out to be her father. She is identified by an amulet that was hanging around her neck when a baby (Smith anticipates "the great god Awto" by having the amulet bear the image of "Yuckla, patron of mirth and laughter"). When he revised the story for resubmission to Wright, he eliminated these elements, which cut approximately fifteen hundred words. Wright accepted the story.[3] Smith received seventy-eight dollars for the story after it appeared in *Weird Tales*' March 1936 issue.[4] At that time H. P. Lovecraft wrote to Smith that the story was "tremendously fascinating—full of a malign sense of hidden horror & aeon-old charnel secrets. I doubt if anything else in the issue can approach it."[5] (Lovecraft had only read Smith's story when he wrote that, as that issue contained the first appearance of Henry Kuttner's "The Graveyard Rats" as well as the penultimate installment of Robert E. Howard's Conan novel *The Hour of the Dragon*.) Smith included the story in *GL*.

It is the opinion of the editors that Smith was correct in eliminating the romantic subplot. It noticeably detracted from the atmosphere and suspense and did not contribute to the tale's unity of effect. The excised material is included in Appendix 4.

1. CAS, letter to DAW, February 28, 1935 (*SL* 262).
2. *BB* item 47.
3. The original version of "The Black Abbot of Puthuum" was given by Smith to R. H. Barlow. It eventually came into the possession of Smith friend and book seller Roy A. Squires. Terence A. McVicker published this version as an exquisitely printed chapbook in 2007.
4. *WT*, letter to CAS, February 25, 1937 (ms, JHL).
5. HPL, letter to CAS, March 23, 1936 (ms, JHL).

THE DEATH OF ILALOTHA

This story, which Smith called a "somewhat poisonous little horror,"[1] was completed on February 22, 1937. He promptly submitted it to *Weird Tales*, but Farnsworth Wright returned it for possible revision, stating that "I like 'The Death of Ilalotha,' and I like the language in which it is clothed. But, unfortunately, there is no story here; for the singularly gruesome ending does not tie in or connect with anything in the story; and the reader is given no hint as to who—or what—it was that had whispered in his ear, making the assignation. Such are my reactions to it."[2] Smith completed the revisions on March 16, 1937, and Wright accepted it upon resubmission, offering forty dollars.[3] "The Death of Ilalotha" was the most popular story in the September 1937 issue of *Weird Tales*, where it was complemented by one of Virgil Finlay's illustrations. When that issue appeared, Smith derived some amusement from a brush with the censors: "I seem to have slipped something over on the PTA. The issue containing ['The Death of Ilalotha'], I hear, was removed from the stands in Philadelphia because of the Brundage cover" [*which depicted a scene from Seabury Quinn's "Satan's Palimpsest"*].[4]

Smith offered Barlow an insight into his state of mind in another letter discussing the story:

Ilalotha is quite good, I believe, especially in style and atmosphere. It is unusually poisonous and exotic. Writing is hard for me, since circumstances here are dolorous and terrible. Improvement in my father's condition is more than unlikely, and I am more isolated than ever. Also, I seem to have what psychologists call a "disgust mechanism" to contend with: a disgust at the ineffable stupidity of editors and readers.[5]

"The Death of Ilalotha" was included in *OST*, apparently at the suggestion of Derleth, and in *RA*. In establishing our current text we consulted two typescripts in the Smith Papers at JHL, a complete carbon of the published version and an incomplete copy of the original version.

1. CAS, letter to AWD, April 6, 1937 (ms, SHSW).
2. FW, letter to CAS, March 8, 1937 (ms, JHL).
3. FW, letter to CAS, March 24, 1937 (ms, JHL).
4. CAS, letter to RHB, September 9, 1937 (*SL* 313).
5. CAS, letter to RHB, May 16, 1937 (*SL* 302).

MOTHER OF TOADS

Just four days after completing the revision of "The Death of Ilalotha," Clark Ashton Smith finished another story that he had begun almost two years earlier. Early in June, 1935, Smith told R. H. Barlow in a letter that "I have started a new Averoigne story, 'Mother of Toads,' which, I fear, will be too naughty for the chaste pages of W.T." E. Hoffmann Price had been regularly selling stories to *Spicy Mystery Stories*, and after looking over a few issues Smith thought that he had gauged its editorial requirements: "This mag wants a combination of the lewd and the ghastly." Smith did not think much of the magazine's contents, but comforted himself with the rationalization that "after all, the genre is classic (vide Balzac's 'The Succubus') and should have possibilities."[1]

The rejection of the story by its intended market fed Smith's growing uncertainties about the writing of fiction:

> "Mother of Toads" is a sort of carnal and erotic nightmare and I can't decide on its merits. *Spicy Mystery Stories* rejected it after holding the ms. for nearly two months. I have now shipped it to *Esquire*, which, judging from the two issues I have read, will sometimes print stuff that would hardly make the grade with an honest pulp.... The magazine seems aimed at a rather naive class of readers who like to feel that they are wicked and sophisticated. I believe that a yarn like "Mother of Toads" would arouse considerable Sound and Fury if printed in that quaint periodical.[2]

But although *Esquire*'s editor seemed "to have considered ['Mother of Toads'] rather favourably, and at least admitted that it was 'well-done'," Smith confronted the reality that *Weird Tales*, despite all of Wright's apparent capriciousness, remained his only real market. Smith set about "gelding" the story, adding bitterly "With certain details omitted or left to the readers' chaste imagination, Wright will no doubt use the yarn as a W.T. filler, and will pay me 25 or 26 pazoors for it some five or six months after publication."[3] Wright did indeed accept this bowdlerized text at the end of July,[4] and it was published in the July 1938 issue. When informing Barlow of the story's acceptance, Smith volunteered that "the tale remains a passable weird, with a sufficiently horrific ending, in which the hero is smothered to death by an army of diabolic toads after which he had refused the second dose of aphrodisiac offered him by the witch, La Mère des Crapauds."[5] It was this version of "Mother of Toads" that was collected in *TSS*.

In order to increase the chances of the story's acceptance by Wright, Smith cut about three hundred words from the story consisting mostly of the more highly charged erotic descriptions. These were restored by consulting and comparing the following typescripts at JHL: Smith's first version (original copy dated March 20, 1937, and the carbon); a complete carbon copy of the published version; and a working text that Smith used to work out the changes. "Mother of Toads" was part of Necronomicon Press' *Unexpurgated Clark Ashton Smith* series, and we acknowledge Steve Behrends' pioneering work on this story; however, we have made some different choices than did Mr. Behrends.

1. CAS, letter to RHB, c. June 1935 (ms, JHL).
2. CAS, letter to RHB, May 16, 1937 (*SL* 301–302).
3. CAS, letter to AWD, June 14, 1937 (ms, SHSW).
4. CAS, letter to AWD, August 1, 1937 (ms, SHSW).
5. CAS, letter to RHW, September 9, 1937 (*SL* 312).

The Garden of Adompha

"I am working on a new weird, 'The Garden of Adompha' which is damnably hard and laborious," Clark Ashton Smith wrote in a letter to August Derleth during the summer of 1937. Smith continued with an ominously prophetic observation: "I don't mind hard work, if the results are satisfactory; but when they aren't, it is certainly discouraging. No doubt most of the trouble is due to the fact that I am below par physically, and suffer from a sense of chronic fatigue."[1] Smith completed the story on July 31, 1937, but his production of short stories, which stood at *none* for 1936 and only three for 1937, was about to stall once again, although he would continue to revise old stories and plot new ones. CAS wrote to Robert H. Barlow that he had sold "'The Garden of Adompha,' a tale which I am inclined to like" to *Weird Tales*, and that Farnsworth Wright "spoke of a possible cover-design by Finlay to go with the story."[2] Smith received thirty-seven dollars for the story.[3] It was published in the April 1938 issue of *Weird Tales*, complete with a cover by Finlay, and was voted the most popular story in that issue by the readers. It was included in both *GL* and *RA*. The current text is based upon a carbon copy at the John Hay Library.

1. CAS, letter to AWD, July 20, 1937 (ms, SHSW).
2. CAS, letter to RHB, September 9, 1937 (*SL* 312).
3. FW, letter to CAS, August 10, 1937 (ms, private collection).

THE GREAT GOD AWTO

Clark Ashton Smith was not fond of modern technology. For most of his life he lived without electricity or indoor plumbing, let alone a telephone, a radio, or an automobile. He harbored a strong dislike of the last listed invention. Consider the following excerpts from his letters:

> I have not heard that the Indians were responsible for the fire; but I did talk with eyewitnesses who saw it start from a lighted cigarette that was tossed into the wayside grain by a passing auto, in which were four boys (unfortunately, not identified).... Crackers were popping merrily in Auburn all day and all night on the Fourth, and also on Sunday. And when I went in Sunday evening, the streets were a torrent of autos. After what I had been through, the reckless idiocy of the merry-making public simply made me boil. I fear that such conditions, and all their accompanying hazards, are going to get worse instead of better.[1]
>
> So Sultan Malik [*E. Hoffmann Price*] has gone into the garage business! Shades of the Silver Peacock and the Hashishins! Well, perhaps he is displaying a modicum of wisdom at that. No matter how serious the depression becomes, the U.S. population will go on running its chariots till the last tire blows out and the ultimate half-pint of gas is exhausted.[2]

And speaking of the Peacock Sultan, Lovecraft referred to E. Hoffmann Price's 1928 Model "A" Ford as "Great Juggernaut." It is apparent that "The Great God Awto" is an in-joke to a considerable extent, but one in which Smith's sardonic and biting humor runs loose like a—, well, like a juggernaut. The story probably dates from the summer of 1937, when CAS wrote that "I have some science fiction (satire) under way at present; but confess that I don't find it very congenial."[4] "The Great God Awto" was collected posthumously in *TSS*. The only surviving typescript among Smith's papers at the John Hay Library was prepared by his wife, Carol, sometime during the 1950s, so the current text was taken from the February 1940 issue of *Thrilling Wonder Stories*.

1. CAS, letter to Genevieve K. Sully, July 9, 1931 (*SL* 155–157).

2. CAS, letter to HPL, c. late February-early March 1934 (*SL* 252).

3. See E. Hoffmann Price, *Book of the Dead. Friends of Yesteryear: Fictioneers & Others (Memories of the Pulp Era)*. Ed. Peter Ruber (Sauk City, WI: Arkham House, 2001): p. 53.

4. CAS, letter to AWD, September 8, 1937 (ms, SHSW).

Strange Shadows

After reading this story it would appear that Clark Ashton Smith was trying to write a story that would be acceptable to John W. Campbell and *Unknown*, but it is not known if any of the three known versions were ever submitted anywhere.[1] Three versions of the story exist, the third of which (with the variant title of "I Am Your Shadow") is incomplete. We present version two, the latest complete version of the story available. The conclusion of "I Am Your Shadow," along with the complete text of version one, may be found in Appendix 5.

1. This would seem to be the case from a letter Smith wrote to Derleth dated November 23, 1941 (ms, SHSW) that states "I am finding it easier to work now and have the ending of a tale (suitable, I think, for *Unknown Worlds*) which has baffled me for close to 18 months." Its position on Smith's log of completed stories would not invalidate this, as Smith would sometimes list a tale in the order it was started, not finished.

The Enchantress of Sylaire

Very little information is available concerning the writing of this story, Clark Ashton Smith's final tale of Averoigne, which saw print in the July 1941 issue of *Weird Tales*. It does not appear in the table of contents for a proposed collection that Smith entitled *Averoigne Chronicles*, although a story with the similar title of "The Sorceress of Averoigne" does appear.[1] An outline for a story with this title, which Steve Behrends dates to October 1930, exists, but it bears little resemblance to the current story outside of the use of a mirror for divination.[2] "The Enchantress of Sylaire" appears to have been written between the summer of 1938 and Farnsworth Wright's firing as editor of *Weird Tales* in February 1940, since Smith mentions that *WT* had two of his stories in its stock of forthcoming stories (see note for "The Coming of the White Worm").[3] The text of the story's appearance in the July 1941 issue of *WT* was consulted, along with its appearance in *AY*.

1. *BB* item 60.

2. *SS* pp. 144–146.

3. CAS, letter to Margaret and Ray St. Clair, February 22, 1940 (*SL* 328).

DOUBLE COSMOS

Although Clark Ashton Smith did not complete "Double Cosmos" until March 25, 1940, he had worked on it at intervals for several years. Back in 1934, when Smith still harbored hopes that *Astounding Stories* might yet become a regular market for his stories, he received a tip about one of Assistant Editor Desmond Hall's pet subjects from August Derleth: "Thanks for the tip about Desmond Hall's medical prepossessions. I am preparing a yarn with a semi-medical interest, dealing with a chemist who invents a strange, terrific drug that enables him to see the reality of the cosmos in toto. The revelation is rather staggering.... 'Secondary Cosmos' is the title: our universe proving but a sort of vestigial appendage of the real world, overlapping into a subsidiary space."[1] Smith apparently drew upon the following entries in his *Black Book*. He called the first one "The Rift:" "A man who sees, following a brain-operation, a rift in the material world through which mysterious beings pass in enigmatic traffic. The rift is visible wherever he goes, as a sort of charm, in streets, buildings, fields, etc." The entry immediately following "The Rift" is even more relevant: "A scientist who, investigating the so-called 4th dimension, discovers that he himself is merely a sort of organ or extension of a being that fruitions in this other world. He is, so to speak, a rather useless vestigial tail or appendix and, at a certain stage in the being's evolution, this organ is to be discarded; this act of shedding entails the death of the investigator." With Smith's typical misanthropy, the title of this one was "The Appendix."[2]

The story was set aside for three years. Smith described his current literary program in another letter to Derleth: "I am trying to finish a science fiction story, Secondary Cosmos, which I began two years ago; and may also add a third tale, The Rebirth of the Flame, to my Singing Flame stories. Other tales, begun and thoroughly plotted, are The Alkahest, and Sharia: a Tale of the Lost Planet. The last-named has great possibilities, I feel. Recent revisions include The Maze of the Enchanter, which I have pruned by more than a thousand words for re-submission to Esquire and W.T."[3]

Smith didn't do much with the story after its completion. He admitted that "None of the present fantasy markets (*Unknown* is the best, I guess) appeal to me greatly...."[4] He later told Derleth that he had given the story to agent Julius Schwartz Jr. to sell, but did not know the story's status.[5] "Double Cosmos" remained unpublished until it was published in Robert M. Price's fanzine *Crypt of Cthulhu* in 1983. It was included in *SS*.

1. CAS, letter to AWD, June 28, 1934 (ms, SHSW).
2. *BB* items 37 and 38.

3. CAS, letter to AWD, August 1, 1937 (ms, SHSW).
4. CAS, letter to Margaret and Ray St. Clair, April 21, 1940 (*SL* 330).
5. CAS, letter to AWD, November 6, 1948 (ms, SHSW).

NEMESIS OF THE UNFINISHED

This is the only instance where Clark Ashton Smith actually collaborated on a story.[1] Don Carter was the husband of Natalie Carter, whose portrait of Smith appears on the back panel of the dust jacket of Smith's *Selected Poems* (1971). The Carters lived in Bowman, California, a small community located just outside of Auburn, and were part of a small network of friends that helped Smith with gifts of clothing and food and the occasional odd job when he needed to earn some cash. "Nemesis of the Unfinished" was apparently written while Smith was recuperating at home from a broken ankle. An outline of the story under the present title (uncredited, but the handwriting is similar to that in known specimens of Carter's handwriting) was found among Smith's papers, so it appears that the basic idea of the story occurred to Carter (undoubtedly inspired by the boxes of papers kept at Smith's cabin).[2] Two different versions of this story exist (an early draft of the first version is dated July 30, 1947). The first version is complete, but the second version, which incorporates significant deviation from Carter's proposed plot, appears to be missing the last page. This version is included in Appendix 6.

1. "Seedling of Mars" was written from a plot provided by the winner of one of Hugo Gernsback's magazine contests, while in the case of "The House of the Monoceros" and "Dawn of Discord" Smith gave completed stories to E. Hoffmann Price with instructions to do with them what he wanted; neither case involved the active interaction of two creative minds.
2. For Carter's outline, see *SS* 40–43, 273–275.

THE MASTER OF THE CRABS

Weird Tales celebrated its twenty-fifth anniversary with its March 1948 issue. In preparation for this, Associate Editor Lamont Buchanan invited Smith to contribute a new story in May 1947.[1] The idea for "The Master of the Crabs" may be found in the *Black Book*:

> A wizard whose legs are trapped by falling rock in a sea-cavern. By hypnotic will-power, he gains control of an army of crabs, and forces them to overpower ship-wrecked seamen and feed him with shreds of flesh torn from their bodies. Tale to be told by one of the mariners, whose companions have disappeared mysteriously. Locale: desert isle. Wizard had perhaps gone there in quest of lost treasure.

Possesses own eternal longevity. Crabs turn on and devour him when he loses his mesmeric power.[2]

This entry predates the story entry for "The Colossus of Ylourgne," which was completed on May 1, 1932, so this story had a long gestation period. Smith wrote out a full outline of this story, which he called at first "The Crabs of Iribos."[3] (Smith may have been reminded of this story when he broke his ankle and was hospitalized for a time during that summer.) *WT* Editor Dorothy McIlwraith accepted the story that October and paid Smith forty-seven dollars.[4] It appeared in the anniversary issue accompanied by a gruesome drawing by Lee Brown Coye. Smith included the story in *AY*.

It was through "The Master of the Crabs" that Smith made a minor but real impact on modern pagan religions. Smith refers to an *arthame* in the story, which is a type of dagger used by ceremonial magicians. He picked this word up from his copy of Grillot de Givry's 1931 treatise *Witchcraft, Magic and Alchemy*. Gerald Gardner (1884–1964), the Englishman who helped bring the Wiccan religion into the public realm, apparently read the issue of *Weird Tales* containing this story while he was visiting America and picked up the word, which he inexplicably spelled as *athame*. According to Ronald Hutton, "There is no evidence to explain Gardner's omission of the 'r' in the word; perhaps he first heard it orally and guessed at the spelling, perhaps he decided to simplify it, or perhaps the error was in a source he was copying."[5] The surviving manuscript of "The Master of the Crabs" was severely scorched in the fire that destroyed Smith's cabin in September 1957. The text from *WT* was collated with the surviving fragments.

1. Lamont Buchanan, letter to CAS, May 7, 1947 (ms, JHL).
2. *BB* item 42.
3. This outline is too long to be included here, but it may be found in *SS* 148–150.
4. See Dorothy McIlwraith, letters to CAS, October 3, 1947 and October 31, 1947 (ms, JHL).
5. Ronald Hutton, *The Triumph of the Moon: A History of Modern Pagan Witchcraft* (Oxford University Press, 1999): p. 230.

MORTHYLLA

Smith had one of his increasingly infrequent bursts of productivity in the autumn of 1953, completing two stories in the later part of September and beginning a third. One of these was "Morthylla", "a tale of Zothique, concerning a pseudo-lamia who was really a normal woman trying to please the tastes of her eccentric poet-lover."[1] Smith had worked out its plot in the *Black Book*:

Valzain, the young voluptuary, weary of feasting and debauchery leaves the house of a friend when the revels are at their height, and wanders forth from Umbri, city of the Delta, to an old necropolis on a mound-like hill half-way between Umbri and Psiom, the twin city. Here, in the moonlight, he meets a beautiful being who calls herself Morthizza, lamia and spirit of the tombs. Half-believing, half-disbelieving, in his weariness of mortality and of fleshly things, he falls in love with her. They meet night after night. His desires begin to revive, but she tantalizes him, refusing corporeal contact. One night, as playful proof that she is a vampire, Morthylla wounds him in the throat with her teeth, saying that this is the only kiss permitted between them. But, as proof of her love, she will not suck his blood. Valzain pleads for a further consummation. Wistfully, she tells him that he must know and love her as she really is before such a consummation would be possible. A day or two later Valzain, visiting the twin city Psiom, sees a woman in the street who has the very features of Morthylla. A friend tells him that she is Beldith, a woman of pleasure, who lately has been absenting herself from the orgies of Psiom, and has been seen going forth at night toward the old necropolis that was once common to both of the cities of the Delta. Valzain, disillusioned, realizes that she is identical with Morthylla, and that she has been playing a game with him. He seeks her out and taxes her with the deception, which she readily admits, at the same time asking if he cannot love her as a mortal woman, since she, all the time, had loved him as a man. Valzain, fearful of the revulsion of the flesh which, for him, has ensued from every carnal contact, tells her sorrowfully of his disenchantment, and without reproaches, bids her farewell. Later, unable to bear the tedium of existence, he commits suicide, stabbing himself in the throat with a sharp poignard at the same spot were Morthylla's teeth had wounded him. After death, he finds himself at that point in time where he had first met Morthylla among the tombs, and the illusion begins to repeat itself for him, presumably with no danger of an awakening. The woman Beldith grows old and grey among the revelries of Psiom; but her intimates note that she seems often absent-minded between the wine-cups; and her young lovers sometimes complain that she is distrait and unresponsive in their arms.[2]

A poetic couplet that was entered a few entries before the above-quoted entry would appear in hindsight to have provided the germ of this idea:

For in your voice are voices from beyond the tomb.

And in your face a shadow risen from vast vaults.[3]

The Relationship of Valzain and Famurza resembles that of CAS and his mentor, George Sterling.

Weird Tales snatched this story up and published it in the May 1953 issue.

The magazine would soon be reduced to digest size and would cease publication in little over a year. Smith included the story in *TSS*. Only a couple of pages of the typescript for "Morthylla" survive among Smith's papers at JHL; most of the typescript perished in the September 1957 fire that destroyed Smith's cabin.

1. CAS, letter to L. Sprague de Camp, October 21, 1952 (*SL* 371 [misdated 1953 in this appearance]).
2. *BB* item 99.
3. *BB* item 94.

SCHIZOID CREATOR

Psychoanalysis and psychiatrists were not subjects near to Clark Ashton Smith's heart. In his 1934 essay "On Fantasy" he listed "Freudianism" as one of the chief forces working against the imagination in modern life[1], and in a 1949 symposium on science fiction he offered the quip "Sometimes I suspect that Freud should be included among the modern masters of science fiction!"[2] One of his epigrams states that "One can postulate anything, and people will accept it as religion, philosophy—or psychoanalysis."[3]

Smith gave full vent to his contempt for Freud's minions in one of two stories he wrote early in the autumn of 1952, "Schizoid Creator." As he described the tale to L. Sprague de Camp, it was "a fantastic satire that mixes black magic with psychiatric shock-treatment (the patient being a demon!)."[4] The "black magic" to which Smith refers is the use of the names of God to compel entities both demonic and divine to do the sayer's will. Two consecutive items in Smith's *Black Book* illuminate this further:

> According to Jewish tradition, when Lilith refused to yield obedience to Adam, she uttered the Shemhamphorash, the ineffable name of Jehovah, and, by virtue of this, instantly flew away. This utterance gave her such power that even Jehovah could not coerce her.
>
> According to widespread belief, the gods have kept their true names secret but other gods, or even men, should be able to conjure with them. To the Mohammedan, Allah is but an epithet in place of the Most Great Name; and the secret of the latter is committed to prophets and apostles alone. Those who know the Most Great Name can, by pronouncing it, transport themselves from place to place at will, can kill the living, raise the dead to life, and work other miracles.[5]

Smith refers to "Shem-hamphorash, the nameless name," in his last poem, "Cycles."[6]

The image of Satan caressing a flayed girl is a homage to his mentor,

George Sterling. In his poem "A Wine of Wizardry" Sterling included the following lines:

> But Fancy still is fugitive, and turns
> To caverns where a demon altar burns,
> And Satan, yawning on his brazen seat,
> Fondles a screaming thing his fiends have flayed,
> Ere Lilith come his indolence to greet,
> Who leads from hell his whitest queens, arrayed
> In chains so heated at their master's fire
> That one new-damned had thought their bright attire
> Indeed were coral, till the dazzling dance
> So terribly that brilliance shall enhance.[7]

Smith submitted the story to *Fantasy Fiction*, a digest-sized competitor of *Weird Tales* that emulated the model of *Unknown Worlds*, where it appeared in the November 1953 issue. Only burned fragments survive of the typescript for this story, and what parts can still be read would seem to indicate that it was an earlier draft—there are differences in the published text, but the differences are cruder and less polished than what finally appeared. The current text is based upon the *Fantasy Fiction* text.

1. *PD* 38: "In short, all pipe-dreams, all fantasies not authorized by Freudianism, by sociology, and by the five senses, are due for the critical horse-laugh...."
2. CAS, letter to AWD, February 11, 1949 (*SL* 358).
3. CAS, *The Devil's Notebook*. Ed. Donald Sidney-Fryer and Don Herron (Mercer Island, WA: Starmont House, 1990): p. 71.
4. CAS, letter to L. Sprague de Camp, October 21, 1952 (*SL* 370). This letter is misdated 1953.
5. *BB* items 21 and 22.
6. CAS, "Cycles." In *The Wine of Summer: The Complete Poetry and Translations Volume 2*. Ed. S. T. Joshi and David E. Schultz (New York: Hippocampus Press, 2008): p. 642.
7. George Sterling, "A Wine of Wizardry." *The Thirst of Satan: Poems of Fantasy and Terror*. Ed. S. T. Joshi and David E. Schultz (New York: Hippocampus Press, 2003): 150–151.

Monsters in the Night

Anthony Boucher (pseudonym of William A. P. White [1911–1968]) had given Clark Ashton Smith's first two Arkham House collections favorable reviews, so when he became one of the founding editors of the *Magazine of Fantasy & Science Fiction*, he would appear to have been a reliable new market for Smith's stories. Boucher even lived in nearby Berkeley, California, where Smith visited frequently to visit his friend George Haas, with whom Boucher was also acquainted.

Smith submitted "Thirteen Phantasms" to Boucher late in 1951. Boucher rejected the story on the grounds that it was too realistic, but took the time to offer Smith these observations, which unfortunately survive only in a burned fragment:

> Personally I've been enjoying & admiring your fiction for twenty years & more—particularly that individually mordant humor that you display in such items as "The Monster of the Prophecy" and "The Weird of Avoosl Wutthuquan." (I just checked & see that I misspelled that... but you'll admit that's doing well from memory!) But your type of highly elaborated & remote fantasy doesn't [*burned*] to be what our readers want. They prefer a more simple treatment, a closer impingement of the fantastic [*burned*] people. [*remainder burned*]²

He concluded the letter with an invitation to drop in for a drink if Smith were ever in Berkeley.

Smith must have experienced a sensation of *déjà vu* at reading this: it was as if Farnsworth Wright were speaking from the next world. When he next submitted a story to F&SF, it was with a newly written story that lacked many of his characteristic rhetorical flourishes.

"Monsters in the Night," one of Smith's most frequently anthologized stories, was the next story that Smith submitted to Boucher. He rejected it with these observations: "Sorry, but—nice idea, this werewolf-vs-robot, but I'm afraid it tips itself to the reader too early, & is too bluntly resolved."³ Boucher responded in a more positive manner after Smith rewrote the story and fixed those defects: "With a very slight change at the end, we want to accept 'Monsters in the Night.' Please advise if you approve of the following, which would replace your last two paragraphs on page 4: [. . .] We think this is quite an effective windup to a highly unique story."⁴ Smith agreed to the change, leading to a story contract, a check for forty-five dollars, and the story's appearance in the October 1954 issue of F&SF (under the title of "A Prophecy of Monsters," which was obviously a nod by Boucher to one of his favorite Smith stories).⁵ It was collected posthumously in OD.

Since Smith readily agreed to Boucher's suggested changes, and since he had a history of being open to such suggestions, we have retained the published ending. For the curious, here is what Smith originally wrote:

"Who—what—are you?" quavered the werewolf.
"I am a robot," said the stranger.

Several different drafts exist of this story. Our text is based upon the type-script dated April 11, 1953 on which CAS had crossed out "Monsters in the Night" and had written in its place "A Prophecy of Monsters," along with "To Fantasy and Science Fiction" and "1100 words."

1. See *FFT* pp. 61
2. Anthony Boucher, letter to CAS, December 6, 1951 (ms, JHL).
3. Anthony Boucher, note to CAS, April 18, 1953 (ms, private collection).
4. Anthony Boucher, letter to CAS, May 17, 1953 (ms, JHL).
5. Robert Mills, letter to CAS and attached legal contract, June 2, 1953 (ms, JHL).

Phoenix

August Derleth invited Clark Ashton Smith to contribute a story to an original science fiction anthology, *Time To Come*, that he was editing for Farrar, Straus and Young. Smith wrote a new story based upon a plot idea he had jotted down in the *Black Book*. Entitled "Phoenix," it described "An expedition sent from the earth to the extinct sun, for the purpose of rekindling it by means of atomic fission. The expedition is trapped by the tremendous gravity of the dead, solid orb but accomplishes its purpose, after sending back to earth a rocket containing reports, messages, etc."[1] He completed the story sometime in September 1953 according to the typescript presented by Smith to George Haas, which was consulted for this text. It was collected posthumously in *OD*.

1. *BB* item 81. The title itself may be found at item 78.

The Theft of the Thirty-Nine Girdles

Smith had entertained the idea of writing additional adventures of Sata-mpra Zeiros when he plotted out a story in his *Black Book* that he called both "The Ancient Shadow" and "The Shadow from the Sarcophagus," but the story never progressed beyond that stage.[1] "The Theft of the Thirty-Nine Girdles" was begun in October 1952, when he mentioned in a letter that he was working on the story,[2] but it was apparently not completed until just before April 25, 1957, when he announced its completion and submission to *F&SF*.[3] Anthony Boucher delivered the news of its rejection in person, probably when they gathered together at George Haas' home in Berkeley, but he typed out a letter putting forth his criticism: "It's good to see the return of Satampra Zeiros after 26 years; but I'm afraid I can't feel that THE THEFT OF THE THIRTY-NINE GIRDLES is really fantasy. The only fantasy element lies in its Hyperborean setting, & the events themselves, in your words (p. 6), 'though extraordinary, are not beyond nature.' Result:

an entertaining crime story in an extravagantly exotic setting rather than, strictly, a fantasy."[4] Smith submitted the story next to *Fantastic Universe*, but apparently editor Hans Stefan Santesson failed to appreciate its subtle humor. Donald A. Wollheim accepted the story for *Saturn Science Fiction*, a short-lived digest magazine, which published it under the less imaginative but also less suggestive title "The Powder of Hyperborea" in its March 1958 issue. It was collected posthumously in *TSS*.

Several different typescripts exist for this story, along with a holographic draft, but none of them appear to represent Smith's final thoughts. We based our text upon the magazine appearance, although we did restore "Lament to Vixeela," which we believe Smith removed on the theory that a 1950s-era sf magazine would not be a receptive venue for his poetry.

1. *BB* item 70. "The Theft of the Thirty-Nine Girdles" may be found in a listing of possible titles at item 210.
2. CAS, letter to L. Sprague de Camp, October 21, 1952 (*SL* 371) [misdated 1953 in this appearance].
3. CAS, letter to AWD, April 25, 1957 (ms, SHSW).
4. Anthony Boucher, letter to CAS, May 22, 1957 (ms, JHL).

SYMPOSIUM OF THE GORGON

This story was completed by Clark Ashton Smith on August 5, 1957. He submitted it to Anthony Boucher at the *Magazine of Fantasy & Science Fiction* and received the following response: "I like 'Symposium of the Gorgon,' but I fear it's too absolute a fantasy for most modern tastes. Our readers seem to prefer a less tenuous liaison with reality, & a little more in the way of plot & character. This has the charm of verse, but not enough bones for fiction."[1] It was accepted by Hans Stefan Santesson for *Fantastic Universe*. "Symposium of the Gorgon" appeared in the October 1958 issue. Curiously enough, the cover features a Virgil Finlay cover depicting the Gorgon and her statuary victims, but it was not illustrating any scene from Smith's story.

Smith expressed some of the same ideas, albeit less acerbically, in his poem "The Centaur."

The Smith Papers at the John Hay Library has no less than two typescripts of "Symposium of the Gorgon," as well as fragments of an autograph manuscript, but all of these are apparently earlier drafts that differ significantly from the published version. These versions are much less polished than the published version, and to perpetuate any of these changes would not be to Smith's credit. Besides *Fantastic Universe*, the editors consulted the story's appearance in *TSS*, but this version had a number of typographical errors.

1. Anthony Boucher, letter to CAS, August 10, 1957 (ms, JHL).

The Dart of Rasasfa

We wish that we could say that Clark Ashton Smith's final story was one of his best, that he went out at the top of his game, but we regret that we cannot. "The Dart of Rasasfa" was commissioned by Cele Goldsmith, editor of *Fantastic*, a digest-sized magazine that under her direction published a great deal of high-quality fantasy, including some of Fritz Leiber's best tales of Fafhrd and the Gray Mouser. Smith was supposed to write a story around a cover by artist George Barr. According to Donald Sidney-Fryer, Smith completed the story in July 1961. Smith was in ill health during that period, having been exhausted both physically and emotionally when he was forced by legal order to have a bulldozer fill in the well that he had helped his father dig years earlier. Steve Behrends quotes Carol Smith's unpublished memoir, reporting that the story's Gernsbackian flavor was meant to be ironic. After reading the manuscript of this story, Goldsmith wrote to Forrest J. Ackerman, who was acting as Smith's agent, expressing her regrets in having to decline what would turn out to be Smith's last story:

> If you read it, I think you can understand why it puts us in the embarrassing position of having to return it. There is no story, no plot, nothing. It would be an injustice to Smith fans and to the magazine audience to think of printing this. It would only detract from the wonderful stories he has written in the past and from the excellent reputation that is attached to his name.

These remarks were written on August 15, 1961. Smith had died from a stroke the previous day, so he never knew that the story was rejected.

1. *SS* 252–254.
2. Cele Goldsmith, letter to Forrest J. Ackerman, August 15, 1961 (ms, private collection).

Appendix Two:
Variant Temptation Scenes from "The Witchcraft of Ulua"

Version I (Rejected by *Weird Tales*)

"There are other things than the pouring of wine for a sottish monarch, or the study of worm-eaten volumes," said Ulua in a voice like molten honey. "Sir Cupbearer, your youth should have a better employment than these."

"I ask no other employment," replied Amalzain. "But tell me, O princess, what is your will? Why has your serving-woman brought me here in a fashion so unseemly?"

"I would have you for my lover," said Ulua. "Behold! my arms are the portals of untold raptures and felicities. The pleasures I give are keener than the pangs of a fiery death. The dead kings of Tasuun will whisper enviously of our love to their dead queens in the immemorial granite vaults below Chaon Gacca. Thaisadon, the black, shadowy lord of hell, hearing the tale that his demons bring to him of us, will wish to become incarnate in a mortal body."

"Nonetheless, I cannot love you," said Amalzain. (*Typescript ends at this point*)

Version III (Published by *Weird Tales*)

"There are other things than the pouring of wine for a sottish monarch, or the study of worm-eaten volumes," said Ulua in a voice that was like the flowing of hot honey. "Sir cup-bearer, your youth should have a better employment than these."

"I ask no employment, other than my duties and studies," replied Amalzain ungraciously. "But tell me, O princess, what is your will? Why has your serving-woman brought me here in a fashion so unseemly?"

"For a youth so erudite and clever, the question should be needless," answered Ulua, smiling obliquely. "See you not that I am beautiful and desirable? Or can it be that your perceptions are duller than I had thought?"

"I do not doubt that you are beautiful," said the boy, "but such matters hardly concern a humble cup-bearer."

The vapors, mounting thickly from golden thuribles before the couch, were parted with a motion as of drawn draperies; and Amalzain lowered his gaze before the enchantress, who shook with a soft laughter that made the jewels upon her bosom twinkle like living eyes.

"It would seem that those musty volumes have indeed blinded you," she told him. "You have need of that euphrasy which purges the sight. Go now: but return presently—of your own accord."

Appendix Three:
"The Traveller"
(Dedicated to V.H.)

"**S**tranger, where goest thou, in the sad raiment of a pilgrim, with shattered sandals retaining the dust and mire of so many devious ways? With thy brows that alien suns have darkened, and thy hair made white from the cold rime of alien moons? Wanderest thou in search of the cities greater than Rome, with walls of opal and crystal, and fanes more white than the summer clouds, or the foam of hyperboreal seas? Or farest thou to the lands unpeopled and unexplored, to the sunless deserts lit by the baleful and calamitous beacons of volcanoes? Or seekest thou an extremer shore, where the red and monstrous lilies are like a royal pageant, pausing with innumerable flambeaux held aloft on the verge of the waveless waters?"

"Nay, it is none of these that I seek, but forevermore I seek the city and the land of my former home: In the quest thereof I have wandered from the first immemorable years of my youth till now, and have mingled the dust of many realms, of many highways, in my garments' hem. I have seen the cities greater than Rome, and the fanes more white than the clouds of summer; the lands unpeopled and unexplored, and the land that is thronged by the red and monstrous lilies. Even the far, aerial walls of the cities of mirage, and the saffron meadows of sunset I have seen, but nevermore the city and land of my former home."

"Where lieth the land of thine home? and by what name shall we know it, and distinguish the rumour thereof, among the rumours of many lands?"

"Alas! I know not where it lieth: nor in the broad, black scrolls of geographers, and the charts of old seamen who have sailed to the marge of the seventh sea, is the place thereof recorded. And its name I have never learned, howbeit I have learned the name of empires lying beneath stars to us invisible. In many languages have I spoken, in barbarous tongues unknown to Babel; and I have heard the speech of many men, even of them that inhabit the strange isles of the sea of fire and the sea of snow. Thunder, and lutes, and battle-drums, the fine unceasing querulousness of gnats, and the stupendous moaning of the simoon; lyres of ebony, damascened with crystal, bells of malachite with golden clappers; the song of exotic birds that sigh like wom-en or sob like fountains; whispers and shoutings of fire, the multitudinous mutter of cities asleep, the manifold tumult of cities at dawn, and the slow and weary murmur of desert-wandering streams—all, all have I heard, but never, in any place, from any tongue, a word or syllable that resembled in the least the name I would learn."

APPENDIX FOUR:
MATERIAL REMOVED FROM
"THE BLACK ABBOT OF PUTHUUM"

The girl, whose name was Rubalsa, dwelt, being parentless, with her grandmother in a village beside the Vos. Regarding her with the shrewd eye of one whose business was the study of women, Simban at once conceived the idea that Rubalsa was no daughter of that outland race. The women of the herders were all swarthy, and, in their youth, most of them were inclined to a not ungainly fatness. But Rubalsa was slender and of queenly height, and her skin was pale as the petals of white poppies, and the undulant blackness of her heavy hair was full of sullen copper gleamings beneath the sun. The eunuch had seen such girls before, but none of them had come from the valleys of the Vos.

[...]

At last the bargain was driven and the price paid, to the sore depletion of Simban's money-bag. Afterward, to satisfy his own curiosity, the eunuch questioned the old woman as to Rubalsa's true parentage. She, fearing that a contrary admission might nullify her right to the money, repeated at first her claim that Rubalsa was the child of her own son, the herder Olot, now dead together with his wife. Simban, perceiving her apprehension, quickly reassured her. He tempted her with a few additional coins, and a leather bottle filled with palm-arrack which he had brought along for his own solacement; and she then told him that Olot, while watering his kine at eventide, had once found a small barge that the lazily flowing Vos had stranded in the mud of the drinking-place; and in the barge was a girl-infant, swaddled with rich fabrics of unknown weave and pattern. Olot had taken the infant home, and he and his wife, being childless, had reared her as their own daughter; and as such she had commonly been regarded. And this infant, in the course of eighteen summers, had grown to be the strange and lovely maiden, Rubalsa.

In proof of her story, the crone brought out the swaddling clothes, which were of fine purple linen broidered with yellow and scarlet silk. She also displayed to Simban a queer amulet of green-zoned jasponyx which Olot had found hanging about the infant's neck. This amulet was carved with the grotesquely grinning profile of the god Yuckla, patron of mirth and laughter. The weft and pattern of the swaddlings and the workmanship of the amulet were not unfamiliar to Simban, and they confirmed his suspicions regarding the girl's nativity. He persuaded the crone to part with those tokens and promptly stored them in a great leather pouch which he carried at all times together with the money-bag at his girdle. He wished to show them to Hoaraph, thinking that the mystery of such matters would add another seduction to Rubalsa's natural charms, and would serve to titivate the somewhat captious desires of the king.

[When the party reaches the monastery they meet another guest, a man in a broidered cloak, who passes out from drink. The following portion occurs at the end of the story after Zobal and Cushara draw lots for Rubalsa.]

An unexpected interruption occurred at that moment, for the man in the broidered cloak, whose very existence all had temporarily forgotten, appeared suddenly from the ruins and accosted Zobal. He seemed as one lost and bewildered, and plainly his bemazement was not wholly due to the after-effects of the heavy potations that had overcome him at the monastery table.

"Surely I have dreamed a strange dream," he said. "Methought that I came to an abbey in the waste, after losing my way in a weird untimely darkness. I was entertained too well by the abbot and his monks, and fell asleep after sundry draughts of their strong amber-brown ale. But I awakened beneath the moon, in a foul pit with crumbling walls, where human bones and fragments of putrefying members were littered about me, like the leavings of a feast of ghouls. I climbed from the pit by a broken stair, to find myself amid this ancient ruin, to which I cannot remember coming."

Zobal recounted succinctly the events of the night, and added, "Thou art fortunate, for mayhaps the fiend Ujuk had intended thee for his ghoulish repast when he had done playing the incubus."

"Scarcely can I credit thy tale," said the stranger. "Yet I seem to remember seeing thee and thy companions at the abbot's table…. Yea, clearly I recall the girl who stands yonder, for she bears a strong likeness to one that was dear to me in the former time."

Then, as if feeling that some further explanation was due, he went on.

"My name is Vadarth, and I hold the post of almoner to King Ilorgh of Tasuun. I am passing through Izdrel on my way to the valleys of the river Vos…. This girl reminds me of the reason of my journey: for she resembles Irali, the wife of my bosom, who died nearly nineteen years agone after giving birth to a girl-infant. The girl was stolen from me at the age of five months by a vengeful servant whom I had dismissed for certain peccadilloes.

I sought long but vainly for any trace of her, and despaired at last of ever finding the child. But only a few weeks since, there came to me a man who had met the kidnapper in a far city; and the kidnapper, who was then at the point of death, had confessed to this man the stealing of my child, which he had come to repent; and he told him that he had fled into Yoros with the babe, and had set her adrift in a barge on the upper reaches of the Vos, and had known nothing of her fate thereafter.

"This tale has revived in me a dead hope: for it may be that the girl still lives. In search of her I shall follow the windings of the Vos and make inquiry among the bordering peoples."

Cushara and Rubalsa had come forward, and they and Zobal were listening to the almoner with open wonderment.

"Verily," exclaimed Cushara, "the marvels of this night are not yet done." He then told Vadarth the circumstances under which he and his companions had found Rubalsa dwelling beside the Vos, and the story that Simban had extracted from the old crone as to the finding by her son Olot of the girl-baby in the barge.

"There were certain tokens that the crone gave to Simban," interpolated Zobal. He stooped down beside the dead eunuch and began to examine the great pouch at his belt, which had been ripped open by Ujuk's claws. A piece of embroidered cloth protruded from the rift, and pulling it forth, Zobal exhibited the swaddlings worn by the infant Rubalsa. Something that had been carefully wrapped in the folds dropped clattering on the flagstones, and before Zobal could recover it, Vadarth sank to his knees with a loud cry and held up the fallen object.

"Truly this is the amulet worn by my lost child, and those are her swaddlings," he said in a voice that trembled. "The amulet bears an image of the god Yuckla, and I hung it about her neck to ward off the assailments of ill demons."

He rose to his feet and embraced Rubalsa, who seemed overcome with astonishment and joy at the revelation that Vadarth was her father.

The almoner turned to Cushara and Zobal. "Will ye come with me to Tasuun?" he inquired. "For this night's work, I shall make ye captains in the service of Ilorgh."

"Thy destination is mine," said Cushara. To this the archer added:

"There is an old saying, that parent should not be parted from child, nor lover from lover, nor comrade from comrade. I also come with thee."

Appendix Five:
Alternate Ending to
"I Am Your Shadow"

J ones went home at the usual post-midnight hour, after getting himself systematically and completely replastered. He prided himself that he had achieved a sort of bland indifference to shadows. Whatever forms they might manifest, were alike inconsequential. He ignored the ebon monstrosity that still companioned him when he turned on the light in his bedroom.

Still, he was glad of the darkness of closely drawn blinds that blotted it from sight and, he hoped, from existence. He lay with eyes tightly shut, waiting the deeper darkness of alcoholic oblivion.

He had almost reached the indefinite verge where stupor becomes sleep. A sourceless voice, a light, thin, sibilant whisper, pierced the gulf into which he was sinking. Jones was roused into a sort of semi-awareness, without knowing whether the voice spoke in his own mind or from without.

"Who's that?" he mumbled drowsily.

"I am your shadow."

"What the hell do you want?" Jones began to awaken now, startled and even a little frightened.

"I shall want many things… in the end. But just at present I can offer to do something for you."

Jones thought: "I certainly must have them now. After seeing things, I'm hearing voices."

However, the bravado of many Martinis had only half evaporated. He said aloud: "What can you do for me, shadow?"

"More than you think," rejoined the whisper. "You have seen the foreshadowing of the crime that your partner meditates: the crime that he will attempt tonight. If you wish I can prevent him."

"You're only a shadow," protested Jones, wondering if the fantastic dialogue were part of some insidious but growing delirium. "You're an ugly bastard: but I'm the only one that can see you. How could you prevent anything?"

"You have made me strong," averred the whisper. "And I have power now over other shadows, both seen and unseen, and can exert myself in the world of physical causes and effects."

"I don't believe it," sneered Jones, feeling even as he spoke a weird horripilation in the mid-region of his back. Something—perhaps a hand or a hoof—was pressing his chest lightly through the bed-clothes. The pressure deepened by almost imperceptible gradations till it became an incubus-like burden that seemed to flatten his ribs and breast-bone and lungs against his spine. He gasped and agonized for breath; and the dreadful weight was withdrawn with insupportable slowness.

"Do you wish further proof of my power?" resumed the whisper, close above him now in the opaque darkness.

Jones was thoroughly terrified by this time; and his terror was complicated by a feeling of nightmare impotence and muddlement.

"No, no!" he cried. "Go away, shadow. Do whatever you want, but don't bother me."

It seemed that a ponderable presence was gone suddenly from the room. There was no repetition of the thin, rustling whispers, no return of the crushing encumbrance. Jones listened awhile with the curious intentness of which only an alcoholic is capable. His fear lightened; his drunkenness came flooding back upon him; and he lapsed by degrees into a slumber without dreams or untoward interruptions.

He awoke only once during the remainder of the night. His mouth and throat were parched with the all-consuming thirst that ensues heavy drinking. He rose and groped his way to the bathroom where, after much fumbling, he found the switch. As he poured himself a second glass of water, he perceived with senses still drugged and sluggish, that no shadow, either natural or unnatural, was cast by his body on the basin and faucets and wall in the light that streamed directly from behind.

"Damn good riddance," he rumbled, as he went back to bed. "Christ, what a nightmare that was!"

A reiterated buzzing, like that of a badgered rattlesnake, awakened Jones to the horrid realities of daylight. It was the telephone on the stand beside his bed.

He lifted the receiver with a none too steady hand. Immediately a feminine voice, shrill with agitation and hysteria, began to babble in his ear.

"Mr. Jones? This is Miss Lamont, in the office next to yours. Come down at once.... Something horrible has happened."

"What? What?" stammered Jones.

"Your partner, Caleb Johnson... dead... found by the janitor... crushed to death…. No one can figure how it happened. Miss Owens… stark mad… in your office…." The babbling became wholly incoherent, till Jones could distinguish only an occasional word or syllable that conveyed nothing of further information to his bewildered mind.

The sun was nearly halfway to its meridian when he emerged on the street. Plainly he had overslept following the strange experience, whether nightmare or hallucination, that had plagued his homecoming.

Heedless, for once, of whatever shadow might ensue or proceed his steps, he reached his office, to find a state of bedlam for which the babbling voice had prepared him all too inadequately with its intimations of horror.

It seemed that all other offices in the three-story edifice had voided their tenants into the hall outside his door. The door itself stood open, with people milling in and out. They made way for Jones, and the hubbub sank to a temporary hush. He entered his office, feeling himself the cynosure of eyes in which some ghastliness beyond belief was reflected.

There were two policeman and a doctor amid the crowd that filled the room as buzz-flies fill an abattoir. Miss Lamont, typist of the real-estate firm in the office next door, detached herself from the clustered group and fluttered toward Jones, still babbling. Jones heard little, and understood less, of what she was trying to say.

Miss Owens, sitting flaccidly in a chair, was moaning and sobbing with the mindless reiteration of a phonograph record. Her eyes were vacant, her face was drawn and distorted as if by some sudden mysterious stroke. The doctor, whom Jones knew by sight as a practitioner in the same neighborhood, was standing solicitously beside her, a hypodermic still in his hand. Plainly he had given her an injection of some soporific drug: her noisy hysteria began to subside, with lengthening intervals of drowsy silence.

Jones gave her only a passing attention. The group of people before the big iron safe had drawn back, turning toward him as if with one accord. Seized and held by an abominable fascination, he gazed at the strange thing that was now revealed.

The legs and hips of a man, wearing the rakish, broad-checked suit that Caleb Johnson had affected recently, protruded at a sharp, stiff angle from the safe door, which had closed on the body like a huge trap. It seemed that the body had been cut virtually in two by this inexplicable closing: since the heavy door was now nearly plumb with its iron and concrete frame. Johnson's coat-tails and trousers were streaked darkly with the blood that had run down and coagulated in a broad pool about his nattily shod feet. It was evident that he had been dead for several hours.

People began to talk all at once, vociferating and expostulating. Bemused with a sense of horror and unreality, Jones gathered by fragments the information they were trying to give him.

The janitor, coming late to work that morning, had heard the cries and sobbing of a woman in Jones' office. Finding the door unlocked, he had entered, to discover Johnson caught like a trapped rat in the safe door, and Miss Owens in a state of shock or seizure that seemingly unhinged her mind. He had been unable to budge the ponderous door of the safe; unable to learn anything from the mouthings of the madwoman; and had promptly called the police and a doctor. The local coroner had also been summoned, but was delayed in coming.

Other people had appeared from the neighboring offices that began to fill at that hour. Many attempts had been made to release the dead and almost bisected body, identified beyond a doubt as that of Johnson by letters in one of his hip pockets. Crowbars had been employed; but nothing could loosen the grip of the massive metal jaws that had closed so unaccountably upon their victim. No one could conjecture what force or agency had caused their closing; certainly no human power could have been responsible. Why they should so obstinately refuse to open was an equal mystery.

As he listened, Jones recalled the eerie nocturnal dialogue in which he had seemed to take part. Could the thin, whispering voice have been more than a figment of dream or delirium? Had someone, or something, offered to prevent the crime that had been apparently foreshown by a pantomime of shadows? Had the frightfully crushing pressure in his chest been something other than a cacodemon of slumber or alcohol?

It seemed all too patent that Johnson, with the connivance of Miss Owens, had planned to rob the safe, and had opened it with the combination known only to himself and Jones. There was no legitimate reason why the pair should have visited the office during what, from all evidence, must have been the late night or early morning hours. What hellish thing had overtaken them, had slain Johnson so hideously in his act of embezzlement, and had driven his companion to madness? Jones stood aghast before the gulf that was opened by such questions and surmises.

At this moment he heard the familiar whispering voice: "You alone can open that which I have closed."

Jones put his fingers into the inch or more of space that remained between the door's edge and the frame. The dialled mass of metal swung outward easily and without sound, and Johnson's body, compressed at the waist to a ghastly hour-glass attenuation, slumped forward into the safe. It lay face downward amid stacks of currency and standard bonds. A rubber-banded roll of twenty-dollar bills was still clutched in the right hand, which had already stiffened a little with premature rigor mortis.

An hour later, Jones locked the empty office in which nothing could have induced him to linger. His feelings were those of one who has just escaped from some inquisitorial ordeal, but is still dogged by more than inquisitorial terrors. The inquest had been a tedious daymare, from which nothing had emerged conclusively except the irrefutable fact that Johnson was dead. No reason, or suspicion of a reason, could be found for holding anyone in connection with his death. His car had been located in an alley back of the building. In it were valises belonging both to Johnson and Miss Owens. Indications were that the pair had planned to elope for parts unknown following the safe-robbery.

Miss Owens had been removed to a local hospital for observation. Reporters had beleaguered Jones with questions that he was, for the most part, honestly unable to answer. Apparently they, as well as the coroner and the police, were satisfied that the whole affair was no less a mystery to Jones than to others. Nevertheless, he was pursued by dark apprehensions, and his feelings of physical shock and spectral horror were tinged by something that bordered on guilt. Walking along the sunbright street with inattentive eyes, he thought that he was not alone—that a presence walked beside him, step by step.

It was the shadow. The thing had changed overnight, assuming new properties. Opaque and tri-dimensional, it paced *between Jones and the sun* like a sable quadruped, rising nearly waist-high above the pavement. It was independent both of Jones and the light: a self-existent entity, a black and bestial doppelganger.

[Typescript of "I Am Your Shadow" ends with this page.]

Appendix Six:
Alternate Ending to
"Nemesis of the Unfinished"

[This version begins following the paragraph that ends "He sat down at the typewriter, determined that he would finish the story to his satisfaction."]

For a while he wrote steadily, without hesitating over variant words or divergencies of plot development. It seemed that some magic lamp illumined his brain, clarifying all that had baffled and eluded him heretofore. The sorcerer, Guillaume de la Coudraie, had procured an ancient chart of mouldy parchment, giving the location of a ghoul-guarded tomb in which were hidden the essential formulæ that he had long vainly sought. The formulæ contained the words of power, the secret names by which the dread kings of the four infernal quarters, as well as many lesser spirits, could be summoned, constrained and dismissed. The procuring of the parchment itself had entailed many obscure perils both to soul and body. The path to the designated tomb, moreover, was fraught with preternatural dangers and deadfalls.

At this point La Porte's inspiration became once more confused and indecisive. He wrote page after page, only to discard them as unsatisfactory. The magic light, illumining the story so briefly, had dimmed and gone out like a necromancer's lantern in smoky darkness.

The day wore on in this frustrating, brain-fettering labor; only to leave La Coudraie still conning the musty, worm-frayed parchment in his tower chamber lined with ponderous tomes of goety and demonology.

At last La Porte abandoned the fruitless task in something that bordered upon despair. It was nearly sunset; perhaps a walk to the neighboring village would refresh his jaded brain.

It was many hours later when he wandered homeward rather unsteadily by the rays of a cloud-strangled moon. Forgetting his usual strict economy, he had consumed numerous brandies at a local bar. He did not care for the people who frequented such places; but he had been reluctant to leave and face again the unsolved problems of his sorcerer, in a cabin peopled with

355

half-written and unwritten fantasies.

He entered, lit the lamp, and seated himself resolutely once more before the typewriter. Removing a partly finished sheet from the roller, he crumpled it, cast it aside, and inserted a fresh one. Then, groping foggily for a sentence with which to resume the tale, he slid into drunken slumber.

Wild dreams came to visit him anon. Eldritch voices shrieked and muttered in his ears, conspiring against his peace and safety; indistinct but nightmarish figures milled around him like the dancers of some demonian Sabbat, swirling and leaning ever nearer with gestures of hideous menace.

In one of the dreams, he was Guillaume de la Coudraie, sitting in his tower with the time-fretted chart, stained with nameless corruption, unrolled before him. He was girt for the journey to the hidden tomb; his scrip was packed with such impediments of magic as he might require; and the *arthame,* the wizard sword of consecrated metal, potent for defense against demons and liches and phantoms, glittered unsheathed on the table close to his right hand. But still he lingered, pondering the chart, whose lines and drawings and letterings, inscribed in the blood of vipers, seemed to shift and change beneath his anxious scrutiny till the route they indicated was another than the one that he had longed yet feared to follow.

By this sign, La Coudraie knew that the powers he had sought to control were working against him. He was mocked by those whom he had dreamt to dominate. He trembled, and peered fearfully about his chamber, seeing now that other signs had begun to manifest themselves.

Curious red and nacarat flames, in the form of reptilian salamanders, had sprung up from the unlit, cinder-choked brazier that the wizard used in his incantations. They seemed to lengthen and lean toward him in uncoiled menace, with heads whitening to intolerable brightness. Pallid vapors, flat as papery tongues, issued from the piled grimoires and swelled interminably, darkening and thickening to the semblance of malign genii whose eye-sockets seethed with lurid fire under night-black brows.

Lowering his gaze in terror, the necromancer saw that the changing lines and ciphers had been wholly erased from the chart before him. In their stead, on the blank surface, appeared the lineaments of a baleful and infernal visage. Though the livid eyelids were shut, the face was that of Alastor, demon of vengeance.... Slowly, dreadfully, it emerged from the flatness of the parchment, rearing on a python-like neck till it confronted La Coudraie on a level with his own face. Slowly, horribly, the eyes opened....

La Porte awakened, or seemed to awaken, from his necromantic nightmare. At least, he was conscious of being back in his cabin, seated before the typewriter just as he had fallen asleep. The profound terror of the sorcerer La Coudraie still possessed him; nor, in the circumstances of his awakening, was there anything to mitigate the terror.

By the light of the oil-lamp, burning stilly beside his Remington, he found himself staring into the same Satanic face that had risen from the sorcerer's chart and had opened its basilisk eyes upon him in his dream. The face was mounted on the same scaled ophidian neck. Algae-green, with ashen mottlings, the neck thickened downward, seeming to issue from the blank sheet of paper, newly inserted, that curved back across the Remington's roller. Clear and rigid as icicles, twin shafts of light poured from the unpupilled eyes, transfixing his very marrow, filling the darkest cells of his brain with their searching, searing illumination.

Inch by tedious inch, like one half-paralyzed, he turned from the direct gaze of the apparition—only to confront the shapes and faces of Pandemonium. Like those that had sprung from the wizard's brazier, burning elementals rose amid the charred logs in his fireplace, breathing smoke and heat as they serpentined outward into the room. Endless vapory scrolls unfurled from between the leaves of his massed manuscripts, dilating into Powers and Dominations. Bloated incubi swam toward him on the air, levitating themselves pronely, quivering like obscene jellies, and lolling their fulsome vermillion tongues from taurine mouths.

Out of all these shapes, that seethed and fumed in perpetual agitation, there pulsed an insufferable horror that centered upon La Porte: a horror older than man, older than the world, deeper than the earth's caverns or the crypts of the brain.

It seemed that he had not awakened from his dream: that he was still the sorcerer La Coudraie, facing the vengeful demons over whom he had secured an incomplete power. And yet he was still Francis La Porte who, metaphorically, had summoned such beings; had imagined and described them in stories that were like unfinished incantations, lacking the spells of compulsion and dismission.

Whether awake or dreaming, he knew the deadly peril in which he stood. A frenzy beyond the frenzy of nightmares mounted within him, and his reason seemed to drown in some abyss of primordial fears. Without knowing whence they came, from what volume of dubious lore he had remembered them, he began to declaim the words of a cabalistic exorcism.

"I adjure ye by the living God, El, Ehome, Etrha, Ejel aser, Ejech Adonay Iah Tetragrammaton Saday Agios other Agla ischiros athanatos—"

The long and orotund formula came to an end. It seemed that the specters had drawn back a little, facing La Porte in a sort of semi-circle. But, without turning, he knew that other visitants had gathered behind him. They guarded the door; they hemmed him in; they barred him from all hope of egress. Truly, he was no sorcerer to dismiss them, entrenched with intricate circles and pentagrams, and armed with the magnetized rod and the cross-hilted knife.

The pulsing horror deepened; the menace quickened like tightening coils....
And yet, among all these formidable shapes, there was nothing that he had
not conceived and depicted in his half-abortive tales. They were, he tried
to tell himself, mere images and ideas that he had never wholly discharged
from his mind. Perhaps there was another mode of exorcism, surer and more
potent than the one that magicians had employed.

Trying to disregard his visitors, he stooped over the Remington and his
fingers began to seek the familiar keys.... [The typescript of "Nemesis of the
Unfinished" ends here. The last page appears to be missing.]

APPENDIX SEVEN:
Bibliography

"The Dark Age." *Thrilling Wonder Stories* 11, No. 2 (April 1938): 95–103. In *AY*.

"The Death of Malygris." *WT* 23, No. 4 (April 1934): 488–96. In *LW*, *RA*.

"The Tomb-Spawn." *WT* 23, No. 5 (May 1934): 634–640. In *TSS*.

"The Witchcraft of Ulua." *WT* 23, No. 2 (February 1934): 253–59. In *AY*.

"The Coming of the White Worm." *Stirring Science Stories* 1, No. 2 (April 1941): 105–14. *Uncanny Tales* 2, No. 11 (December 1941): 10–17. In *LW*, *RA*, *SS*.

"The Seven Geases." *WT* 24, No. 4 (October 1934): 422–35. In *LW*, *RA*.

"The Chain of Aforgomon." *WT* 26, No. 6 (December 1935): 695–706. In *OST*, *RA*.

"The Primal City." *Fantasy Fan* 2, No. 3 (November 1934): 41–45. *Comet Stories* 1, No. 1 (December 1940): 102–6. In *GL*.

"Xeethra." *WT* 24, No. 6 (December 1934): 726–738. In *LW*, *RA*.

"The Last Hieroglyph." *WT* 25, No. 4 (April 1935): 466–77. In *OST*, *RA*.

"Necromancy in Naat." *WT* 28, No. 1 (July 1936): 2–15. *Narraciones Terroríficas* No. 8 (1939): 14–25 (as "Nigromancia en Naat"; trs. unknown). In *LW*, *RA*.

"The Treader of the Dust." *WT* 26, No. 2 (August 1935): 241–46. In *LW*.

"The Black Abbot of Puthuum." *WT* 27, No. 3 (March 1936): 308–22. In *GL*.

"The Death of Ilalotha." *WT* 30, No. 3 (September 1937): 323–30. In *OST*, *RA*.

"Mother of Toads." *WT* 32, No. 1 (July 1938): 86–90. In *TSS*.

"The Garden of Adompha." *WT* 31, No. 6 (June 1938): 393–400. In *GL*.

"The Great God Awto." *Thrilling Wonder Stories* 15, No. 2 (February 1940):111–114. In *TSS*.

"Strange Shadows." *Crypt of Cthulhu* No. 25 (Michaelmas 1984): 22–31. In *SS*.

"The Enchantress of Sylaire." *WT* 35, No. 10 (July 1941): 25–34. In *AY*.

"Double Cosmos." *Crypt of Cthulhu* No. 17 (Michaelmas 1983): 35–41. In *SS*.

"Nemesis of the Unfinished" (with Don Carter). *Crypt of Cthulhu* No. 27 (Hallowmas 1984 [special issue: Untold Tales]): 1–4. In *SS*.

"The Master of the Crabs." *WT* 40, No. 3 (March 1948): 64–71. In *AY*.

"Morthylla." *WT* 45, No. 2 (May 1953): 41–46. In *TSS*, *RA*.

"Schizoid Creator." *Fantasy Fiction* 1, No. 4 (November 1953): 78–85. In *TSS*.

"Monsters in the Night." *The Magazine of Fantasy & Science Fiction* 7, No. 4 (October 1954): 119–21. In *OD*.

"Phoenix." In August Derleth, Ed. *Time to Come: Science-Fiction Stories of Tomorrow*. New York: Farrar, Straus & Young, 1954, pp. 285–98; New York: Berkley, 1954, pp. 18–29. In *OD*.

"The Theft of the Thirty-Nine Girdles." *Saturn Science Fiction and Fantasy* 1, No. 5 (March 1958): 52–62 (as "The Powder of Hyperborea"). In *TSS*.

"Symposium of the Gorgon." *Fantastic Universe Science Fiction* 10, No. 4 (October 1958): 49–56. In *TSS*.

"The Dart of Rasasfa." *Crypt of Cthulhu* No. 27 (Hallowmas 1984 [special issue: *Untold Tales*]): 5–8. In *SS*.